SPARTAN SLAVE, SPARTAN QUEEN

SPARTAN SLAVE, SPARTAN QUEEN

◆

A TALE OF FOUR WOMEN IN SPARTA

A NOVEL

HELENA P. SCHRADER

iUniverse, Inc.
New York Lincoln Shanghai

Spartan Slave, Spartan Queen
A Tale of Four Women in Sparta

iUniverse books may be ordered through booksellers or by contacting:

iUniverse
2021 Pine Lake Road, Suite 100
Lincoln, NE 68512
www.iuniverse.com
1-800-Authors (1-800-288-4677)

Because of the dynamic nature of the Internet, any Web addresses or links contained in this book may have changed since publication and may no longer be valid.

This is a work of fiction. All of the characters, names, incidents, places, organizations, and dialogue in this novel are either the products of the author's imagination or are used fictitiously.
Cover title type face is ACROPOLIS NOW, copyright P22.com

ISBN: 978-0-595-47067-9 (pbk)
ISBN: 978-0-595-91349-7 (ebk)

Printed in the United States of America

FOREWORD AND ACKNOWLEDGEMENTS

This book practically wrote itself. Having completed *Are They Singing in Sparta?*, I realized that I wanted to tell more about what happened to some of the minor characters in that book. Leon and Kassia demanded more attention. The two captive girls took on lives of their own almost from the moment I described them and started writing. At no time was I unsure what either they or the leading Spartan characters would do. The book was written easily and rapidly, but I did not like the result. On the one hand, in principle, I do not like sequels, and on the other this book seemed particularly limited in its appeal. It is very much a woman's novel, focused on women's issues such as sex appeal, love, marriage, and childbirth. It also seemed a rather simple story. I hesitated to publish it.

Thanks to the encouragement of my editor, Christina Dickson, I decided to go ahead after all, and, with some modifications suggested by her, release this book. I was encouraged, furthermore, by the number of visitors to my website, **www.elysiumgates.com/~helena.com**, who came to the website searching for information about "Spartan Women." I am very grateful, therefore, to Kythera Grunge of Crystal Cloud Graphics, who has maintained this website, posting up-dates and keeping track of the visitors.

The central theme of this book—the impact of physical beauty on human interactions—is, however, a universal one. It is quite independent of any cultural or period context. This is a topic that has long fascinated me, and one deserving more sophisticated attention in literature. Too often it is taken for granted that beauty is something positive, or—worse—that physical beauty is equated with inner beauty, virtue and all things good. I hope this book will provoke readers to a more differentiated reflection on what beauty is and means.

Oslo, Norway
August 2007

PART I
THE CAPTIVE BRIDE

PYROS, MESSENIA

AT THE END OF THE 1ST YEAR OF THE 30TH OLYMPIAD
THE 7TH YEAR OF THE SECOND MESSENIAN WAR

CHAPTER 1

The sun had set behind the island of Sphacteria, leaving the island a black bulk against the luminous blue-purple sky. The air was beginning to cool, and the evening sea breeze rustled the leaves of the olives on the long slope up from the coast. The wild birds calling in the orchard set the captive birds in their gilded cages chirping and fluttering about in agitation.

Niobe went to the cage containing the beautiful, bright-feathered bird that had been one of Aristomenes' many wedding gifts to her. She clucked to him and called him by name, trying to soothe his agitation. But he looked at her coldly with his white-rimmed eye and then flew to the other side of the cage, grasped the bars with his talons, and bit at them with his beak. Niobe knew better than to reach out her finger. Instead she drew back and looked up at the patch of sky visible through the skylight of the peristyle.

She could see a single star. Aristomenes said sailors could navigate across the expanse of the seas by following the stars as they moved, but she found that hard to imagine. Her eyes sought the familiar and slid down the painted pillars supporting the roof around the pool in the middle of the paved peristyle. The paint was fresh, a bright ox-blood base with bright blue capitals on which palms were painted in yellow. Kallisto said that Aristomenes had had the women's quarters redecorated entirely for her. "He must have spent a fortune," Kallisto told her young mistress in wonder, adding, "which shows that all the rumours about Lacedaemonian successes in recent years are rubbish. If Aristomenes was losing the war, he couldn't afford so much luxury."

Niobe didn't know enough about politics or war to know if this were true, but she did not think her father, King Aristokrates of Arkadia, would have given his favourite daughter to a man he did not think would be king one day. Aristomenes was of royal blood and the unquestioned leader of the Messenians, but he would only be king if he could regain his city's freedom from the Lacedaemonians.

Three generations ago, after a long and bitter war, the last Messenian king, Aristodemos, had killed himself when he realised all further resistance was hopeless. His demoralized subjects had capitulated and been turned into Lacedaemonian subjects. But at least back then, Niobe's father had explained to her, the Lacedaemonians had been ruled by the Spartan kings. Now the Lacedaemonians had adopted new laws and although they still had kings, their kings were almost powerless. Instead, the country was ruled by the common citizens, who met every month in Assembly and decided what to do based on whatever the majority wanted.

The men of good family in Messenia might have been willing to accept the leadership of Sparta's kings. They, after all, were descended straight from Herakles himself, but the nobles of Messenia were not willing to be ruled by the whim of mere Spartan citizens. As her father had explained to her, some of these Spartan citizens had been landless nobodies before a land reform had cut up all the great aristocratic estates into equal parcels and given each of the citizens a plot of his own. Now the Spartans called themselves "equals" or "peers," but it was obvious to anyone who could think (as her father said) that most of these "peers" were just jumped-up peasants. It was inconceivable that men of royal blood like Aristomenes would submit to be ruled by what the majority of these peasants voted once a month!

That was why the Rebellion began almost ten years ago. The Messenians had attacked the Lacedaemonian administrators and when the

Lacedaemonians sent an army to put them down, they had defeated it and sent the Lacedaemonians scampering back behind the safety of the great Taygetos mountain range. The Lacedaemonians, however, would not admit defeat. So for nearly ten years the war had dragged on with many casualties and hardships for both sides, Niobe's father said.

In all those years, Aristomenes had proved the most brilliant and audacious of all leaders on either side—like a hero from the *Iliad*, Kallisto had told her young mistress as she prepared her for her wedding. He had once raided right inside Sparta itself, and dedicated a shield at the Temple of the Bronze Athena on the Spartan acropolis. The number of times he had slipped out of the hands of his pursuers and enemies was both legion and legend, Kallisto said—and he certainly had a large number of scars, Niobe thought blushing.

She still found the thought of his body—and what it did with hers—slightly embarrassing. She had only been married for three months, and most of that time Aristomenes had been away from her. They had spent just five days together in idyllic seclusion after the wedding, and then he had left her in the care of a large household, which was moved slowly and with considerable hardship from Arkadia to Pylos in Messenia. Here he had visited her shortly thereafter to "make sure everything was all right," but he had stayed only one night before he rushed off again. The women who had been in the household for a long time said that was typical of him. "It's the kind of war he's fighting," they explained; "he never strikes twice in the same place. The Lacedaemonians have many more troops than we, and he can't risk a fixed battle."

The women who had been with Aristomenes' first wife said that sometimes he was gone all summer, but Niobe hoped he would be more attentive to her. After all, his first wife had been nearly 40 years old when she died and he'd been married to her for more than 20 years. She had given him six children—which was admirable, of course, but everyone admitted it had also made her very fat. Niobe was

16, and all her life she had been told that she was by far the prettiest of her father's many daughters.

More important, Aristomenes seemed to find her very attractive indeed. In fact, when Aristomenes was with her he made the most extravagant declarations of adoration, and certainly he showered her with gifts. The morning after her wedding, he had presented her with a beryl ring set in gold that was so massive it was uncomfortable to wear. He had given her reams of purple silk, sandals with lapis beads, a diadem of ivory and gold, and a bottle carved out of crystal with a gold filigree stopper. And yet, for all his adoration when he was with her, he still left her entirely on her own for months at a time. She didn't understand that any more than she understood his peculiar behaviour last night.

Last night he had swept in very late and with no warning. She'd had no time to prepare herself for him. He had simply appeared out of seemingly nowhere, and in a very strange mood. Although she was almost ashamed to think this of the man her father had given her to, she could not avoid noting that he had behaved very much like he was intoxicated—although he claimed to have drunk no wine in days. He had literally burst in on her laughing, and declared, "This time I got him! I took that arrogant son-of-a-whore completely by surprise. You should have seen their faces! All of them cozy around their fires and we came at them out of the deep. Those Lacedamonian land-lubbers are afraid of the sea! They don't understand it is the greatest highway in the world. We overran their whole camp and threw their dinner into the bay! It will be the next new moon before they get their gear collected, let alone threaten me again! The asses! And we were away before they could even blow their silly flutes!" He had laughed until the tears glistened in the corners of his eyes.

Then he'd sent all her slaves away and made love to her in a rush of passion. He hadn't even taken the time to bathe first, and he had smelled of sweat and been dirty and covered with various minor scratches and scrapes and dried blood. His hair had been a snarled mess, still damp, and the blond strands were stiff and rough with salt. "You married a warrior, not a philosopher, girl," he told her when she protested.

That experience had left her confused and bruised and even a little frightened. She still hurt from the way he had taken her, but Kallisto said it was a compliment. "See! He wanted you so much, he just couldn't wait. You should be happy your husband is so ardent. You have no idea how many young brides weep away their nights alone, while their husbands prefer drinking companions, flute-girls or pretty boys." But Niobe much preferred it when Aristomenes paid her compliments and begged for her favours in the language of her father's court.

Niobe was frowning slightly in the gathering dusk. Aristomenes was sure to come to her again tonight, and she had to work out a strategy to teach him to treat her—a king's daughter!—better than the girls he presumably had while out campaigning. Niobe wondered if she should be very cool and distant to him tonight. Not actually deny him, of course. She had learned long ago that that could be dangerous. One of her father's concubines had tried that trick and she had promptly been sold to a brothel. Not that Aristomenes would dare do that to his bride and the daughter of a king, but after last night Niobe knew enough to know that she didn't know Aristomenes as well as she'd thought she did just 24 hours ago. She knew she shouldn't take dangerous chances.

A sound at the door made her turn and there was Kallisto. Kallisto had been her slave for as long as Niobe could remember. Even as a very little girl, Kallisto had always been there to take care of her. Her mother was only a distant, vague memory. She had died in childbed when Niobe was hardly more than a toddler. Kallisto had raised her.

Niobe had no idea how old Kallisto was, but she had streaks of grey in her hair and her face was deeply lined. It had never been a particularly pretty face—square with a flat nose. Kallisto came from the lands beyond Ionia and had been captured as a little girl by slave traders. She said all she remembered of her homeland was that it was very dry and dusty. She remembered, she said, standing in the door of a tent, and the wind blew the dust sideways and there were horses and shouting, and then the dust got in her eyes and someone grabbed her.

Now she was carrying a fat bronze jug full of steaming water. "Come, child, we must get you pretty for your lord husband," Kallisto called as she staggered under her burden into the bedchamber opening onto the peristyle.

Niobe followed her into the bedchamber. The ceiling beams here were brightly painted with red-and-yellow spirals. The walls themselves were a bright blue and painted with a broad band of dolphins dancing in stylized waves. The tiled floor was completely obscured by rich woven carpets in rust and straw-coloured geometric patterns. There were carved and painted chests all around the room containing those parts of her dowry which were movable and her personal things: her clothes, linens for beds, curtains, rugs, lamps, candelabra, pottery, jewellery and so on. There was a large bed with rich covers and the curtains drawn back. Niobe felt her pulse race slightly at the sight of it and hastily looked away to the dressing table with a chair before it. Then she focused on the small terracotta bathtub set on a woven mat. Kallisto had carried the water to the bath, and Niobe followed her there.

"Your lord husband is having a feast with his companions, but he is sure to come tonight. You want to look your best for him," Kallisto declared.

Niobe nodded. Of course she wanted to look her best for him—especially if she wanted to make him regret the haste and roughness of the business last night. She must make him admire and desire her so much that he would be anxious to please her and fulfil her whims. Niobe could remember how she and all her sisters and half-sisters used to fight over the only mirror they owned or study themselves in the surface of the pool trying to see if they were pretty or not. That she was the prettiest had been established early on and was reinforced by her father's obvious favour. Her father had always called her "my pretty darling," and she was always the first of his daughters that he kissed or took onto his lap. Moreover, Aristomenes had been the oppo-site of disappointed when he removed her veils on their wedding night and looked her up and down with a smile that grew wider and wider. But what good was beauty if it could not secure consideration for one's wishes?

Kallisto efficiently unpinned Niobe's peplos at the shoulders and removed the heavy gold pins with the goathead clasps. She unbuckled Niobe's belt with the knot-of-Herakles set on the buckle, and her mis-tress' peplos fell to the floor. Frowning, Kallisto turned and called over her shoulder in an irritable voice, "Mika! Where have you got to, you lazy bird-brain? Come quick and help me!"

At once the curtains of a little chamber opening off the back of the bedroom were pushed aside and Mika, the second of Niobe's personal slaves, emerged. Mika was much younger than Kallisto, probably Niobe's own age, and had been given to Niobe by her father as part of her dowry. Mika was very skinny with brown hair cut very short, pale brown eyes, colourless lips and no feminine curves at all. Her figure was rather that of an underfed teenage boy, while her face was ruined by warts all around the chin and lips. Niobe had been shocked by the sight of her, but her father explained that it was exactly this defect which made it certain that she would never be an object of desire. As such, the king told his teenage daughter, Niobe could be certain she would not "make trouble"—as slave-girls who were too attractive did. Who needed a slave who was pregnant all the time? Much less, one who might seduce the master of the house himself?

Mika darted in with a guilty expression and a hasty, "I'm sorry, Mis-tress" to Niobe. She hastily picked up the discarded peplos and started to fold it up to put it away.

"Brush it out first, you stupid girl!" Kallisto ordered with a frown, adding to Niobe as if Mika couldn't hear, "Really, the girl doesn't seem to have a brain in her head. You have to tell her absolutely everything!"

"That's not true!" Mika protested at once, but Niobe waved her silent with a regal gesture she had learned from her father's chief concubine. She addressed Kallisto herself in a patient voice, "She's just a barbarian from somewhere north of Macedonia. She doesn't know how to take proper care of things yet. My father warned me I'd have to train her properly."

"Well, I can see why no one wanted to keep her!" Kallisto declared, with a hateful look at the younger girl who was brushing out the peplos with a resentful expression on her face. "I know your father wanted someone young, someone who'll be there for you when I'm gone, but there must have been many more suitable girls in the markets than that!" Kallisto cast another look of distaste at Mika and ordered the younger slave to fetch lamps, adding, "Can't you see it's getting dark?"

Mika opened her mouth to answer, her face turning red with resentment, but already Kallisto had turned her attention back to her mistress. "Step into the bath, child, and let me sponge you down with rose-water."

Niobe stood in the bath with her arms outstretched. Kallisto took a sponge and dipped it into the steaming water that she had carried into the chamber. This was heavily perfumed with extract of roses. She wiped Niobe down with this water from her chin to her toes (grunting a bit as she bent over the rim of the tub to reach Niobe's feet). When she finished, she snapped her fingers and called "towel" with her hand stretched out. Mika all but threw a towel at her, but Kallisto ignored her contemptuously. Instead she dabbed the remnants of water away from Niobe's nubile body and then threw the towel back at Mika, who had to jump aside not to be hit by it.

Niobe ignored the silent bickering of her slaves. Her father's wife had advised her not to take notice of what her slaves said or did among themselves. She stepped out of the bath and went to stand beside the dressing table, knowing the routine. Kallisto had prepared her for her wedding and on every night of her brief "honeymoon" in exactly the same way. Only last night had he come too unexpectedly for there to be time for this.

Meanwhile Mika lit all the lamps on the five prongs of the bronze candelabrum standing beside the dressing table. They cast a gentle light that glittered on the carved crystal bottles of perfume and on the gold clasps of the various ivory, inlaid and pottery boxes. Kallisto opened one of the ivory boxes and removed the little pot of henna paste. She smeared the paste carefully onto Niobe's nipples, making them appear much larger. At 16, Niobe's breasts were still a little under-developed.

Next she had Niobe sit down and released her hair from the ribbons and pins that held it up on the back of her head. Niobe had rich, red locks of hair, not truly curly but wavy, and Kallisto felt they were best set off by bands of gold ribbon she braided into the locks before winding them upon the back of Niobe's head. This she proceeded to do, finishing her work with the gold and ivory diadem set above Niobe's brow.

Next came rouge for her lips and cheeks. Kallisto applied the lip rouge sparingly. Niobe had full lips and they did not need to be exaggerated any more. Her eyes, in contrast, were a pale grey-blue, and so Kallisto took a fine coal pencil and, dipping it frequently in one of the little pots of oil specially made for this purpose, very carefully outlined Niobe's eyes. She dipped her baby finger in one of the pots containing a fine blue powder and then applied this to Niobe's eyelids, smearing the powder up to her eyebrows. Using the coal again, she darkened Niobe's eyebrows and then stood back to consider her work critically. Kallisto dabbed again here and there until she was satisfied, before smearing perfume on the base of Niobe's neck and between her breasts.

At last she snapped her fingers for the towel, and when Mika handed it to her, she wiped her smeared fingers clean. Then she rummaged through the large, ivory jewellery box until she had found the amber and gold-pellet earrings and the matching necklace she was looking for. The necklace had pieces of rolled amber set between gold beads and one large drop of amber hanging from the centre. She set this around Niobe's neck and then hung the earrings from her ear-holes. She selected a gold bracelet with panels of embossed gold and an amber ring in addition to the rings Niobe always wore: the amethyst with Aphrodite carved into the surface given her by her father and the beryl set in gold from Aristomenes.

At last Niobe was coifed, perfumed, made-up and bejewelled.

Kallisto snapped at Mika to bring the mistress' rust-coloured silk gown.

Mika removed the requested peplos from one of the chests and brought it to Kallisto laid across her outstretched arms. Kallisto carefully spread the peplos on the floor so that Niobe could step into it. Then she lifted the gown by the shoulders and pulled it up over Niobe's naked body. Mika was already standing by with the gold shoulder pins and the belt. Kallisto deftly fastened the peplos with these. Last of all, Niobe's sandals were brought to her. These had golden and rolled lapis beads sewn on top of the leather. Kallisto bent to lay them before her mistress, who stepped into them daintily.

"Now! See how pretty you look?" Kallisto held up the polished silver mirror for Niobe. Niobe studied herself avidly. She certainly looked sophisticated when Kallisto was done with her. She hoped that in so much finery she would remind Aristomenes of who she was—a king's daughter and not some captive to be rolled in the straw!

"I'll go see how the symposium is coming along," Kallisto announced. "Mika, clear away all these towels and then fetch water and wine to set out beside the bed—and some figs and bread as well."

Niobe was left alone again. It was now completely dark and the birds were silent. Only the sound of crickets came from outside. She left the bedchamber to wander around the peristyle again. From the front of the house came the sound of male laughter and she sighed, wondering how long it would be before her husband came to her. She remembered that her father's parties could go all night, but surely Aristomenes would be eager—

The sounds from the front of the house had changed abruptly. Someone was shouting. Not happy shouting, joking and boasting and the like, but urgent, frightened shouting. More voices joined in, louder now and more alarmed.

"We're under attack!" A man fell into the peristyle, blood streaming from a wound in his side, and collapsed right there as if he were dead. Niobe's hair stood up on the back of her neck as she heard a scream that sounded like someone in pain. She couldn't believe it, though. The peristyle itself remained so still and lovely in the darkness.

Kallisto came up from behind her. "What is it? What is going on?"

"It seems to be an attack. That man said something about an attack." Niobe pointed to the man crumpled up on the opposite side of the peristyle holding his side.

"Here? That's impossible!" But Kallisto's eye took in the bleeding man and her ears, too, heard the shouting and clamour. She put her arm around her mistress protectively and urged with unmistakable unease, "Come back into your chamber until Aristomenes and his companions have driven them off."

The screaming and shouting had taken on a new quality; rather than urgency there was rage and hatred in the voices. The sound of things smashing and clattering started to reach them. Niobe looked over her shoulder from the threshold of her chamber, but all she saw was women, boys and clerks of household rushing into the peristyle.

"Lacedaemonians!" one of them gasped out.

"They're all over the place!" cried out the next.

"They've seized the kitchens and slaughtered everyone there," a woman gasped out as she sank onto her knees breathlessly, her hair torn from her pins and hanging around her face.

Niobe stared, but Kallisto pulled her inside her chamber, slamming the heavy oak door shut behind her. Kallisto's face was white and her eyes darted about the room as if she were looking for something. Shooing her mistress before her, she drove her through the curtain to the slaves' chamber. Here two straw pallets were on the floor, each with a crumpled blanket, and there was a wooden crate on which a chipped pitcher stood, along with a scattering of personal things. With a single gesture, Kallisto knocked these off the crate and told Niobe to sit there. "Whatever you hear, don't move! Don't move or speak. Stay right here until I come for you!"

Then Kallisto was gone. Niobe waited. It all seemed very unreal to her. She knew the Lacedaemonians had attacked, sacked and burned various estates throughout Messenia over the years, but mostly those on the west side of the Taygetos or on the broad Plain of the Five Rivers. They had never ventured this far west before. And Aristomenes was not alone here. He had at least 100 of his companions with him and various attendants and light infantry as well. Niobe saw in her mind's eye Aristomenes as she had last seen him, on the way to dinner tonight: his long blond hair had been freshly washed and had lifted on the wind while his chiton fluttered behind him as he strode out. She had loved the way he looked, because in his light indoor clothes you could see his firm, muscular body. But now her heart missed a beat. He was unarmed *and unarmoured*. What if they *all* were? But surely a watch had been set? The watch would be able to hold the Lacedaemonians long enough for Aristomenes and his companions to arm themselves. Surely....

The palms of her hands were starting to sweat, and yet she was very cold. She strained to hear something beyond the curtain and the closed door, but although there were noises, they were confused and indistinct, nothing she could really identify. After what seemed like a long time, the noises grew dimmer and then faded away. Niobe sighed with relief and got up from her chest. She peered around the curtain. Nothing. She stood indecisively in the cramped chamber, but then decided to do what Kallisto had told her to do. She returned to the chest, sat down and waited.

At last the door to her chamber banged open and she jumped up eagerly. But something made her catch her breath and stand still. The voices she could hear were *male*, unfamiliar male voices. And no Messenian man would dare enter Aristomenes' bedchamber.

"Aha."

"Very nice."

And then without further ado, the curtain was pulled aside and a fully armoured man, his helmet still covering his face, looked in. He started visibly at the sight of her, but then gestured and ordered simply, "Come with me."

Niobe's throat went dry. Her heart was pounding furiously. The man had still-wet blood all along his right arm. Blood had splattered the bronze of his breastplate. She could smell his sweat in the confines of the little chamber. He was wearing Spartan scarlet under his bronze.

He stood back to let her out of the chamber and pointed out of the chamber toward the peristyle. Niobe managed somehow to put one foot in front of the other, although her joints seemed like jelly. Her head was spinning and her breathing was shallow. Everything was happening too fast. She couldn't believe what she was seeing with her own eyes.

Crowded into the peristyle were what appeared to be the entire household: the laundry maids, the kitchen boys, the cook and the clerks, the household slaves of both sexes. Kallisto gave a little cry at the sight of her beloved mistress and dropped her face into her hands, but Mika was nowhere in sight. From the other rooms around the peristyle, other Spartan hoplites were driving the wives of Aristomenes' companions and their slaves to join the crowd. Niobe had never realized how large the household was until she saw it all collected here together—there were about a hundred of them. And not a single fighting man.

"Aristomenes?" she managed to breathe out, addressing her question generally, while her eyes darted about for someone who might know what had become of him.

"Don't worry. That coward thinks of his own skin first. He got away as usual." The answer came from the hoplite who had found her. He shoved his helmet back onto his brow, revealing a surprisingly normal face. He looked about 40 and could have been a farmer anywhere, with a thick brown beard and kindly wrinkles around his eyes. He left her with the others and went purposefully down the corridor by which Niobe had last seen Aristomenes leave for dinner only hours earlier.

Kallisto worked her way through the crowd to Niobe. She put her arms around her mistress protectively, but her hands were trembling.

Niobe looked at the women around her. On all their faces was the same stunned horror. They were captives. Slaves. No, not that. Not her. She was a king's daughter, the wife of the man who would be King of Messenia.

"They'll spare you," Kallisto whispered to her, as if reading her thoughts. "They'll spare you for your father's sake. They can't risk his anger. You're worth a huge ransom. They won't dare lay a hand on you."

No, Niobe nodded unconsciously, they won't hurt me. But what about the others? Surely Kallisto was too old, but her eyes went to the wives of Aristomenes' companions. They were noblewomen like herself. On their faces was the same disbelief that she felt. Their husbands and fathers would pay huge ransoms for their freedom, too. No, they had nothing to fear. But they looked as terrified as Niobe felt.

What if these Lacedaemonian peasants, who called themselves "peers," didn't respect noblewomen? After all, if they could take away the land of their own nobles and divide it up among themselves, then maybe they didn't respect nobility at all?

But she had one shield that the others did not have: beauty. Lifting her chin a little higher, she reminded herself that even barbarians respected beauty. All her life she had seen that a woman's beauty could tame the beast in any man. She had to use that weapon now.

A small commotion drew Niobe's attention back to the corridor leading from the front of the house. A tall man in plain armour and a black-crested helmet emerged into the atrium flanked by two younger men. One of these was in the most splendid embossed armour, while the other was in worn leather armour and holding a torch, apparently only a low-born infantryman. They were followed by a half-dozen other heavy infantrymen, including the man who had found her.

Although his armour was much simpler than that of several of his companions, all eyes were on the tall man at the head of the little group. There could be little doubt that whoever he was, he was in command here. He was exceptionally tall, even without the black crest of his Corinthian helmet. He was lean. The veins of his arms stood out so prominently that they were visible even by the dim light of the lamps and torches. His nose had a large bump on it, and his eyes glittered with predatory coldness over a short dark-blond beard. Niobe felt a shiver go down her spine. He didn't look like the kind of man who had much sense for beauty.

Raised on the *Iliad*, there was not one woman in the peristyle at Pylos who did not know that the conquerors had their pick of the captive women. Even the Queen of Troy and her priestess daughter had not been spared. But *they* had had no fathers, brothers or husbands left who could pay a ransom, Niobe reminded herself as she tried to calm her rising panic. She failed. All she could think was that the first pick of women went to the most senior of the enemy—and that could only be this lean killing machine with the predatory eyes. And of course he would pick the prettiest of the captives....

Suddenly from the corridor to the front of the house came a crash, a curse, and high-pitched screaming in both bass and soprano. Everyone turned to stare as a burly hoplite emerged, carrying over his shoulder a kicking, struggling and screaming Mika. "Let go of me, you motherfucking bastard! Put me down, you shit-head!"

Niobe was shocked and mortified to see her own personal slave not only stark naked but behaving like an absolute savage and using that kind of language. The man carrying her, meanwhile, cursed her back in similar language, but she had no chance of escape. Mika was far too weak and small to escape his massive, muscular arms. When he flung her down into the pool in the centre of the peristyle with a huge splash, Mika was defeated. She staggered up out of the water, gasping for air and wiping water and hair out of eyes as everyone—not just the enemy—laughed.

"Zeus! Would you look at that!" the hoplilte who had brought her exclaimed with a look of distaste. "The ugly thing had no need to hide. None of us are *that* desperate!"

There was laughter again. Mika crouched down, clutching her knees to her chest and her arms around her knees. She was clearly trying to hide her tiny pointed breasts and pubic hair from public ridicule, and then she bowed her head and pressed it to her knees to cover her ugly wart-covered face as well.

The laughter died away and the predatory eyes of the commander swept across the collected household. They returned and focused on Niobe—just as she had expected. Her heart was pounding furiously. She felt as if the enemy commander were stripping her with his eyes, and became abruptly aware that she was not only unveiled but also dressed for the intimacy of her bedchamber. No strange male had ever seen her like this before. Her head and neck were bare except for the necklace, her arms naked, the silk of her gown so sheer that the form of her torso and legs must be visible even in the dim light of the lamps that hung all round the peristyle.

Kallisto could stand it no longer. She flung herself forward onto her knees in front of Niobe. "Mercy, Master! My mistress is the daughter of King Aristokrates of Arkadia, the wife of Aristomenes—"

"What? Another one? How many of these 'wives' does he maintain?" The question came from the young man in the splendid armour who stood just one pace behind the commander.

The commander turned his head slowly to look at the young man, but did not reply. Still, the laughter of the other men confused Niobe. She heard someone remark, "He must keep 'wives' the way we keep post-horses—one every 20–30 miles."

Another man was saying, "This is the second of his concubines we've captured in the last year."

"But she's his *wife*," Kallisto called out desperately; "his wife, not his concubine. Her father is King Aristo—"

"Yes, and we know how many concubines *he* keeps! He must have a stable of bastards he can give away to his friends," the young man in the splendid armour cut her off. Then, turning to his commander, he remarked, "I fancy this one, Agesandros; you wouldn't object to me taking her, would you?"

Niobe was so terrified she couldn't breathe at all. Both men turned to look at her. There was no doubt about it now: the man with the bump on his nose and the predatory eyes was the infamous Agesandros, the man Aristomenes hated more than any other, the man he claimed to have surprised and sent running only yesterday. He was supposed to be so confused he couldn't attack for a month....

Niobe's found herself praying to all the gods at once: anyone but him, anyone! She let her eyes shift to the young man in the elaborately embossed armour, pleading to him with her eyes to rescue her.

He was stocky and muscular with a square, clean-shaven face, dominated by a short pug nose. Despite being nearly the opposite of Aristomenes in every way, he was undoubtedly handsome. And he was young—21 or 22, Niobe guessed—half Aristomenes' age.

Agesandros took his time, but then he answered in an even, emotionless tone, "It's your right, my lord, to take first pick."

"After you, sir," the young man stressed with a vigorous nod.

Agesandros dismissed this with an irritated flick of his hand, already turning away from Niobe as he said, "I'm a married man." His next remark was to one of the other men. "We're going to need a thorough inventory of what we've taken here. We should sell the bulk goods and livestock in the harbour and send only the slaves and important valuables back to Lacedaemon. Have Onatas report to me with the inventory and his estimates on its value as soon as possible. I don't want to spend more than another day here." He paused and looked over his shoulder at the crowd of women and slaves and added, "And have one of the perioikoi commanders look into hiring a cargo ship to send the lot back to Lacedaemon. I don't like the thought of having to provide an escort for them all the way home."

Agesandros was moving toward the corridor out of the women's quarters again, followed this time only by the young man with the torch. He paused just before leaving the peristyle and addressed the torch-bearer. "You can stay, Leon. You have a right to the spoils, too, you know."

"That's all right, sir. I've never done it with a girl who didn't want it. I—" Niobe could see the embarrassed way the youth looked down, not meeting Agesandros' predatory eyes, "I don't think I could."

To her astonishment, Agesandros didn't laugh or mock the youth. Instead, he laid his hand on his shoulder and she thought she heard him mutter, "You're a better man than I am," before they continued out together.

Niobe jumped as her wrist was seized. She had been so fascinated by Agesandros, she had not noticed that the young man who'd claimed her had moved up directly to her. "No point pining after Agesandros. He's madly in love with his wife. I'll give you a better time. Where was Aristomenes' chamber?" His eyes were already sweeping along the doors opening off the atrium.

Kallisto, still on her knees, flung her arms around his legs and made one last attempt to stop him. "Please, Master, please spare her. Her father will pay a huge ransom for her safe return."

"Good. If I don't like her enough to take home, I'll take the ransom instead. Now, let go of me." As he spoke he looked down at Kallisto with a cold-blooded authority that withered the resistance of the old slave woman. She released his legs slowly, but she kept her eyes fixed on his face, hoping he would change his mind.

He didn't.

Mika had been in the kitchen fetching the bread and figs for Niobe's bed-side table when the attack occurred. Her first panicked reaction at the sight of men with bloody swords had been to hide. As she had learned to do as a child, she rushed to climb a tree, but her chiton got in her way. In her panic, she had tossed it aside. Thus when the hoplite pulled her down and dumped her in the pool in front of everyone, she had been naked. She was so ashamed, she wanted to die. She knew her body was nothing to be proud of, but she had never exposed it like that to hundreds of eyes. And no matter how true the remarks about her ugliness were, it still hurt to hear the mockery. Worse: people who she'd thought were her friends laughed at her in her humiliation.

Still, despite her own humiliation, she had been shocked when she saw Niobe, the beautiful king's daughter, led away. And then, one after another, the other young and pretty women were claimed. She heard the noble wife of one of Aristomenes' companions sobbing and crying out in despair from the room next to Niobe's. She heard another women begging "please not that" from another chamber, and soon she began to fear in a way she never had before.

After the pretty women and youths were divided up, it was the turn of the older men and less attractive women, girls and boys. This was done more rationally and yet more heartlessly. It was a matter of adding up specifications: age, race, sex, skills, defects. Most of the men didn't even bother to ask Mika about her skills. They took one look at her, grimaced, and moved on. Late in the night when she was falling asleep with her head on her knees, she heard the men around her talking. "No one wants that one. We'll have to try to sell her with the livestock in the market in town tomorrow."

"She won't bring much."

"What else should we do with her? Something's better than nothing."

"The Lady Alethea could use her."

Mika jumped at the sound of a new voice and turned to look at the speaker. A slender young man came into the light of the torches still burning around the atrium. He was very dark. His straight eyebrows almost met over his fine, straight nose. His eyes were a dark brown, warm even at that dark hour of the night. He was clutching his himation around him against the chill of the night—and to Mika he seemed the most beautiful young man she had ever seen.

"Have you had a close look at her?" one of the other men answered the youth in obvious disbelief.

"Yes," he answered simply.

"You're an odd one, Leon. If there's any wife who doesn't have to surround herself with ugly slaves, it's the Lady Alethea. She's got Agesandros so hog-tied to her, he doesn't even look at the captives that throw themselves at him."

The youth smiled at that, a quick flash of even white teeth, but then insisted, "She's still short-handed." The others shrugged, and so the youth came and touched Mika on the elbow. "Your hair's soaking wet and you've got nothing on. You've got to come in out of the cold and get some clothes on you. You have nothing to fear."

Mika was at once grateful for his consideration, and more embarrassed than ever. Being naked beside such a good-looking young man made her doubly aware of both her nakedness and her ugliness. At least it was dark and there was no one else around to gawk at her. To her horror, however, the youth led her to the very chamber where the infamous Agesandros, the Scourge of Messenia, was sleeping soundly on a reed cot in his cloak. The youth gave Mika one of his own chitons and a himation from a knapsack hanging on the wall, and then spread out a blanket on a mat on the floor.

"My name is Leon," he whispered; "you don't have to worry. Neither of us will misuse you. Lie down and try to get some sleep." He lay down himself, carefully wrapped in his own himation, and turned his face to the wall as if to demonstrate he meant what he said.

Mika was too frightened to think of doing anything other than what he ordered. She dropped down onto the mat and stretched herself out. But how could she sleep? The full impact of what had happened fell upon her like a great weight. Her beautiful princess-mistress was now a slave and she was herself in the hands of the Spartans. Her beautiful world, her beautiful fairytale world, had come crashing down around her ears. She had never been so happy as she had been here with the beautiful princess, and Sparta was bound to be more horrible than anything that had gone before.

Not that she knew anything about Sparta except what Kallisto and the other slaves had said, but they said that in Sparta the women went around naked all the time and wrestled like men and went barefoot just like slaves. And the men—well, they were these horrible killers, more interested in war than in their wives or even their children. Spartans knew nothing about love, that was certain, and Mika was reminded of the sobs and whimpering that had come from the chambers of the captured noblewomen.

She knew she ought to be glad that none of them had wanted her, but there was little comfort in the fact that she now belonged to them nevertheless. And what did they want with her? The future was a horrible black nothingness and she was so cold that she started shivering. After a moment, her teeth started chattering, too. Terrified of waking the men on either side of her, she clamped her jaw shut.

It was too late. The youth on the floor beside her grunted slightly, turned over, and without even appearing to wake up pulled her into his arms—not like a lover, more like a brother or a comrade. "Try to sleep," he murmured sleepily.

Mika could not remember being held in anyone's arms before. She was amazed at how quickly the warmth from the youth warmed her back and stopped her shivering. The feel of his warm breath on her shoulder was like a warm, gentle breeze and the sound of his steady breathing was calming. Very gradually, the tension eased and she surrendered to sleep.

CHAPTER 2

Niobe woke feeling stiff and sticky, bruised and still bewildered beside the young man who had claimed her as his prize. She was desperately thirsty and almost as desperate for a bath. But she was afraid to leave the bed, afraid it would wake the man snoring on his back beside her. She was afraid that if he woke up, he might want to do it yet again. All she wanted now was to get away from him and clean herself up and then cry in Kallisto's comforting arms. She wanted it all to be over. She wanted the nightmare to end.

Abruptly, with a single knock and hardly an apology, a short-legged man with a long beard broke into the chamber and announced, "Agesandros wants the inventory this morning." Niobe's new master grunted and rolled over with a groan. He sat up in bed, rubbing his eyes and indifferently pulling the covers off Niobe in the process. She gasped and managed to pull a corner of the bed sheet to cover at least her breasts and pubic hair from the eyes of the old man. But neither her new master nor the auditor paid her any attention.

The auditor had gone to the chest nearest the door and started pulling the contents out. He noted each item he found on a wax tablet he carried. His stained accountant's hands felt the quality of the silk and his near-sighted eyes inspected the quality of the embroidery with a cold-bloodedness that chilled Niobe. To him, the white silk chiton with gold embroidery that she had worn at her wedding was nothing more than a commodity. She watched him empty every chest in the room, spilling all her treasures and all her memories onto the floor with heartless efficiency, and a knot started to grow in her throat until it became hard to swallow. In the light of day, watching this strange servant callously catalogue her treasures impressed upon her her new status more than the rape of the night before—or maybe the shock was beginning to wear off.

When the auditor started going through the jewellery boxes, Niobe's master left the bed and went to look over his shoulder. At the sight of the coral and gold necklace, which had been a gift of one of Aristomenes' uncles to her, he reached out his hand and fastened it over the fist of the clerk. "You don't have to write that down. I'm keeping it for my mother."

The auditor turned and stared up at him in amazement. Then without a word he continued with his list and left.

Scratching at his crotch and yawning, Niobe's master came back to the bed, and for a moment Niobe was afraid he was going to start all over again, but he stretched instead and announced, "I better get dressed and find some breakfast." He paused and with a crooked smile remarked, "You look funny with all that paint on your face smeared about and your hair looking like a rats' nest. You need some practice before you're really good, but I think I'll keep you. Your father wouldn't want you back now anymore, would he?" He laughed at his own joke and then bent and took his chiton off the floor to pull it over his head.

He had almost finished dressing when a Spartiate in scarlet and bronze burst into the chamber scowling, "Anaxilas?" So that was his name, Niobe noted. Anaxilas. "What's this I hear about you trying to pocket valuables for yourself?"

Anaxilas didn't even look at the speaker as he casually finished fastening his baldric. "Who said that?"

"Onatas. Don't be a fool. Give me the necklace."

"Why? I want it for my mother." He looked over at last and reminded the intruder, "The Kings have a right to double the normal share of loot."

"Only after the loot has been collected and valued and the portions set—not before. Besides, you aren't king yet. Your father isn't even king yet. But if Agesandros finds out about this, your *grandfather* will hear of it, too—and *he'll* have your hide!"

Anaxilas squirmed uneasily and, scowling, went to the dressing table. He picked up the necklace, but he did not turn it over to the other man. Instead he asked, "Why should Agesandros hear of it?"

"Agesandros hears of everything that happens in his battalion sooner or later—"

"Sooner, in your case." Agesandros himself was in the doorway, fully armoured with his helmet on his brow. "Stealing from your comrades-in-arms is not the best way of winning their respect, Anaxilas. I'd try to remember that, if I were you." The green-gold eyes of the commander shifted to the bed and Niobe pulled the covers up higher and closer, ashamed that she was lying there naked, her make-up smeared and her hair in disarray. It made her feel so cheap, and for the first time since her capture, tears filled her eyes. Agesandros saw them and his eyes lingered on her for a second longer with a strange expression on his face. Then he turned back to Anaxilas. "You had your prize when you took Aristomenes' concubine. Everything else is common spoils." He held out his hand and Anaxilas very promptly turned over the necklace.

"Take the rest of the jewellery off the girl," was the next order, and Anaxilas docilely went to the bed and removed the amber necklace and earrings, the gold bracelet and Niobe's various rings—including the rings her father and Aristomenes had given her after her wedding. The tears were now trickling down her face, and Anaxilas scoffed loudly, "Isn't that just like a woman! It hurts her more to part with her trinkets than her virtue."

"I hope your grandfather and father both live long enough for you to grow up," Agesandros remarked dryly, and then was gone.

"Who the hell does he think he is!?" Anaxilas burst out furiously. "Agesandros, son of an illiterate drunkard—"

Anaxilas was cut off by the other Spartiate. "He's the man who captured Phigalia, the youngest battalion commander in the Spartan Army, the protegé of the Supreme Polemarch—but most important of all, he's a Spartiate peer. I'd think twice about insulting him for expressing an opinion *all* the men in this battalion share." The other man was gone, and Anaxilas in fury swept everything off the bed-side table so that the pottery shattered on the floor, spilling what was left of the wine onto the pretty rug. "Clean it up!" he ordered Niobe, and then stormed out of the chamber.

Mika, too, soon found herself face to face with the Scourge of Messenia. She had woken to an empty room and sat on the floor completely bewildered, thinking she had been abandoned—so worthless that she wasn't even worth taking along or selling. But then the youth had returned with some bread for her to eat, a comb for her hair and a simple leather belt. "Make yourself as presentable as possible," he urged. "Agesandros will be back any minute."

She did her best, but when Leon returned with Agesandros a few moments later, the latter did not look terribly pleased by the sight of her. Although his expression was less marked by aversion than Aristomenes' had been when she had been presented to him the first time, nevertheless Agesandros frowned and remarked to the youth, "I said last night that you had a right to a prize, Leon, but what makes you think Alethea will want to have the girl around permanently?"

"She's very short-handed in the kitchen and Sybil can hardly get up and down stairs anymore, and Kassia is now at an age when she should have a maid-servant of her own," Leon answered earnestly.

Agesandros' eyes shifted to him, and there was something very like amusement in them even as he scowled. "She's your prize, Leon. Do with her as you please—but if Alethea objects, you'll have to come up with another solution."

Leon grinned, "Yes, sir."

Agesandros was gone again, and Leon smiled at Mika. "Now you're safe," he told her with what sounded like a touch of relief. He added with apparent urgency, "They are sending all of the captives back to Sparta this very afternoon, by ship. You'll be on the manifest as the property of the Lady Alethea; but remember, if anyone tries to lay a hand on you or treat you badly in any way, tell them you are *Agesandros'* prize. Tell them he is sending you home to serve his lady. No one will dare harm you then."

It was one of the clerks that informed Niobe that the captives were to be taken by sea back to Sparta. She was told she would be allowed to take with her only what she was wearing—that is, only one set of clothes. Niobe managed to seize one of her prettiest peplos, a richly decorated himation and a good belt, but in her haste to claim them before they were taken away from her, they did not match well. She also snatched her favourite set of sandals just before some men came to pack away the plunder for shipment.

When the captives were rounded up in the courtyard for departure, Niobe noticed that some of the other noblewomen looked even worse off than she. One woman was so dazed that she just shuffled along still wearing her torn and dirty finery of the night before, while others had apparently been forced to put on the robes of their own slaves—coarse, homespun garments without adornment of any kind.

Then she caught sight of Kallisto across the courtyard, and although the old slave woman did not look as if she had been abused, her eyes were full of agonized questions. The sympathy in her expression reminded Niobe again of the humiliations of the night before, and tears stung her eyes, but there was no time for self-pity. The captives were being herded out of the palace and down to the port where a large sailing vessel was tied to the quay.

Niobe had never travelled by sea before, but she had watched with pleasure the vessels with their bright-painted prows and sails ply in and out of the harbour ever since she'd come to Pylos. She had noticed the passengers that stood on deck under stripped canopies, and she looked forward to the journey. After all, since the Spartans weren't coming with them, there could be no repetition of last night. And now that she knew she had been claimed by a king's grandson, she expected she would be treated well. Anaxilas might be able to do with her as he pleased—as indeed any man could with his women, whether wives, concubines or slaves—but surely no one else would dare lay a hand on a prince's prize?

But when they got down to the quay, Niobe was not separated from the common slaves. Instead, despite her protests, she was crowded together with the others in the hold. This had a bed of old, stale sawdust and nothing else. Next the hatchways were nailed shut.

Niobe was still in a daze of shock and fear when Kallisto at last managed to push and wriggle her way through the others to reach Niobe's side. She took her poor, stunned mistress in her arms, and they sat side by side in the darkness waiting for what would happen next. From overhead came the sound of sailors running on the deck. They heard creaking, thumping, flapping, and clanking, none of which made any sense to them. And then, with a lurch, the ship started to move. Indeed, it started to toss the helpless passengers from side to side without warning. They cried out in fear and outrage as they were flung against the sides of the ship or the foot of the mast or crushed together. But if their cries were heard on deck, no one paid the slightest attention.

Then, without warning, the vessel abruptly leaned hard on its side, causing the passengers to scream in panic. Like the others, Niobe thought they were capsizing and screamed hysterically. But apparently the ship had only just cleared the harbour and skirted the island of Sphacteria, because it steadied on a steep heel and started to plunge and swoop its way forward over the waves.

Within minutes the first of them was seasick, and the smell and sound of retching soon made the others sick. Kallisto stroked Niobe's hair and wiped her face clean with the hem of her own skirt after she was sick. Then she had Niobe lie down with her head in her lap, and soothingly tried to comfort her. Kallisto had learned that Niobe's master was the grandson of one of the Spartan kings, and so she assured Niobe that even as a slave her life would be far from bad. "As a prince, he'll have fine apartments in his father's palace. All you need do is please him, little one. And how can you not please him? So pretty as you are! You'll see. You'll live there just as you did at home—think of your father's concubines. You'll even have slaves to wait on you." Kallisto's throat grew tight, thinking that she wouldn't be there to serve Niobe.

Niobe was too miserable to even hear the pain in her nanny's voice.

They were given water but nothing to eat for the night-long voyage to Gytheon. At Gytheon the hold was opened and the passengers were ordered out. Hardly any of them could do more than crawl by that stage. They were stiff, weak, hungry, filthy and stinking. The bright sunlight blinded them after the darkness of the hold, and the fresh air after the stuffy stink below deck was almost intoxicating. They stumbled and staggered on cramped limbs as they tried to shield their eyes from the sun.

A crowd had collected on the quay, and they were greeted by loud exclamations of "Oooh! They stink!" or "Are all Messenian women so ugly?" and the like. Their escort, which consisted of helot auxiliaries, officiously ordered the crowd to stand back. The captives were ordered to sit on the deck and a half-loaf of bread and a hand-sized hard cheese was given to each of them. They ate ravenously. Even Niobe, who had never before in her life eaten with dirty hands and no knife, tore into the bread with her teeth as the others did.

To leave the ship, they were roped together for the first time. There were 10 different ropes, each with 8 or 9 slaves bound around the waist and a guard at each end. They were led off the ship and through the town.

Everywhere people came out of the shops or hung out of the windows to see them and call down insults. "Filthy Messenian sluts!" "May your husbands and sons rot unburied!" "Misbegotten whores of Messenian bastards!" Niobe had never dreamed there was so much hatred anywhere—much less aimed at innocent girls and women like herself and her companions. It seemed particularly unfair that most of the insults were directed at the women rather than the boys and men in the slave-column.

They were led to a sloping beach on which many fishing boats and one penteconter were pulled up. The guards led them straight into the shallow water and ordered them to clean themselves up. Like the others, Niobe squatted down until the water came up to her neck and rubbed herself as clean as she could with sand and the skirts of her peplos. The pretty things she had chosen for herself just the day before were completely ruined already.

The tugging at her waist told her, even before the orders were shouted, that it was time to wade out again. With their clothing clinging to them so that every feature of their bodies was revealed, they were again led through the city. But this time added to the insults and jeering was a new torment: the sun was starting to beat down mercilessly. Niobe, who had never been exposed to it before, felt it burning her skin.

Then the real torture began. They were led up the steep incline of the hill on which the town was built, and as they passed through the walls outside the gate, it began to dawn on Niobe that they were expected to walk all the way to Sparta. Although she had no real idea of where Sparta was, she knew it lay far inland, nowhere near the sea. Just the climb up the slope of the town left her gasping for breath, her heart pounding and her face bright red. Niobe, who had never walked farther than from one chamber to another of her father's place, was exhausted within the next hour. Added to this was the fact that her pretty little sandals were ill suited for walking on a rocky road. Every pebble and every stone bruised her tender feet. She was soon lagging, holding the other women on her rope back, and some of them—mere slaves who had once bowed to her and jumped to fulfil any whim—were muttering insults and complaints. Niobe could not understand how they could be so unkind. She had never done them any harm that she could remember.

The guards, noting the problem, took her out of the centre of her rope and put her at the front, next to one of the guards. He then took hold of the rope at her waist and pulled her forward with his own strength, holding her up when she stumbled.

She was grateful to him until they finally stopped for their first break. Then the guard sat down beside her and said she owed him a "quickie" for all the help he'd given her. Niobe was so shocked, she was speechless. It was bad enough that Anaxilas had not made special provision for her transport back to his palace in more suitable fashion, but it was unthinkable that she should be treated like a common whore. She was still a king's daughter! Besides, this was an ugly, middle-aged helot!

The man seemed to take her stunned silence for consent. He pushed her over backwards as if he intended to have his way with her right there at the side of the road in front of everyone. Niobe screamed, and one of the other guards called out sharply, "I wouldn't do that if I were you. She belongs to Prince Anaxilas."

"Shit! Just my luck! Fucking whore!" he responded in frustration. Then he stood and kicked her hard in the thigh before stalking off in shame, while his comrades laughed at him.

On the next stage of the journey, of course, he made no attempt to help Niobe. Instead he poked and shoved at her to make her walk faster, although by now her feet were blistered from the straps of her sandals, her thigh hurt from his kick, and her legs were so exhausted that she simply couldn't go any faster. At last the woman behind her took pity on her and pushed her forward for a while, but she too was unused to walking such distances. When Niobe tripped and fell down, the other woman didn't have the strength to help her up.

Niobe wept openly. She had ripped a knee open with the fall, and the bone itself seemed so bruised she wondered if it was broken. When she tried to straighten her leg, the pain made her gasp and cry out.

The man commanding the escort came back and pulled up her skirts to look at the injury without any regard for her modesty. Niobe blushed and closed her eyes in shame, but he only grunted. "She's slowed us down enough already. Kallias, run up to the next kleros and borrow a mule. Simon, take her on your back until the mule gets here."

Niobe was untied and heaved onto the broad back of a stinking, hairy giant. The sun was hotter than ever now, and the man was soon drenched in sweat, soaking the front of Niobe's dress. Eventually a donkey arrived, and Niobe was heaved onto the bony back of the little animal. The animal had been lying in his own manure, and no one bothered to brush it off before she was ordered to sit on him. The dirt of the stable rubbed into her only peplos and soon the insides of her thighs were bruised from the spine of the piteous animal. By nightfall, Niobe was so exhausted, bruised and aching that she could hardly eat the bread and cheese they gave to her. The skin of her arms and her face was burnt bright red and ached continuously. She lay in the straw of the barn in which they had been locked for the night and wanted to die.

Kallisto lay down beside her and whispered, "Your lover will be furious with them when he finds out what they did to you. Tomorrow when we reach Sparta, you'll be cleaned up and taken care of. Tomorrow night you'll sleep in a fine, soft bed again, and everything will be fine."

But she would have to get through tomorrow first, Niobe thought miserably, still unable to understand how it could have come to this.

Mika, too, was miserably seasick during the voyage, but after the meal and the wash in the sea she started to feel better. Walking was no problem for her. Her feet were better soled than the best shoes in the world, because she had never worn sandals in her life. Her skin had long since tanned a dark, protective brown, and although the sun was very hot it did not bother her excessively. She was used to hunger, too.

Mika's parents had been poor and they had often gone hungry. Her father was a lumberjack, working in the forests, and they lived from what her mother could grow in a small, rocky kitchen garden and from what they could gather in the forest: mushrooms, berries, and nuts. In bad years they ate bark.

But that was long ago. Mika had spent much of the last two and half years in slave caravans like this, tied at the waist to others being herded, like her, to an unknown future. There was nothing strange about it anymore, nor any humiliation really. What was there to be ashamed of?

She had been sold by her uncles as soon as her father died. She had fought like a wildcat and almost got away from them once, but then they bound her in a sack so she could hardly breathe and dumped her over the back of their only mule. By the time they let her out, they were camped in the middle of a dense forest filled with wild animals and she hadn't the faintest idea which way was home. When they reached the city on the coast, she was far too intimidated by the strange people in their funny clothes, communicating with a babble of sounds that had nothing to do with language as she knew it, to try to run away. She had been inspected, poked, stripped and rejected by what seemed like dozens of men before her uncles finally found a buyer. And then her uncles had gone away cursing each other and passing the blame back and forth for the bad price they'd got.

After that she'd been sold again and again, never kept for long by any master or mistress. At first she had been rebellious and sullen, earning frequent blows, beatings and even days locked in a damp, cramped cellar without food or water. Even after she'd been broken and *wanted* to please her owners, she had lacked the language and hadn't understood what they wanted of her. Gradually she picked up enough Greek to understand and make herself understood, but still she had failed to please, although she had done many things.

One of the worst times had been a short spell with a blacksmith where she had done nothing but squeeze the bellows all day in oven-like heat. Because she fainted more than once, he'd sold her. She'd belonged briefly to a fuller, and had had to tread cloth in the dye-pools for hours on end. But he sold her because the fumes from the dyes made her sick to her stomach and she'd vomited into the dye. For months after that her feet and lower legs had been dyed an ugly brown-grey. Eventually, again the property of a trader and travelling in a slave caravan, she came to a place in the high mountains that was cold and rainy. Here she had stood shivering in the middle of the marketplace when with great fanfare, an enormously fat man surrounded by dozens of slaves appeared. The man was dressed in rich-coloured, elaborately woven and embroidered gowns, and his hands were weighted down with rings. His slaves spread carpets before him so he did not have to step in the filth, and he sat down on a chair they had carried for him. The slave-girls were brought to him one at a time, and from the awed whispers of her companions Mika learned that he was the King of Arkadia.

Since the king demanded young female slaves, the trader thought he was after bed-mates and did not even send Mika forward for inspection. But he regretted his decision. Scowling, the King shouted angrily, "Have you no *ugly* slave-girls?!"

"Ugly?" asked the astonished slave trader.

"What does my daughter want with a pretty slave?" the king had retorted. "I want a girl so ugly, not even a notorious lecher like Aristomenes would want to touch her." And so the trader had grabbed Mika with delight and shoved her forward in obvious excitement at his good luck. The King had been no less delighted and had paid a handsome price—more than anyone had ever paid for her before.

Abruptly, Mika found herself in the household of a king's daughter. She found herself in a world she had never known existed. Even as a slave, her standard of living was beyond all her wildest dreams. She had a warm, dry bed, enough food to eat and fresh, clean water to drink any time she wanted. She was given a wool chiton for winter and a flax chiton for summer. She'd even been given a discarded leather belt and a comb for her hair. And her duties were light, even pleasant—dusting and polishing beautiful things, brushing and folding fine gowns, fetching and carrying the precious little objects that a maiden wanted. The worst task, cleaning out Niobe's chamber pot, was hardly a burden at all to the hardened Mika. And Niobe herself was so beautiful and removed from the world Mika had known that Mika admired everything about her—the way she looked, moved and even smelled. Mika was awed by her graceful gestures, her dainty feet and mincing step.

Mika had also enjoyed being part of a large household. She loved sleeping with the other slave-girls in the warm loft above the hearth room and she loved sharing hearty meals in the kitchen. But most of all, she loved the nights in the slave's hall listening to the others talk. At last she felt like she belonged somewhere—until they all laughed at her when she was thrown naked into the pool of the peristyle like an unwanted cat.

Because of her warts, she thought, and her hands automatically felt the warts on her chin. She had not always had warts. When she was very little, she could even remember her father smiling at her. The warts had come only after she was 9 or 10. Her mother had tried all sorts of remedies, but nothing worked. Instead, the warts spread from her hands to her chin and lips. Her father had stopped smiling at her and started to shout at her. He cursed her mother and said they should have "drowned this one rather than the others." Her mother cried a lot, and answered that it must be the will of the gods.

Mika supposed it was. The gods were full of surprises. Niobe, who had seemed almost like a goddess, was now only a slave like herself. Niobe, who had been carried in a litter whenever she left the palace, now had to walk with the rest of them. And her beautiful, soft white skin was burned bright red like a boiled crab. It was the way the gods were. Cruel and capricious.

As they made their way up the valley beside a broad, muddy brown river, Mika accepted that, wonderful as her short service amidst the luxury of a royal palace had been, it was over. So she looked with interest at the countryside around her, noting that it was as rich and green and cultivated as the richest lands she had ever seen. She was surprised by the way the farmsteads came at regular intervals, and even if these were not palaces, they seemed peaceful and content in their broad valley at the foot of majestic, snow-capped mountains. Mika started imagining herself living on one of them, and she smiled at the children that came to stare at the passing slave caravan.

CHAPTER 3

It was dusk of the second day before they reached the southern out-skirts of Sparta, the once independent town of Amyclae. Here, too, the people stopped to stare at the bedraggled files of women, boys and old men stumbling along on their ropes. People called out and asked the guards where they had come from, and the guards proudly reported, "Agesandros took them right out of Aristomenes' palace at Pylos!"

That made some of the boys hoot and clap. At some point they were met by young men with very short hair—like Anaxilas—but in simple leather armour and black rather than scarlet cloaks. When they heard the news, one of them stripped naked and started sprinting back up the road ahead of them, apparently to bring the word to the city officials. As they advanced closer, more and more people lined the streets to gawk at them. There was less cat-calling here than in Gytheon, but because only Niobe rode, more attention was directed at her person-ally. Again and again the escort responded to questions, saying she was "Aristomenes' whore" or more seldom, "Anaxilas' prize."

Niobe was far too exhausted, dehydrated and hurting to take note of her surroundings particularly. It was almost dark by the time they were collected in a square flanked by colonnades and temples. There she was shoved off her donkey and she collapsed onto the paving stones like all the others, her knee hurting fiercely and her skin as tender as if she'd inserted her face and arms into a bread oven. Now she did not even have Kallisto to comfort her. About the middle of the day, the faithful slave woman had been removed from the slave caravan and taken to one of the outlying farmhouses where she was to serve the bedridden mother of her captor. Feeling utterly alone and abandoned, Niobe was so miserable that she could only await what would happen next with more apathy than interest.

Eventually, men with torches started moving among them, asking each their name. Shortly thereafter, people out of the crowd started coming and taking this or the other captive away. Niobe saw a young man in a black cloak address Mika. She nodded, stood and followed him out of the square. Finally, a tall, well-dressed man with a long white beard loomed up over her. "Niobe, daughter of Aristokrates?"

She looked up with a flicker of renewed hope. They had acknowledged she was a king's daughter. "Yes."

The man made a grimace, but then signalled, "Come with me."

Niobe struggled to her feet, gasping from the pain in her knee.

"What's the matter?"

"My knee. I stumbled and hurt it," Niobe told him with hope of sympathy.

"Show me?"

She lifted her skirts modestly, exposing the swollen, discoloured knee with the growing scab.

The man made another grimace but announced, "The royal palace is just around the corner. You'll have to hobble that far." Nevertheless, he walked slowly, pacing himself to her slow, painful gait. At last they reached an imposing building with a long colonnade raised three steps above street level. There were guards in scarlet and bronze flanking the door, their helmets down over their faces. Niobe, however, was led around the corner and along the side of the building to a back entrance. Here she entered a dim corridor and was led to a cobbled courtyard cluttered with household articles. Laundry hung flapping from lines; a hand mill stood in a corner; baskets were heaped near the door for some unclear purpose; empty amphorae leaned against one another along one wall. Light spilled from a room that opened on the far side of the courtyard.

The man led Niobe, limping, into the room. At once all activity and conversation stopped and everyone stared at the newcomers. Niobe noted that the walls were roughly plastered and grey with smoke. Hooks lined the wall nearest the door where the slaves left their cloaks, while their outdoor clogs and sandals (if they had any) were lined up under a crude wooden bench. On the other walls, rough wooden shelves held the chipped, unglazed pottery used on the large, solid table with benches on each side at which the slaves took their meals. Benches around the outside of the room provided places for the slaves to sit, as now, drinking and gossiping after dinner. This was not the fine quarters provided royal concubines. It could only be a common slave's hall—such as she had never set foot in before.

"This girl was taken captive in Messenia," her guide announced to the astonished company, "and Anaxilas sent her home to his grandmother. Get her cleaned up so she may be presented to the queen." Then he was gone.

Niobe stood waiting for something—words of welcome, comfort, even pity. They just stared at her. Gradually the meaning of the man's words sank in to her stunned brain: Anaxilas had sent her home *to his grandmother*, not for himself.

"Get her cleaned up, he says! A lot easier said than done," a hefty older woman exclaimed at last, her hands on her knees as she looked Niobe up and down like a stray dog.

"He sent that to his *grandmother*?" one of the men asked with a laugh. "My ass he sent that to his *grandmother!*" The other men joined in his laughter, but the older woman, who had opened the commentary, heaved her well-padded body to its feet and snapped at the men, "That's what Hekataios said, and that's the way we're going to treat her. Gyrtias, Nais, get off your fat backsides and come give me a hand. Come on, you, what's your name?" she demanded of Niobe with a penetrating stare.

"Niobe."

"What sort of name is that? Messenian? Never heard it before."

"Arkadian," Niobe answered, anxious to explain who she was. "My father—"

The woman cut her off with a sniff and announced, "It don't matter here who your father was, girl, and we'll see if the mistress lets you keep some fancy, foreign name like that. I'm Thratta, and that there is Gyrtias and that is Nais. Oh, and big mouth over there is Kylon, our cook. Keep out of his reach or he'll be feeling you up every time you ain't looking."

Thratta grabbed a lamp and led Niobe back out into the courtyard, and then into another cramped little area open to the sky and separated from the courtyard by only a crude wall, but with neither door nor curtain. Here a big stone basin collected rainwater and a wooden tub evidently served as the slaves' bath. Niobe was told to strip and get in the bath.

"Where'd you get such pretty pins and this pretty gown?" one of the younger girls asked, picking up what Niobe removed. "The patterns are woven right in and it's the same colour all over!" She spoke in wonder, holding the cloth close to the lamp to see better.

"It was the only one of my gowns I was allowed to keep," Niobe told her sadly, thinking of all the others dumped on the floor of her chamber by the heartless Lacedaemonian auditor. "And the pins belonged to my slave—"

The girl looked over at her with narrowed, angry eyes. "Oh? Were you some kind of fine lady or what? Well, you ain't that any more! You ain't nothing but a slave now and we are free-born helots, do you understand? We ain't slaves. *You* are, and you got—"

"That's enough of your mouth, Gyrtias!" Thratta cut her off. "Get the bucket and dump it over our fine lady here."

Gyrtias put the gown aside and sullenly picked up one of the small buckets beside the trough. She dipped it into the trough and with open malice dumped it over Niobe. After the fourth bucket, Thratta decided, "All right, that's enough. Nais, go fetch one of your peplos, some wooden pins and a cord. Gyrtias, fetch me some tar to smear on that banged-up knee." The younger girls disappeared.

Thratta stood with her hands on her hips and shook her head. "You don't got a lot of brains, do you, girl? Bragging about being some fine lady! As Gyrtias said, you're a slave now, and just because young Anaxilas fucked you, don't mean you're gonna get special treatment. Anaxilas fucks a lot of girls. He thinks it makes him a man. Besides, he's with the army and won't be seen back here 'till the campaign season's over, when the passes to Messenia close."

"But I was Aristomenes' *wife*," Niobe protested, unable to stand it any longer. "I'm the daughter of King Aristokrates!"

"Sure you are. Tell that one to the mistress, but don't try it on us, girl. You heard Gyrtias. We ain't slaves. We're helots. No one can buy or sell us, and we marry who we like and have families of our own. *You* ain't any different from the cattle. The master or mistress can use you any way they like, and no matter how many brats you give Anaxilas, they ain't yours—they're his."

Niobe stared at Thratta. She was shivering, her teeth were chattering, and no one offered her a towel, much less a cloak. She had to clutch herself as she stood naked in the night air. This couldn't be happening! She was a king's daughter—the prettiest of all the girls in King Aristokrates' household. How could these helots treat her like she was beneath them? She felt the lump in her throat again, but the tears wouldn't come. Why didn't anyone believe who she was? And how could Anaxilas—after what he'd done to her—send her back to be just a common slave?

Thratta turned and pocketed the simple—but silver—pins that had once belonged to Kallisto, but which Niobe had been allowed to keep for her peplos. Then she tossed Niobe a rough, none-too-clean cloth that she was evidently supposed to use as a towel.

Gyrtias was back first, and Thratta expertly heated up tar over the lamp and then smeared it over Niobe's knee. It hurt and stung, bringing the tears that hadn't come earlier, but Niobe knew it would help her, too. At last Nais was back with the oldest, most threadbare peplos she owned. She handed this over with the question, "Do I get to keep her peplos, then?"

"No. I won't have you two fighting over it. I'll keep it myself—"

"But you can't wear it!" both younger girls protested simultaneously. "You're too fat—I mean, tall."

Thratta smacked the impudent girl carelessly, remarking, "I'll keep it to reward whichever one of you gives me less mouth next month."

The girls moaned and grumbled, but Thratta ignored them as she pinned Niobe's peplos at the shoulders with crude pins whittled from light wood. Then, pulling a wooden comb from the pocket of her own peplos, she vigorously set to combing out Niobe's wet hair. It was frightfully tangled and wet, but Thratta worked systematically. "I don't reckon the mistress will let you keep all this hair."

"Anaxilas likes long hair," Nais remarked knowingly.

Thratta shot her a disapproving look and remarked, "That's why you got your head shaved off last year, little tart!"

Niobe's heart missed a beat. They couldn't do that to her, could they? Take away her very hair? Nais had hair so short it clung to her head and made her look almost like a boy—like Mika. The thought appalled Niobe almost more than any of the other humiliations. To take away her hair was to attack the very substance of her own self-image: her beauty.

That night Niobe slept on a straw pallet in the loft above the helots' hall. All the female helots slept here, with Thratta at the top of the stairs to be sure none of the girls sneaked down to the men who slept in the hall below. Niobe was given only a coarse, dusty blanket to cover herself. She woke stiff and thirsty. Her muscles ached and her limbs were heavy. Her eyes and throat burned from the perpetual smoke that hung here in the rafters over the hall. Already the room was very warm and uncomfortable and most of the other women and girls were gone.

Thratta stood over her and shook her out of her deep, escapist sleep. "The mistress wants to see you, girl. Hurry and get dressed!"

Niobe's knee seemed utterly unbendable, and the mixture of smoke and sweat made her feel dirty again already, but Thratta gave her no chance to wash. She went down the steep wooden stairs sideways, her stiff leg first, and then limped along behind Thratta through long, cool corridors that became increasingly well plastered, painted and tiled. Abruptly she was in a peristyle. The sun poured down to sparkle in a pool with a little fountain. Pots of flowers hung between the bright white of the columns. Potted palms waved their fan-leaves leisurely in the wind.

Here was beauty and luxury again, and Niobe's heart cried out in anguish: this was where she belonged! But then she realised with a new rush of hope that all she had to do was convince the Queen of Sparta of the truth. A queen would have respect for a king's daughter. She would understand that it was wrong to anger a king as powerful as Aristokrates. She would tell her husband that their new slave wasn't a slave at all, but a princess. A girl worth a ransom. She would intervene. All she had to do was make her believe the truth.

Thratta passed beyond the peristyle into a gracious, high-ceilinged room which faced a garden on the far side. The breeze swept from the open doors on the peristyle through the chamber and out into the garden, keeping the chamber remarkably cool. The tiles under Niobe's naked feet were cool (she had lost her ruined sandals at some time during the journey). The sound of water gurgling and splashing in the peristyle behind her was soothing. Loose woven curtains billowed from the tall doorways. Birds chirped from the lemon and almond trees in the garden. The room smelled not of smoke and rancid oil and stale wine as did the helot's hall, but of lavender and thyme.

Thratta was bowing before a woman seated at a desk, and Niobe turned her attention from the beautiful surroundings to this woman who would decide her fate. She had not expected anything in particular, and yet she had subconsciously pictured a woman of Kallisto's age and dressed like her father's wife in bright, gold-encrusted gowns and laden with jewels.

She was taken aback to be confronted with a lean, grey-haired woman without any make-up, wearing a very fine but almost severe peplos. Although the peplos was the coveted purple colour of the most expensive dye in the world, it was adorned only by a very thin embroidery border in white. Her only adornment was a pair of earrings in the shape of hoplite shields and a necklace of miniature spearheads. On the middle finger of her left hand she wore a heavy ring that was clearly more functional than decorative. Even as Niobe waited, the queen used the ring to set her seal on a wax tablet. Then—only then—did she turn her attention to the two women before her.

"Mistress, this is the girl who arrived last night with the slave transport. Your grandson Anaxilas sent her to you."

"Hm." The queen leaned back in her beautiful chair with carved lion's feet for legs and ram's heads on the arms. "I'm told you claim to be the daughter of King Aristokrates of Arkadia and the wife of Aristomenes."

"Yes, my lady," Niobe said at once with an inner sigh of relief. "I am—"

"Who was your mother?"

"Antinoe, my lady, she died—"

"She was a concubine. I know your father's legal wives. As to being Aristomenes' wife, that is—shall we say—difficult to prove. He keeps a great many women. Only Aridaios was ever recognised as his wife—"

"But she died six months ago, my lady, and I married Aristomenes three months ago," Niobe pointed out desperately.

"Were you taught to interrupt older women in your father's house?" was the cool, disapproving reply.

Niobe flushed hotly. It wasn't fair to treat her like this! She wasn't a child—she was the wife of a man who would be king one day. And she had a right to tell her story! How else could she make this woman understand that she shouldn't be treated like a common slave? But even without all the gold and make-up, this woman was clearly not one to be taken lightly. As she had learned to do with her father's wives, Niobe bowed her head and answered dutifully, "No, my lady."

There was a long silence, and Niobe could feel the Spartan queen studying her. Finally she resumed the conversation. "I presume my grandson slept with you."

"Yes, my lady," Niobe whispered. She sensed that this severe woman was not going to favour her for this.

"Well, believe me, that hardly makes you special. You were not the first and will not be the last. It is not the tradition in Sparta, however, for her kings—much less her citizens—to keep concubines. You are here not as my grandson's plaything, but as a slave pure and simple. Do you have any useful skills at all?—besides lying on your back, I mean."

Skills? Niobe had never been asked such a question in her life. Skills were what craftsmen and slaves had—not noblewomen. She was a king's daughter. Men wanted her for beauty, for the ties to her father, for the children who would be blood relations of the King of Arkadia....

"Well?" the Spartan queen prompted impatiently, her fingers drumming on her desk.

Niobe tried to think what she could do that would count as a skill. "I can spin, weave and sew a little...."

"Of course. Can you also wash and press clothes? Do you know how to clean bronze and silver? Can you polish wood? No, I presume not, but I'll give you the benefit of the doubt and assume you can learn—if you have more brains than a bird." Without giving Niobe another chance to speak, she turned to Thratta and instructed, "She will be familiar with precious cloth and metals, so you can have her dust and polish in the royal apartments. Once you've instructed her, she can probably be trusted to wash, press and repair my own and Archidamas' silk and linen garments or the household linens. Let her weave herself a couple more peplos from the household wool. She may put modest decoration on them if she likes, but keep a sharp watch over her. I don't want her sleeping around. Dismissed." And she returned her attention to the documents on her desk without even watching Niobe and Thratta bow and depart.

Mika hadn't started to feel nervous about her future until the slave column reached Amyclae. Then, as the time came nearer for her to meet her mistress, she found herself afraid. She had waited with the other slaves in the large square, and searched the growing crowd of Spartans who came to collect their unexpected spoils. She tried to imagine what the wife of the fearsome Agesandros might look like, and she was quite taken by surprise when a youth addressed her, "Are you Mika? Agesandros' prize?"

She looked up at a lean youth with curly dark hair cut very short. He would have been very handsome—if she hadn't at once compared him to Leon and found him wanting. Proudly she answered the question, "I'm *Leon's* prize. He sent me home to serve the Lady Alethea."

The youth grinned at that. "Leon's first prize? Well, well!" He sounded pleased as well as amused. "Come with me. The Lady Alethea is my mother. I'll take you to her."

Mika scrambled hastily to her feet and followed the long-legged youth readily. She decided he must be Leon's younger brother. Not that they looked similar, but it would explain why Leon was sleeping in Agesandros' chamber and had sent her back to serve Agesandros' wife and it explained why he had told her to call herself "Agesandros' prize" when she was really his. Apparently Agesandros was his father, although the infamous "Scourge of Messenia" hardly looked old enough to have grown sons, not to mention that both youths were dark and Agesandros blond.

They left the city behind them, and Mika found herself on a country road leading straight toward the tall, rugged mountains, black and threatening against the luminous night sky. The youth at first set a fast pace, but then seemed to remember himself and slowed down. "I'm sorry. You must be tired. What's your name? And where do you come from?"

"Mika. I come from up north. I think you Greeks call it Illyria."

"Is it true you were taken in Pylos? In Aristomenes' own house?" Niko asked eagerly.

Mika nodded.

"But Aristomenes got away?"

Mika nodded again.

"How does he do it?" Niko asked angrily. "Agesandros must be furious."

"But he took a lot of loot—almost 100 slaves, including Aristomenes' wife," Mika pointed out.

"Aristomenes' wife? I thought she'd died last winter?"

"That was his *old* wife. He married again—my mistress, Niobe—three months ago. She's only 16 and very pretty. She's the daughter of the King of Arkadia—" Mika remembered too late (as usual) that slaves weren't supposed to speak unless they were asked a question.

Niko stopped and looked at her in evident astonishment, but then he whistled briefly. "She should be worth something." Then he seemed to remember he was in a hurry and pressed on, adding as he walked, "I'm Nikolaidas, son of Euryanax, but you can call me Niko like everyone else does."

Mika was perplexed. How could he be the son of Euryanax if his mother was the wife of Agesandros?

The mountains loomed up darker and darker, blocking their way, and Mika was beginning to fear she was going to have to start up the steep slopes. Just before the slope started, however, Niko led her off the road down a drive through orchards of mirabelle and pear trees. From ahead came the sound of a gurgling stream, and through the trees the white of a house at last shimmered.

The house sat snuggled between the stream and the face of the mountains. Hounds barked wildly as they approached, but Niko called to them by name, and the tone of the barking changed at once from threat to welcome. The gate swung open and a maiden stood silhouetted against the gentle light of oil lamps. She called out with a tremor of alarm in her voice, "Niko, is that you?"

"Yes. Agesandros raided Pylos and has sent back a slave to my mother."

The girl ran out to greet them. She was barefoot and in a simple homespun peplos that opened far up her thigh. She flung herself into Niko's arms. He kissed her rather hastily, as if embarrassed, Mika thought. "Chloe—not here. Someone might see us," Niko whispered urgently, looking about guiltily.

"I can't help myself. You come to me so seldom."

"You know I have to sleep in barracks. I come as often as I can."

Chloe was pouting. "You could come during the daytime. Other melleirenes do. My friend—"

"Don't start that again, Chloe. I'm not free to do what other youths do. I nearly got thrown out of the agoge once already. If they catch me at anything 'irregular' again, I'm finished. You've got to understand that."

"I'd love you even if you weren't in your stupid agoge," Chloe assured him passionately.

"If I don't graduate from the agoge with the rest of my class and get my shield and cloak with them, I'll *kill* myself," came the uncompromising answer of the young man.

With that Niko shook himself free of Chloe and strode through the gate, with Mika hurrying to keep up. Mika found herself in a cobbled yard with somewhat run-down-looking buildings with crude wooden porches on her left, a solid two-story building ahead of her, and on her right a raised colonnade before a stone façade of pale limestone.

In the doorway of the two-story house a woman stood with her hands on her hips. "What now?" she demanded in a sour tone.

"A slave-girl to help you in the kitchen, Phoebe," Niko answered lightly. "Where's my mother?"

"How should I know? I've got enough to do without keeping track of where your mother is! Come here, girl!"

Mika glanced uncertainly at Niko. She'd been told she was being sent to the Lady Alethea, and this was very certainly not her. But Niko indicated with a nod that she should do as she was told. She advanced timidly and, as usual, as soon as the woman could see her warts by the light of the huge fire burning in the hearth, she grimaced and exclaimed, "Has Agesandros sunk so low he sends us only the dregs of what he collects? I swear there must have been stronger, healthier slaves! Why couldn't he send one of *them* back, rather than a worthless little runt like this?!"

The words hurt. They always hurt. No matter how often similar things had been said over the last years of her life, Mika was wounded every time. She lashed out in self-defence, "I'm not worthless! I served Aristomenes' own wife! I know all about how to clean real copper and bronze and how to tend silk and make rose-water—"

Laughter cut her off. A crowd had collected in the kitchen hall. There were a handful of men and twice as many women, most of them young, all of them amused.

From the door Niko was explaining, "She's Leon's prize, actually, and no doubt he didn't get first pick, so be thankful he sent her back here at all."

"Leon? Since when does he get a prize?"

"Since he carries a javelin and serves in the Lights," came Niko's cool answer, and it silenced the others. "Come on, Mika, let me take you to my mother."

Mika gladly fled the gawking crowd and attached herself to Niko's shadow as he mounted the steps and passed under the colonnade.

"Orsippos and Phoebe work the kleros for us. Phoebe's a bit of a bitch, I admit, but you'll just have to get used to her. The others are all right."

They went down a short, dark corridor that suddenly opened onto a broad peristyle, and Mika caught her breath. In Pylos the columns had been brightly painted but the peristyle paved and barren. Here the columns were pure white, but the peristyle had been turned into a garden overflowing with flowers. Mika couldn't begin to identify them all, certainly not in the poor light offered by a pair of oil lamps hung on opposite sides of the garden. Niko, seeing the way she gazed, smiled. "My mother loves her flowers." Then, nodding to light spilling onto the black-and-white mosaic tiles of the walkway, he suggested, "My mother is probably in there."

Not only light was coming from the chamber, but also the sound of a lovely, high voice singing to the accompaniment of a cythera. Mika thought she had never heard anything so beautiful. There had been musicians and flute-girls in Pylos only when Aristomenes was there, and Mika had only heard them from a distance, the music jumbled and overlaid by the clatter of dishes and the drone of male voices.

To her amazement, the music was coming from a maiden with bright blonde hair and a face more beautiful even than Niobe's. Mika stopped in astonishment as the girl looked up and exclaimed with obvious delight, "Niko? What are you doing here? Who's that?"

"Her name's Mika, and Leon set her back to Mom. She was captured in Pylos and claims she was in service to Aristomenes' wife."

"Did Agesandros finally run him to earth?" The maiden put the instrument aside and jumped up in excitement that was quite unladylike. Although she was more beautiful than Niobe, she was dressed only in a simple peplos, opened far up her thigh, and her hair was pulled back in a simple pony tail. Her skin had been tanned by the sun and was an even bronze colour against the white of her gown. Nor did she move with Niobe's languid graciousness, but with the energy and self-confidence of a youth. Mika didn't know what to make of her. Her clothes and tan suggested she was unfree and her beauty suited her for the role of concubine, but Mika had never seen a concubine who was so direct and unself-conscious in the presence of a man.

"No, apparently the bastard got away again, but Agesandros took over a hundred slaves and quite a treasure—according to rumour, anyway. They were saying in town that he's taken enough loot to outfit a pentaconter—as he's been begging to do for months. Where's Mom?"

"I don't know. Maybe in the garden. Shall I go—"

She didn't have to. From the second door of the chamber a lady entered, and both young people turned to her and called out, "Mom." So the maiden was Niko's sister and a daughter of her new mistress, Alethea, Mika noted.

Alethea was no longer young, nor had she ever been the beauty her daughter was, but she was attractive nevertheless. She was not as richly dressed as Niobe, but there was no denying her elegance and dignity. For the mother of two grown children, she was slender, though no longer fragile and willowy like a girl. She had rich, dark, curly hair like her son rather than the bright blonde of her daughter. She wore it pinned up but with curls about her face. She had fine eyebrows over intelligent eyes and a fine, long nose. She wore a lilac peplos with a simple dark border running down the left side. She had a himation wrapped loosely over her arms and—to Mika's astonishment—she was barefoot. She nodded to her children as they explained about Mika, but kept her eyes fixed on Mika herself. Then she turned to her son. "Do you have leave for the night?"

"No, just to deliver the goods."

"Not even time for a glass of wine?"

"Mom, don't—"

"All right, forgive me," she dismissed him, and at once he seemed to become confused. He crossed the room to her, gave her a quick kiss, and promised, "Next year when I'm an eirene, it'll be different."

"When you're an eirene everyone will be watching you more closely than ever," his mother countered; but then she relented, smiled and kissed him before sending him away with a wave of her hand. Then she moved deeper into the room, gesturing for Mika too to come closer. "What did you say your name was?"

"Mika, Mistress."

"Well, Mika, you have come a long way and must be very hungry and tired—not to say a little frightened and bewildered." She turned to her daughter. "Kassia, go to the helots' hall and ask Phoebe to send a nice hot meal in for Mika."

Kassia made a face. "Phoebe will make a fuss—"

"I know, and it's time you learned how to deal with impudent and sullen helots. Now, go and do as I say."

Kassia sighed, but left the chamber.

Alethea looked around and found a stool, which she pointed to. "Bring that over here and sit down so we can get acquainted."

Mika was almost dizzy with amazement. Not once in all her life in slavery had any of her owners, male or female, ordered a meal brought to her and then suggested she sit down. She found herself sitting on the stool, clasping her hands between her knees in embarrassment. She had seen the way the Lady Alethea studied her face from the doorway, and now those eyes, which were a penetrating blue, seemed to burn into her face, making each of her warts sting under her gaze.

"How long have you had those warts, Mika?"

"I think it's five years now, Mistress," Mika whispered in shame. "I was nine or ten when the first ones came—on my hands. And then they spread to my face."

"Hm. We'll have to see what we can do about them, but that's not important right now. Start by telling me more about yourself. Were you born in slavery?"

"No, Mistress. My uncles sold me into slavery in the spring of the year two winters ago—"

"Your uncles?" She sounded shocked.

"My father was crushed by a tree, and so they married my mother and sold me."

"That's horrible!"

Mika didn't know what to say. She'd thought it was horrible at the time, but that was in a different world. Two years of slavery had taught her that her fate was neither uncommon nor the worst one could endure. Just look at what had happened to poor, beautiful Niobe.

The Lady Alethea sighed and continued. "What did your father do for a living? Was he a poor man?"

"He cut trees, Mistress, and we lived in the forest. We rarely had enough to eat. In the bad years we had to eat bark and the wolves would come down right to the fence of the garden. Once—" Mika stopped herself. What she was she running on about? No one was interested in her childhood. She looked down and waited.

"Did you have herds? Livestock?" Alethea asked, after waiting to see if Mika wanted to say more.

"No, Mistress," Mika admitted, feeling inadequate, and to make up for it she tried to tell about what she could do. "But I worked for a fuller and learned all about treating wool and getting out stains, and I worked for a blacksmith, too—but he only let me work the bellows. But another one of my masters taught me to weave mats and baskets—not the fancy ones, of course, but simple baskets or flat things—" There she was, running on again, which was not at all what a good slave was supposed to do. She should have learned at least that by now. How often had Kallisto slapped her for not "holding her tongue"? A slave was supposed be heard as little as possible and only answer with the absolute essentials. Guiltily she looked down at her hands, biting her lower lip and waiting for a reprimand.

It didn't come; instead her new mistress asked calmly, "So you can clean and cord wool. Can you spin?"

"Oh yes, Mistress! And I learned all about removing stains from cloth, and brushing it and—" Alethea was smiling at her, and Mika was so confused by so much attentiveness she fell silent again.

Alethea had to prompt her, "How old were you when your uncles sold you?"

"I was about 13, Mistress. I hadn't started my monthly flux yet, and nobody would have taken me to wife anyway. That's why my uncles decided it was better to sell me. They said I would eat more and more, but I would never be as much use to them as a boy. My mother was pregnant by one of them by then and they were sure it would be a boy, although I hope it wasn't."

Alethea laughed at that, adding, "I hope so, too. But now tell me, how did you come to be in Pylos in Aristomenes' household? Niko said something about serving Aristomenes' wife; is that true?"

"Oh yes, Mistress! The King of Arkadia bought me to serve his daughter and he gave me to her as a wedding present, and then I went with her to Messenia and lived in the palace with her and served her day and night. I know I still have a lot to learn about taking care of good things, Mistress, but I'm not stupid or clumsy like Kallisto says. If you just show me what you want me to do, I'll do it *exactly* like you want me to. Really, I will! I want to do things right, Mistress. It's just that everything is very new and I don't always understand all the words people use sometimes. But Leon said that Kassia is old enough to need a personal maid, which I'm sure I could do…." Mika noticed too late that she was running on at great length. Somehow it was so easy with this woman.

Alethea was smiling and she prompted in an amused voice, "What else did Leon say?"

Mika looked up. Over the last three days, Mika had re-pictured in her mind over and over again the few short minutes she had consciously spent with Leon. She could remember every single word she had ever heard Leon say, and repeated them all a hundred times in her head. "He—he said you were very short-handed in the kitchen and that Sybil can hardly get up and down stairs anymore and that Kassia is old enough to need a personal slave…."

Alethea laughed. "How very perceptive of him!" She paused, looking at Mika gently. "Niko says you were Leon's prize. Did he take you in *every* way?"

Mika found herself blushing, although she didn't know why. The question was the most reasonable in the world. Most people didn't bother to put it so delicately. But strangely it hurt to admit that Leon—just like all her other masters and slave-traders—hadn't *wanted* her in that way. She knew it would be horrible to be raped, but to be not even wanted…. She shook her head in shame, not daring to meet Alethea's eyes.

Alethea nodded knowingly, and then she said in a lighter tone of voice, "Well, Leon was right in all respects. I am short-handed, poor Sybil is no longer young and needs help, and Kassia is getting to an age when she could have a maid of her own. So, you see, you are indeed welcome here."

She paused and then continued, "Since you come from far away, there are some things you may not know about our customs. First, the other men and women who work on this estate, or kleros as we call it because it is a state allotment, not private property, are free helots. They are not chattel slaves as in other Greek cities. They are not citizens and have no political rights, but they cannot be bought or sold, either. Orsippos and his wife Phoebe have lived on this estate longer than I and they will pass it on to their son and his sons, just as my Niko and his sons will live here as their "masters" but not their "owners." You and Leon are the only slaves on the kleros—"

"Leon is a slave?!" Mika was so shocked she forgot herself.

"Yes. Didn't you know?"

"But—"

"He technically belongs to me, but I've loaned him to my husband and Agesandros has trained him into a good squire. Agesandros tells me he is now good at tracking and scouting and—so it seems—fighting as a light auxiliary as well."

Leon had made a very strong impression of Mika. It was much more than that he was so handsome; it was that he had been so kind to her. She had gone to sleep in his arms very frightened, and woken up—well—in love with him. But at the time she had thought of him as her master. Discovering he was a slave made a world of difference, because in a way it made them equal, and equals—at least in theory—could fall in love with one another. Couldn't they?

"Leon has a long, complicated story, but you'll have to hear that another time," Alethea was saying. "What you should know for now is only that he is very well liked and respected in this household and you can be, too. Tomorrow I will show you around and introduce you to Sybil. She has been my personal maid since I was younger than Kassia, and is also the head laundress. You can start off by helping her and learning all she can teach you. Now here's your dinner." Alethea looked up toward Kassia coming in with a tray. "After a good night's sleep, we'll get you cleaned up and find some new clothes for you as well." With a smile and a twinkle in her eye, she added, "Leon doesn't have so many chitons that he can afford to give them all away."

CHAPTER 4

Niobe reached for the kettle hanging over the burning coals to pour over the silk stained with red wine. She was concentrating on keeping the queen's silk gown stretched over the basin with her left arm, and reached without looking. Her fingers grasped the metal of the kettle itself, rather than the wooden handle. With a cry of pain she jumped back. The kettle fell onto the coals and spilled its contents onto the floor in a sudden rush. The splattering, boiling water burned Niobe's arms and legs so that she jumped back crying out again, as the queen's peplos slithered into a heap on the wet floor of the washhouse.

Niobe couldn't take any more. She sank down onto the tiles, crying in misery. It was too much! It was too much! She'd been up since before dawn, chased from one task to the next. The queen wanted the bed-sheets changed, and her husband's chamber had to be completely aired and dusted and the rugs beaten. She even insisted that the clasps and locks on the chests and cupboards be polished. "Do you think I want my husband to come home to a chamber that looks neglected?" the queen had asked in astonishment.

It had taken so long to get everything ready to the satisfaction of the queen that Niobe had missed lunch—and that after she'd lost her breakfast. For days now she couldn't keep her breakfast down and felt sick every morning when she woke. But nobody here even seemed to notice, much less care, that she might be seriously ill.

Niobe started crying harder than ever. She was so alone here. None of them were ever kind to her. Instead, they kept to themselves with their inside jokes and their stories about people who meant nothing to her. All her life Kallisto and the other slaves of her father's household, her sisters and half-sisters and even her father, had been concerned about whether she was healthy and happy. The first sign of a little cold or a stomach ache and she had been put to bed, a doctor called, special foods made for her.

Here they didn't care if she was dying—much less if she was happy. How could she possibly be happy? She was sure she would never be happy again.

In just three months her hands were covered with burns and cuts and calluses. Her feet, which were denied any protection, were so ingrained with dirt she couldn't scrub them clean even when she did get a chance to bathe. She had bruises on her arms and shins. Her knee was scarred from the fall during the trip here. Her hair had not been cut off, but she could wash it so seldom that it languished from lack of care. She was sure she was losing her beauty. She must be, since no one here seemed to take any note of it—unless you counted that lecherous goat, Kylon.

Niobe cried even harder, giving in to despair for the first time since her captivity. None of the fantasies she fed herself at night in the last months could help her any more. Aristomenes wasn't going to raid Sparta as he had two years ago, rescuing her from her captors and taking revenge on them for all the humiliations and abuse she had endured. Nor was her father going to storm down from Arkadia with an army at his back, demanding the return of his precious daughter and an indemnity for the injustice and misery she had suffered. Apparently not even Anaxilas was going to come and lift her out of the drudgery of slavery to the luxury of concubinage. No one, no one at all, was going to help her.

Gradually her crying wore itself down to a piteous whimpering as she lay curled in a ball on the floor. She might as well just throw herself off the bridge she had seen over the broad river, or maybe if she stopped eating altogether—

"What's going on here? Good heavens! That's the mistress's best peplos! And the coals have gone out!" Thratta was standing over her, the smell of garlic oozing from every pore and sweat drenching the side of her peplos. She reached out and grabbed Niobe's arm, yanking her to her feet. "Pull yourself together or I'll give you something to cry about!" Niobe had never seen Thratta this angry, and now she shook Niobe violently to underscore her threat.

"The vanguard's already passed Artemis of the Goats. King Anaxandridas will be here before sunset—and you're lying about on the floor feeling sorry for yourself!"

"I'm sick!" Niobe wailed in self-defence. "Haven't you noticed? I'm sick to my stomach. I haven't been able to keep my breakfast down for days—"

"When did you last have your flux?"

"Not since I've been here. I'm sure—"

Thratta had a hand on her belly, pressing it cruelly. Then she snorted and drew back with a sour look on her face. "For your sake, I hope you can convince Anaxilas it's his and not Aristomenes'. Now, get that peplos off the floor, fetch burning coals, and see that you get those stains out and the gown freshly pressed before the queen calls for it. She will want to wear it to receive her husband tonight."

Dazed, Niobe staggered out of the washhouse toward the hall to fetch burning coals. Pregnant? She was pregnant? The tears welled up again. This was supposed to be a moment of supreme joy. How often had she imagined telling Aristomenes that she was carrying his child? She had imagined his face—surprise and then delight and gratitude. Of course he already had a son by his first wife, a youth of 17 or so, and he had no less than three daughters, but Niobe had been certain he would be grateful for her gift of love. Her father had always been delighted when one of his concubines grew big with child. Her father said a king could never have too many children. Her father had told her to send word to him the "very same day" she was certain she had his grandchild under her heart.

Aristomenes! Niobe cried out silently. How could you abandon me? How could you run away and leave me to your worst enemy? If my father had thought you would discard me like a pretty bauble, he would never, never, never have given me to you! Never!

She had the coals and, half-blinded by tears, stumbled across the cobbled courtyard back to the washhouse. She hung the kettle on the hook again, shovelled the red-hot coals into the stone basin, and then bent and picked up the peplos. It was very beautiful, a two-toned weave such as could only be imported from Phoenicia and beyond. It shimmered even in the dim light of the washhouse in two tones of blue, and the embroidery was of such exquisite precision that it must have been done by a very talented hand. It was a gown fit for a queen, but it would not make the bitter old hag who was one of Sparta's queens any prettier, Niobe thought bitterly.

She stopped abruptly. It wasn't just the king who was returning; Thratta had said "the vanguard" had passed some sanctuary or other. The entire army was coming home. The campaign season was over. Anaxilas would be returning, too.

The water in the kettle was starting to simmer, and Niobe again stretched the silk so that the wine-spots were over the bowl. Anaxilas was just as likely the father of her baby as Aristomenes. More likely, really, since he was so young and virile he had taken her twice in that single night.

She took care to get the kettle by the wooden handle and poured very slowly, although the weight of the kettle strained her arm, making it tremble. The steam made the sweat drip from her forehead. At last the kettle was empty and the stain much less obvious. She poured fresh water into the kettle and set it on its hook.

Anaxilas was her last hope of rescue from this drudgery. She simply *had* to make him love her. But how could she hope to do that sweating and barefoot and with dirty hair?! She almost started to cry again, but then she closed her eyes and took a deep breath. She had a child to think about. She had to find a way to make herself pretty again. After all, she had access to the queen's chamber. She started to work out her plan.

King Anaxandridas returned with the main army, but not Anaxilas. He was with Agesandros, whose irregular unit was called the "secret army," or *kryptea*, and operated independently. It was almost a fortnight after the main army was in garrison before Agesandros brought his battalion home for the winter. By then Niobe was ready for Anaxilas.

Niobe knew enough about Sparta by now to know that all male citizens, including the kings, were required to eat in messes called *syssitia*, and that youths and young men were required to live in barracks until the age of 31. But princes, at least those in the direct line of succession, were allowed to sleep at home. As Niobe now knew, Anaxilas was firstborn to the crown prince, Archidamas, who maintained his own household in Messenia as part of a permanent garrison there. Because Anaxilas was in direct line to the throne, although one step removed, he had not attended the agoge, nor did he sleep in the barracks with the other men on active duty. Thus although he first went to his mess, he returned to the palace after dark. On arrival he went to his grandparents' chambers, where he talked late into the night with both of them.

Niobe, meanwhile, went to the slaves' bath after her own dinner and washed herself and her hair thoroughly. Then she put on the prettiest of the two peplos she had been allowed to make herself. It was very simple by the standards of her past, but it was new and pretty enough, a bright blue with a red border. She had frequently sneaked looks in the queen's mirrors while cleaning out her chamber and was certain the colours were flattering to her. Meanwhile, she had also managed to replace the ugly wooden pins Thratta had given her that first night with some bone pins she had found, as if discarded, behind one of the chests in the chamber of Anaxilas' younger sister. She had also replaced the cord they had given her for a belt with one she had woven herself in the same red as the border of her gown. She brushed out her hair as it dried so that it was full and the waves came back. Then she very slowly and softly made her way into the main house. The helots in their hall were busy with themselves as usual, and no one seemed to notice that she hadn't returned from her bath.

Niobe tiptoed up to the royal apartments and paused with pounding heart before the closed door of the king's chamber. Light oozed out under the crack and Niobe could hear the king's deep voice declaiming in an angry tone: ".… not the first time such stories have come to my ears! We don't live in the age of Herakles, and wars aren't won with reckless acts of childish bravado! Learn your place in the rank and file—"

"Then why didn't you send me to the damn agoge? You can't ask me to know in just a few months what the rest of them have learned in 14 years!" The sound of Anaxilas' voice reminded Niobe all too vividly of their first encounter. She had to swallow down her bile and block out the memories. It didn't matter what she had felt then; that had been a different world. She had only one hope now, and that was to make this man love her. Just as her father's concubines, often gifts or prizes themselves, had learned to love her father, even if they too had cried and been sorry for themselves at first. Niobe had never understood why the silly girls were not pleased to be chosen by a king. Now she forced herself to focus on the fact that Anaxilas would be king one day.

Niobe tiptoed further along the corridor. She went particularly cautiously by the queen's chamber, but it was empty. This induced her to take one further risk. The image of one pretty girl being made ready for her father came to mind. She had been weeping, and the slaves had had so much trouble getting the make-up to stick. "Do you want to insult him?" the older women had asked indignantly. "You silly goose! If you insult him, he can send you to the sculleries!" It had sounded worse than the galleys or the mines, even to the child Niobe. Now she knew that was true, because that was where she had been. She had to escape, and for that she needed all the skills her father's concubines had taught her in her youth.

With all her nerves on edge, she slipped into the darkened chamber and by feel more than sight found her way to the queen's dressing table. She felt very, very carefully for the bottles, found one of the perfumes and applied it behind her ears and down the front of her gown. Then, with a glance toward the connecting door to the chamber beyond, from which the voices still came muffled but unmistakable, she found the little pot of rouge that the queen never used, and applied it with the help of a mirror to her own lips and cheeks. Then she tiptoed back out of the queen's chamber and found her way to the room she herself had scrubbed, dusted, polished and aired for Anaxilas.

Here she paused, utterly unsure of where she should await him. She did not want him to see her immediately, not when he first came in. After all, he might be accompanied by someone else—an attendant or even one of his grandparents. She had to be hidden. She could crouch down behind a chest or—should she climb onto the bed itself? She gazed at it with a certain trepidation, memories of the repeated rape at Pylos causing her to tense despite her efforts to block them out. She reminded herself that she *had* found pleasure with Aristomenes, and the thought of her wedding reminded her of Kallisto's advice as she prepared her for her marriage bed: "The way to a man's heart, my precious bird, is to convince him that his love-making is the most wonderful in the whole world. No matter what you feel, you must make him *think* you are dazed with ecstasy. You must make him think you want him in your bed more than you want jewels or slaves or life itself. If you make him think that, my pretty little bird, than he will give you your every wish and you will rule his kingdom as much as he does himself."

Niobe went to the bed and stood before it. If she were going to wait for him in bed, she wondered if she should be dressed at all. Her gown was not *that* flattering, but Kallisto had told her long ago that the act of disrobing was particularly arousing for a man. Maybe she should not only wait on the bed, but in it? Then she could be naked but covered at first. Yes, she decided, that seemed a good idea. What better way to convince a man that she wanted him in her bed? She removed her peplos and hid it from sight behind the bed. She climbed into the bed and pulled the curtains closed. Not a minute too soon.

Already the voices from the king's chamber had grown louder as the door was opened. She heard Anaxilas wish his grandparents good night and then she heard the queen's voice, "Your grandfather is right in this. You must earn the respect of the peers—"

"Peers! Men raised in the gutter! All these new laws, Mother, I tell you they are against the gods!"

"Delphi explicitly approved them," came the cool reply. "Remember that. And your great-grandfather accepted them on his deathbed. Don't think you are cleverer than he or the Oracle. Now, let me get some sleep."

Niobe was holding her breath. She heard the queen close the door behind her and Anaxilas' footsteps as he continued toward his own chamber. He came in carrying a small lamp, which he set down on a chest by the door as he closed it. Then he kicked off his sandals and, apparently still in a bad temper, pulled his chiton off over his head and threw it aside. He dropped his loincloth where he stood and yanked back the curtains around his bed in irritation.

Then he went stock still. Niobe saw his eyes widen in surprise. The smile came slower, but it came. "I'd forgotten all about you."

"But I could never forget you, Master," Niobe smiled at him languidly, and then she deliberately and slowly lifted her arms to run her hands through her hair so that the covers slipped off her breasts.

His eyes fell as they were supposed to and he knelt on the bed. "They're bigger than I remember them." His hand cupped one, his thumb rubbing the nipple as he remembered, "No paint this time?"

"They're growing to feed your child, Master."

"My child?" He looked up sharply and for a moment Niobe was afraid that he was displeased, but then his smile broadened. "Are you certain? No chance it was Aristomenes?"

Niobe managed to laugh. She had expected this and carefully prepared an answer. "Aristomenes? Don't you remember my surprise the first time I saw your—your manhood? Surely you guessed the truth? Aristomenes is twice your age. He was impotent."

"Then I was your first real man?" Anaxilas clearly liked the thought.

Niobe nodded and reached out her arms to him. "And I've missed you so much. I'm so hungry for you. You can't imagine what torture it has been dreaming of you night after night and no hope of having you in me—until now."

Anaxilas didn't need any further encouragement

Alethea had taken it into her head to trim back the plum trees. Orsippos was opposed to the idea, but Alethea insisted. Reluctantly Orsippos and his eldest son took pruning shears and ladders out to the orchard. The two helots climbed into the trees while Alethea gave instructions from the ground.

She was dressed in a simple wool peplos and had wound a himation in a figure eight around herself against the chill of the autumn. She wore a scarf tied at the back of her head to keep her hair out of her eyes, and her feet were in sandals because the earth was damp and cold at this time of year. There was frost at night and the peaks of Taygetos were white with snow.

Sybil, shaking out the bed sheets from the balcony of Kassia's room, saw him coming, and she waddled back inside to lean over the gallery and call down to the peristyle urgently. "Mika! Mika!"

Mika was on her hands and knees with a scrub-brush and a bucket of water, trying to clean the mosaics of the walkway. She looked up, wiping her hair out of her eyes with the back of her arm. "What is it, Sybil?"

"Run fetch the Mistress. Agesandros is coming!"

Mika jumped up, leaving her bucket and brush where they lay. They had been waiting for this day ever since the regular army returned—and no one more anxiously than Mika herself. With Agesandros would come Leon.

Mika jumped down into the courtyard and ran as fast as she could out into the orchard. She could see them now, Agesandros in scarlet and bronze and Leon beside him in his leather armour and black himation. They were coming up the road from town.

Mika left the drive and dashed across the grass between the rows of trees to the far corner of the orchard where she could see Alethea pointing with her arms.

"Mistress! Mistress! They're coming!" Mika called out long before she reached them.

Alethea turned around startled, and then she turned and started back toward Mika, smiling. "You're sure?" she asked, but her gaze was already searching the distance. Then she was moving on, picking up her skirts so she could move better. Mika turned and watched her. She could see Agesandros between the trees, coming up the drive. Alethea called to him and waved. He looked over, startled to have her emerge from that direction, but then he turned and started towards her with a long, purposeful stride. She started running, and he caught her up in his arms and pulled her clear off the ground.

Mika watched with fascination. Alethea had always seemed so dignified and proper up to now. But at this moment, she was like a young girl. In her simple clothes and scarf she could have been any farmer's wife. Except that Mika couldn't think of any farmer who would greet his wife like this. They kissed without any shame. Then Agesandros slipped his arm around his wife's waist and they started back toward the house, talking and laughing together. Mika had never seen two people in such apparent harmony in her life. Certainly her parents had never laughed with one another like this. Her only memories were of them fighting and shouting at each other. Aristomenes and Niobe had made love together, but they had rarely talked much. At least Niobe hadn't talked much. Yet Alethea was clearly talking now and Agesandros listened to her, nodding and smiling and laughing. As Mika watched them walking away, she saw the infamous Scourge of Messenia pull his wife closer, kiss the top of her head, and laugh again. Alethea looked up. He dropped her another kiss on her lips.

"Mika?"

She jumped and found Leon beside her. He was more beautiful even than she remembered. He was cleaned up now. His hair shone in the sun, his face was freshly shaved, and he smelled of fresh water and clean leather. Mika's heart was in her throat as she looked up at him.

"Are you all right? Is everything all right?"

"Oh, yes! It's wonderful here. I've never been so happy in all my life. My parents were very poor and even when I was free, you see, I never had clothes as good as this." She looked down and held out her simple but sturdy peplos. "And the food is fantastic. Phoebe's a great cook even if she's a terrible bitch, but I help Sybil most of the time and so keep clear of her!"

Leon was smiling at her, and too late—as usual—Mika realised she was running on like a river in flood. She bit her lower lip at once and stood helplessly in front of Leon, slowly flushing as she remembered her warts and ugliness.

"I told you the Lady Alethea was kind," Leon said into her silence. "I was sure she wouldn't send you away. I need to bring this stuff up to the house. What were you doing out here?"

She noticed only now that Leon was loaded down with Agesandros' and his own gear in a large leather knapsack. "The Lady Alethea wants the plum trees pruned. She says it will make them grow better next year. Do you think that's true? It seems strange to me, and Orsippos didn't like the idea either—" She was doing it again. Talking a blue streak.

Leon was smiling at her, but he answered seriously. "I wouldn't question anything the Lady Alethea suggests—certainly not when it comes to plants. She understands plants and trees and flowers as if she could talk to them." Leon had started walking up the drive again, and Mika fell in beside him without thinking. "Tell me the news here," Leon suggested. "Has anything happened while I was away?"

Mika thought for a bit, and then decided on the most important item. "Well, Chloe's pregnant and Niko is the father."

Leon stopped dead in his tracks. "What!? Agesandros will kill him!"

"The Lady Alethea was quite upset, too," Mika admitted. "She told him it was a disgrace, but I don't really see why. After all, Chloe is pretty and she's not a whore or anything. I'm sure she hasn't had other lovers—well, not since I've been here, anyway. And this farm is so rich, you can afford to raise a baby here. Not like at home, where we had to kill some of the babies my mother had because we couldn't afford to feed them—" This time she stopped, not just because she'd been running on so long, but because of the way Leon was staring at her. "Did I say something wrong?" she asked after a bit, frightened by the way he was looking at her.

Leon shook himself. "No, of course not." He took a deep breath, but his eyes remained shaded, as he tried to explain. "It's different here. Niko shouldn't have taken liberties with a girl in his mother's household. That's not considered—" he searched for the right word—"proper for a Spartiate in the agoge."

"But she wanted it!" Mika protested. "I'm sure she did. More than he did. I'm sure she loves him," Mika added earnestly.

"That's not the point. You see, Niko—well, he ran away from the agoge some years back. If Agesandros hadn't convinced him to return, he would have lost his right to citizenship. Even now, he can't be sure they won't hold it against him. He ought to be very careful not to do anything the elders disapprove of."

"But I don't understand. Why should the elders care if Niko sleeps with one of his helots?"

Leon sighed. "I don't know really, but I think it's because the elders are afraid that if Spartiates form attachments to helots—particularly those on their own estates—then they will one day want to see the children of such liaisons recognised and admitted to the agoge and made citizens. The elders don't want other peoples admitted to citizenship. Only Dorians."

"Oh," Mika answered, still not understanding.

"I think," Leon repeated uncertainly.

They had reached the house, and ahead of them the entire household had crowded around Agesandros, who had Alethea in one arm and Kassia in the other. At the sight of Leon, several of the younger helot girls left the outer fringe to come to cluster around him. They offered to take his knapsack or to get him water, and Mika found herself cut off from him. She stopped and watched as Agesandros mounted the steps of the main house with Alethea and Kassia and the helots went together with Leon into their hall. For the first time since her arrival, she felt like an outsider.

CHAPTER 5

At first things went very much as Niobe had hoped. Anaxilas was not sated that first night, but explicitly ordered her to return to him the next.

"I'm not sure Thratta will let me, Master," Niobe replied in a mock-timid voice as she pulled her peplos on at the first light of dawn. "I had to sneak away and hide here. But tonight she'll be watching for me—"

"Who the hell do you think I am? No old hag of a helot can stand in my way. If I say I want you here tonight, then Thratta has no more right than you to say no!" Anaxilas countered with youthful self-assurance.

Niobe smiled to herself, but kept her head down humbly and her eyes lowered. "But she won't believe me, if I tell her—"

"The hell she won't. You tell her that if she doesn't let you come, she'll have me to answer to."

Niobe did as she was told, and although Thratta shook her head and sighed and Nais cast her looks to kill, they did not stop her. She waited for Anaxilas as before, naked and in bed. He came sooner, knowing she would be there, and he was as eager as a schoolboy.

Niobe was relieved, even if she sensed his ardour was not love. On the first night, back in Pylos, he had made it all too clear that raping her was his way of fucking Aristomenes. It was also clear that he had liked the idea of having a princess for his personal slave. As he

71

explained things to her, all he had had up until then had been helots and other captives who were of lower birth. By the end of the first week after his return to Sparta, however, Niobe thought her plan was working perfectly. He seemed determined that she should not only be at his disposal whenever he wanted, but that she should be freed of any tasks that might harm his child or her attractiveness. He had even started talking to her much as Aristomenes had done.

As Niobe soon learned, Anaxilas was convinced that nobody was treating him with the respect he deserved—whether in the baths or the gymnasium, or even in the chorus he'd joined. He even complained to Niobe that the others made fun of him behind his back. They certainly didn't make any effort to befriend him. Anaxilas was suspicious that Agesandros was spreading evil rumours about him. He complained to his grandmother, but she dismissed his allegations with an impatient gesture. "Nonsense. Why should he? You're no threat to him." When he went to his grandfather he got the even blunter answer, "Royalty doesn't bring popularity. You have to *earn* that. That's why I had you assigned to Agesandros' unit: to learn how a man—who was once scorned and ridiculed—wins men's admiration and trust."

Niobe comforted her misunderstood lover. "The others, especially Agesandros, are just jealous of you, Anaxilas," she assured him, remembering the way Kallisto had comforted her when the other girls hadn't wanted to play with her. "They can see you're superior to them, and that makes them feel uncomfortable and jealous."

But then one day Anaxilas came looking for Niobe in the morning. He found her on her hands and knees in his mother's room, trying to sweep under the dressing table. The sight of her well-formed hindquarters sticking out from under the dresser was too inviting. Niobe was taken by surprise, but not unpleased with his ardour. She felt she was gaining increasing power over him, and his obsession with her was growing.

Unfortunately, the queen walked in on them.

"What is going on here!?" she demanded.

Anaxilas jerked back and sank onto his heels. Sobbing for breath, sweat running down his face, he gazed at his grandmother in a daze. Niobe fell forward onto her face and lay gasping for breath, not daring to move. She knew the queen would be furious, but it was up to Anaxilas to defend her. He dragged himself to his feet, reeling slightly and still out of breath, and faced his grandmother with a crooked smile. She waited. He shrugged. "I'm taking a piece of ass, that's all. It belongs to me, after all."

"I didn't question your right to her—only the appropriateness of place and time. You're keeping her from her duties. Remove yourself from my chamber."

And Anaxilas went. Just like that. Without another word.

Niobe pulled her skirts back down and scrambled onto her shaking legs. Her breathing was short. Her face was still bright red. She kept her eyes down, not daring to look into the face of the Spartan queen. It wasn't her fault that she'd been found like this. None of it was her fault. She hadn't asked to be captured or sent here, but she was Anaxilas' slave and she had no right to say no to him. Why did she feel so ashamed?

"Pull your skirts up. I want to see your belly," the queen ordered in a cold tone.

Niobe, the blood rushing to her head again, dutifully pulled her skirts up to expose her round belly. Still she did not dare look the queen in the face. Her eyes were fixed on the other woman's feet instead: well-filed toenails in simple but sturdy sandals. "You're with child," the queen remarked at last.

"Your grandson's child, Mistress," Niobe whispered, hoping against her instincts that this cool, efficient woman had some motherly feelings. Her instincts proved correct.

"So what if it is? What my grandson spawns on the likes of you has no relevance for the Kingdom. But I suppose it suggests he's at least virile enough to sire children. Finish what you were doing—before my son distracted you."

The queen departed, and Niobe was at first bewildered and then relieved that there were no severer consequences to the incident. That was, until the next day.

Right after breakfast, when Niobe was collecting the dust-cloth and other things she usually took to clean the royal apartments, Thratta stopped her. "The queen says she doesn't want to see you in the royal apartments again. She says I'm to find you other duties. Go fetch a bucket of water and come with me."

Thratta led her to the entrance hall of the palace where petitioners, visitors, guards and officials came and went. Coming from the outside, they tracked in dirt on the marble floors. "Clean that up," Thratta ordered.

Niobe stared in horror. There was mud everywhere—not to mention bits of straw, horse hairs, feathers, manure—anything that could be brought in on the soles of men's sandals when they came from the streets. "When you're finished here, do the front porch and then the waiting rooms."

Finished? Niobe could see from the start that she would never be finished. No sooner had she finished one portion than someone would enter and walk right across the still-wet marble, smearing it anew with mud. Niobe had to fetch clean water every half-hour or so. Soon her shoulders ached from carrying the water nearly as much as her knees hurt from kneeling on the marble floor. She was exhausted by mid-day and she went to take her meal, trying to find some way of telling Thratta that she couldn't continue. She was met by Thratta holding a large hydria. She thrust the large pottery vessel into Niobe's hands with the order, "Take that to the fountain and fill it up. We're running short of water in the kitchen."

Water was piped into the royal palace in two places, the royal baths and the washhouse. Most days, there was sufficient water in the washhouse to meet all the needs in the kitchen as well, but Niobe knew that some days, when the laundry was heavy, they ran short in the kitchen.

Then someone was sent to one of the public fountains in the city, but Niobe had never been sent before.

"I don't know where it is," she pointed out, as if this would exempt her.

"Then it's time you learned, ain't it? Ask anyone. Hurry!"

Niobe took the heavy hydria and ventured out into the street with trepidation. Never in her life had she gone out in public on her own. Even the nightmare of her transport from Pylos to Sparta had been in company and under the "protection" of the guards. Suddenly she was being asked to go into a completely strange city without any kind of protection or chaperon. She didn't even have a shawl to cover her head. And her peplos was wet and dirty from scrubbing the floors all morning. She was ashamed to go out.

She stood just outside the doorway, cowering in the gutter and watching the people rushing past, intent on their business. There were helots leading pack animals and helots driving donkey-carts, helots loaded with things on their backs, and even a boy herding a flock of squawking geese in front of him. There was a merchant on an ox-cart, a man on a shaggy old horse, and a younger man on a fine, high-strung stallion that pranced and danced its way down the street. To Niobe's amazement, there was even a woman driving a chariot! She stared after this apparition for a long time, but then it was gone and she was still there with the hydria.

What was she supposed to do? Go up to a perfect stranger and ask the way to the nearest public fountain? It was unthinkable. What choice did she have? At last she saw a woman on a donkey cart come around the corner, and she thrust herself forward. "Hello! Hello! Excuse me! Can you tell me the way to the nearest public fountain?"

The woman stared at her as if she were mad. "Where did you come from? Just back there on Herakles Square." She pointed vaguely behind her and Niobe had no choice but to strike off in that direction. Soon she found herself in a very busy square, where the shopkeepers were starting to pack their things away and fold up their tables. On the far side was a small fountain house behind a simple portico with two pillars.

Water spluttered into the deep stone basins from no less than nine brass spouts in the three walls. Other women were bending over to dip their hydriae into the basins or reaching over to hold them directly under the lion-head spouts. Niobe bent and scooped water into her hydria as she saw the other women doing, but when she went to pull it out again, she gasped. It was so heavy it sent a wrenching pain through her back and belly. This couldn't be good for her, she registered with shock. Hadn't she heard the women at home say that a pregnant woman shouldn't fetch and carry heavy things? Hadn't they said that bending and lifting was the worst thing a woman could do when she was expecting? She rested the foot of the hydria on the edge of the basin and caught her breath. But she knew she somehow had to get it back to the royal palace. She had to.

Collecting all her strength, she set out. The hydria seemed to grow heavier and heavier. She couldn't find a way to carry it comfortably. Her belly got in the way if she tried to carry it in front of her in both arms. But it was far too heavy and bulky for just one arm. She stopped again and again to put it down and catch her breath. But that meant lifting it again, and part of her brain said that lifting was more dangerous than carrying.

At last she made it back to the royal palace. She staggered into the courtyard and just as she was about to enter the kitchen, she tripped on the steps and fell. The hydria shattered on the cobbles, spilling its contents everywhere. The shouts and curses that rained down on her were nothing compared to the pain in her knees and elbows. What was more, she had also cut herself on one of the shards and was bleeding profusely from her palm. But no one showed the least concern. Nais was openly laughing, saying, "What a pity Anaxilas can't see you now! You look like a drowned rat! I bet he wouldn't want to fuck you if he could see you now!"

Thratta was shoving another hydria at her. "Fetch that water and be quick about it! We don't have all day."

"I can't!" Niobe wailed out. "I've hurt myself! Can't you see? And—"

Thratta slapped her twice across her face. It hurt, of course, but the shock of someone doing that to her was greater than the pain itself. Niobe stared, holding the back of her hand to her cheek. "That's enough of your mouth! You ain't no fine lady anymore! Ain't you got that into your thick head yet? You got to do as I say, whether you like it or not! Now fetch that water quick!" To make sure Niobe had got the message, she gave her a smack on her backside for good measure.

Niobe, drenched, bleeding from the scrapes to her knees and elbows and the cut in her hand, stumbled back out into the street, blinded by tears. They had never been this cruel to her before. At the back of her brain, she was beginning to understand that the queen was behind this. She hadn't just been banned from the royal apartments; orders had evidently been given to make her life miserable. A warning voice suggested that the queen even *wanted* her to miscarry the baby, that she was intentionally being given tasks that would endanger her child. Niobe stumbled forward down the street, lost in her thoughts and sobbing miserably.

"Stop! Wait!" A young male voice called out, and Niobe gasped and looked about herself in terror.

A youth with dark brows that nearly met over his forehead was suddenly beside her. She tried to back up, but found herself already pressed up against the wall of the palace. "Leave me alone! I'm just going to fetch water. Leave me be! I—I—"

"But you're bleeding. Your hand is cut. You need to bind it up. Let me see if I have something." Already he was slinging the knapsack off his back and rummaging in it.

Niobe stood staring at him in wonder. He seemed vaguely familiar, but she couldn't place him. She was far too stunned and confused to resist when he pulled a roll of bandages out of his knapsack with a triumphant smile and said, "Hold out your hand."

She did as she was bid, timidly but without hesitation. Not since she had been captured had anyone been so considerate or kind.

The youth, his tongue sticking out of his mouth as he concentrated, worked with gentle efficiency, and then glanced up as he finished. The look in his eyes was shy and his cheeks were a little flushed as he asked, "Is that all right? Not too tight?"

She shook her head and looked down at the bright white bandage, neatly tied at the back of her hand. "Thank you," she murmured, not knowing what else to do or say.

The youth, too, stood awkwardly before her. Then his eyes went to the hydria she had set down to let him bandage her hand. "Did you say you were going to fetch water? Shall I help you?"

"No, no, it's all right," Niobe remembered herself. What was she doing talking to a strange youth? If Anaxilas found her here, he would surely beat her. When one of her father's concubines had been caught with another man he had had her flogged in front of the other women. Niobe had heard her screams and sobbing even though Kallisto told her to put a pillow over her head. The woman had been feverish and unable to sleep for weeks. She would be scarred for the rest of her life, Kallisto said—and she was sold, of course.

Niobe grabbed the hydria and started toward the fountain, refusing to look at the youth, but he had fallen in beside her. "You shouldn't be out in this cold without a himation—certainly not when you're soaking wet."

"I fell and broke the other one and that's why I have to hurry and fill this one up," Niobe found herself explaining, still not looking at him. "The sooner I'm finished, the sooner I can get changed and warm."

"Then let me help," he insisted gently. She felt his warm, firm hand on hers as he took the hydria away from her. "You weren't raised to this kind of work."

"How do you know that?" she demanded, stopping to stare at him.

He stopped and met her eyes. "You were Aristomenes' wife—in Pylos. I recognized you at once."

At Pylos. He'd been at Pylos. She searched her memories again. Of course; the youth with the torch. The youth who had left with Agesandros because he "couldn't do it with a girl who didn't want it." And he called her Aristomenes' "wife," not concubine.

"Yes," Niobe whispered in answer, unsure what to make of all this.

He smiled at her. "Come, you mustn't catch cold." He led her to the fountain, and dipped the hydria in and out of the water as if it weighed nothing at all. He had the broad, well-muscled back of a warrior, Niobe noted, nearly as broad as Anaxilas', although his face seemed younger than the prince's. She swallowed, the fear returning. "I belong to Anaxilas now," she whispered, hoping the youth would understand what that meant, that she couldn't be seen with him.

"I know." He was carrying the hydria for her, and she couldn't bring herself to demand it back. She let him carry it all the way to the entry to the slaves' court of the royal palace. There he paused and they looked at each other. "My name's Leon," he told her simply. "I serve Agesandros. If you need me for anything, just send for me." He carefully returned the hydria to her and stood watching her as she turned, still somewhat dazed, and carried it back inside.

Since her capture, Mika had never been so miserable as after Leon came home. For months she had looked forward to his return. She had imagined all sorts of scenarios, but they all ended with Leon "claiming" her, as was his right. And now he was here, and he didn't take any more note of her than he did the other girls on the kleros. Some days, Mika felt like he paid her even less attention than the others.

Not that Leon was in any way unkind. If he had been, maybe she would have fallen out of love. But Leon always had a smile for her, and he would stop to listen to any nonsense she wanted to tell him. Mika, however, wasn't blind. She could see perfectly well that he had a smile for all the helot girls, too. And when *they* chatted with him, they could talk about a common past and common acquaintances—they *shared* things. When she tried to talk to Leon, Mika had the feeling that she was from a different world. He listened politely to her, but he never joked and teased as he did with the others.

And Mika knew why. She was ugly. Not that the helot girls were beautiful like Niobe or Kassia were, but they weren't blemished as she was. Most of them had softer, more feminine figures and long hair, too.

As long as she didn't get sold, Mika was confident of growing out her hair. They only cut it off when she got lice or fleas, which usually happened in the crowded conditions of slave-trader stations or transports. She even had hopes that her figure was improving, since her flux had started and she was developing breasts. But the warts were the real source of men's aversion to her, and Mika became obsessed with trying to get rid of them.

Glauce, one of the kitchen maids, suggested that Mika make a paste of stinging nettles, fat, and garlic to rub on her warts, but that had only resulted in discomfort and a rash. Then Eunice, the other kitchen maid, said she should burn the warts off by heating up a sharp metal object and applying this to each individual wart.

It took a long time to work up the courage for this or find the right object, but Mika eventually decided on a skewer and one night after everyone else was in bed, she crept back down into the kitchen and stuck the skewer into the coals. From her time with the blacksmith, Mika knew the metal would get red and then start to glow. Holding the other end wrapped in the corner of her himation, Mika heated up the skewer and then in the dim light of the coal embers, she tried to aim the glowing end at a cluster of warts at the base of her thumb. But the heat was so intense that as the skewer approached it her hand flinched and shuddered of its own accord. Mika lay her hand on the table so it couldn't flinch and tried again. This time she grimly brought the hot skewer to the cluster of warts, but the searing pain was too much to stand more than a couple of seconds. Sobbing with pain and frustration, she dropped the skewer and rushed to plunge her burned hand into the water in the kitchen basin. Then she put the skewer away and crept back up to bed.

She slept poorly because of the pain in her hand, and in the morning not only were the blisters big and ugly, but she couldn't move her left thumb at all. She managed to hide her hand from everyone during breakfast, but no sooner did she join Sybil in the laundry, than the older woman asked, "What's wrong with your hand?"

"I—I burned myself."

"Let me see." Sybil held out her fleshy hand and Mika had to put her own into it. Sybil was sometimes gruff and moody in the morning, but she was a kindly soul at heart and Mika trusted her. She secretly hoped for help.

Sybil didn't disappoint her. She made a face and exclaimed with heartfelt sympathy, "That's a terrible burn!" Unfortunately, Sybil was also familiar with everything that happened in the household. Her next questions were, "How did you get it? Don't tell me you listened to that silly goose Eunice and tried to burn the warts off? I thought you had more sense than that!" And then, even before Mika could answer, she added, "We better show this to Alethea."

"No, please, no! I don't want her to know—"

"I can understand that," Sybil agreed, with a firm grasp on Mika's right wrist and starting to pull her out into the courtyard. "I'd be ashamed of being so stupid, too, but you've managed to do yourself real harm and we have to show Alethea."

Mika was struggling with all her strength to break free of Sybil. Precisely because Alethea had never said an unkind word to her, Mika was furiously determined not to reap her criticism now. She wasn't afraid of punishment so much as ashamed of disappointing. It was clear to Mika that her clumsy attempt to remove her warts could easily be seen as self-mutilation. Some slaves did that to avoid work. She didn't want Alethea to think that of her.

With her violent writhing and pulling, Mika managed to break free of Sybil just before they started up the steps into the main house. Sybil shouted after her as she ran away, "Come back here, you stupid goose! Where can you run to? Come back!"

Mika fled straight out the gate, because Eunice and Glauce were already peering out of the kitchen door to see what the commotion was. Mika ran to the orchard, away from the helots tending the fowl and pigs in the adjacent pens. She ran, as she always had as a child, to the trees and started to climb one. Unfortunately, with her damaged hand, she couldn't really get a grasp on the branches, and after several futile attempts she collapsed against the trunk and burst into tears.

Eventually Mika cried herself out. When the worst was over, she sat hiccupping and wiping her running nose on the back of her good hand, and the instinctive fear that had made her run started taking articulate form. She had been sold for lesser faults than self-mutilation. What if Alethea were angry enough to sell her? Mika felt her stomach cramp at the mere thought.

She was happy here. Happier even than in Pylos. The kleros was not a palace, but the people were nicer to her. Eunice and Glauce were real friends. They'd taken her into town with them on market days, and they included her in their gossip and even shared their things with her. Although Phoebe was a sour old bag, she wasn't as bad as Kallisto because she was short-tempered to everyone, not just Mika. And Sybil was truly kind. She'd taught Mika her duties with patience and encouragement, and had started to teach her things like table manners and good behaviour and good grammar. "You can't hope to serve Kassia until you know how to act like a lady," Sybil was fond of saying. Mika liked the idea of being allowed to serve a lady. She remembered the relationship between Kallisto and Niobe, and she thought it would be wonderful to be a trusted confidant of someone rich and beautiful.

And then there was Leon—even if he didn't take any particular interest in her. If she were sold, she would never see him again. The tears started swelling up again.

The sound of Alethea's voice behind her made her jump clean out of her skin. "Its starting to rain, Mika; you'd better come back inside and let me see to your hand."

"Oh, Mistress, I'm sorry!" Mika declared earnestly, scrambling awkwardly to her feet. "I didn't mean to hurt myself so bad I can't work proper. I—I just wanted—I thought—Eunice said—Please don't sell me, Mistress. I'll make up for any work I don't do now. I promise—"

"I'm not going to sell you, Mika—certainly not for something like this. Come inside. I don't want to get wet, even if you don't mind."

Mika looked up at the grey sky, astonished to see that Alethea was right and it was starting to rain. She dutifully walked back to the house beside her mistress. They didn't speak, but Mika kept repeating in her mind what Alethea had said, that she wouldn't sell her. She didn't care what else Alethea did to her, as long as she didn't sell her.

Alethea led her into the main house and to the back of the peristyle, to a small room beside the bath. It had high windows opening toward the walled orchard behind the house, a tiled floor, two naked beds, a chair, a lamp hanging from the ceiling and some wall cabinets. Alethea nodded for Mika to sit down on one of the two beds. "Let me see."

Mika dutifully held out her hand, holding her breath and biting down on her lower lip.

Alethea inspected the damage Mika had done to herself with a stoical calm. Then she took a deep breath. "I feel responsible for this," she declared as she went to open one of the cabinets. "The day you arrived I said we should see what we could do about those warts, and then I completely forgot about it. That was very remiss of me. Have you tried to burn them off in the past?" She turned to look at Mika as she asked this.

Mika shook her head vigorously. "No, Mistress. It was Eunice's idea. I just—" She cut herself off and bit down on her lip again, not daring to meet Alethea's eyes.

"What other methods have you tried?"

"Glauce suggested stinging nettles and fat and garlic, but it didn't work."

"What else?"

"My mother tried some things, but I don't remember what they were—and wouldn't know the Greek words for them anyway."

"But what else have you tried? Besides these last two methods?"

"Nothing, Mistress."

"In all the years after you left home? Nothing until now, in the last month?"

"But it wasn't important before—"

"Before what?"

"Before—I came here." Mika suddenly saw a new danger. Alethea's deep, understanding eyes might understand too much. She started speaking in a rush to distract attention. "The King of Arcadia bought me for his daughter because I was ugly, Mistress. He said that I would serve his daughter better because no one would want me and so I wouldn't get pregnant. He—he knew about Aristomenes, you see—that Aristomenes liked to sleep around even with the women of his household. They said in Pylos that he even seduced the wife of one of his companions. And of course he'd had all the pretty slave-girls. The King of Arcadia didn't want his daughter to be insulted by her husband sleeping with her personal slave, so he chose me because I was so ugly. Everyone said Aristomenes would never want me."

Alethea sighed and shook her head slowly, but she was not distracted. "But surely you know that even if we don't value you *because* of your disfigurement, we don't value you *less* because of it, either? You know that, don't you?" She looked hard at Mika, expecting an answer, and Mika could only look down in embarrassment.

Alethea waited for a little while but when Mika made no reply, she took another deep breath. "I have an ointment here to ease the pain of the burn and then we'll bandage the hand so it stays clean, but I'm going to ask a surgeon friend of mine if he knows any remedy for warts. Meanwhile, for the next few days, I want you to wait on Kassia and help me with the spinning."

Mika soon discovered that serving Kassia was very different from serving Niobe. For a start, Kassia took no interest in her looks whatever. She owned no bottles of perfume, no eye shadow or liner, not even any rouge, much less henna. When Mika came to help her dress the day after she burned her hand, she found that there was nothing she could do for her but brush her hair—and even then she was impatient.

"But I know lots of fancy ways to put up hair, Mistress," Mika protested, anxious to prove her worth and secure her future.

"Whatever for?" Kassia replied. "It just takes time and then it all falls down again as soon as I *do* anything. Just brush it out and tie it at the back of my head, please."

"But you'd be even *prettier*, Mistress, if you put it up like your mother does, with a diadem or—"

"I don't *want* to be any prettier, Mika. It's bad enough as it is. If I go anywhere, people *stare* at me. I *hate* it! It makes me feel like I'm just an object—a statue or a racehorse. I want people to see me as a person, not a thing. I want them to listen to what I *say*, not just gawk at my hair, my face or my legs. My music is what's important to me. I'm a poet. I *write* poetry," she stressed to the evidently still confused Mika.

"But you're so lucky to be pretty, Mistress," Mika protested, baffled.

"I don't think so, and would you please stop calling me 'Mistress'—it makes me feel like an old woman. I'm only 17, and I'm still a maiden."

Mika couldn't understand why a beautiful girl was still not married at such an age, but was afraid to ask an impertinent question, so she asked instead, "But what should I call you, Miss—"

"Kassia, of course."

"Oh, I couldn't do *that*, Mistress—people will think I'm disrespectful."

"What people?" Kassia countered. "All the helots call me Kassia."

"But they knew you from when you were little. What does Leon call you?"

"Leon?" Kassia stopped to think. "I think he calls me 'ma'am'—but that's no better than Mistress. It's what the boys at the agoge and the young men call married women. Look, Mika," Kassia said as she turned around on her stool to face her new maid, "it's all very well that Mom thinks I should have a maid, and I know you mean well, and I'm sure you did a wonderful job with Aristomenes' wife or concubine or whatever she was, but you aren't going to turn me into something I'm not. Now please just do as I say and brush my hair into a ponytail."

Mika soon discovered that the hardest part of serving Kassia was cleaning and mending her peplos, himations and sandals. It seemed that when Kassia was "composing," she liked to go for long walks—even in the worst weather. Because she was lost in her poetry, she never seemed to watch where she was going enough to avoid getting mud and dung on her hems—not to mention the dog hairs she collected, because she usually took one or more of her brother's hunting dogs with her. This explained why she had only a very few pretty peplos at all; Alethea said it was an absolute waste to give her daughter anything of silk or with embroidery on it.

After she had been serving Kassia three or four days, Mika's curiosity got the better of her, and she finally asked, "What kind of poetry do you write? May I hear it?"

"Of course!" Like all artists, Kassia was delighted by interest in her work. She launched at once into a poem, and Mika's eyes widened and widened with each line. Even if she didn't understand it all, she could hear that it was *real* poetry—metered and rhymed and lyrical.

"That's beautiful!" Mika exclaimed sincerely as Kassia finished, and Kassia beamed. Mika's future was secured.

"Thank you." Kassia gave Mika a quick hug and then enthusiastically added, "It will be better to music. Tyrtaios has promised to write a melody for it. I used to write my own music, but he's much better than me."

"Who's Tyrtaios?"

"Our Supreme Polemarch, appointed by Delphi. He'll come visit one of these days, and you can meet him. He's short and fat and near-sighted and balding and lame—but he's a wonderful poet and writes divine music. You'll hear it at the next festival when the age-cohorts graduate."

Before that, however, another curious figure made his appearance at the kleros: it was the surgeon's apprentice, Pharax, and he came to look at Mika's warts.

Mika was back in the laundry by then. She still helped Kassia dress and undress and took care of her things, but for most of her day she helped Sybil. She had been pressing bed linens when Kassia stuck her head into the laundry and called, "Mika, Mom says to come to the infirmary and let the surgeon see you."

Mika carefully replaced the heavy iron on the marble shelf and used the towel hanging on a hook by the door to wipe the sweat from her face and under her arms. For some reason, the very thought of facing a surgeon made her throat dry. They didn't have surgeons where she came from. Like fountains and sailing ships, they were part of "civilization."

"Put your snood on properly, girl," Sybil admonished as she started out, and then came and gave her a hand, taking the scarf off entirely and re-tying it at the back of her head. "The surgeon is a Spartiate citizen, so be on your best," she warned. "No bad words." Then she gave Mika a smile and sent her out with a kindly pat on her shoulder.

Mika hesitated on the doorstep of the infirmary and waited there for someone to notice her. Alethea was leaning against one of the two beds, and a young man who looked no more than 30 stood opposite her, leaning on the other bed. To Mika's horror, he had only one leg, the other being cut off below the knee and replaced with a wooden peg. A walking crutch was leaning against the bed beside him. He had a slight paunch and his arms and chest were soft and round rather than hard and muscular. He had a round face, exaggerated by a fringe of red beard, but it was a jolly face, and he was smiling and laughing as he talked to Alethea. They seemed to be sharing an old joke, because Alethea was saying, "And then he said, 'Why not?!'"

"'In case you've forgotten, you were bleeding to death at the time!'" the surgeon supplied the answer, and they both laughed delightedly. The surgeon recovered first. "Really, it's a good thing he doesn't put himself in the way of thrown javelins often!"

"Well, hopefully my sons are past the age for running away," Alethea noted with a sigh.

"They're all right, ma'am. You've got nothing to worry about. They're both all right—but what have we here?" The surgeon had caught sight of Mika and he focused his bright blue eyes on her and smiled—although at once something darkened his eyes as he took in her disfiguring warts.

"This is Mika," Alethea announced, standing upright and signalling Mika to enter. "Mika, this is Pharax. He was one of my husband's best men—"

"Don't anger the gods with lies, ma'am. I was one of your husband's worst men, but thanks to him I'm only a cripple and not under ground."

Alethea replied blissfully, "Agesandros says you were an excellent hoplite, and I don't question him on such things." She continued to Mika, "After Pharax lost his foot and was retired from the army, he started learning about medicine from one of our best physicians, Kleonymus. Kleonymus is ageing and didn't feel up to coming all the way out here, so he sent Pharax instead."

"Do you mind if I take a look?" Pharax asked in a friendly tone.

"I'm just a slave," Mika blurted out, confused by his polite tone.

Pharax glanced at Alethea, but then looked back at Mika and said steadily, "I know, and I'm just an apprentice doctor."

Mika glanced again at Alethea, who nodded to her. Then she cautiously went to stand before him, torn between instinctive fear of a surgeon and trust in a man who was so nice. He inspected her face and then her hands and asked her a lot of questions: when the warts first appeared, if they hurt or stung, what methods she had used to try to remove them. He inspected her hand with the burn scar particularly closely. The warts were definitely gone, but they had been replaced with a scar: "Hardly a solution which warrants repetition" was his comment to Alethea. "The same problem applies to surgical removal. It is appropriate if the warts occur, say, on the soles of the feet or between fingers and toes and so cause discomfort—but for facial warts it is not a viable alternative. I will have to come up with something else." He turned back to Mika. "I'm sorry I can't offer an immediate solution, but I promise I will try to rid you of this problem. You know," he tilted his head and smiled, "you'd be a pretty girl without them."

Mika looked down confused. No one had ever said that to her before.

Pharax stood up and took his crutch. Turning back to Alethea he remarked, "Give my regards to Agesandros. I'll be back when I have an idea what to do for Mika."

CHAPTER 6

As Niobe soon learned, just after the winter solstice there was a festival in Sparta to mark the graduation of youths from one age-cohort to the next. From the other helots, who evidently looked forward to the event with excitement, she learned that there were competitions at archery and javelin, wrestling matches and—clearly one of the highlights as far as the helots were concerned—a fierce ball game between the Melleirenes (graduating 19-year-olds) and the 20-year-old eirenes.. There were also races for each of the age-cohorts *of both sexes* of the agoge, and chariot races among citizens in which, she was told, women or maidens sometimes did the driving. Niobe found herself looking forward to seeing such exotic things. But most important, since they had the entire day off and were allowed to attend the festivities, Niobe was certain this festival would at last give her a chance to speak to Anaxilas.

Since the day she had been banned from the royal apartments, she had not seen him. Niobe knew this was the queen's doing, and she kept telling herself that if she could only remind Anaxilas of herself and her child that she could yet talk him into helping her—even if it were only to send her to another household where they could meet secretly.

Yet things proved more difficult than she had imagined. It turned out that Anaxilas had entered a chariot in one of the races. As a result, he did not attend the other events to which the household flocked. Then, after he lost the race and Niobe was on the brink of rushing forward to comfort him, the queen swept up and insisted that Anaxilas personally escort her to some choral performance. Anaxilas was clearly not pleased, but there was nothing Niobe could do but tag along behind with the others. She could hear him raving about the race to his grandmother.

"The fool! The idiot! I swear he did it deliberately!" Anaxilas insisted loud enough for everyone in the entourage to hear.

"Keep your voice down. You're making a fool of yourself," his grandmother hissed under her breath. They had reached the theatre and the Spartan queen led her son to a seat reserved for them at the very centre and one row behind the kings and council. The helots, of course, had standing room only, but Niobe managed to squeeze herself onto one of the steps on the right-hand aisle where she could keep her eye on Anaxilas—and hear what he was saying loudly. "I swear my driver was bribed—"

"I'm sure none of the citizens can afford to pay him more than you can," his grandmother hissed back.

"Pay him? Why should I pay him? He's a nothing but a slave! In the name of the Twins! I had to pay Klearchos a bloody fortune for him, but I'm not going to pay my own property. Klearchos must have known he wasn't to be trusted, otherwise he wouldn't have sold him and let a mere boy drive his own chariot—"

"An eirene is not a boy, and besides, he is Klearchos' sister's son. Now, forget the race. A man who cannot lose graciously should not compete in athletic events at all."

"I had the much better team. Surely, you—"

"Hush, the chorus is ready to begin."

At last Anaxilas turned his eyes to the stage with a frown, his thoughts evidently still on the race he'd lost. Niobe, too, turned her attention to the stage. She had never seen anything like it. Adolescent girls of apparently marriageable age were on the stage unveiled and in full view of all the men of the city. It was as if they were all on display like wares at a market, Niobe thought in abhorrence, and she looked around her in distaste. But the faces of the audience seemed strangely passive, not leering as she had expected or as she had seen on the faces of her father's guests when he produced female entertainment for them at his elaborate feasts. (Niobe knew this because she and her sisters had often snuck around to watch these events themselves from the safety of the gallery.)

Then the soloist came onto the stage, and even Niobe caught her breath. The girl was stunningly beautiful, with the bright blonde hair Niobe had always wished she'd had—the colour of hair men invariably liked best. This must have been the way Helen looked, Niobe registered with an alarmed glance at Anaxilas.

And she saw her worst fears affirmed. Anaxilas was staring at the soloist as if he needed her to keep him breathing. The girl was dressed for this performance in a pale blue silk peplos with dark blue trim, and her hair was fastened loosely to the back of her head, while an ivory diadem kept it out of her delicate, oval face. Anaxilas swallowed and licked his lips.

When she stepped forward to sing, the slit on the side of her peplos revealed—if only for a brief second—a slim, well-shaped leg, and Niobe could see the way Anaxilas watched avidly for another glimpse. When the soloist took deep breaths, her small breasts rose, and Niobe could see that Anaxilas kept swallowing as if his throat were dry.

When the performance ended, no one applauded more enthusiastically then Anaxilas, and even before the clapping had died out he was demanding of his grandmother, "The soloist: who was she?"

"Your second cousin, Kassia, daughter of Euryanax."

"*The* Euryanax, who died commanding the rear guard after Hysiai?"

"Yes, that's right."

"How old is she? She must be out of the agoge!"

"Long ago; but Tyrtaios likes her voice and almost always has her sing his solos. I'm surprised you haven't noticed her before—but then, you don't appreciate music and usually avoid the choral events, don't you?"

"I never guessed what I was missing! Is she spoken for?"

"I don't think so. If I remember correctly there was some understanding with a cousin on her mother's side, but the young man was killed while still an eirene, in Aristomenes' raid several years back. Why? I thought you only had eyes for that Messenian baggage you sent home from Pylos." She added the latter remark with a contempt that made Niobe wince in outrage.

"Niobe? Why she is nothing but a crude, cheap bauble compared to that maiden—like painted glass beside a real jewel!" Anaxilas assured his grandmother emphatically. "Besides, Niobe is just a slave, and that is a citizen's virgin daughter. By Herakles, she's the right girl to follow in your and my mother's footsteps! She'd do Helen herself credit!"

Niobe could only sit petrified and chilled to the bone, conscious that she had been defeated by her own best weapon. This girl was prettier than she.

Mika couldn't understand what was happening at first. A very distinguished-looking older man with long, white braids, whom she had never seen before, arrived at the kleros and closeted himself with Agesandros and Alethea. The helots explained to Mika that the visitor was Leobotas, a member of the Council of Elders and, more important, the uncle of Alethea's first husband and so guardian of her children by her first marriage. His arrival at once sparked speculation about what the mistress' boys had done *now*; Mika gathered rapidly that both had been in trouble in the past. Suspicions seemed to be confirmed when only a few minutes later they heard Agesandros' angry voice, followed by the low tones of Alethea in evident distress. Everyone was speculating hard about whether it was Sandy or Niko who had gotten in trouble this time, when Alethea came looking for Kassia. Kassia?

"Prince Anaxilas has asked for her in marriage," Alethea explained, looking as if she were dazed rather than happy. Mika couldn't understand that—or why Agesandros sounded angry. Surely it was a great honour, even in Sparta, for a prince to want to take the daughter of the house to wife?

In any case, Leobotas insisted on speaking to Kassia alone, without either Agesandros or Alethea present, and then he went away again looking very satisfied. But what followed was dreadful: there was a terrible fight between Agesandros and his stepdaughter. Neither made any effort to keep their voices down, and the entire household heard most of what transpired—or at least the things they shouted at one another.

Mika didn't know entirely what to think. While it was uncommon for a maiden to be defiant of a father, Mika already knew Kassia well enough to know she was not the kind to be intimidated even by a man of Agesandros' stature. Besides, he was only her stepfather and had no say over her future whatsoever. Which, as it turned out, was exactly the problem.

Agesandros was outraged to learn that Kassia had agreed to marry the Eurypontid prince and was demanding that she withdraw her consent. Kassia kept challenging him to give her "one good reason why." Agesandros called Anaxilas (his prince!) all kinds of rude names and insisted Kassia would not be happy with him. Kassia retorted that he couldn't possibly know what would make her happy. The whole terrible scene reached a climax with Kassia screaming at Agesandros that he wasn't her father and had no right to interfere in her life. Then she ran out of the hall where the discussion had taken place and rushed up to her chamber, almost trampling on Mika, who was sitting outside her door awaiting her duties.

Mika didn't know what to do. She was supposed to help her mistress undress and go to bed, but she was rather afraid of her in this mood. She fussed around outside the door for a bit and then she heard sobs coming from inside. Realising that Kassia was crying, she decided she had better go in and see if she could help her in some way. She knocked timidly and then pushed the door open and peered inside.

Kassia was stretched out on her bed, sobbing into her pillow. Mika tiptoed into the room. "Mistress? Kassia? What's the matter?" When she got no response, Mika crept right up beside the bed and crouched down. "Kassia? What's the matter? The master can't stop you from marrying. You'll get your prince."

"Oh, Mika!" Kassia wailed in despair and sat up to face her. "You don't understand! Nobody understands! Not even my mother—much less that interfering bastard Agesandros! Damonon is dead and I'm never going to love another man, so I might as well be married to a prince! Uncle Leobotas explained it all so clearly. He says he's had dozens of offers for me already! Can you imagine that?!" Kassia sounded incredulous, whereas Mika found it only natural. After all, in Mika's experience most girls were married at 14 or 15—at least the pretty ones were.

"And your uncle didn't think the others worthy of you?" Mika asked timidly.

"That's not the problem. I gather they were all good peers, but Uncle Leobotas said that to give me to one would make the others jealous. He said he had the same dilemma as Tyndareus when trying to marry off Helen. He said that he had no choice but to follow Tyndareus' solution: to give me to the most powerful of the suitors. And that is Prince Anaxilas. It makes perfect sense to me, and I don't understand why Agesandros is making such a fuss about it. It isn't as though *he* had another suitor for me he prefers. He couldn't think of a single name when I pressed him! He's just being unreasonable—as if he were jealous of me marrying into the royal family just because he came from such a poor family himself. I really don't think that's the least bit fair. After all, it isn't as if I asked to marry a prince, but if I have to marry anyone other than Damonon, why shouldn't it be a prince?"

"But, Kassia, who is Damonon and why can't you marry him?" Mika asked anxiously, frowning in her effort to understand.

Kassia stared at her blankly for a moment, and then to Mika's utter amazement, she pulled Mika into her arms and started crying again. "Oh, Mika, you don't know! He was the most wonderful young man in the world. My cousin. We had promised to marry each other when we were still children, and he was so good! But they killed him! The Messenians stabbed him 23 times. They crept in in the dark of night when the army was away and they attacked the children in their school-beds. Damonon was an eirene at the time, and he—like all his classmates, every one of them—was killed trying to defend his charges.

"So you see, Mika," Kassia pulled back and looked at the slave-girl earnestly, "I can't love anyone else, and if I'm not going to love my husband, then I might just as well be Queen of Sparta. After all, as Sparta's queen, no one can stop me from writing my poetry, and people will have to respect me and listen to me. I won't just be a *female*" (she said it as if it were something despicable) "but a *person*. That's what I want most, Mika; I want to be a person that people listen to and take seriously. If I can't be that, I'd rather be dead." She said it so definitively that Mika winced inwardly.

"When I lost Damonon, I wanted to die," Kassia was continuing. "I tried to kill myself four different times, but someone or something always got in the way and saved me. It was so frustrating! But then Tyrtaios came and showed me that my poetry really is good. He gave me a reason for living again—even without Damonon. But only if I can be someone that people listen to! So you see, it doesn't matter what Anaxilas is like, really; all that matters is that I will be a queen one day and people will have to take me seriously."

Mika nodded solemnly, because obviously Kassia felt very strongly about this, and certainly she knew better than Mika did. But Mika couldn't help thinking that it would be nice to at least *like* the man you were married to.

In the days following the festival, Niobe started to truly fear for her future. Until that horrible moment following the choral performance, she had hoped that—at the latest, when their baby was born—things would improve. Now Niobe feared things would change for the worse.

And she was right.

Just four days after the festival Thratta came into the hall and announced in a loud, triumphant voice, "Well, have you heard the news? Anaxilas has been betrothed to his second cousin Kassia, daughter of Euryanax." She looked pointedly at Niobe and announced maliciously, "I guess he won't be needing the likes of you or your brat much longer, girl. Everyone agrees that Kassia is the most beautiful creature to be seen in Lacedaemon since Menelaos' Helen was buried."

The very next day the new treatment started. Niobe was again sent to scrub the entrance hall, and when she was finished there, she was told to scrub the floors of the next room and the next and the next. She was kept on her knees all day long. Dragging water in a bucket to wherever she was working, scrubbing the terracotta, mosaic or marble floors, wiping them dry, fetching more water. By the end of the day, her hands were red and wrinkled from the water, and her knees were bruised black and blue and hurt so much she could hardly straighten them. Her shoulders ached oppressively, and the pain in the small of her back was almost unbearable. But as she staggered exhausted into the hall, Thratta met her with an outstretched arm, pointing to a fat hydria. "Take that and fetch water. We're almost out."

"I can't," Niobe protested, sinking onto the nearest bench and wiping strands of hair out of her face. "I'm exhausted and my back aches—"

"Don't give me any of your mouth! Move!"

"But I've been scrubbing floors all day!" Niobe whined indignantly.

"What do you think the rest of us have been doing? Sitting on our backsides? We're all tired! Get on with it!"

"I wasn't born to this like you were!" Niobe lashed out, unconsciously echoing Leon's words. "I was raised to be a lady. I had two personal slaves to wait on me day and—"

From all around the kitchen came hooting and mocking voices: "Poor little princess misses her slaves!" "Princess wants to be waited on!" "What is it ladies do? Lie on their backs and fuck all day?"

"I *can't*!" Niobe whined louder; "My back is killing me—"

"Killing you, is it? Well, if you don't get off your backside fast, you'll *wish* you were dead!" Thratta threatened, her hands on her hips.

"I *can't*!" Niobe insisted more emphatically than ever. The tears were swimming in her eyes and her voice was tight.

Thratta grabbed her and yanked her up off the bench, pulled her out the door of the hall, and then shoved her down the stairs into the courtyard. With a cry, Niobe fell on her hands and knees; her whole body was jarred by the impact. The pains in her back increased sharply and spread to her belly. She screamed in pain and terror. But Thratta was already standing over her, thrusting the hydria into her arms. Pulling her to her feet with one hand, while smacking her buttocks with the other, she ordered, "Get that water now, or I'll have you flogged!"

Niobe fled in tears. She stumbled, doubled over with pain down the corridor to the street, and then came to a halt. Leaning against the wall, she tried to catch her breath. Up to now they had always sent her for water at noon, and every day Leon had been waiting for her. He had taken the hydria from her, walked with her to the fountain, filled it and carried it back to the doorway for her. But now it was after dark. The dinner hour was over. Leon must long since have gone home with his master to his kleros. The streets were almost deserted. There was no one to help her.

Niobe was crying, whether from pain or hopelessness she didn't know. She staggered down the street, unable to walk a straight line with the hydria in one arm and the other trying to hold her belly. The pains were getting worse. So much worse they were blotting out all her other aches and pains. By the time she reached the fountain, she was almost blinded by pain. Part of her knew that this was serious. That something terrible was happening. Although she had heard of it in her father's house, her brain still resisted facing it: she was losing her baby.

She dunked the hydria into the water, grateful for the feel of the icy water all the way up over her elbows. When she tried to straighten her back, she collapsed with a long, drawn-out scream of protest instead.

She must have blacked out for a few minutes. When she came to, she was still on the floor of the fountain house, but there were women crowding over her. "Where is she from?" "I've seen her here before." "Doesn't she usually come with Agesandros' squire?" "No, she comes from the Eurypontid palace." "Shall I fetch the midwife?" "Yes. Run!" "No, there's no time." "Doesn't Pharax live just around the corner?" "What does he know about miscarriages?" "He'll have a pain killer." "We need to get her out of here."

Niobe groaned aloud and then cried out in pain as various women grabbed her arms and legs and started to carry/drag her out of the fountain house. "We need some light." "Let's get her inside somewhere." "Knock there and ask them to let us in—" Suddenly there was a male voice, vigorous and commanding: "Put her down!" They dumped her onto the paving stones and Niobe groaned again. The man was leaning over her, feeling her belly with his strong, cool hands. Niobe cried out. She heard the murmur of voices. "It's too late. Nothing to do now."

"Silence!" the man ordered. "Dexippos, come quick." Niobe heard the footsteps and smelled sweat and garlic. Then a man slipped his arms under her knees and shoulders and she was lifted off the pavement, carried into a house, and set down on a bed. Lamps spun over her head. She saw a man with a silly red beard looking over her. She felt him pull up her skirts, but it didn't matter any more. Any sense of modesty or dignity had been lost in the consuming pain and the gush of blood and stench that enveloped her as she passed out again.

PART II
THE RUNAWAY
AND THE SURGEON

IN THE 2ND YEAR OF THE 30TH OLYMPIAD
THE 8TH YEAR OF THE SECOND MESSENIAN WAR

SPARTA, LACEDAEMON

CHAPTER 7

When Niobe did not appear with the hydria the first day after Kassia's betrothal, Leon thought nothing of it. Some days they didn't need extra water or one of the other girls was sent. But when after three days in a row she had failed to appear, he began to get concerned.

At first his concern was vague and swung between fear that she had taken ill and fear that Anaxilas had finally prohibited her from being given a task that endangered her health. Leon told himself that he ought to be glad if the latter were true, but he wasn't quite as selfless as he wanted to be. The thought of not seeing her again discouraged him. Somewhat at a loss, he wandered to the fountain itself and after hanging about there a bit, he asked one of the other women if she knew where Niobe was.

"Niobe? Is that her name? The girl you always came here with?"

"Yes; have you seen her recently?"

"Isn't that the girl who was big with child?" one of the other women asked, setting down her own hydria. "You aren't the father, are you?" There was nothing so odd about the question, really. Leon and Niobe were both slaves.

Leon, however, reacted as if he'd been insulted. "Of course not! I wouldn't have laid a hand on her! Surely you know she was Aristomenes' wife?"

"That murdering bastard's wife? If I'd known that, I wouldn't have lifted a finger to help her," another woman called out indignantly.

"Help her? I would have kicked her belly to be sure his brat was dead!" another woman pitched in furiously.

Although Leon understood the hatred that Aristomenes aroused in the women of Lacedaemon, he was nevertheless appalled to hear it extended to Niobe. "It's not Niobe's fault that Aristomenes slaughtered the children of the agoge. She wasn't even married to him then," Leon told the women firmly. "She's just a girl. Haven't any of you seen her recently?"

"Sure. She lost her baby—right here, practically. We got her outside and then Pharax had her taken to his place, but it was too late to do anything."

"The gods took care of Aristomenes' brat even without my help," the woman who had promised to kick Niobe's belly declared triumphantly.

Leon was horrified. "Is she all right?" he asked urgently, remembering how often women died in childbed or were sick or even crippled afterwards.

The women shrugged collectively and looked at one another.

"How should we know? She hasn't been here since," one of them finally answered.

"How long ago did this happen?" Leon pressed them, his worry growing by the second.

"Four or five days, I'd guess," one woman suggested, and the others nodded agreement.

"You took her to Pharax?" Leon pressed them anxiously. He hated the thought of asking after her at the Eurypontid palace; Anaxilas might misinterpret things.

They nodded, and he set off at once. He did not know the surgeon's apprentice very well, but they had met. Agesandros had brought the wounded Pharax to Alethea's kleros three years ago. That was the night Agesandros and Alethea met, and Kleonymus had amputated Pharax's leg. After that, Pharax had spent more than a month at the kleros recovering. At the time, Leon had been a slave in Alethea's household.

When Pharax tried to kill himself once, it was Alethea and Leon who together had managed to prevent it. Then Pharax had been removed to his mother's care and Leon had seen almost nothing of him. He wasn't even sure if Pharax would recognize and remember him, but his concern for Niobe overrode his own reluctance to face the Spartiate surgeon. She might be dead or ill. Certainly she must be devastated by the loss of her child. He remembered her telling him that she was only 16, and it was her first child.

He knocked on the door, composing his face and the wording of his request with trepidation. When Pharax had been brought to Alethea's kleros wounded, Leon had been a runaway. He had been recognized by one of Agesandros' men, and they had almost killed him on the spot. Only Alethea's furious intervention had stayed the knife after it was already slicing the skin on his throat. The memory of that moment made Leon break out into a sweat even now, almost three years later. There was still a scar from that knife on his throat.

The door opened and he found himself confronting a giant of a man with a shaggy beard, unkempt long hair and breath that reeked of garlic. "What do you want?" the man demanded roughly.

"I've come to speak to Pharax about Niobe," Leon explained.

"So who the hell are you?" the man demanded.

"Leon, Agesandros' squire."

"You come from Agesandros? Why didn't you say so?" The man backed up and gestured for Leon to enter. He slammed the door shut behind him and then led down the corridor and into a courtyard. Here the man stopped and, lifting his head, shouted toward the gallery of the one section of the house that was two-storied, "Master! Agesandros' squire is here to see you."

A moment later, Pharax limped to the railing and waved down at Leon, smiling. "Come on up," he invited.

Pharax's servant pointed him toward the stairs, and Leon went up feeling increasingly guilty about penetrating the privacy of another man's home under false pretences. Pharax thought he'd come on Age-sandros' business.

Pharax was sitting on a stool with his peg leg stretched out before him. He had changed a great deal since he'd been brought in wounded. Then he'd been on active service, which meant he was clean shaven with short hair. He'd also been in peak physical condition, muscular and overly lean. It was strange to see him tending to flabbiness and with a funny fringe of red beard.

In front of him now was a large table overflowing with parchments, wax tablets and papyrus. In wonder, Leon took in the floor-to-ceiling cubby-holes filled with yet more documents. There were even parch-ments stacked on the floor, while others were held rolled open by rocks or weights.

Pharax followed Leon's gaze and apologized with a helpless shrug and a grin. "I know it looks a bit chaotic. If Agesandros saw me here, he'd write me off as completely crazy." Pharax laughed at the thought. "But in fact, it's all his fault. He was the one who gave me the idea of studying medicine in the first place. You know the story?"

Leon shook his head.

"You remember how I tried to kill myself?"

Leon nodded.

"Well, Agesandros found out about it, and when the campaign sea-son ended he came to see me. I was living with my mother at the time, feeling sorry for myself and wasting away with self-pity. I'd been a run-ner, you know, before I lost my foot. I thought athletic and military ability were the only qualities that did a man credit. Agesandros was angry with me for sulking. When I told him losing my leg had been the worst thing that could have happened to me, he blew up. 'You think that was the worst thing? I'll show you something worse,' he said. Then he drew his sword and grabbed my wrist as if he wanted to hack off one of my hands. Of course I struggled and tried to stop him. He got me pinned down and then said, 'You've still got your hands and your head! Why don't you use them?' He added, 'Any fool can get his men wounded and killed, but it takes a great man to save lives. It's embarrassing to think Kleonymus wasted his skills on a thick-skulled fool like you!' Then he stormed out again, but it got me thinking.

"I was never going to fight or run again, but Agesandros was right that I still had my hands and my head. And thinking about Kleonymus, it was clear that he used these and not his feet to help people. So I went to the surgeon and asked him to teach me all he knew about healing. He's done what he can, but he's the first man to admit he doesn't know everything. Since his eyes are gradually failing, he turned his whole library over to me." Pharax gestured grandly to the documents in all forms filling the room around him. "Now I can learn from others as well. All this," Pharax gestured again to the clutter of papyrus and parchment, "is what other men have written down about their own efforts to cure human illness."

Leon looked about the room with even more wonder than before. He was illiterate. It was hard for him to understand how squiggles on papyrus could contain the key to helping cure illness.

"I'm trying to find a cure for warts," Pharax continued cheerfully, "to help the girl you brought back from Pylos."

"Mika? Do you think there is a cure?"

Pharax scratched at his stubby, stiff beard. "Well, I can't say my research has been very encouraging, but I'm not going to give up yet. In some cases warts have been known to disappear, but the causality is very hard to determine. But that's not what you're here about, I warrant. What can I do for my old benefactor?"

Leon looked down guiltily, but then he collected his courage and looked squarely at Pharax. "I'm sorry, sir, if I gave the wrong impression. Agesandros didn't send me. I came on my own—to find out what happened to Niobe. The women at the fountain house said she'd lost her baby and that you had had her brought here. I wanted to find out if she was all right."

Pharax considered Leon for what seemed like a long time. His eyes seemed to be assessing him very critically. Leon was sure that the Spartiate was remembering that he was a runaway. He found himself swallowing hard, but he kept his eyes fixed on Pharax.

At last Pharax answered, "I couldn't help her. It was too late when they called me."

"Is she dead?" Leon asked in alarm. He couldn't bear it if she were dead! Anything but that.

"No, no," Pharax reassured him. "I meant it was too late to save her baby. It's so frustrating! Women keep these things to themselves until it is too late. If only she'd come to me earlier."

"But she didn't know anyone here," Leon defended Niobe ardently. "She's a complete stranger in the city. Besides, she was raised differently. She says in Arkadia noblewomen don't go out at all. And she was a princess, you know. She was kept completely secluded and protected in the women's quarters. She even had her own personal slave, who looked after her and did all her shopping for her."

"You seem to know her quite well," Pharax observed, and Leon blushed.

"Not really, sir. I was there the night of her capture, and so I recognized her again at the fountain house. I helped her once or twice, and we talked a little." He shrugged in awkwardness.

Pharax nodded. "You know she is Anaxilas' concubine?"

"Yes, sir. He claimed her at Pylos." Leon spoke steadily, but he did not meet Pharax' eye.

Pharax sighed and shook his head. "Anaxilas has not done right by her. Even if he couldn't be expected to treat her like a precious toy—certainly not with his grandmother running the household!—he should at least have seen to it she wasn't given tasks like fetching water or scrubbing floors." Pharax shook his head again and grimaced. "You don't have to study medicine to see that work like that endangers an unborn child. But if you would allow me to give you some friendly advice, Leon"—the citizen looked hard at the young slave, and Leon felt the scar on his neck burning—"you'd do better not to take such an active interest in a prince's concubine."

"But Anaxilas is now betrothed to Kassia. He won't be able to keep Niobe after he's married." Leon blurted out his deepest wish without thinking.

Pharax broke eye contact and fussed with the papers on his desk in obvious agitation. "You may be right, but that's not the point. I was only trying to give you some advice, but I guess it's not my place. So, have I answered your question?" At last he looked back at Leon, but he didn't quite meet his eyes. "Niobe is all right. She returned to the palace two days ago. I gave orders for her to be given only light work for at least another month, but—" he sighed and threw up his hands—"who knows if my 'orders' will be respected. I'm only an apprentice physician, after all."

"Thank you, sir," Leon answered sincerely. He knew he ought to be relieved that Niobe was all right, but somehow the whole conversation had depressed him. It was a long time since he had been made so acutely aware of his status.

Not long afterwards, Pharax drove to Alethea's kleros with his first experimental ointment for Mika's warts. On account of his leg, he could not stand in a chariot, and rode instead on the seat of a cart pulled by an ageing gelding. It was a grey day and the peaks of Taygetos were lost in overcast, but the air was noticeably warmer and the olives were ripe.

The noise coming from the olive orchard at first startled Pharax, and then he laughed. Alethea had evidently commandeered the entire class of 10-year-olds that her son Niko commanded as an eirene to help with the harvest. The boys were scrambling about in the branches of the olive trees, shaking vigorously at the limbs. Pausing to watch the spectacle for a few moments, Pharax noted that Agesandros, Leon, Orsippos and Lampon, all stripped down to loincloths, were working the heavy nets spread under the trees to collect the olives that were shaken down. Working in teams of two, they pulled the nets in and emptied their contents into waiting baskets. Two more men whom Pharax didn't recognise, probably helots from Agesandros' own kleros, were loading the baskets onto a waiting mule cart. Niko was standing at a table and apparently keeping some kind of score, as if he had divided his boys into teams who now had to compete. Pharax nodded his approval. By turning this labour into a competition, Niko was encouraging ambition even at menial and unpleasant tasks, just as the agoge was meant to do. Pharax resolved to put in a good word for Niko at the next opportunity. Clicking to his gelding, he continued up the drive toward the house.

Here the activities were, if anything, more feverish than in the orchard itself, as the women prepared to feed the horde of hungry boys and the other harvesters. The smell of fresh-baked bread hung pleasantly in the air, and lamb was roasting somewhere. They were starting to set up tables and benches in the courtyard, and Phoebe angrily gestured for Pharax to take his cart to the stables beside the house. Pharax guided his cart to the wooden out-buildings that clustered behind the walled farm complex.

With all the men out helping with the harvest, there was no one here to help him down or unhitch his cart. It was at moments like these that Pharax still felt a flash of resentment about his leg. He hated being helpless. Then he reminded himself that it had been his choice—mistake—not to bring Dexippos along with him. He'd chosen Dexippos as his personal servant precisely because he was strong enough to lift Pharax up when necessary.

Pharax was so busy finding a good hold for his hands and letting himself down carefully onto his peg leg that he didn't notice anyone had come out to the stables until a girl said, "I'll take care of your horse."

Pharax jumped. Her voice was breathy and weak, not at all what one expected of a girl who could sing like a siren. Nor was she dressed as he had seen her last, at a public performance in silk with a diadem, but rather in a simple linen peplos, hardly better than what the helots were wearing. She had her hair confined under a snood, and she was barefoot. For a second Pharax wondered what Anaxilas would think if he could see his future bride like this, but then he dismissed the thought: she was still the most beautiful creature he'd ever laid eyes on. He quickly looked away, embarrassed. "Thank you, thank you. I didn't realise it was harvest. I probably shouldn't even be bothering you at a time like this." Indeed, why was he? Why didn't he just climb back up and drive away? The ointment for Mika could wait a few more days or months or years....

"Why not? Join us for supper. We have plenty this year. Agesandros has brought back so much livestock from his raids that we've more than restocked the herds which Aristomenes slaughtered and drove off three years ago." As she spoke she had efficiently unhitched his gelding, and now led him to an empty stall and closed the stall door behind him. Pharax watched her supple, easy movements with admiration. She was clearly at ease with horses, and although her arms were thin they were muscled. For all her petite, blonde beauty she was not as fragile as she looked on the stage of the theatre.

"I guess I should congratulate you," Pharax managed when she was again standing before him.

"Why?"

"On your betrothal," Pharax answered, confused.

"Oh, that," Kassia shrugged. "Uncle Leobotas arranged everything. We won't be married until after the winter solstice next year when I'm 19. I'm told Anaxilas didn't want to wait that long, but his grandfather was—ah—*persuasive*." She flashed Pharax a sly smile, and he found himself laughing unexpectedly.

"Have you met your intended?" he asked cautiously when their laughter faded naturally. Kassia shrugged, and Pharax was was puzzled by her apparent indifference to her wedding and bridegroom. Most girls preened and beamed at the prospects of an imminent marriage—much less one to a prince. "Didn't he meet with your approval?" he asked her.

"I don't know. It was a formal introduction at the palace with Uncle Anaxandridas and Uncle Leobotas and Uncle Charillos—not to mention Queen Eupolia, Mom and Agesandros—all looking on. If Anaxilas had so much as touched my hand, I fear Agesandros would have gutted him on the spot. Mom was close to fainting the whole time, and Uncle Charillos looked like the cat that had just swallowed the canary. Actually, it was hilarious." Kassia giggled, covering her mouth with her hand. And suddenly Pharax was laughing with her—as if they had known each other all their lives.

"Do *you* know Anaxilas?" Kassia asked pertly, recovering first.

Pharax didn't know what to say. If he admitted he knew Anaxilas, she'd want to know his opinion, and that was so bad that he couldn't possibly confide it to a young bride. He didn't have to.

"Never mind. Your opinion can't be worse than Agesandros'. To hear him tell it, I'm being sacrificed to a wild beast. Well, not quite. Agesandros doesn't describe Anaxilas as wild exactly. I think the phrase he uses most frequently is 'brainless boor.' Is that the way you'd describe him?"

"A brainless boor!?" Pharax was shocked, and yet in some way the description was so apt that he had to laugh. Then he remembered himself and, choking back his laughter, he started to apologize. "I'm sorry. I didn't mean to be so insulting. It just—"

"That's all right. If Agesandros can say it, why shouldn't you laugh at it?"

Sensing a certain tension, not to say resentment, between stepdaughter and stepfather, Pharax felt he ought to defend his former commander. "You know he didn't mean to be insulting, but no one has ever accused Agesandros of being diplomatic."

That took Kassia by surprise, and she giggled in delight, her hand over her mouth again. "How true!" Then, sobering somewhat, she continued, "Anyway, Anaxilas didn't act that badly at our meeting. He was very attentive, actually, and full of compliments. He gave me a beautiful beryl ring—but it's much too big to wear. It's so heavy it drags my whole hand down and gets in my way. But it was a nice gesture and he meant well. You know, it seems to me that you men think being good at killing people is the only thing that matters." She said this in a tone that was so reproachful that Pharax was reminded of her late father, a very idealistic man, who had been inclined to lecture everyone. "I'm sure that's the reason Agesandros doesn't like him, but I don't think that's important at all." She was very definitive—as only a teenager can be. "My cousin Damonon wasn't much good at arms either, and my uncle Charillos made his life hell because of it, but Damonon was the kindest, gentlest and most wonderful man you can imagine." She flung this at Pharax, daring him to deny it. He hastened to assure her that she must know best.

"Just because Anaxilas is a clumsy hoplite is no reason to look down on him. I would much rather marry a man who can create—like Tyrtaios—than just kill, kill, kill!"

"I didn't realise Anaxilas was a poet," Pharax replied in astonishment. He never would have suspected it.

"Oh, he's too humble to share his work with anyone yet. He says it isn't good enough, but I hope I'll talk him into sharing with me soon."

"Ah, so," Pharax nodded, hating Anaxilas all the more for such a transparent lie to gain Kassia's esteem.

"I've told him we can ask Tyrtaios to put his poetry to music, just as he does mine, and I can sing it—am I boring you with this? You must have come for a reason. Shall I help you into the house?"

"No, no. I can manage." Pharax had almost forgotten how beautiful she was while they talked, but as she moved closer to give him a hand, it jolted back into his consciousness and embarrassed him. He felt infinitely inadequate beside it. "I've just brought an ointment for Mika," he told her, pulling his crutch out of the back of the cart and then reaching for his leather satchel with the jar of medicine he had put together. "I don't know if it will work," he admitted. "I couldn't find

any source that offered a cure with confidence. But there were a number of ingredients that came up again and again. I thought—am I boring *you*?"

"Not at all. I think it's wonderful you would go to so much trouble
for Mika."

"Because she's a slave?"

"No," Kassia looked at him with a puzzled frown; "what does that
have to do with anything? After all, if Mom and the helots hadn't held
Aristomenes in the courtyard during the raid three years ago until the
perioikoi auxiliaries arrived, maybe I'd be a slave. Mom told me to kill
myself. She even gave me one of Niko's hunting knifes, and told me
how to gut myself. I know I would have tried to kill myself if the Messenians had broken through Mom's line of defence. Anything would
be better than being taken by the Messenians alive. But if something
had gone wrong—if they'd come in the back and taken me by surprise—then I might not have had time. After all, other Spartiate girls
have been captured and were enslaved for a while—even if they were
ransomed and returned to their fathers later."

Pharax didn't know what to say, but he didn't dare look at Kassia,
either. In the almost 10 years of war with Messenia, Aristomenes had
managed to capture Lacedaemonian women several times. The worst
incident had been a raid on the Temple of Artemis Karyai, when the
Messenians had taken all the virgins serving at the temple. Not one of
the girls was a virgin when they were returned to their fathers. And
none of them had looked like Kassia.

Meanwhile Kassia was saying, "I think it's wonderful that you want
to help Mika, because most people don't seem to notice that it's only
her skin that makes her look ugly. I like her. I hope you can help her."

What else could he say but: "I hope so, too. Where is she?"

"Oh, she's helping out in the kitchen." Kassia nodded toward the
house as they started back together, but already she was giggling again
behind her hand. "Actually," Kassia shared the joke, "she wanted to
climb the trees and help the boys. She loves trees. I guess she grew up

in a forest. Trees mean safety to her. You heard about how she tried to hide from Agesandros' men by climbing a tree?"

Pharax shook his head, but he was smiling already because Kassia's giggles were infectious.

"Well, she told me, when she saw 'bronze men'—as she called the hoplites—with bloody swords coming out of the kitchen at Pylos, her instinctive reaction was to climb a tree. But her chiton got in the way so she stripped—" Kassia couldn't continue for laughing so hard.

Pharax waited, not quite as amused as Kassia. He felt sorry for Mika.

Kassia had hold of herself. "I'm not as callous as you think, but you have to admit no Greek would have done that. You remind me of Leon."

"What!?" Pharax could not imagine any resemblance between himself and the former runaway. He was flabby, red-haired, and crippled; Leon, slender, dark and in superb physical condition. What was more, he was becoming a very scholarly man, and Leon was illiterate.

"Leon is very protective of Mika, too. He says one of the cruellest things he ever saw was the way everyone laughed at Mika in Pylos. It was Leon who brought her here, you know? She was his first prize."

Pharax was slightly shocked. He didn't approve of Leon sleeping with Mika and yet taking such an active interest in Niobe. Then again, he noted cynically, he was only imitating his betters. Wasn't Anaxilas sleeping with Niobe while courting Kassia?

They were at the entrance to the courtyard. The tables and benches had been set up, and Phoebe, Mika and the kitchen maids were all lugging pitchers of water, platters of celery and carrots, and baskets of bread onto the tables. He saw Mika with a pitcher that seemed far too large and heavy for her, but she was laughing and calling something to one of the other girls.

"Mika!" Kassia called out, and the slave girl looked over readily. Kassia waved, and Pharax saw Mika's eyes widen as she saw and recognized him. The joy fled from Mika's face, replaced by apprehension. That hurt him a little, but she came dutifully.

"Pharax has brought an ointment to help get rid of your warts." Kassia explained.

"It's just an experiment, really," Pharax emphasized humbly. "No source I've found offers a sure cure, but I've put something together. I thought we should try."

"Yes, Master," Mika said dutifully.

Pharax seated himself on the nearest bench and started rummaging in his leather satchel, looking for the jar with the ointment. Mika waited, but then with a cry of "Don't, Chloe! Let me!" she ran away. Pharax looked up astonished to lose his patient, and saw her rush to take a heavy pitcher away from a girl who looked considerably bigger and stronger than herself. Then he noticed that the other girl was pregnant.

The parallels to Niobe were too obvious to ignore. Pharax watched with fascination the way not only Mika but also one of the other girls hastened over to help. The pregnant girl was being scolded and told to sit down. She was handed something to do by her sour-faced mother—but something she could do sitting down.

Mika was back. "I'm sorry, Master."

"How many months pregnant is your friend?"

"Chloe? It's her sixth month."

"Is she married?"

"No, Master, of course not. It's Niko's baby."

Kassia frowned and hissed furiously at Mika. She clearly knew this fact would not do Niko any credit with the peers. Pharax reassured her, "Don't worry, I won't say anything. I was only curious. Recently I had another case of a girl with an illegitimate child and she was sent to fetch water every day. She lost the baby. I can see you're taking better care of Chloe, but would you promise me one thing?" He glanced up at Kassia as he spoke. "Will you send for me if she starts to have pain or bleeding—anything at all that indicates trouble?"

"But there's a midwife just up the road," Kassia replied in surprise.

"How can a doctor learn to help, if you women won't let him?" Pharax responded with a touch of irritation. "Whenever a midwife is at the end of her wits and doesn't know what to do, she sends for a doctor, but how is a doctor supposed to know what to do if he's only brought in at the last minute? I hadn't been with Kleonymus more than a month when we got a call from a woman in childbed and Kleonymus refused to go. I was shocked, but he said to me, 'They only call me when the midwife has failed. You go if you like, but I've seen enough women die in childbed already.' Of course I went, and of course the woman died. And since then I've seen at least another dozen women die and I don't know how many babies. I'm tired of it. I want to learn how to help."

Kassia stared at him, and Pharax suddenly remembered himself and that he was talking to a beautiful virgin, and looked down in confusion. He'd never talked about this particular passion to anyone before—not even Kleonymus. How could he blurt it all out to a girl who had only just been betrothed and shouldn't be thinking about the risks of childbearing? He was a fool! What had Agesandros called Anaxilas? A brainless boor. That's what he was. Embarrassed and not daring to look up at Kassia, he said almost harshly to Mika, "Now, hold out one of your hands, Mika, and let me apply this."

Mika bit down on her lower lip and held out her left hand as if she were going to be beaten. The ointment was cool and not even evil smelling. "But it doesn't sting," Mika exclaimed in astonishment.

"Why should it sting?" Pharax asked back.

"But how can it do any good if it doesn't sting?" Mika wanted to know.

Pharax looked at her, and then in perplexity he stole a glance at Kassia. All the awkwardness of a moment earlier was already past. Kassia couldn't help herself, and started giggling again. As before, Pharax found her laugh infectious, and then even Mika started laughing, although she clearly wasn't sure what they were laughing about. When the laughter had died down, Pharax tried to explain. "The idea is to gently dissolve the warts, not burn them away. I don't want a solution that leaves scars or marks."

Mika looked at her hand where the ointment had almost disappeared, and then back up at Pharax with scepticism. "Do you really think it can work?"

"I think it's worth a try. Here, keep this and rub it on your hands twice a day, morning and night. I'll come back in a month and see how it worked."

"Thank you, Master."

They could hear the boys of Niko's unit approaching in a ravenous horde, and Phoebe called out angrily, "Mika! What are you doing? Come give Eunice a hand with the platters!" Mika jumped up and was gone. Pharax watched her for a moment, and then turned and looked up at Kassia.

She was watching the boys pour in through the gate, and something terribly sad had come over her face. The look in her eyes was that of an old woman rather than an 18-year-old maiden, and it all but broke his heart. He wanted to ask her what was wrong, but he was too shy. It wasn't his business anyway. She was already bespoken to another man. She would be his queen one day. What was he doing sitting here wondering about the secrets of her young heart?

Pharax pulled himself to his feet and would have liked to slip away, but Kassia turned back abruptly, and he could clearly see the tears swimming in her eyes. "Don't mind me. I was just remembering the year my cousin Damonon brought his unit to help with the harvest. It was the happiest day of my life."

"You're only 18," Pharax countered with all the compassion he felt. "You'll have many, many more happy days."

Kassia pulled her lips into a smile, but her eyes still swam in tears. "I wish I believed that. At least Mika makes me laugh. Excuse me, I better go help Mom." She left, he guessed, as much from embarrassment as from a sense of duty.

Agesandros was coming towards him, wiping sweat off his face with the back of his forearm and looking surprised and pleased to see him. Pharax's attention was already on his former commander when he heard from behind him Kassia's breathy voice, "I will send for you when Chloe gets near her time, Pharax. I think it's wonderful that you want to help."

CHAPTER 8

Leon waited before the Council House for Agesandros. The passes to Messenia were opened at last, and those officers commanding independent units, the five lochagoi, the guard commander, and Agesandros, as commander of the krypteia[1], had all been summoned to the Council. The details of the summer deployment against the Messenians were being discussed, and that generally took the better part of the afternoon. Leon knew the routine, because this was the third year in which Agesandros had commanded the krypteia.

It was a bright spring day and the sun burned in the open, but after the cold and damp of winter, Leon welcomed it. He sat on the steps before the Council House and watched the life of the city pass before him. Soon he would leave the city behind him. He and the others in the krypteia would live in the open, camping most nights under the stars, cooking for themselves over open fires whatever they managed to hunt. It was an uncomfortable life of long marches, sudden skirmishes, unrestful nights on improvised bedding and interrupted by guard duty. They would wash only in cold streams, and their clothes would get worn and dirty and ragged. Their leather armour would get stained

---

1. By the 5th century, the krypteia was a kind of "secret police" that murdered suspicious or rebellious helots by stealth. The origins of the unit are not recorded, but just as the yearly declarations of war against the helots had their roots in the Second Messenian War, I hypothesize that the krypteia also had its roots in this war. The explanation offered here is plausible, but not based on historical record.

and scratched and stiff with sweat; the bronze would tarnish. There would be accidents and casualties, and some of them would not come home when the autumn came.

Leon couldn't say he was looking forward to it, but he was fiercely proud to be facing it. It was a life worthy of a man. Unconsciously, he glanced over his shoulder in the direction of the public baths. When he had been a very little boy of 5 or maybe 6, his mother had sold him to the bath-master. For roughly a decade he had worked in the baths. At first his principal duties had been scrubbing out the public latrines, crawling in the corners and underground passages too small for adults. When drains clogged or pipes were blocked, he had been ordered to try to clear them with his small, thin hands. His body had been covered with slime and excrement so much of the time that the smell of it never left him—even when he swam in the river for hours. They kept his hair shaved, because otherwise it just collected filth.

When he became too old and big for cleaning the drains and pipes, he had to keep the baths themselves free of slime, worms, insects, debris and leaves. He had to chop wood delivered as massive logs at the south entrance into blocks small enough for the ovens. Or he had to feed the ovens themselves, bent over and dripping sweat for hours on end.

Not that life in the baths was all bad. He had three chitons and two himations at the city's expense, and there was always enough to eat and drink in the slave's mess, and a warm, dry bed at night. He even had a degree of freedom, since no one particularly cared where he went or what he did before or after opening times. But Leon had never been happy there. He had never felt he belonged there, and in his free time he wandered over the bridge to watch the men and youths of the agoge at drill. On holidays, he loved to watch the athletic competition and the sword dances. But nothing in the world excited him as much as the sight of one of the Spartiate units in full battle array when they paraded in or out of the city at the start or end of the campaign season.

Leon knew he could never be a hoplite, because only freemen, citizens, were hoplites, but he could not have been more than 8 or 9 when he learned that every hoplite had at least one and sometimes two attendants—and these men were *not* free men. Most were helots, but some were slaves, captured or bought. From that day on, Leon dreamed of being one of them.

Not that he had much of a chance. Most of these men were helots who worked on the estates of their masters. They were younger sons, superfluous to the farming, who were selected as much by their own fathers as their masters to serve in the army. That way they stayed single and the inheritance didn't get divided up or the estate burdened with too many children. They tended to be a "rough" crowd as a result. "Honest" girls didn't want to have anything to do with them. But for all that, they were men in a way that bath slaves weren't.

It was impossible not to notice the difference. These men weren't just muscled and tanned, hardened and scarred, they were proud and self-assured. They did not cower or grovel even to their own masters, let alone other men. Leon knew that they were sometimes harshly punished—some of them had scars from that, too—but they were punished like men and the youths of the agoge. The bath-slaves were soft and plump and, so Leon increasingly felt, slimy. They sought to please, to wheedle and flatter and win favour, always angling for the extra tip—even if it meant bending over and letting a customer fuck them quickly in a corner.

With puberty Leon's dissatisfaction grew, but even so, he had never *planned* to run away. On the night that Aristomenes came down from Taygetos and raided in the Eurotas valley, however, Leon had been seduced by opportunity.

Unable to sleep because of all the excitement, he had gone out onto the pier behind the baths, planning to take a midnight swim to cool his blood and tire himself out. He had heard a voice calling for help and discovered one of the youths from the agoge, roughly his own age, splashing about in apparent panic. When he succeeded in pulling the boy onshore among the reeds, he discovered that the youth had been so badly flogged that his limbs had cramped and failed him as he tried to swim across the river. Leon's first reaction had been to fetch a doctor, but the youth stopped him. He was AWOL from the agoge, the youth explained. He'd run away from the eirene who had flogged him so mercilessly because, he said, his mother and sister were on one of the kleros that had been set ablaze by the raiding Messenians. He begged Leon to take him there.

Leon had been unable to resist the temptation. What made the proposition so irresistible wasn't that Niko offered him a reward (which he did), but the prospect of helping a real Spartiate. In Leon's imagination, that night he was already a hoplite's attendant carrying his wounded master out of danger.

When he had finally managed to carry Niko all the way to his kleros, however, they found half the outbuildings gutted and burned and his mother tending three wounded helots while the dead Messenians still littered the courtyard. It seemed the Messenians had burned the mill beside the kleros first, then forced the gate and plundered and burned the storerooms, apparently looking for wine. Meanwhile, Niko's mother and her helots had defended the main house until the perioikoi auxiliaries arrived and drove the Messenians off.

The survivors were overwhelmed by the tasks facing them. They had to tend the wounded, feed the survivors, bury the dead, patch up the worst damage, take stock of what had been lost and damaged and try to rescue what was left. Niko's kleros had lost all livestock, and the amphorae containing the entire harvest of olive oil had been shattered and the contents spilled into the earth. Although the sacks of barley had been split open, they managed to rescue much of it by scooping it up and putting it in new containers, but with three of the helots wounded and Niko in bed, someone had to get the hay harvest in. That summer it had seemed that no sooner was that finished, than the barley harvest began. Meanwhile, Leon found that there were a thousand other things that needed doing on a farm, and it made little difference that he had never done them before. He was young and strong and willing, and the wounded helots were happy to give him instructions and advice while he did what they could not.

Leon had never worked so hard in his life, and each night he fell into bed so exhausted that he slept dreamlessly. He never seemed to have time to consider the fact that he *ought* to have returned to the baths. No one asked him about it, and he couldn't bring himself to bring it up. Why should he? For the first time since he had been sold, he felt he belonged where he was. The people on the kleros called him by name and looked him in the eye when they spoke to him. They not only seemed grateful he was there, but they acted as if they *liked* him. He worked as hard as he could to make sure they wanted him to stay.

It wasn't until the night that Agesandros arrived with his wounded that Leon had been exposed as a runaway. Agesandros' men had nearly killed him on the spot. The law said that a runaway could be killed at capture or returned to his master—whatever circumstances made most appropriate. When the hoplite took him and wrenched his arms behind his back, Leon had thought he was dead. He felt the blade of the knife at his throat and he heard the words, "This is that runaway bath slave." Although the words were spoken just inches from his ear, it was as if they were said at the far end of a long tunnel.

He hardly knew what happened. Alethea shouted at the Spartiate to let him go, and the man obeyed so promptly that he fell on his knees, his legs no longer capable of supporting him. Alethea sent him upstairs "out of the way" and he cowered in the darkness, aware only vaguely that a surgeon was sent for while a whole platoon of Spartiate hoplites and their attendants made themselves comfortable at "his" kleros.

He crouched in the dark on the floor of the stairwell waiting. He didn't think. He was too frightened. The sky was grey with dawn and he was cramped from crouching unmoving for hours when Alethea suddenly loomed up before him. "Leon?"

He tried to get to his feet. She waved him still and went down on her heels before him. She looked him deep in the eyes. She was so exhausted that for the first time since he had met her, she looked old enough to be Niko's mother. "Is it true? Are you a runaway?"

At that moment, Leon wished they had slit his throat. He had never admired anyone as much as he did Alethea. Seeing the shock and distress in her eyes, he wished that he could have been spared telling her his crime. He tried to speak, but at first nothing came out. Only on his third try did he manage to squeak out "yes." There was no way he could have found the words or strength to try to explain himself.

He hadn't needed to. Alethea understood. She had put her arms around him as his own mother never had, and she had held him as he shook and cried all the shock and terror and shame from his young body. Then she had promised to find a way to "put things right."

She had kept her word. As soon as the Spartiate hoplites were gone, she had sold some of her personal valuables and used them to buy Leon from the bath-master.

Later, Leon sometimes wondered if he had made the right decision to leave Alethea for Agesandros. He had been with Alethea roughly 8 months when Agesandros offered him the opportunity to serve as his attendant. By then Orsippos, Lampon and Hegylos had recovered from the wounds they had received during the Messenian attack. Almost a year of harvests were in, and Alethea's need had not been so acute as when he'd arrived. Agesandros had, of course, asked Alethea first and she had given her consent. The lure of his old dream had been too much. Leon had jumped at the opportunity to serve with the army.

At the time Agesandros still had another attendant, an ageing man who had been born free, but captured by the Athenians as a young man. Enslaved, he had served in the silver mines and on merchant galleys and even had a short spell as an outlaw before he fell into Spartan hands. He had been Leon's trainer, tormentor and friend in his first year of service to Agesandros, but he had died suddenly last spring. After that there was no going back. Agesandros needed him, and Leon—for all that he loved life on the kleros—knew he couldn't leave Agesandros.

He got to his feet now as the commanders emerged in a group from the Council House and stood chatting together in the shade of the portico. Leon felt taller seeing the way Agesandros ranged a full 6 inches over all the others, and he felt stronger when the other, senior officers nodded to Agesandros in farewell as if he—a man 10 years their junior, and a rank below them—were their equal. But he felt proudest in that moment when Agesandros looked about as if he missed something—until he caught sight of Leon.

Agesandros' short smile, flashed at Leon, was replaced by his more habitual scowl as soon as Leon came up beside him. "You'll never guess what's happened now? Anaxilas has decided he 'needs' to become familiar with 'regular warfare'—the ass! Oh, well, I won't miss him. I rather pity Polydektes, who will now be his Regimental Commander, but he's an old aristo and should be able to deal with blue-blooded boors better than I."

"No doubt, sir," Leon answered, invigorated just trying to keep up with Agesandros' long strides.

"What are you grinning at?" Agesandros demanded suspiciously. Agesandros had never been able to understand how Leon could be so good-tempered despite the injustice he had suffered. Agesandros had confided to Alethea that if *his* mother had sold him, he would have hated the whole world—and not rested 'till he'd killed his heartless mother with his own hands. He certainly could not fathom that Leon enjoyed just watching him.

"I was wondering if Anaxilas knew what a stickler for regulations Polydektes is."

Agesandros threw back his head and laughed, but when his initial surprise was passed, he eyed Leon suspiciously. "You're getting good at answering me, but I sometimes wonder if you're telling me the whole truth."

Leon smiled at him blissfully. "But why shouldn't I be, sir?"

Polydektes commanded the vanguard, and they were the first unit to deploy to Messenia. Knowing that Anaxilas was safely beyond Taygetos, Leon decided to risk going to the Eurypontid palace and asking after Niobe. He had waited every noon for Niobe since his talk with Pharax, but when she did not appear he was certain that it was because Anaxilas had prohibited her from fetching water. He supposed Anaxilas had a guilty conscience after Niobe had lost her baby—although secretly he hoped that wasn't true.

Despite his determination, Leon found it surprisingly hard to just knock at the door to the slaves' quarters. What reason could he give for wanting to see Niobe? He could hardly say he was concerned for her health, because her health was no concern of his. But he could say he had a message for her from Mika. It wouldn't matter that he had none. Once he was face to face with Niobe, he could tell her the truth. The problem, he was sure, was getting to see Niobe.

Fortunately, just as the door opened to his knock, he remembered Niobe complaining about a certain "Thratta," so he asked to speak to her rather than Niobe and was admitted instantly. In the helots' hall he was told to sit down and a plump girl offered to fetch him something to drink, adding with a coy smile, "I haven't seen you here before."

Leon was familiar with the look and avoided meeting her eyes, saying, "No, I serve the army."

That had the desired effect. No self-respecting helot girl wanted a friend in the army. She wanted a man who would inherit his own kleros and be able to provide for her. The girl disappeared and a hefty woman, taller than Leon himself by a good 4 inches, bore down on him. "You wanted to see me, young man?"

"Are you Thratta?"

Leon was already feeling sorry for Niobe. Hadn't she said that this woman hit her? Leon was appalled. "I've come about Niobe."

"What about her?" the woman demanded, crossing her arms on her chest with open hostility.

"I have a message for her from Mika—her former personal slave."

"Oh? She really had one? So what do you want with me?"

"I thought—I mean—may I have permission to speak to Niobe?"

"How should I know? You'll have to ask her master that."

"But Anaxilas has already deployed. I thought in his absence—"

"Niobe don't belong to Anaxilas anymore," Thratta interrupted him with an annoyed gesture. "The mistress wanted her out of the house before his bride comes next winter." Thratta turned her back on him and shouted to the plump girl, "Get off your backside, you lazy girl, and get back to work," and was gone.

Leon looked around bewildered. "But where is she?" he asked generally. An old man who was repairing a harness on the bench only shrugged, but the plump girl trounced out of the kitchen and told him in a lofty voice, "Niobe? She wasn't good at anything but spreading her legs—so the mistress sold her to a brothel."

CHAPTER 9

Mika had known ever since Leon arrived that he would go away again when the campaign season started. From the day Sybil started teaching her to weave—not at the loom but on a hand-frame—she had conceived of the idea of making new straps for Leon's knapsack. The old straps, she had had the opportunity to see when washing the knapsack soon after his return, were all but worn out.

The weather had turned abruptly warm and the snows had melted just as suddenly. The news that the army was re-deploying almost immediately had taken everyone a little by surprise. Mika sat up late two nights in a row to get the second strap finished. She was bursting with pride in her work and wanted to give it to Leon as soon as he came home.

Usually he and Agesandros were home by early afternoon, but when by mid-afternoon Mika remarked that it was "strange" Agesandros wasn't home yet, she learned that Agesandros had "too much to do" to get his battalion ready. No one expected him until after dinner. Naturally Leon was with him, Mika reasoned.

So Mika didn't go out to wait at the foot of the drive until after her own dinner. It was dusk by then and nearly dark before Agesandros at last came into sight—alone. Mika couldn't understand it. Leon always came home with Agesandros, if not before him. When Agesandros was abreast of her, she separated herself from the trees and gave even the hardened veteran a momentary fright. "Master? Where's Leon?" she asked without coyness. She still tried to disguise her love for Leon from the women of the household, but there was no reason to hide it from Agesandros.

"Leon? Isn't he here? I told him not to wait for me while I had dinner at the syssitia. I assumed he'd returned." Agesandros sounded surprised but not concerned. Mika was afraid to say any more.

All night Mika listened for Leon's return. Not that she would have left her bed to speak to him in the middle of the night; that would have been too forward. Still, she couldn't help wondering where he was. The most reasonable explanation was that he had a girl in the city and had decided to spend this last night before the campaign season with her. Mika was furiously jealous and deeply hurt, and hopelessly discouraged because she knew she was ugly and there was nothing she could do to make herself worthy of him. The ointment the surgeon had given her didn't work a bit.

But when he was not back by the morning, Mika started to worry. Leon had to go with Agesandros into the city. He would get into trouble if he didn't. He had never failed in his duties before.

Just as she had feared, Agesandros was angry when he learned that Leon was missing. Scowling, he demanded, "How could he do this to me? He knows how much we still have to do! If he's run away again, I'll kill him!"

"Don't be ridiculous," Alethea countered in a calming voice. "Leon has never done anything to deserve such a suspicion—"

"He ran away from the baths—"

"You can't blame him for that. He's been more than loyal to us."

"Then where is he when I need him?"

"He's probably waiting for you at the barracks. Don't make such a fuss. If anyone has the right to a night out on his own before you deploy, it's Leon."

But Leon wasn't waiting at the barracks. Worse, Agesandros was promptly told by one of his men, "Leon is in the stocks." Before he could even reach the jailhouse or the public pillory, Agesandros had run into and been told by dozens of (amused or disapproving) citizens that Leon had been arrested for disrupting the peace, breaking and entering, resisting arrest, and assault.

Leon?

Agesandros' irritation was instantly gone, replaced with an uncomprehending worry. For two years, Leon and he had lived side by side, in peace and war. They had shared rations, shelter, dreams and fears. They had bound each other's wounds, kept each other's secrets, and corroborated each other's lies. Agesandros knew he did not *understand* Leon. He did not understand how he could be so consistently good-humoured even in the worst weather, after the longest marches or in the most hopeless situations. He could not fathom his lack of bitterness and his willingness to try to make the best of a status he had not been born to. There had also been times when Leon's consideration for others annoyed Agesandros into a foul temper, but whether he understood him or not he felt that he knew him as well as himself. Despite what he had foolishly blustered this morning, there was no one except for Alethea—not even his own mother—whom Agesandros trusted as much as he trusted Leon.

Turning drill over to his deputy and leaving all the other tasks he had set for himself undone, Agesandros made straight for the jailhouse. He was far more familiar with the procedures for releasing prisoners than he would have liked. Leon's predecessor had had the habit of going off on drunken binges every now and again. When he was drunk he picked fights and broke things, and as his owner Agesandros was liable for all damages. Pyrros had drunk himself into these rages when he couldn't stand life anymore. He seemed to hope he would go so far that someone would finally kill him, or that he would kill someone himself and be executed for it. When Agesandros collected him—sometimes only after he'd let him stew for a few days—he was usually still badly hung over and even more foul-tempered than usual. Agesandros understood Pyrros better than he did Leon, and he had never worried about him. Pyrros had been old enough to be his father, while Leon was as young as Niko—barely 20—if he were that.

At the sight of Leon in the stocks, Agesandros' worry turned to anger—he just didn't know whom to be angry with. Leon's wrists and ankles were clamped between wooden boards, and his body hung off the back of the stocks as if it were a broken rag. He had bent his head forward, resting his forehead on the board that confined his hands, but as Agesandros approached a pack of boys ran up, flinging missiles at the object of ridicule. Leon's head jerked up as the unpleasant things splattered on his back. His face was a swollen mess of broken lips, bloody nose and blackened eyes.

Agesandros blew up. He stormed into the jailhouse shouting, "Let that boy out of the stocks before I have the lot of you tanned alive!"

Duty at the jailhouse, like the watch at public buildings or patrolling in the streets at night, was done by melleirenes, 19-year-olds from the agoge. They were supposed to come to their feet for any citizen, and they jumped up sharply at the sight of a battalion commander of Agesandros' standing. But they were commanded by a citizen. This man, a good fifteen years Agesandros' senior, was not so easily intimidated.

"Calm down, Agesandros," he admonished in a tone that was almost contemptuous, as he slowly got to his feet. "You know as well as I do you can't just storm in here giving orders. Your slave broke the law—or rather several of them—and he has been duly sentenced—"

"In two days my battalion takes to the field and I need Leon, and I need him today, and just what in the name of Castor is he supposed to have done to justify what you've done to him?" Agesandros demanded.

"*That* should have been your first concern," the older man countered in a tone of open disdain, and Agesandros' fury increased to such a level that he was suddenly very calm.

He cocked his head and leaned against the door as if he had all the time in the world. From the outside he looked relaxed, but the inner tension was so great his nerves were humming. "Of course. By the looks of him, Leon must have committed sacrilege, treason and threatened the very survival of the city. Just how did the boy manage all that in a single night?"

"Save your sarcasm, Agesandros. He tried to break into a brothel, assaulted the proprietor, and when the watch came at the cries of his victim, he resisted arrest. Even your father never behaved in such a rowdy fashion merely for the sake of a piece of ass."

Even the melleirenes stiffened at the insult, and they looked sharply from their own commander to the famous founder of the krypteia, known throughout the agoge as the Scourge of Messenia. Everyone knew Agesandros' father had been a troublemaker and drunk. In fact, his father was credited with causing riots, disrupting the Assembly, vandalising the Council House and assaulting more than one citizen. He had certainly died in a gutter, stinking of stale wine. But this was not something people usually drew attention to any more—certainly not to Agesandros' face.

It took him several seconds before Agesandros was sure he could answer in a tone of sufficient nonchalance. "True. My father forced the kings to restore lands to the disinherited and give citizenship to the disenfranchised. He was a threat to land thieves like *your* father. If all Leon wanted was a piece of ass, then I dare say Lacadaemon was not endangered."

"I should have known you have little respect for law and order, Agesandros son of Medon."

"None whatsoever," Agesandros countered, and then turned and left the jailhouse. He had no choice but to appeal to the ephors[1] directly.

---

1.   Officials elected yearly to act as public officials. Among other duties, they acted as judges in cases involving helots and perioikoi.

It took Agesandros nearly two hours to secure Leon's release. By then it was almost noon and Leon had been in the stocks nearly 12 hours. He collapsed onto the paving stones with an involuntary groan when he was abruptly released. Despite Agesandros' help he couldn't seem to get his feet under him; all circulation had left them.

Leon clamped his teeth shut and made another attempt to get up, and another. Eventually he succeeded, but he stood swaying and sweating and clinging to Agesandros as if he might fall down again. Agesandros waited until Leon himself made the first tentative attempt at a step. He helped him out of the square to sit in the shade of a stoa. Agesandros then went for water from the nearest fountain. Only after Leon had drunk and Agesandros had wiped the dried blood off his face did the youth recover enough to whisper, "Thank you, sir," but his eyes were so swollen he couldn't seem to keep them open. He dropped his head and held it in his hands in complete despondency.

Torn between alarm and perplexity, Agesandros finally demanded an explanation. "Are you going to tell me what happened, or am I supposed to believe this was all about some prostitute?"

"Prostitute?" Leon gasped, jerking his head up and managing despite his swollen lips to sound outraged. "You can't call Niobe a prostitute! No more than Kassia!"

"Kassia?! What the hell does she have to do with this? Have you gone completely mad?!"

"I mean, sir—if Kassia had been captured—in the raid. If—she had fallen—into Messenian hands." Leon was having trouble speaking with his split and swollen lips.

Understanding began to dawn. "Niobe? She's Messenian?"

"Aristomenes' wife! You must remember her, sir. The poor girl Anaxilas claimed."

"Oh, yes." Agesandros started to remember vaguely.

"She was sold—to a brothel. A king's daughter! And hardly more than a girl! She lost her baby barely a month ago." In his distress, Leon was forcing the words out, although they came slurred and indistinctly from his swollen mouth.

Agesandros was trying to remember her. He remembered being disgusted with Anaxilas because the prince tried to keep more than his share of the spoils. He remembered Anaxilas sneering at his prize for weeping over the loss of her jewels, apparently too dense to appreciate what a trauma the girl had just endured. But for the life of him, Agesandros couldn't remember the girl herself. She was just a blur, a dazed, frightened, weepy girl with smeared make-up like hundreds of others. Mika had impressed him far more, fighting like a wildcat, and he had been pleased when Leon selected her.

"Sir, you've got to get her out of there," Leon was suddenly urging with desperation, and Agesandros stared at his slave in disbelief. "Please, sir. Whatever it costs—you can deduct it from my spoils. But we can't leave her there for another day. Please, sir!"

"Have you forgotten we deploy two days from now! I've lost half a day already getting you out of the stocks!" Agesandros was scowling again, remembering all his own problems.

But Leon knew him far too well to be discouraged by his expression or his tone. "It won't take long to free her, sir. You know all a brothelmaster cares about is gold. Please, sir."

"Not now! We have work to do!" Agesandros growled back, getting to his feet, and Leon sighed with relief. Agesandros would do it.

Agesandros, lacking time, asked Alethea to find out from her uncle's wife, the queen, exactly what had become of Niobe. Alethea went directly to Queen Eupolia, who willingly told her that Niobe had been given not to a brothel, but to an aging helot whom she had wanted to reward for years of loyal service. She told Alethea which kleros the man worked and said that of course she was free to ask about purchasing

Niobe, but also warned against purchasing her. "The girl has not accepted her new status and will only make trouble in your household. All the helots hated her. She's lazy, unskilled, and stuck up."

Alethea sighed. She too had her doubts about the wisdom of taking a former princess into her humble household, but she felt they owed it to Leon. Knowing that Eupolia would not take a slave's affections into account in her own household management, Alethea tried to explain herself in other terms. "I am short-handed, you know. One of the helot girls is 7 months pregnant, and Sybil is ill."

"Surely you have household helots old enough to marry. Native helot girls are much better workers than these captive Messenians. They are all resentful, homesick and self-pitying, even the best of them."

Alethea sighed again. Her uncle's efficient wife made her feel foolish and sentimental.

"You're too soft-hearted, Alethea," Eupolia told her bluntly. "I do hope Kassia has some of her father's hardness. In your case, your excessive mildness only makes your own life more difficult; but in a queen, too much softness can be dangerous for the entire city."

Alethea supposed Eupolia was right, despite an inward resistance to the thought of Kassia having anything from her father besides his blond beauty. She left the royal palace and went to Leobotas' townhouse to borrow his chariot for the drive down to the kleros where Niobe's new master lived. As a girl, Alethea had been an ardent rider, and as a maiden and young matron she'd turned to driving as a substitute for the riding she was no longer allowed to engage in. But she had lost both her chariot and team in the Messenian raid in which her kleros had been attacked three years ago. Agesandros, coming from a poor family, neither liked nor trusted horses and had not yet provided her with replacements. But Leobotas kept a team in town and was happy to loan them to her—although naturally, he wanted to know why.

He too was sceptical about her plans. "Do you really think it is wise to buy this girl for Leon?"

"You know how much I owe Leon. He saved Niko's life. He's never asked for anything in return—until now."

"His reward, my dear, was his own life—which he'd forfeited by running away from the baths. You saved his life, and any debt you owed him for saving Niko's was paid then."

"Maybe, but what about all the help he gave me when I had almost no one else? He, who knew nothing about farming, worked harder and longer than any of my helots. You know, too, what a good squire to Agesandros Leon has become," Alethea countered.

"I do, but that's exactly the point: he is a squire. Most squires don't marry, and there's a reason for that. Husbands and fathers have other priorities than dying for their masters."

Alethea looked slightly shocked, as if she had never seen it from this perspective, but she was quick to retort, "By that measure, Sparta should not want her hoplites to marry either."

"Technically, my dear, men on active service *aren't* supposed to marry. Why do you think there is a law requiring all men on active service to live in barracks where they are subject to evening and morning roll call? The Law was *meant* to prevent marriage until citizens went off active service. The fact that young men nowadays openly violate the spirit if not the letter of the law by 'stealing' their brides after curfew and sneaking out to visit them night after night in the dark is something we elders have come to tolerate. It was not Lycurgus' intention."

"If the Spartan Council is helpless in the face of young men's ardour, how can I, a mere woman, be expected to be more steadfast?"

Leobotas laughed and shook his head. "Take the chariot, my dear, and I wish you luck."

Alethea looked about the muddy yard with distaste. She did not often have dealings with poorer helot families like this. They existed mostly on estates where the Spartiate masters for one reason or another had not built country houses and lived permanently in the city. Agesandros' kleros, for example, had been carved out of a much larger estate at the time of the Land Reform. There had been no house on it when it was deeded to his father. Only since their marriage had Agesandros started talking about building a proper house, and meanwhile the helots who worked it had built a cottage similar to this.

Still, Alethea, who had visited Agesandros' kleros once or twice, could not remember it stinking quite like this one did. Nor was the thatch on the cottage of Agesandros' helots' house this mouldy. Here not only did everything stink and seem vaguely foul, but the air was laden with mosquitoes as well. Alethea had already been bitten several times by the time she had tied the reins and stepped down. She had only one hand free to wave away the ominously droning insects, because with her other hand she clutched her skirts to keep them out of the mud.

A woman with unkempt hair and a filthy grey peplos was staring at her from the doorway of the cottage, but made no move to greet her.

"Hello. I am looking for Niobe, a Messenian girl captured last fall and claimed by Anaxilas." It did not occur to Alethea that this filthy, broad-faced woman might be the spoiled royal beauty that Mika had described, Anaxilas had been so keen to possess, and Leon loved.

The woman's dark eyes instantly narrowed and she eyed Alethea suspiciously. "What you want with her, Mistress?"

"First, I'd like to speak with her. I may be interested in purchasing her."

The woman's eyes lit up greedily as she announced, "She's out back," and hastened to lead the way. Around the back of the cottage, a crude twig fence enclosed the kitchen garden. Here a young woman was kneeling in the mud beside a wheelbarrow filled with cow dung. With her bare hands, she was taking lumps of dung from the barrow and packing it into the holes that had been neatly dug in rows. She was dressed in a peplos that was—remarkably—even dirtier than that of her mistress. It hung somewhat askew at the moment, revealing a small, bony shoulder that looked bruised as well as dirty. Her hair was an exotic coppery colour, but it was as filthy and unkempt as that of her mistress, and hung in greasy strands as she bent over her work.

"Niobe!" Sinope called out. "Come here, slut!"

The woman on her knees looked over her shoulder with a frightened start. She had big, pale blue eyes set in a haggard face smeared with smoke through which drips of sweat trickled, leaving trails. All along the hairline, down her neck, and on her arms were red lumps and unsightly scabs from scratched mosquito bites. At the base of her throat was an ugly bruise. She got to her feet with apparent difficulty, trying to keep her filthy hands off her clothes and so treading on her skirts. When she approached, Alethea could see she was trembling. She kept her face averted from Alethea and she held her manure-caked hands awkwardly in front of her.

"She's young yet," Sinope started praising her wares, "but she'll grow. She just needs to harden up a bit. She was spoilt before, see, but if you work her hard enough, she'll toughen up. I won't let her go for less than the price of a goat."

"Niobe?" Alethea addressed the girl herself, so shocked by the sight of her that she still couldn't bring herself to believe that this listless, battered and filthy creature could be an Arkadian princess and former concubine of Prince Anaxilas.

The captive's head moved in a gesture that might have been acknowledgement or denial. The eyes remained averted.

"Are you Niobe, daughter of Aristokrates of Arkadia?" Alethea asked more explicitly.

The girl looked over sharply. Hope flared up in her eyes and then was extinguished by fear. She glanced with open nervousness at Sinope. "Yes," she squeaked out, and then raised her eyes to Alethea pleading and frightened at once.

Alethea only sighed. Even if Leon hadn't begged this favour of her, there was no way she could leave a king's daughter here in these conditions. Regardless of how useless she turned out to be, Alethea felt she could not return home knowing that a gentle-born girl was being kept in filth like this.

Turning to Sinope, Alethea announced, "I'll give you this silver bracelet." She removed a simple silver bangle from her right wrist and shoved it into Sinope's hand. She felt a little guilty paying so little, less than a tenth what a healthy—not to mention allegedly pretty—slave-girl could bring in a real market. The fact that Sinope had only asked for a goat, however, suggested that she did not have much appreciation for the value of slaves. Besides, Alethea had the bracelet with her. If she offered a higher price, she would have to return with the balance or send someone else. She wanted to get this over with as quickly as possible.

Turning to Niobe, she said simply, "Come with me," and then started back toward the chariot.

Sinope rushed after her, shouting, "Wait!" She held the bracelet out and angrily demanded, "What good is this? I want something useful. I want a billy goat."

"That's silver," Alethea told her. "You can trade it for about ten goats in the market." She was already untying the reins of her chariot.

"Ten?" Sinope's mouth dropped, but then her eyes narrowed with suspicion. "First I trade the bracelet, then you get the girl." She grabbed Niobe roughly by the hair just as she went to get on the back of the chariot. Niobe let out a cry and fell onto her knees.

"Take your hands off my property," Alethea ordered with all the inbred dignity of a Eurypontid, and Sinope dropped her hand and jaw in sheer astonishment. "I am the wife of Agesandros, the daughter of Kleodacus. I do not cheat and I do not lie. If I said that bracelet was worth ten goats it is worth at least that," Alethea told her in a tone of voice to make Sinope start bobbing her head and apologizing instinctively.

Alethea ignored her abruptly subservient babbling. She bent and helped Niobe onto the chariot.

Niobe's arrival caused a minor crisis in Alethea's little household. Phoebe refused to let the stinking girl inside the kitchen or helots' hall until she had been thoroughly cleaned, and she insisted the girl not be washed in the household baths, either. "You don't know what vermin the girl has. She could infect the whole household! Look at those bites! She probably has lice!"

Mika had experience with lice and it was she, talking soothingly to her former mistress about how everything was going to be all right, who scrubbed her clean in the stream by the ruined mill. There was no way to save her hair, however. It was not only crawling with lice, it was so matted that combing was impossible. Sybil had to shave it all off as Niobe sobbed helplessly.

The younger girls, Glauce, Eunice and Mika, each gave the newcomer one of their own peplos. Chloe loaned her a belt (she couldn't use one in her condition), and Phoebe herself loaned her some pins. Horrified by the state of her delicate former mistress' feet, Mika even begged a pair of worn-out sandals from Kassia. "She never went barefoot before she was captured," Mika told Kassia, still wide-eyed with horror at the state Niobe had been in on arrival. "Not even to cross the room to the privy. I had to have her slippers ready for her every morning when she swung her legs down off the bed."

"That's silly," was Kassia's practical answer. "Mom and I always go barefoot inside the house, and I know I refused to have anything on my feet until I was six or seven. But go ahead take that pair to her if you like."

The washing ritual had, of course, revealed not only the scores of ugly insect bites, but also many bruises all over Niobe's body. Sinope was responsible for most of them, but Niobe had also bruised herself—dropping wood on her toe, for example, or banging her shins on the fence when she'd been sent to feed the pig. Her once tender, white breasts, however, were so suffused with swaths of black, blue and red internal bleeding that even the usually hard-hearted Phoebe was shocked. "What did they do to you?" she demanded in a horrified voice.

Niobe looked away, but then she admitted in a low, shamed voice, "He liked to—suckle—gripping them in his hands and chewing on the nipples."

When she was cleaned up, shaved, and dressed in her borrowed clothes, Phoebe took her to Alethea in the main house. "Here's the new girl, ma'am." Her look and tone said plainly, "I hope you knew what you were doing when you bought her."

"Thank you, Phoebe. Sit down, Niobe."

She indicated a stool, just as she had for Mika roughly nine months earlier. Niobe sank down on it and crouched there in a pose of cowed terror. Nervously she kept feeling her shaved scalp, still unable to grasp that all her hair was gone.

"It will grow back—thicker and healthier than ever," Alethea assured her.

Niobe abruptly realised what she had been doing, and clutched her hands between her knees.

"You have nothing to fear here, Niobe. No one is going to abuse you. First you need to get your health back, and then we will see how best you can fit in. You can weave and sew, I presume?"

"Yes, mistress," Niobe whispered.

Alethea nodded, "Good. You can help my daughter Kassia as well. She needs a personal maid." The name Kassia seemed to make Niobe flinch, but Alethea wasn't sure. When further attempts to get Niobe to open up and speak failed, Alethea decided to let it go for now and sent her back to the helots' hall for a hot meal.

It was there that Leon found her. He bounded in with relief and eagerness, calling excitedly, "Niobe? Niobe?"

Leon's eye sockets were still discoloured, his nose swollen and lips scabbed from what the watch had done to him, but he smiled so broadly that all his teeth showed.

Niobe caught her breath at the sound of her name and looked over sharply. At the sight of Leon approaching her with outstretched hands and a wide smile, she jumped to her feet and started backing away. "Leave me alone. The mistress said no one would touch me here. Leave me be!"

Leon stopped dead in his tracks. Around them, Phoebe and Chloe and Mika all protested in various tones of outrage. Phoebe called to Niobe in an irritable voice not to be "a silly goose!" while Chloe protested in amusement, "But Leon's the one who rescued you. Who do you think asked the mistress to buy you?" Mika, however, called out in outrage, "Don't you remember Leon? Leon wouldn't ever hurt anyone!"

Niobe stood with her arms crossed over her chest, staring at Leon as if he were something hateful.

Leon's smile faded. "I would never hurt you," he echoed Mika in a soft, hurt voice. "I—" He didn't finish, just turned and left the kitchen.

Behind him the other members of the household started lecturing Niobe on who Leon was, but Mika ran after him. "Leon, Leon!"

For the first time since they had met on that night in Pylos, Leon spoke to Mika in a harsh tone. "Leave me alone!" he ordered, and hastened out across the courtyard and out the gate.

Mika stared after Leon with a horrible twisting in her stomach. He was in love with Niobe. He kept his distance from the helot girls. They were no real rivals to her. But he was in love with Niobe. Everyone loved Niobe, Mika realized, the tears coalescing in her throat. Niobe—even shaved and battered—was still prettier than she.

Alethea found Leon sitting on the cracked steps leading down from the ruined mill. Weeds were sprouting between the cracks, and the crickets were screaming all around them as the air grew damp and chill.

"Leon."

At the sound of her voice, Leon started to get to his feet, but she put her hand on his shoulder and stopped him. "Sit still," she murmured as she sat down beside him instead. At first she just sat there, her chin on her hand looking at the way the gurgling stream reflected the moonlight.

Leon was tense beside her. She could feel how he sat unmoving and yet wound up like a cat preparing to pounce. She could smell his tanned skin, the oiled leather of his armour and a whiff of dried sweat from his chiton. She could sense the hardness of his young muscles. He was so like Niko, and she wished she could lay her arm over his shoulders as she would have done with her son. Leon's mother, she reminded herself, had sold him into slavery when he was just a little boy. What sort of mother had she been before? Had she ever taken him in her arms to comfort him? Certainly no one had done it since—until she herself had held him the night Agesandros' men would have killed him. Was it any wonder that he wanted a wife to give him all the caressing and affection his unnatural mother had denied him?

"Leon, you mustn't take Niobe's reaction personally."

Leon made a sharp, dismissive gesture, and his face was hard and resentful. If she hadn't been his mistress, Alethea was certain he would have told her to mind her own business in no uncertain terms. But he did not want to risk offending his benefactor and held his tongue.

"From what Phoebe and Mika said, Niobe was not only beaten and worked mercilessly, she was brutally raped by all three of the men in the household—apparently many times."

Leon flinched and caught his breath, but he stubbornly refused to look at her. He had his arms crossed on his knees and his chin on his arms, and he stared at the rushing water dancing in the moonlight.

"You know yourself how she was raised. You know that, whatever else one says against Anaxilas, he is a good-looking man with the manners of a prince." Leon grimaced slightly, but he kept his eyes fixed on the water, his head on his arms.

"But those helots, Leon, they were of the very worst kind. Not comparable to Orsippos and Lampon in any way. They were even worse than Agesandros' helots. It seems that the younger son was as big as an ox and hardly more intelligent. Niobe was the first girl his father let him have. Niobe is so bruised and sore from what he's done to her, that she just can't bear the sight of any man. She needs time to recover. She needs to regain her strength and health, and forget the abuse and the fear."

Leon still refused to speak or look at her, but his expression had eased from animosity to doubt.

"You leave tomorrow with Agesandros and will be gone all summer. We women will be among ourselves. No one will hurt her or frighten her here. The half-month of abuse and brutality that she endured with that helot family will become less and less important to her. When you return in the fall, see if she doesn't run to greet you eagerly and gratefully."

Leon swallowed and at last turned to look at Alethea, his chin still resting on his arm. "Do you really think so?"

"Yes, I do," Alethea assured him confidently, thinking that a girl would have to be mad not to want this fine youth whose heart was a beautiful as his body.

Leon did not look convinced, but he wanted to believe her. "She didn't even try to stop Anaxilas. Her slave pleaded for her, but she didn't resist him."

"How could she? The blood of her husband's guard was still dripping from your swords!" Alethea reminded him reproachfully. "Besides, if she had only known her husband, no doubt she had not learned to fear. It was the brutality of these helots that has taught her fear."

"But she knows I'm not like them, ma'am," Leon protested. "I bandaged her hand and I helped her carry water, and I never once laid a hand on her. She *must* know I'm not like them."

"I'm sure she does know in her heart. But the other experiences were just too raw and recent. Give her time, Leon. I'll bet she looks forward to your return in the fall almost as much as I long for Agesandros." She gave him a quick, motherly hug.

Leon was so disconcerted by her gesture that he blushed bright red and almost pulled away, but Alethea was used to confused youths. She let her lips brush the top of his head, and then let him go as abruptly as she'd embraced him. "You know all the girls in the household vie for your favours, Leon. Why should Niobe be any different?" she asked in a laughing tone.

Leon only looked down in confusion and shrugged, but to himself he said: because she's a king's daughter, and because she's been a prince's wife and a prince's concubine, and I'm only a slave. But maybe—the thought came to him quite unexpectedly—but maybe if I could prove I was braver than Anaxilas and Aristomenes.... The thought gave him courage. He sat up straighter and took a deep breath. "Thank you, ma'am."

They stood and returned to the house together.

CHAPTER 10

The news that Chloe was in labour reached Pharax at a most inconvenient moment. Kleonymus had already sent for him. There was a boy with what appeared to be acute appendicitis and they had to hurry. Inwardly cursing the timing, Pharax sent a message back to Alethea that he would come as soon as he could, and hastened to the first patient.

The boy, a 13-year-old from the agoge, was in his barracks, and his eirene stood out in front with the other boys looking pale and frightened in a group around him. At the sight of Kleonymus, the eirene came forward anxiously, describing the symptoms again. Kleonymus nodded as he swept into the dim barracks where the boy was laid out on his couch, clutching his himation around him as he squirmed and sweated in agony.

Kleonymus was snapping orders to his helot assistants as he pulled his own himation off and flung it onto a nearby couch. He stopped and waited tensely for Pharax to limp to the far side of the couch, and then he turned to the young patient and gently but firmly pulled the himation away. "We need to know exactly where it hurts most. Do you understand? We *want* you to cry out when it hurts. No stupid games now. No nonsense about hiding the pain. We must *know* when it hurts."

The boy nodded, squirming miserably on the coach. Rather than probing with his fingers, however, Kleonymus stepped back and ordered Pharax, "You do it."

Pharax gently but confidently began probing, zeroing in on the suspected source of the pain. When the boy cried out as expected, he only glanced up and Kleonymus nodded once before challenging, "So?"

Pharax rattled off the procedures. Again Kleonymus nodded and then turned and gave orders to their assistants. Boiling water, wine, bandages, pans and surgical equipment were brought or unpacked respectively. The patient was deftly knocked out with a clinical blow to his head. The scalpels were cleaned in boiling water. When everything was ready, Kleonymus asked his apprentice, "Where would you cut?"

Pharax traced the course of the suggested cut very lightly with his finger. Kleonymus nodded and handed him the scalpel. "Do it."

Pharax caught his breath and held it for a second. This was not the first time Kleonymus had turned an operation over to him, but it was the first time in an emergency. Although he had gained familiarity with the scalpel by practising on animal cadavers and then performing minor, secondary operations on extremities, this was the first time he was being asked to cut into a human torso near the vital organs. To be sure, he had watched Kleonymus do this exact operation at least a half-dozen times, and yet his throat was instantly dry. He glanced up at his mentor, and Kleonymus scowled angrily and commanded, "Do it! Every second counts!"

Pharax took a deep breath, turned his attention back to the scalpel in his hand, and began the operation. Once the first incision had been made, Kleonymus gave running instructions. There was no time to inquire after Pharax's opinion. This was a case of Kleonymus' knowledge guiding Pharax's hands. But there is no better instructor than experience.

After they were finished and were washing their hands, Pharax abruptly started shaking so badly that he had to sit down. He wiped the sweat off his brow and tried to get hold of himself, but his knees were knocking together and his hands trembled. Kleonymus watched him for a moment before he at last remarked, "Don't worry. As long as the shakes hit you afterwards, you'll make it."

Pharax looked up at his mentor in wonder. "How could you risk it?"

"I had to." He held out his own hands. They too were trembling. "They're like that more and more. You're going to have to be my hands from now on."

Pharax ran a hand through his coarse, long hair and thought what that meant. His gaze went back to the boy on the couch. He was so pale and still that he could have been dead, but Kleonymus was confident that they had saved him. The boy's mother could be heard demanding admittance from out in front, and Kleonymus raised his voice to tell the eirene to let her in. She rushed in, her hair in disarray. "What happened?" she demanded. "They said he collapsed while running. What—??" She caught sight of her son on the couch and cried out, thinking he was dead.

"Hush!" Kleonymus admonished, moving quickly to stop her from falling on her son in grief. In a low, professional voice he explained the situation to the distraught mother, while Pharax managed at last to stand and wash his hands. The shakes were gone as suddenly as they'd come. It was only then that he remembered about Chloe's baby.

Excusing himself, he went back out where Dexippos was waiting with his wagon and set off to Alethea's kleros. It was now mid-afternoon, and the day was bright and hot. The fields were green with barley, and wildflowers brightened the side of the road and the edges of the fields. From a distance the bright red of the poppies dominated, but up close there were dozens of other flowers feeding the bees. Pharax looked across the blooming valley and toward the still snow-capped crests of Taygetos, and he marvelled at how good the gods had been to him. Today he had saved a boy's life. Not alone. He knew he couldn't have done it without Kleonymus' constant instructions, and yet they were his hands that had done it. His hands, the hands he had taken for granted when he still had two good legs, the hands he had almost failed to value—if Agesandros hadn't reminded him.

Dexippos was driving, and Pharax lifted his hands and held them before his face, turning them this way and that. They looked ordinary. Short-fingered, soft, white and even a little plump. They were not particularly beautiful or strong, but they had the strength to save lives. It was a wonderful, awesome feeling.

Pharax told Dexippos to drive right around to the empty stables behind the walled complex. One of the kitchen girls appeared at once from the hen house, a basket on her arm, and waved to him with self-important urgency. "Chloe is in labour, Master," she told him with obvious excitement.

"That's why I'm here," Pharax declared with pride, and the girl looked shocked; birthing was women's business.

The courtyard was deserted, and Pharax put his head into the kitchen to find someone. To his astonishment he discovered Niobe chopping onions, parsley and celery at the heavy table. Her shaved head was sprouting a short fuzz of bright red hair. She wore a clean but simple peplos bound at the shoulders by tin pins. Sweat was running down the side of her face and shimmering on her arms as she worked rather listlessly. She started at the sight of someone in the doorway, and her eyes widened as she recognised him. "Pharax?"

"Niobe! What are you doing here?" Pharax stepped into the kitchen. It was very hot and humid. Not only were both the hearth and bread-oven burning, but a huge kettle was slowly simmering over the hearth, filling the air with steam.

"Didn't you hear? Queen Eupolia gave me away—to a *helot*." There was so much bitterness and hatred in that one word that Pharax, who knew many good helots, raised his eyebrows slightly. Nor did the answer explain what she was doing here.

"You mean to Orsippos?" He tried to make sense of it.

"No, to Lampis and his sons Deidas and Kapros. You can't imagine what it was like," Niobe told him, her voice tight and almost accusatory. "They—they lived liked pigs. They never washed and they—they poisoned my insides with their filth."

Pharax was shocked as much by her tone and as by what she was saying. The bitterness was understandable, but the bluntness discomfited him nevertheless. "What makes you say that?" he asked carefully, seating himself slowly on the bench opposite her.

"I—I'm oozing filth all the time. Not my monthly flux, just stinking filth!" She flung the words at him without looking at him, but that was understandable. She was ashamed to talk of such things to a man. She kept her face averted from him as she continued, "And nobody cares. Not even here." Tears were in her voice now.

"How did you come to be here?" Pharax pressed again softly.

"Oh, Leon found out I'd been sold and told his mistress. She bought me away from Lampis, but only to keep me here like a common slave. She expects me to work just like the others. Just as they did at the palace. She knows I'm a king's daughter, but she's no better than Queen Eupolia. She treats me like a slave."

"You *are* a slave," Pharax reminded her gently but firmly. No one could criticise Alethea in his hearing and expect sympathy. Alethea and Leon had saved his life, no less than he had saved that boy this morning.

"No I'm not!" Niobe cried out, the tears shimmering in her eyes as she turned a hot, angry face to him. "I'm a king's daughter! How many times do I have to tell you all that? I was raised to be a queen. I never lifted my finger to do any work. I never took a step without slippers. I never even combed my own hair or dressed myself. I had a slave who cared for me from the day I was born, and when I married I had two personal slaves and the whole household jumped to do my bidding and please me. Why should I be cutting onions for a bunch of helots?" In a gesture of furious indignation, she shoved the cutting board and knife aside with childish rebelliousness.

"Because your husband abandoned you to his enemies," Pharax told her in a low, firm voice.

Niobe stared at him in shock, as if she had never grasped this simple fact, but then she shook her head and the tears spilled down her hot, sweating cheeks, as she insisted, "But it's not *my* fault he had to flee so suddenly. Agesandros took us by surprise. Agesandros shouldn't have been able to attack. Aristomenes had defeated him just two days earlier. That's why he and his companions were unarmed. He...." She stammered to a close, aware that Pharax was just like all the other Lacedaemonians. He had no respect for what she'd been. Leon was the only one who understood her. She dropped her head in her hands and started sobbing in self-pity.

Pharax let her cry for a few minutes, glancing over his shoulder impatiently, anxious to get to the real patient. When he thought Niobe had calmed down enough, he got to his feet again and told her, "If you collect the discharge you are having on a cloth and give it to me before I leave, I'll see if I can identify it. I suspect it is a light infection that we can quickly cure. Now—"

Mika burst into the kitchen with a fat hydria in her arms, and was half way to the kettle before she saw him. Pharax was pleased that this time her expression brightened rather than darkened at the sight of him. "Oh, Master Surgeon" (that was what she'd started calling him at some point), "have you come to help Chloe?"

"Indeed I have. I would have come earlier, but I had another patient, an emergency. How are things going?"

Mika bit her lower lip and admitted, "I don't know. They won't let me in the sickroom. I just fetch water when they send for it." Reminded of her duties, she at once turned away from Pharax and lowered her hydria into the kettle of steaming water. She was so small and thin that Pharax automatically reached out to help her, but she shook her head confidently. "I can manage." And sure enough, with surprising ease she pulled the now-heavy hydria out of the kettle again. The process was not effortless, however, and she at once set the hydria down and used the back of her arm to wipe sweat from her brow as she caught her breath. She looked at Pharax with wide, trusting eyes, but Pharax noted that her warts were if anything worse than ever.

"The second ointment hasn't worked any better than the first, has it?"

"No, Master Surgeon," she admitted, looking down, and her shoulders hunched automatically when she remembered herself.

"Well then, we'll just have to try something else," Pharax assured her. "I'm not going to give up.."

She looked up at him as if she wanted to hope, but didn't dare.

He smiled to encourage her. "But first take me to Chloe, all right?"

"Oh, yes, Master Surgeon." She picked up the heavy hydria and led him out of the kitchen and up the steps to the main house. They passed under the colonnade and down the corridor to the peristyle, and here Pharax had to catch his breath at the splendour of the garden. Pinks spilled from the hanging pots, peonies bloomed along the edge of the walkway, and rose bushes spread their splendour in the sun at the centre. He was so taken by the beauty of the garden that Kassia was almost upon him before he saw her in the shade of the walkway.

She was barefoot as usual in the house and her hair was pulled back in her usual ponytail, but she was dressed better than for the harvest, in a pretty linen peplos with a palm-leaf border. "Thank you for coming, Pharax," she greeted him earnestly, and her face looked strained for her young years.

"Of course I came. I asked you to send for me. I would have been here sooner, but Kleonymus had already called me to another patient. A boy from the agoge had acute appendicitis and we had to operate at once. He is going to be fine, and how is Chloe doing?"

Kassia shook her head and admitted in a near whisper, "I don't think things are going right. They won't let me in but—but she's been in labour almost 24 hours."

Pharax was shocked. "But I didn't get a message until this morning—"

Kassia was waving her hand in agitation. "I know. I know. Mom didn't wake me and so I didn't learn that Chloe's labour had started until I got up this morning, but she started last night just after we'd all gone to bed."

Pharax calculated that was about 16 to 17 hours earlier. Not an excessive time yet, so he smiled at Kassia and told her, "That's not unusual. Certainly not for a first child. She's in the sickroom?"

Kassia nodded and stepped back to let the surgeon pass. Mika had hurried on ahead while they talked. At the door to the sickroom, Pharax announced himself and requested admittance. Kassia waited tensely, her hands clasped together. She had been the one to send for Pharax and she knew that the midwife would resent it. It took Pharax a few minutes, but finally Alethea prevailed on the midwife and he was admitted. With a sigh of relief, Kassia went back to watering her mother's flowers.

Eunice and Glauce, with some help from Mika and Niobe, managed to get dinner ready for the household without Phoebe shouting at them. The midwife left the sickroom long enough to come take a meal, but to the anxious questions from the rest of the household she refused to say anything more than "Difficult, but she's a healthy girl." When she returned to the sickroom, Phoebe came to eat something, but she said nothing at all except to order Niobe to help with the washing up and Glauce to do the milking.

As soon as she'd gulped down her own meal, Mika loaded a tray and took it to the main house for Kassia and Alethea. "Should I serve the Master Surgeon in the andron, Mistress?" Mika asked as her mistress sank down exhausted before the meal.

"I don't think he'll leave Chloe right now," Alethea replied, her head on her hand.

"What's the matter, Mom?" Kassia pressed.

Alethea seemed to pull herself together. "It's a difficult birth, that's all. I'm reminded of Niko's. It lasted longer than this and I was sure I was dying, but you see I didn't." It was supposed to be a joke and she tried to smile, but she was too exhausted.

"Maybe you should lie down and rest, Mom," Kassia suggested in concern. "Now that Pharax is here."

Alethea waved her hand in an ambiguous gesture. "Pharax means well, but he's no help. He's just learning about birth."

"But he's learning so he can help," Kassia pointed out indignantly, as if her mother had in some way insulted the surgeon.

Alethea had no nerves for teenage over-sensitivity, and she just waved her hand vaguely. She was so tired, much more tired than she ought to be.

When it was time to go to bed, Chloe still had not delivered successfully. Alethea told the younger girls to refill the kettle, stoke up the fire and then go to bed. Niobe, who had replaced Mika as Kassia's personal slave, at once left the kitchen to help Kassia undress for the night. As Kassia's personal maid, Niobe slept in her mistress' chamber rather than the helots' hall. Here she had a low bed with a real mattress and clean linen sheets, almost as good as at home. Exhausted from the long day, she was in a hurry to get to bed. But Kassia was not. Kassia lingered in the gallery, looking down to where the light from many lamps spilled into the peristyle from the sickroom, and Niobe was forced to wait for her. With every second, Niobe's dislike for Kassia grew.

"Something's really wrong, isn't it?" Kassia commented, frowning with worry as she watched Sybil waddle out of the sickroom, pushing Alethea before her.

Niobe shrugged, adding in a reproachful tone, "How should I know? I lost *my* baby at 7 months."

Kassia showed no interest in Niobe's tragedy, which made Niobe dislike her even more. Kassia didn't have any of the qualities that made a good queen, Niobe found herself thinking. Right now, for example, she was leaning over the railing, obviously trying to hear what Sybil was saying to her mother. No queen would have tried to eavesdrop so openly—not to mention hanging over a railing like a boy. No, Kassia wasn't fit to be the wife even of a palace official, much less a king, Niobe thought, remembering the elegant and dignified way her father's legal wife had glided about the palace, trailed by a half-dozen attendants carrying her train and her distaff and her caged bird.

At last Niobe had had enough waiting and reminded Kassia in a resentful tone, "There's nothing we can do. We might as well go to bed."

"Shhhh!" Kassia hissed, frowning and straining harder to hear what Sybil was saying to her mother. All she heard, however, was the hissing and clucking of the old servant, while her mother wiped her face with her hands.

Niobe stiffened and waited. Anaxilas was going to regret marrying this self-willed little brat, she thought. Kassia was pretty enough in her way, but when you saw her like this—not dressed up as she had been on the stage of the theatre—you could see all her defects as well. For a start, her skin was burned brown from the sun, and her feet had hard soles from walking about barefoot, just like a slave. But most obvious to Niobe, as a girl who had grown up among her father's concubines, Kassia's sexuality was so underdeveloped that it would have been pitiable in anyone other than this little bitch who had stolen Anaxilas' affections from her.

Sybil had apparently convinced Alethea that she should rest, because the two older women were making their way around the peristyle toward the stairs. Kassia pulled back from the railing and said to Niobe, "I can take care of myself. Go help Sybil with my Mom, will you?"

Would they never let her get to bed? Niobe thought bitterly. Without answering, she went to the top of the stairs and waited, listening to the sound of Sybil huffing and puffing as she made her way up one step at a time. Alethea emerged first. She looked so astonished to see Niobe that Niobe felt she had to explain. "Kassia told me to help you, Mistress," she declared in a sullen voice, hoping that Alethea would notice how tired she was and send her to bed.

"Has she gone to bed?" Alethea glanced toward her daughter's door, but all was dark and still. "Good. I'm just going to lie down for a bit, maybe—"

"You go fetch some hot water for the mistress," Sybil ordered Niobe, coming out of the stairs and dabbing sweat from her brow. "She needs to wash and change. She hasn't been out of her clothes for almost two days now and hasn't had a wink of sleep either. And bring some wine as well," Sybil called after Niobe.

How was she supposed to carry both wine and water? Did they think she had four hands? Niobe went into the kitchen and to her relief Mika was still there, carefully arranging the logs under the kettle so they would burn as long as possible. At once she ordered, "Take a hydria of hot water up to the mistress so she can wash," and started toward the cupboard where the wine flasks were kept.

Mika spun about in surprise, and with all the resentment she felt toward the beautiful Niobe who had stolen Leon's heart, spat out, "I don't have to take orders from you anymore!"

Niobe turned about in amazement. How could this ugly little slave dare to talk to her in that tone of voice? Her astonishment quickly gave way to outrage. "How dare you! Have you forgotten who I am? All I did for you?" Niobe remembered how she had defended the ugly, clumsy slave from her husband's insults and Kallisto's accusations. To make sure Mika remembered, she added, "You never would have lived in luxury if it hadn't been for me. Aristomenes hated the very sight of you, and Kallisto told me about all the things you broke and ruined." Part of her couldn't believe that this was all the thanks she got for being so nice to Mika: Mika talking back to her when she was exhausted and needed help.

"What do I care about Aristomenes and Kallisto?" Mika spat back, stamping her foot. "They aren't my masters—any more than you. You're no better than me!"

"How dare you say that! You know I'm a princess!"

"You're a slave just like me!" Mika shot back, louder.

"I'm a king's daughter!" Niobe returned louder still. "Just because I was captured by these Laconian-barbarians, doesn't change that I was *born* a princess. I'm not a barbarian slave like you!"

"I was born free!" Mika screamed in frustration.

"Your own parents sold you—that's how worthless you are!" Niobe sneered. "You ugly little toad! Not even your own mother could love something as ugly as you!"

Mika launched herself at Niobe, her hands held like claws, with the intention of scratching out her rival's eyes—or at least leaving scratches on her pretty, sneering face. She screamed as she attacked, "Your husband abandoned you! He didn't care if his worst enemy fucked you! That's how much he loved you!"

"That's a lie! You hideous toad!" Niobe screamed back as she defended herself, fending off Mika's hands with one arm while grabbing her hair with the other and trying to tear it out.

Mika was struggling like a wildcat. She tried to kick Niobe's shins while trying to claw at her face.

"Ugly little toad!" Niobe screamed again. "No one can stand the sight of you!"

Neither of the opponents even heard the shouts of Orsippos calling for order, or the giggles of Glauce and Eunice. Niobe and Mika's shouting had drawn all the helots from the hall and loft, and the rest of the household craned their necks and muttered among themselves, debating who would win, while Orsippos shouted at the rivals to stop fighting, but didn't risk trying to separate them. From the doorway to the courtyard Kassia too shouted, "Stop it!" but her high, breathy voice carried no authority. Finally Phoebe stormed in, and her voice pierced the air as she grabbed one protagonist in each hand and hauled them apart with a jerk. "You worthless wretches! My girl's dying, and all you can do is fight like two wild bitches!"

"Dying?" Orsippos and Lampon said in unison, their jaws dropping.

"Oh, get out of my sight, all of you!" Phoebe screamed, but in the next instant she collapsed onto a bench and started sobbing her heart out into her hands. For a second everyone just stared at her. Then her husband rushed over to her and—after a moment's hesitation because Phoebe usually rejected any sign of affection in public—put his arm tentatively over her shoulders. The fact that she did not shake him off shocked everyone as much as what she'd said. When Phoebe hunched over more and sobbed harder, they gazed at one another in dawning comprehension of impending tragedy. Orsippos looked over at his son in horror and then sat down beside his wife and held her; but he was helpless in the face of weakness on the part of his dominant wife. Lampon was no more comfortable with this sudden weakness of his mother, and he followed the rest of the household who, confused and disturbed, tiptoed back to their beds. Only Niobe, Mika and Kassia stood staring a moment longer.

Kassia came to herself first and hissed at the two slaves, "What were you doing fighting like that? My mother is still waiting for the water and wine you were sent to fetch, Niobe. Hurry!"

Niobe opened her mouth to protest. Here she'd been attacked by this wild beast Mika, was cut and scratched and bruised, and she was still supposed to fetch everything herself. Everyone else had gone to bed and she was expected to rush around fetching and carrying. Why didn't they ask someone else to do anything?

Mika, however, was filling the hydria unasked, and she shoved Niobe aside as she took it out of the kitchen, leaving Niobe to fetch the wine. That way she was the first upstairs and into Alethea's chamber. Sybil had helped Alethea out of her clothes and she was lying naked on the bed, her arm over her eyes. At the sight of Mika in the doorway, Sybil rushed over, scolding, "Where's Niobe? What took so long?"

Mika was sniffling, and wiped her nose with the back of her arm as soon as Sybil had taken the hydria away from her. "It's not right, Mistress," she declared defiantly. "Niobe's got no right to order me around anymore. It's not fair. I do my share of the work here. I do everything you tell me to do. It's not fair that Niobe gets to serve Kassia and orders me around like I was still *her* slave—"

"What is this all about?" Sybil cut her off angrily. "Can't you see the mistress is exhausted? And poor Chloe's near the end of her strength. This is no time to start wailing and complaining—"

"It's all right, Sybil," Alethea declared, sitting up but pressing her hand to her forehead. "Niobe has no right to give you orders, child. I'll—"

"Mom." Kassia had been on Mika's heels and now came into her mother's chamber with a worried expression. "Phoebe says Chloe is dying."

Sybil hissed angrily at Kassia, but Alethea waved her silent. "She's exhausted, and the baby just won't come. No one knows what to do anymore. We're all at our wit's end."

"But Pharax—"

Alethea waved her silent. "What can he do that the midwife can't? Go to bed. All of you."

At last Niobe arrived with a pitcher of wine. Her mouth was set in a sullen pout as she set the pitcher down on Alethea's bedside table while all the others stared at her. She could feel the stares and didn't understand them. She looked around herself and felt the hatred of Mika, the contempt of Sybil, the anger of Kassia and the weary disappointment of Alethea. They're all against me, she registered. It was so unfair.

As soon as she was gone, Kassia declared, "Mom, I don't want Niobe to serve me any more. I want Mika, she—"

Alethea let out a little sigh, and Sybil hissed angrily at Kassia, "Must *you* start that now?!"

Kassia bit her tongue and looked contrite.

Alethea lay back on the bed and covered her eyes with her arm again. "Just let me sleep a little."

"Of course, of course." Sybil pulled the linen sheets up over her and tucked her in like a child.

Kassia was woken by the birds at her window. With a start she sat up in bed. Bright sunshine slanted steeply into her chamber. It must be mid-morning, she thought, flinging off the covers and looking about her room. Niobe was sleeping soundly on the pallet at the foot of her bed. She grimaced, remembering the way she had called Mika an "ugly toad."

In her agitation after the fight last night, Mika had told Kassia how Niobe had also tried to order her around. Kassia believed her. Niobe was nothing if not lazy. It was because Sybil complained about having to chase after her all the time that Alethea had decided she should serve Kassia. But Kassia didn't want her anymore, either. Even last night, after all the commotion, she had simply gone to bed *ahead* of Kassia. When Kassia had entered her chamber, her slave was lying with her face to the wall and made no move whatever to help her. Kassia didn't need help and she hadn't asked for it, but Mika never would have done that. It wasn't fair that Niobe had been "rewarded" with the more pres-tigious position and lighter work than Mika because she was *less* deserv-ing. That offended Kassia's sense of fairness.

Determined to see that Mika and Niobe got what they each deserved, Kassia pulled a peplos over her head, combed her hair into a ponytail and slipped out of her chamber onto the gallery. She was star-tled when Mika jumped up with a little gasp.

Mika had been sitting just outside Kassia's door, clutching her knees in her arms. Her short hair was a tousled mop, and her face was swol-len and streaked with tears. "Oh, Mistress!" she cried out, and at once a gasp escaped her lungs. "It's terrible! Chloe is dead! The baby wouldn't come out. She's dead and the baby's still inside her! It's dead, too!"

Tears streamed down Mika's face, and she helplessly wiped her run-ning nose on the back of her dirty hands. Kassia was so taken by sur-prise that she just stared. Then she looked over the railing into the peristyle. Now she could make out the keening of at least two others, and noticed that Eunice and Glauce were already dressed in black as they moved along the side of the peristyle, apparently on some errand from the sickroom.

"When?" Kassia stammered, still not really believing it.

"Just after dawn, Mistress," Mika sobbed out, trying now to wipe her nose on the inside of her elbow.

"Is my Mom …?"

"She's down there trying to—Phoebe—I've never seen her like this. And—oh, how could it happen? Chloe was so strong and healthy!"

"My brother," Kassia whispered; "someone has to get word to Niko. She was his girl and—the baby is dead, too?"

"It's still inside her," Mika repeated, trying so hard to hold back her tears that she was hiccuping.

And Pharax? Where was he? Why hadn't he been able to help? Kassia ran down the stairs and around the peristyle, but at the entry to the sickroom she faltered. The midwife was gone. Pharax was nowhere to be seen. Phoebe was collapsed on the floor beside the bed on which her daughter's corpse lay, and Alethea was holding her in her arms as she sobbed, swaying back and forth in agony. Who would have thought the sour helot woman would grieve like this? Kassia was sobered by the sight of her. Sybil was using a cloth soaked in fragrant oils to wash down the corpse and keening as she worked. The corpse—naked and limp, arms hanging off the bed and legs spread under the enormous belly—sent a shiver of horror down Kassia's spine. Chloe was her own age. Just two days ago she had been full of life and looking forward to motherhood. She had chattered about the different names she wanted to suggest to Niko. Unlike Kassia, she had been so certain that Niko would be a proud, doting father.…

Kassia started into the room. "Mom—"

Alethea looked up, and the sight of her ravaged, sagging face gave Kassia a new shock. Her mother looked 20 years older than usual.

"Thank the gods Agesandros can't see her now," Kassia thought. She looked *old*.

"Not now, Kassia," Alethea got out in a hoarse voice. "The corpse isn't ready yet. This is not for you."

Kassia glanced once more at the bloodless corpse with the huge, distended belly. Repulsion sent a shudder through her and she gladly turned away. She wandered along the side of the peristyle, and all the bright, happy flowers of her mother's garden seemed an insult to the dead girl behind her. She wandered aimlessly through the empty rooms and then decided to ask in the kitchen where Pharax was.

Although it was well past breakfast time and Glauce and Eunice were cleaning up, Orsippos sat on one of the benches in a state of shock. His hair was almost completely grey, Kassia noted with surprise. Had it been like that yesterday and she had simply failed to notice? Or had the loss of his bright, happy teenage daughter aged him overnight? He sat, his hands hanging between his knees and his jaw slack, just staring at nothing. Glauce and Eunice nodded to Kassia but said nothing.

"Have you seen the surgeon?" Kassia asked, automatically lowering her voice to a near whisper.

The helot girls shook their heads. Kassia went out to the stables, thinking Pharax must have left already, but his wagon and gelding were still there and his helot was helping with the mucking out. "Where's your master?" Kassia asked Dexippos.

The man shrugged and then gestured vaguely toward the stream. "Wandered off that way."

Kassia hesitated. She was barefoot and not prepared for a long hike, but then the surgeon wouldn't have gone far with his peg leg and crutch. She took the path toward the mill. It was the obvious thing. Not rebuilt since the raid in which the Messenians had attacked her kleros, the charred ruins of the old mill sat amidst the sprouting weeds. The grass was long. The poppies blew bright along with centaur's foot, meadow sage and lavender. On the cracked, broken steps down to the stream, the surgeon sat with his head in his hands.

Kassia caught her breath and stopped. Once, a long, long time ago, she had sat here with her cousin Damonon while the rest of the household feasted after the olive harvest. She had been 15 and he had just turned 20. She had snuggled up against his tanned, hard body and felt like a woman when he put his arm around her. They had kissed for the first time—not like cousins but like lovers—and three months later he was dead. Slaughtered as he tried to defend his 7-year-old charges from the Messenians, who had crept into the city like foxes into a henhouse. Damonon had not had time to put on any armour. He had died naked. His body had been lacerated with stab-wounds. She had clung to his body, unable to accept that it was empty of that precious life. And when they had taken it away from her and buried it underground, she had tried to follow him. She had thrown herself into this very stream—but a shepherd had seen her do it and rescued her. She had tried to goad a bull into goring her, but Orsippos had distracted the bull. Then she had decided on going into the caves behind the house and taking one of the trails that led into the underworld itself—but one of the bitches had bayed so loudly that she'd been discovered before she got halfway up the trail to the caves. So, for all her promises, Damonon was still waiting for her….

Kassia stood so long, lost in her memories, that Pharax sensed her presence and jerked upright, looking over his shoulder in alarm. His face was pale and his eyes wide with distress. At the sight of him, Kassia forgot her dead cousin. "Oh, Pharax. It's not your fault. I'm sure it wasn't your fault."

"But why?!" he cried back in a wounded tone, his eyes strangely wild. "Why? Why? Why?" His hands were balled into fists and he was pounding them on his knees. "It can't be what the gods want. It can't be!" Pharax was talking now without even looking at Kassia. His eyes were on the river, and he spoke in a flood. "I've seen women die because they were old and worn out. I've seen them die because they were half-starved and too weak to endure. I watched one child—a girl of just 12, raped by her own uncle!—die because her immature body couldn't respond to the unnatural situation. I've seen women give up in the middle of a normal birth because they didn't *want* another mouth to feed—or a child from a man they didn't love. Every death I've found an explanation for—until today. Chloe was strong, healthy, young, and built like a heifer. She had the hips and build for child-birth. And she wanted that baby. I know she did. I can't explain it." He was pulling at his beard in agitation.

Kassia sat down beside him primly. She was careful not to sit too close to him, not as she had sat with Damonon more than 3 years ago. But she was not frightened by Pharax's ravings, either. She too stared at the river, and shivered at the thought that Pharax didn't know why Chloe had died. If there wasn't a reason, then there was no way she could protect herself from the same fate.

"There was nothing *wrong* with Chloe," Pharax insisted, running his hands through his coarse hair yet again. "She never gave up. To the very end she kept *trying*. She held her mother's hand and pressed so hard, her mother's fingers are black and blue. Chloe did everything any woman could—and more. It makes no sense. No sense at all." He dropped his head in his hands and fell silent.

Kassia waited a bit without speaking. At last she whispered in her breathy voice, "Will you tell my brother."

Pharax seemed to jump nearly out of his skin. He looked over at her and his eyes widened. Only now did he really see—or at least regis-ter—*who* was beside him. "Oh, my lady, I'm terribly sorry." He reached for his crutch, his hand feeling about helplessly in the long grass. "What have I been raving on about? This is not for your ears. I must have gone mad. Forgive me. Forgive me. I don't know what's the matter with me. I'm over-tired. I'm so sorry." He managed to find his crutch, got it upright and hauled himself to his feet.

Kassia rose with him, but she was frowning in puzzlement. "Why shouldn't you talk to me? I'm a person, aren't I? A woman? I have as much right to know about these things as any other woman. It might be me in there in a year or so." She nodded, still frowning toward the house.

Pharax got even paler. The thought was abhorrent. Kassia dying in agony with Anaxilas' child. Asclepius and Hygeia, help me! He prayed.

"Will you tell my brother? He has a right to know."

Pharax nodded helplessly. "Of course, of course."

Kassia, still frowning, picked up her skirts, revealing her bare feet and calves, and left him standing there as she returned at a brisk pace to the house. Pharax stood for a long time, catching his breath and collecting his thoughts. He was an idiot. What was that phrase? A brainless boor—or was it boob? Yes, a brainless boob. Was there not one of the gods that would help him?

And just yesterday he had been so pleased with himself for saving the boy with appendicitis....

Suddenly Pharax wanted to scream. Would They kill a happy teenage mother and her infant to punish *him* for his pride? Could They really be that petty and vindictive?

Pharax lifted his face to the heavens and screamed silently at the gods, "If you're so petty, I will never make another sacrifice to you, never pour wine in your honour, never burn incense. Never, never, never again will I send my thanks or my prayers to you! Barbarians! Monsters! Beasts! I hate you! Do you hear me?! I hate you!"

CHAPTER 11

Alethea lay staring at the ceiling of her chamber, one hand on her belly. It was going to be another bright, sunny summer morning. From the open doors onto her balcony the still, cool air wafted into the room, carrying the sound of birds chirping and trilling, and the gurgle of the stream. Bright sunlight also streamed into the room, giving warning of a hot day to come, and lighting up the cracked and crumbling plaster on the ceiling. Something would have to be done about that, Alethea-the-manager registered, but at once she thrust the thought aside. When and where was she to find money for major repairs to the kleros?

With Chloe dead, they were more short-handed than ever. Mika was hard-working and cheerful, but she was slight of build and had her hands full helping Sybil in the laundry. Niobe ought to have been more help, but a girl who did everything slowly and without a will was almost more trouble than she was worth. Phoebe was still in shock over the loss of her daughter, but Alethea could already hear the nagging, complaining and shouting that would ensue when Phoebe was back to normal.

And now this. Alethea swallowed down the bile in her mouth, and tried again to find another explanation for the morning sickness that had plagued her for days. But in her heart she knew there was none. She was pregnant. At 40.

When she had taken Agesandros to her bed two years ago, she had never dreamed that this might happen. Nobody had. Indeed, the most serious objection to their marriage on the part of the Council and ephors had been that she was too old to give Agesandros sons. Agesandros had deftly parried this official criticism by indirectly reminding them that Spartan law recognized all children sired by Spartiate fathers on Spartiate mothers as legitimate—regardless of whether the parents were married to each other. Namely, he had retorted bluntly with the words: "I'll sire sons on someone else's wife, if you like."

And now she was pregnant and didn't want to be. It was as simple as that. She loved her three children. They had been the joy of her life during her loveless marriage to their father. They had been her life itself in the years of widowhood following her husband's and parents' deaths. But three children were enough. They caused her enough worry, and both Kassia and Niko were old enough to give her grandchildren. What did she need all the hectic, sleepless, unceasing care of a baby for? She simply didn't have the energy to care for small children any more. She no longer had the strength to go through it all again. She had a right to a little peace and quiet and rest. She'd only just found love and a man she wanted to grow old with.

And instead she was going to die, just as Chloe had.

The thought was there no matter how much she reasoned against it. The thought pressed down on her chest and she wanted to weep. She was going to die as Chloe had done, in agony and exhaustion, before she ever saw another spring.

By her own calculation the baby would come in the darkest part of the year, in winter. It would come when the men were home. She was glad that she would see Agesandros again before his baby killed her. She would probably also see Kassia wedded first. That would be a comfort after the terrible time she had had with her after Damonon's death. Alethea still could not understand how such a beautiful young maiden could try to take her own life, but clearly Kassia was highstrung and needed a clear purpose for living. Even if there was much to say against Anaxilas, Kassia seemed to want to be queen, and Alethea thought it would be good for her to have taken up her new duties before she was confronted with her mother's death. Otherwise she might over-react.... Maybe, if she were lucky, Alethea calculated, and the baby came late, she would even live long enough to see Niko receive his citizenship. She'd like that. She closed her eyes and swallowed the nausea down again.

The sound of the door opening did not disturb her. She had been expecting it all along. Besides, Sybil's footfall was heavy these days, and each breath was wrung from her lungs audibly; you could hear her coming all the way along the gallery.

"Not feeling well again?" the older woman diagnosed instantly from a look at her mistress. She then put into words all that Alethea had been thinking: "That young bull you married was stronger than nature itself, it seems." Sybil chuckled with open approval. "Who would have thought a barren field could be brought to new life after 15 years? But I should have known the Master would do it." Sybil chuckled again, and Alethea cracked her eyes to consider the old woman.

"Did it not occur to you, Sybil, that I'm too old—if not to conceive, then to bear this fruit to ripeness?" Alethea admonished now with just a hint of bitterness. It seemed so obvious to her that she was going to die that she resented her maid's unmitigated delight with her pregnancy.

"May all the gods protect you!" Sybil exclaimed in horror—looking as if she'd never even thought of this possibility. She lifted both her hands heaven-wards in a gesture of supplication, and a silent prayer was sent. Then she looked at her mistress with a frown of reproach. "You should know better than to even say such things! Of course you will bear this fruit to ripeness! You mustn't fear for a minute." Sybil was all smiles again, and with her plump, callused hands she stroked Alethea's cheek as if she were just a sick child with nightmares. "Why shouldn't you carry this child safely to birth? You never had any trouble with the other three."

"I nearly died with Niko, in case you've forgotten; and furthermore, I was a healthy young woman when the others were born—"

"And you're a healthy mature woman now!" Sybil told her in no uncertain terms. Clucking and scolding, she added, "Lots of women give birth at a riper age than 40! Good heavens, I had an aunt who was 51 when she dropped her last baby—easy as a ewe. Now stop thinking such morbid thoughts. Here, nibble on these before you sit up. It will settle your stomach." Sybil handed Alethea several dried biscuits which she was carrying in wide pockets of her peplos, and then with an audible grunt Sybil picked up the hydria again and went into the adjacent nursery to pour the steaming water into the laver.

After nibbling a bit, Alethea felt well enough to sit up. She went to the laver and took the sponge, soaked in warm water and rosemary oil, which Sybil offered.

"What do you want to wear?" Sybil inquired, moving back into the bedchamber and opening the clothes chest painted with palms and lilies. Without waiting for an answer, she reminded Alethea, "Now that Chloe is under ground, it is time you wore something other than black." Only family members wore mourning the entire 11 days allowed in Sparta.

Alethea agreed, adding, "But something sober. The mustard-and-rust cotton peplos would do. How are Phoebe and Orsippos?"

"Orsippos is working like a madman. He's been up since dawn hammering at the goat shed, and he has a list of repairs so long it will take him 'till the troops come home to finish half of them."

Alethea nodded. Work was a healthy way of banishing grief. "And Phoebe?"

"Phoebe...." Sybil hesitated and sighed, "she's not herself yet. She just shrugs at everything. She can't even get angry, it seems." Sybil shook her head as if in disapproval, and Alethea shook her head over the contradictory nature of man; Phoebe's perpetual sour temper had been a bane to them all, and suddenly they missed it.

"I don't think it would be fair to make things harder on her by having Niobe in the kitchens," Alethea ventured cautiously.

At once Sybil caught her breath and straightened to her full height. "I won't have that whiney girl in the laundry all day. She doesn't just get in my way, she makes me sick with all her tales of what a fine lady she was and how she had much prettier dresses than you have and how Kassia isn't fit to be a queen's handmaiden, let alone a queen. Honestly, child, if you heard what she drivels on about all day, you'd sell her tomorrow." Sybil was so indignant about the perceived insults to Alethea and Kassia that her face was flushed just talking about it.

Alethea sighed inwardly. "Well, then, Glauce will have to help Eunice and Phoebe in the kitchen, and Niobe will have to take over all of Glauce's duties in the house."

Sybil snorted, "You'll spend your whole day chasing after the girl. I warn you, you won't have a moment's peace until you get rid of the little minx."

"Yes, I will, because I will make Kassia responsible for seeing that Niobe does everything she is meant to do properly."

"Ha!" Sybil said with a smug expression. "Now that's a good idea! I should have known you were cleverer than me. Though I dare say, Kassia may be as unhappy about the arrangement as Niobe."

"Kassia will be in my aunt Eupolia's household in less than a year. I can't let her go there thinking life is all about song, can I?"

Sybil agreed vigorously. Much as she liked Kassia, she thought Alethea had let her prolong her childhood more than was sensible. Kassia was old enough to have two babies at her knee, and yet she was more child than woman even now.

Pharax found Mika in the washhouse. It was late afternoon and although the sun had slipped behind the heights of Taygetos, casting a cooling shadow over the entire kleros at the foot of the steep slopes, the air trapped in the washhouse was a good 10 degrees warmer and humid. Mika had just finished with a washload, and a heap of sheets and towels sat in a basket oozing water onto the tiled floor. Mika, her arms and hands still bright red to her elbows from working in the hot water, was wringing out a sheet, twisting it over and over on itself so that the water splattered onto her bare feet and the terracotta flooring of the washhouse. Sweat dripped down the sides of her bright red face and glistened at the base of her throat. She was wearing only a short, sleeveless chiton for working and her legs were bare from the knee down. The linen of the chiton—soaked with wash-water or sweat—clung to the front of her body.

Pharax noted that she had developed pronounced if small breasts and a little rounded belly. The stick-like, almost boyish figure she had had on arrival in the slave convoy had given way to the figure of a lithe, athletic but nubile maiden. It was as if she had abruptly grown up in the last 12 months, without becoming soft or spoiled. Her arm muscles stood out in her tanned arms as she wrung the water from the sheet with efficient determination, and her calves were hard and slender. Her hair, now chin-length, was a silky, light brown with natural curls. She kept it clean and out of her face, and although it was not as glamorous as Niobe's red hair or Kassia's bright blonde, it was healthy. Except for her warts, she really was pretty, he thought again.

With a little gasp and a start, Mika realized she was being watched. "Master Surgeon! What are you doing here?" Sybil had done much to improve her grammar and pronunciation, but Mika still said exactly what she thought. Seeing Pharax in the doorway leaning heavily on his crutch, Mika thought he looked sick. "Are you all right?" she asked at once, and dropping the sheet, she came over to Pharax. "Come out where it's cooler and sit down. Shall I fetch you some water?"

Pharax was embarrassed by the solicitousness of the young girl. "No need; I have a new ointment I wanted to give you. I'll wait at the mill."

"You can sit right out here," Mika suggested, indicating a wooden bench just outside the door that leaned against the washhouse, facing the courtyard, but Pharax shook his head and insisted, "I'll go to the mill."

Mika had been a slave too long to think of contradicting a freeman, and simply hurried with her work, wringing and then hanging out the sheets and towels in the courtyard. Being short, hanging the sheets on the line was hard work for Mika. She had to fling each sheet just right to get them up over the lines that were stretched two feet over her head. Then she pulled the bench under the lines and climbed up on it to stretch the sheets straight. Only when she was finished with them did she take a satchel of clothes pins over her shoulder and climb onto the bench again to hang up the towels. When she was finished, she shoved the bench back against the wall and started out of the courtyard. But she stopped herself, went back to the washhouse, pulled her peplos on over her chiton, and then went down to the old mill at a run.

Pharax was sitting on the broken steps, his hands resting on the crutch he held propped between his knees and his chin on his hands. The stream was in shadow at this time of day, and it looked black and ominous. The gurgle it gave seemed deep and mysterious.

Mika slowed down as she approached and considered the surgeon's apprentice. He looked sad. "What's the matter, Master Surgeon? You look sad."

Pharax looked over sharply, lifting his head in astonishment at her candid remark. Then he nodded very slowly, "Yes, Mika; I can't get over how Chloe died for nothing. Come sit down. Let me give you this." He reached around and pulled his leather satchel off his back, removed a jar with a cork stopper and handed it to Mika, who dutifully seated herself beside him. She took the jar from him and sniffed at it, wrinkling her nose slightly in distaste.

"I know. It smells a little bitter, but I want you to try it."

"Of course, Master Surgeon." Mika wouldn't have dreamed of refusing. Even if she had little hope of finding a solution to her warts, she was determined to try anything she could. Besides, it would have been an insult to the kind surgeon to refuse. Dutifully she removed the cork stopper, and Pharax automatically reached over to help her apply the ointment to her hands and then her face. "It's a bit yellowish, I'm afraid. It will make you look worse at first," he admitted, "but promise me you'll try it for 10 days. I think I may have found the key."

Mika nodded, but looked at her stained hands dolefully.

"Mika," the surgeon started in a low voice, "I need your help."

Mika looked up baffled. His tone of voice was so serious that she instinctively knew he didn't mean he wanted her to fetch him fresh water or wine or do his laundry. But what else was she good for? "My help?" she asked uncertainly.

"Yes. You see—this is very hard for me. I—Mika—try to understand. I want to be a good doctor. Kleonymus has taught me so much. As much as he can. But he's a military surgeon. He's taught me how to prevent infection in and sew up puncture wounds and cuts, how to close even lung and gut wounds, how to amputate poisoned limbs," he gestured toward his own peg leg, "how to remove organs like the appendix and kidney when they malfunction, and how to remove the skin that grows over an old man's eye. But he can't teach me about childbirth because, you see, he doesn't know. He spent his whole life with the army. Only in later life did he go into general practice. He knows very little about women's illnesses, and nothing really about childbirth."

Mika nodded, because that seemed perfectly normal to her.

"But Mika, don't you see? A midwife can only help so long as things go right. When something goes wrong—as it did with Chloe—then only a surgeon can help. Can you understand that?"

Mika nodded a little uncertainly, a puzzled frown playing over her features. She didn't really see how a surgeon could help even then. "Do you mean you can cut out a baby like a liver?"

Pharax smiled, delighted by how quick-witted she was. "Maybe! But before we can help," Pharax continued in his low, patient voice, "we have to know exactly how a baby sits in the womb, and how it ought to sit. We have to understand what goes on inside a woman's womb before and during childbirth." His tone of voice was both urgent and tortured. Indeed, his voice was a little raw, as if he were suffering from a cold. He had bags under his eyes as well, Mika noted. She nodded, as much out of sympathy as understanding.

"Mika, I have to find out what was wrong with Chloe."

"But she's dead and buried," Mika whispered. "We buried her yesterday."

"I know," Pharax said, in a voice so low it was almost inaudible over the sound of the stream. Then, pulling himself together, he continued in a low but somewhat louder and firmer voice, "I can't help Chloe now, but maybe—if I find out what went wrong with her—I can help another woman."

"But how can you find out what went wrong when she's already dead?" Mika asked.

Pharax dropped his voice again, but he looked so intently at Mika that she seemed to hear his words inside her own skull, and they made her hair stand on end: "By cutting open her corpse and seeing what happened inside the womb."

Mika was so terrified by what he'd said that she didn't have the courage to breathe, much less speak or move.

"Mika," Pharax continued urgently, "Chloe's soul has gone on to where-ever souls go. Her body is already starting to rot. It has nothing to do with her—but it holds the key to what killed her. If I find out what killed her, then next time—and there will be a next time—I will be able to intervene before it's too late. I saved a boy with appendicitis. I'm sure I could have saved Chloe if only I'd known what the problem was. Maybe something was blocking the exit to the womb that only needed to be removed. Maybe the child lay wrong in the belly—that's what the midwife said. She said that the child lay crosswise and needed to be turned in the womb. But we couldn't do that from outside. Do you understand? The midwife tried to massage Chloe's belly, to push the child around, but it wouldn't move. She may even have killed the baby with her efforts. But if I knew enough about how the womb is positioned and the child in it, maybe I could help. Do you understand?"

Mika was frowning at him. She understood only two completely contradictory facts: that he wanted to mutilate a corpse and that he wanted to save women's lives. She shook her head ambiguously.

"Think of Kassia. She could be lying in childbed a year or two from now—young and full of hope and promise, a gifted singer, a poet, a young wife and mother of an unborn child. And just because no one can make the right cut, because no one knows how to remove the obstacle to birth, she could die in agony. Do you want that to happen?"

"Mistress Alethea is pregnant already," Mika remarked, because she still couldn't deal with what the surgeon was saying.

"What? At her age?" Pharax looked alarmed.

"It's bad at her age, isn't it?" Mika asked, watching him intently.

"It's dangerous—particularly after such a long barren period. Sandy is going on 15, I think." Pharax sighed and scratched at his fringe of red beard in distraction. Then he turned his blue eyes back on Mika. "Won't you help me?"

"How?" Mika squeaked out in a tiny voice, hoping that there was nothing she could do.

"I need to know where Chloe is buried, and then I need to come in the dark of night and dig her up. I need to take the corpse somewhere where I can open her womb and inspect it, and then I will put her back into her grave. I will only need to have the corpse a couple of hours, and I could inspect it almost anywhere—this mill would do." He gestured to the half-ruined building beside them. The roof had burnt off and the ceiling beams, still charred, had fallen into the naked room. Dead leaves and various forms of other natural rubbish collected in the corners. The native terracotta tiles were cracked by the falling beams and the heat of the fire. Weeds grew up between them, but the adobe walls were still largely intact. "I need a table on which to work, and lamps. Dexippos will come with me to carry the corpse and can bring a table, water and towels and can hand me my instruments, but someone has to guard the door. That's all I ask of you, Mika; show me where Chloe is buried and tonight, when I come, watch outside the door and warn me if someone is coming. Would you do that for me?"

Mika sat clutching her knees almost to her chin, not daring to look at the surgeon. She didn't like this at all, but she didn't know how to say no. She nodded and stood up, still avoiding his eyes. She gestured with her hand. "This way. She's not far."

Chloe had been buried only a short way from the mill under a tamarisk tree—symbol of youth and beauty. The last of its pink blossoms had just faded and lay in a browning carpet around the fresh grave. Pharax and Mika stood in silence before the freshly turned earth and low mound. Then Pharax turned and limped away on his crutch with Mika beside him. As they neared the main house he asked in a low voice, "Will you wait for me tonight in the mill, after the moon has set?"

Mika nodded, but she shivered inwardly.

Kassia was in a very bad temper by the time she went to bed. She hadn't had any time to work on her latest poem, nor had she been allowed to take her brother's hounds out for a long walk, because Sybil had insisted there was too much to do in the house. Sybil had taken her aside and lectured her on the fact that her mother was pregnant and should do absolutely *no* lifting or heavy work. "You have to take over from her as much as possible," Sybil insisted. "And keep your eye on her to make sure she doesn't over-do herself."

Kassia didn't mind that in principle. She, too, was concerned about her mother and didn't want to think of her doing anything that might endanger her health. But she didn't see why she had to spend every minute at home. When Alethea worked at her loom, for example, she sat in peace for hours. Plenty of time for a walk with the hounds. But no, Sybil insisted, while her mother was at the loom, she should check on Niobe. Niobe had been sent to clean the latrines hours earlier and had not been seen since.

Kassia found Niobe lying and dozing in the shade of a plane tree. She had spread her himation under her and plucked lavender from the bank of the stream, which she crumbled and held to her nose. The latrines had had some water poured down them and thrown onto the floor, but they hadn't been scrubbed clean. Kassia was furious. "What are you doing lying about? There's work to do," she admonished in a breathy, indignant tone.

Niobe started up and looked about herself for a moment. A faint frown then clouded her face as she started to get to her feet, brushing off her skirts. "I just lay down for a minute to rest. I'm not used to so much work."

"What work? You were sent to clean the latrines hours ago and you've done nothing at all!"

"That's not true," Niobe defended herself, her lower lip jutting out slightly in an expression of resentment. "I scrubbed the latrines and my peplos was soaking wet. I had to dry it out a bit in the sun. I'm still sick, you know, and the doctor says I should rest as much as possible."

Kassia had seen Pharax talking to Niobe earlier in the day, but that only made her more annoyed for some reason she couldn't explain. She frowned harder and declared, "You didn't scrub anything. You just threw water at it so you wouldn't dirty your dainty little hands. You probably held your nose the whole time. Do you think the rest of us are stupid!?"

The more Kassia thought about it, the angrier she got, and she ended up exploding at the innocent Mika as she prepared for bed that evening. "Why does everyone treat me like an idiot?" she raged in her breathy voice, kicking off her sandals. "Sybil tells me I mustn't let Mom do anything, and then insists she's in no danger at all. If she's not in danger, why should we coddle her? It's the same way Agesandros threw a fit and ordered me to withdraw my consent from the marriage to Anaxilas, but refused to name even *one* good reason. When I asked him why I shouldn't marry Anaxilas, all he could do was stammer a bunch of nonsense about not showing a sense of camaraderie with his fellow hoplites! What does that have to do with marriage? If he really wanted me to change my mind, why didn't he tell me the *real* reason he's against the marriage? I hate it when people treat me like am too stupid to reason! Mom acts as if I don't know what goes on in a marriage bed, and—Aphrodite's my witness—I've seen every farm animal mate, not to mention that Niko and Chloe weren't exactly *discreet* doing it out in the orchard by full moonlight! While Pharax treats me as if childbirth was none of my concern!"

The mention of Pharax and childbirth made Mika jump so guiltily that she jerked at Kassia's hair. The ill-tempered teenager cried out "Oouch! That hurt! Pay attention!"

"Yes, Kassia," Mika said miserably.

"Don't sulk. I have a right to complain when you yank at my hair like it was a weed you were trying to tear up by the roots."

"Yes, Mistress," Mika said more miserably still.

"Don't start *that* again," Kassia groaned, turning around on her stool to confront Mika. "What *is* the matter with you tonight? You're all nerves."

Mika jumped again, feeling as if she'd been caught in the midst of a crime. "Nothing," she protested like a child, but at Kassia's suspicious look, she crumbled. "It's Pharax," she squeaked out.

"What about him?"

"He's going to come tonight," Mika whispered, her eyes wide.

"Why should he come tonight? He was just here this afternoon. You can't mean he's—" Kassia was frowning. Mika was behaving like a girl who was afraid of something, but she couldn't imagine the Spartiate surgeon trying to seduce the disfigured slave—especially with the yellow stains all over her face and hands.

Mika was relieved to be able to share her terrible secret. She lowered her voice, but she gazed at Kassia with trust. "He's going to dig her up."

"What? Who? Why?"

"Chloe."

"Pharax is going to dig up Chloe?!" Kassia finally understood. Mika nodded. For a moment, Kassia was so shocked she was terrified. For a wild instant she remembered vague stories Sybil told of demons dressed as men who plundered graves or drank blood, but she shook the images away. Pharax was the least demonic person she had ever met. "Why?" she asked instead.

"He wants to cut her open and find out what blocked the birth," Mika repeated, still not really understanding.

"Of course!" Kassia jumped to her feet, and suddenly her heart was pounding. She was frightened and strangely elated at the same time. With a shiver, she recognized that his need to know *why* Chloe had died was so great that he was willing to do the unthinkable. She was awed by that dedication. "Tonight? You said he's going to come tonight?"

Mika nodded, bewildered by Kassia's tone of excitement.

"Did he say when?"

"He said I was to wait for him in the mill after the moon is down."

Kassia flung her arms around Mika and gave her a quick hug. "Thank you for telling me. Thank you!"

Kassia's enthusiasm soon infected Mika. She still didn't like the idea of what they were assisting, and as the darkness deepened she was more and more afraid of ghosts. But helping Kassia after all the rest of the household was asleep was like a privilege, too. Suddenly they were two conspirators—almost equals, certainly friends. And Mika had never had a friend before.

Kassia was visibly excited. She whispered instructions and darted about like a moth around a candle. She put on her sandals, then took them off, chose first one and then another—darker—himation. She told Mika to bring her two baskets and together they loaded them with towels, wine, bread, dried figs and cool water. "Oh, and bring a lamp as well—or should we take two? Yes, two. Oh, and do you think—no. All right. Let's go."

They tiptoed out of the courtyard and down the path behind the sheds and stables. The dogs barked happily at the scent of Kassia, but she called to them to be quiet. When one of the bitches persisted, Kassia went and let her out of the kennels and the hound trotted along beside her, thinking they were going hunting. At the mill all was still, and they sat side by side on the steps. Mika shivered and Kassia put her arm over the younger girl's shoulder. "There's nothing to be afraid of," she whispered. But secretly, Kassia was glad to have Mika with her. "Shall I recite some of my poetry?"

Mika nodded—anything to stop her from listening to the wind.

They had been waiting the better part of an hour when at last they made out a wagon moving slowly between the trees of the orchard. It stopped still on the drive, and a burly man clambered down and hoisted a table deftly onto his back. With this burden doubling him over, he came toward the mill. At the sight of the two girls, he only grunted and continued into the ruin. With a loud crash he let the table down, and both Mika and Kassia hissed out furiously, "Be quiet! You'll wake the whole household."

The man only grunted and went back to the wagon. Here Pharax had dismounted slowly and the two men consulted. Pharax turned toward the mill and waved. Mika ran forward and then when he started for the grave, she ran back to Kassia and whispered. "He said to watch the house and be sure no one comes out. If someone comes, I'm to whistle a warning."

Kassia nodded, satisfied. The girls watched long enough to see Dexippos bring a spade and start digging, but then they lost their courage and took refuge in front of the mill where they could watch the house, their backs to the sacrilege taking place behind them. Kassia looked very white in the darkness, Mika noticed, and Mika herself felt a strong urge to urinate when they heard the heavy tread and breathing of Dexippos.

Through the wall they heard Pharax say, "Put her down on the table."

"I didn't lug the thing here to dump her on the floor," the helot answered in a growl.

Pharax ignored the impudent tone. "Bring the light and my tools."

The helot went back to the wagon, grumbling the whole way. He returned with the doctor's satchel and a lantern closed on all sides with little sheets of metal. Holding hands, the girls listened as Pharax gave instructions to hold the lantern up. They could hear him sorting through his tools. Then there was only silence. The girls held each other and hardly dared breathe. Their value as watchmen was minimal as they strained to hear what was happening in the mill behind them. Once or twice Pharax told Dexippos to move the lantern this way or that. Once he exclaimed, "Ah! Look at that!"

Dexippos growled back, "I'd rather not. May Persephone have mercy and bear witness that I am a poor slave."

"All right," Pharax silenced him. "Just a few moments more."

They could hear the helot sigh audibly, and it seemed a long time to the girls clutching each other in the dark. Finally Pharax said, "That's it. Take her back and lay her carefully in the grave just like you found her." With a grunt the helot apparently took the corpse back into his arms, and Mika and Kassia closed their eyes until the helot with his burden was out of earshot. Then Kassia pulled her courage together and, picking up the nearest basket, she went around the side of the ruin and stepped inside.

Pharax had moved the lamp under the table to minimize the risk of discovery and was wiping his hands on a towel. He glanced over, sensing more than hearing someone in the doorway. Kassia had her dark himation up over her head, covering her blonde hair, so it was not surprising that as she was much the same build as Mika, he mistook her. "Is everything quiet?" Pharax asked.

"Yes, we brought you some bread and wine and figs. I thought you might—"

Pharax staggered backwards at the unmistakable sound of her high, breathy voice, which was so different from Mika's low foreign tones. He almost lost his balance in the process and grabbed the table. "Kassia? What are you doing here?"

"Why shouldn't I help? Did you find out?"

"What?" Pharax was still in a state of shock at being discovered here by Kassia with the blood still on his hands.

"What killed Chloe?"

"The midwife was right. The baby lay wrong—not head-first. I think," Pharax found himself explaining, too excited by his discovery to hold back in the face of such genuine interest, "the midwife's inept attempts to get the baby to turn actually killed it. Once it was dead in the womb, lying crosswise, nothing Chloe could do could save her."

"Then nothing could have saved her?" Kassia asked, and her voice was more breathy than usual, almost tremulous.

That made Pharax answer more decisively than was perhaps warranted. He didn't want Kassia to go away without hope. It was not arrogance that made him so decisive, but the fact that he wanted her to believe what he said next: "*I* could have saved her—if I could have opened her womb while she was still alive. I could have removed the baby—just as I would a sick organ or a spearhead—and sewn her up again."

Kassia shuddered visibly and clutched her himation closer around her. "But why do babies sometimes lie wrong?"

"I don't know," Pharax admitted. "It may have to do with the way a child is conceived. Depending on the position of—ah, the—" How had he got himself into a discussion of positions for copulation? "I don't know," he said hastily and looked down at his hands.

Kassia stepped deeper into the room and offered her basket to him. Pharax took the goatskin gratefully and drank a little wine. That soothed his agitated nerves a little. "It's late and dark and this no place for you, Kassia."

"Why? It's my mill and my kleros. If anyone shouldn't be here, it's you."

Her regal tone caught him by surprise and made him laugh briefly. "Don't be angry with me, Kassia." He hastened to dispel the frown of indignation that had at once settled on her delicate features. "You are right, of course. You hold my future in your hands. If what I did tonight came to the wrong ears—"

Dexippos was back with a grunt. "If you don't want to be discovered, then let's get the hell out of here," he urged practically. He turned his back to the table and deftly hefted it onto his shoulders to depart.

Mika was in the doorway hissing, "Hurry! I think I saw a light up by the house—from the mistress's room."

Pharax leaned and blew out the lamp at once. They all waited tensely in the dark.

"I'll go back and tell her I just went for a walk," Kassia decided. "Come on, Mika." Together they left the mill and Kassia whistled to the hound, who was sniffing about contentedly for rabbits or pheasants in the nearby oleander bushes. With Mika beside her, she walked confidently back toward the house.

Pharax gestured for Dexippos to put the table down and wait. He peered out of the doorway but could not see the main house. He heard Kassia raise her lovely, high voice and call, "It's just me, Mom. I couldn't sleep and went down to the mill to talk to Damonon."

He could not hear Alethea's answer, but he could imagine her dismay. What mother would be pleased to hear that her 18-year-old daughter communed with shades three years dead? What mother could rest easy thinking her betrothed daughter sought midnight trysts with ghosts rather than her bridegroom? But would she have preferred the truth? What was the truth? Why had Kassia come to such a grisly rendezvous unasked?

Pharax didn't understand it, but to his own discomfort, he realized it had increased his admiration for her. His feelings for her were already inappropriately strong. This wasn't good. He shook his head.

This wasn't good for anyone. He heard a bang, like a door closing, and then silence. He waited a little longer, but all was peaceful. He nodded to Dexippos to take up the table again, and they returned to the waiting wagon and drove away.

CHAPTER 12

Agesandros' battalion had made camp in a meadow beside a stream that was now only a narrow, splashing trickle. The grass of the meadow had long since gone to seed and the sun had parched the green out of it. Among the rugged limestone crags of the slope behind them, however, thistles, gorse and wild thyme bloomed. Goat and sheep dung was strewn plentifully amidst the grass, and they could hear the bleating of sheep and the clang of bells from the trails near the crest of the surrounding hills.

Campaigning Spartan military units had a set routine for setting up camp. The periphery was defined, sentries posted, and then weapons were stacked to be ready at hand. Meanwhile the attendants spread out in search of firewood while the cooks set up their tripods and got out their pots and pans. Meat, onions, oil, and other supplies were taken from the baggage train. The hoplites staked out their places around the cooking fires. They spread out their straw pallets and their himations. Then they fetched water, refilling their goatskins for the next day. Some stripped and washed themselves down. Some rinsed out their sweat-soaked chitons. Others just sat with their feet in the running water cooling off their soar feet. The cooks mixed wine with water in the kraters, and soon the first fires were lit and the sound of sizzling oil and the smell of smoke, grilling meat and fried onions filled the little meadow.

Once the fire was started, Leon set off again, following a goat track up the slope in search of a wild fig tree among the scattered vegetation. A light breeze rustled the bushes and the stunted oak, myrtle and ash trees. The clatter and voices of the battalion settling in for the night faded into the haze at his feet. "Are they real *Spartiate* hoplites?" a young voice asked out of seemingly nowhere.

Leon started and looked about himself in mild alarm. The voice was not itself threatening, but the fact that he could be taken by surprise unnerved him.

The shepherd boy emerged from the shadows of a grove of stunted ash trees. He was scrawny with a mop of unkempt hair and his bare feet were filthy. His arms and legs were scratched by briar and thorn. But it was the awe in the boy's eyes that made Leon feel taller and stronger.

"Yes," he answered. "We're the krypteia under Agesandros."

"Agesandros? Himself? Is *he* down there?" The boy peered toward the meadow below them.

Leon smiled and nodded.

"Nah! You're just putting me on," the boy decided, but his eyes were filled with a longing that it be true.

"He's down there. Do you want to meet him?"

The boy seemed to light up. "You think I could?" But then he changed his mind. "I better go tell my Dad. We live just over there." He pointed vaguely and Leon followed his finger, but could see nothing.

"You can't see the house from here," the boy explained, seeing Leon's look. "I'll go get my Dad." He started away.

"Wait!" Leon called after him. "I'm looking for wild figs. Do you know where I could find some?—For Agesandros."

"There's a pair of trees over there," the boy pointed a bit farther up the slope, but then added, "You don't really know Agesandros *personally*, do you?"

"Of course I do. I serve him."

The boy considered him and then shook his head, "Nah, I don't believe you. You're too young."

Leon laughed. "What good is an old attendant?"

"But *Agesandros*—isn't he a terrible master?"

"Why?"

"I mean—is it true he can fly?"

"Fly?" Leon laughed. "Of course not."

"But he can get from one place to another so fast, and they say he turns up wherever he's least expected. He can see in the dark, can't he?"

"No better than you or I," Leon assured the boy, smiling.

"But there must be *something* different about him. How else could he do what nobody else can?"

Leon didn't have a ready answer and the boy didn't seem to expect one. He turned and ran with the ease of the goats he tended along the narrow, rock-strewn trail.

Leon continued in the direction the boy had pointed. He found the fig trees and a few ripe fruits. These he carefully loaded into his satchel and then returned to camp. By now the men had collected around the cooking fires and were holding their bowls ready for their portions. They joked and grumbled among themselves, depending on their temper. Agesandros was standing with Ikarios, one of his company commanders.

"Where did you get to?" Agesandros asked with a scowl at the sight of Leon, who answered by extracting a fig from his satchel.

Ikarios laughed and with a nod withdrew. Agesandros and Leon went together to their cooking fire. Leon opened a folding stool for Agesandros, and then fetched their mugs and bowls from his knapsack. Agesandros dipped their mugs into the krater while Leon held their bowls out to the cook, who filled each with a portion of stew. Leon settled himself on the dried grass beside Agesandros' stool.

It was nearly dark now in their little valley, although the sky overhead was streaked with purple clouds against a luminous blue dome sprinkled with stars. The cooking fires were burning bright across the little meadow, making the surrounding shadows darker. Agesandros was about to speak when a sentry gave a cry of challenge, and Agesandros at once lifted his head and looked in the direction of the cry. Although the voices that followed the challenge were relaxed and peaceful, Agesandros did not really turn his attention back to his meal. He ate with his ears cocked.

A few moments later they saw men coming toward them, and Agesandros set his meal aside and got to his feet. There were three strange men and the shepherd boy, surrounded by curious hoplites and attendants. As they came within the light of Agesandros' fire, it was possible to see that two of the strangers were weathered, but not bent, by a life in the sun and wind, and the third man was still in his prime. The lines on the faces of all were deep, their eyes alert. They were obviously ill at ease among the hoplites and their attendants.

Episthenes, the sentry, indicated Agesandros and announced, "That's the commander, Agesandros."

The men bowed their heads respectfully and shuffled their feet uneasily, while the boy gazed in wonder. Leon grinned at him, and the boy's eyes shifted for a moment to Leon before fixing again on Agesandros.

"Master Agesandros," one of the men started, "I'm Xenarkes, son of Prytanis, and this is my brother-in-law Cheirisophes and my son Talmides. We're helots keeping the herds of Diagoras, son of Ikkos."

Agesandros nodded, satisfied that these were honest helots.

The youngest man held out a burlap sack. "We brought this for you," he announced, and at a gesture from Agesandros, Leon stepped forward and took it from the shepherd. He glanced inside. It was full of goat cheese.

"Thank you," Agesandros replied without knowing the contents. "Is there something I can do for you?"

The three shepherds looked at one another. Then finally the spokesman cleared his throat and announced, "Well, Master, we—we wanted to tell you about some thieves—"

His brother-in-law ribbed him and hissed, "Rebels."

"Rebels, thieves," the spokesman frowned irritably, "what's the difference? They've killed or stolen three of our kids and took a she-goat as well, and just the other day they attacked a merchant on the road and left him naked, gagged and bound. And now my woman says she's seen strange men lurking around the spring, just waiting to pounce on a girl that suits their fancy. She's afraid to send our girl for water, seeing that she's 13 and getting pretty."

"And my wife's frightened, too," the younger man announced. "She says one of these men came down to the house asking for fire, but he really just wanted to see what we had in the house and leered at her like she weren't a decent woman—even though he could see the baby right there."

His father waved him silent with an irritated frown. "They robbed an old shepherd from up the valley of everything he had and left him with his head half broken in."

"Have you seen them?" Agesandros asked.

"Only from a distance," the brother-in-law answered, adding, "They're a rough lot."

"Are they heavily armed?"

"Oh, yes, they all have bows and javelins and swords—an ugly lot."

"Are the men armoured?"

All three men shook their heads.

"What dialect do they speak?"

"We haven't talked to them."

"But your wife did," Agesandros reminded them, turning to the younger man.

He nodded, but added, "She didn't say nothing about them sounding funny."

"How many of them?" Agesandros asked next.

"A dozen at least," the spokesman answered.

"And they've built themselves a little fort of rubble and wood overlooking the road," his brother-in-law added.

"They attack any traveller that looks weak. Just the other day some people came looking for a relative who was missing. He must have been killed by these men," the youngest continued.

The spokesman scowled and waved his son silent. "We don't know that for sure, but it's clear they feed themselves by theft. All the shepherds hereabout have lost livestock, and then there was the old man we just told you about."

"This fort they've built. You can lead us to it?" Agesandros inquired.

"Oh yes." They all nodded vigorously.

It was agreed that the youngest of the three men would return at dawn and lead Agesandros to the fort, which was reportedly only about three hours away.

When the shepherds were gone, Agesandros' deputy, Klearchos, a man 15 years older than himself with greying hair and beard, remarked in a low voice. "Are you sure we should waste time with this? It sounds like nothing but a bunch of thieves to me."

"Agreed. But why shouldn't we help loyal helots by eliminating this band of thieves that frightens and preys upon them?"

Klearchos shrugged. Their mandate was tracking down Messenian rebels and destroying their bases and supporters, but on second thought Agesandros was right. If they didn't help the loyal helots when they could, they might well turn rebellious. This operation could be put down to "preventive action."

So in the morning they found themselves winding their way over the goat tracks in single file. Agesandros kept near the front of the leading company, and Leon kept close beside him. When he had first joined Agesandros, he had lacked strength and stamina in his legs and had barely managed to keep up with the baggage train. After two years with Agesandros, he had no trouble keeping up with his master. Today it was particularly easy because he was dressed only in a chiton with a leather pilon cap on his head while Agesandros, in anticipation of a clash with the robbers, was in armour. Not that Agesandros wore full hoplite panoply on these irregular campaigns. He wore only a leather breastplate and carried a wooden training shield slung on his back, but he had his greaves on his shins and wore his crested helmet shoved back so that the nosepiece rested on his forehead.

By mid-morning they had reached the alleged fort. From a distance, it was difficult to be sure the piles of white rocks jutting out on a spur of land were man-made. At most the structure looked like a ruin, but the shepherd insisted that this was where the thieves returned after their raids. The merchant they had found bound and gagged claimed to have seen them both descend from and return here—loaded with all his wares.

Agesandros and Leon, with a number of others, went down onto the main road and looked up at the alleged fort. From the road it was completely invisible, obscured by a large, naked bluff that jutted out over the narrow road and by the dense vegetation around that bluff.

Agesandros consulted with his company commanders. Ramphias was for surrounding the fortress and attacking at once. They had enough men for this task, and they were fully armoured hoplites with little to fear from thieves possessing only a rag-tag collection of weapons. Ikarios pointed out, however, that the bulk of the thieves were probably absent at this time of day. It would be better to wait until night. Klearchos reminded them that they were rather obvious. It was hard to hide an entire battalion in this landscape. It was therefore decided to position the bulk of the battalion on the road, as if they were a regular unit in transit from Laconia to Messenia, while Agesandros took a platoon and selected light troops on reconnaissance.

By now the sun had reached its zenith and the day had become oppressively hot. Sweat soaked the sides of the armoured hopliltes and crawled in their hair and beards. Agesandros found his own enthusiasm for the task waning rapidly. They had plenty of time. They could do the reconnaissance later when there would be more shade.

"Smoke," one of the men pointed. Although difficult to see at first, there could be no doubt that smoke was indeed smearing the sky just above the pile of rocks they had come to think of as a fortress.

"Someone is there."

"Probably just the women-folk."

"The smoke's not coming from the fortress itself, but more to the left," the platoon commander pointed out.

Agesandros looked again and had to agree. The smoke appeared over the fort only because it was being blown on a southerly wind. Agesandros' stomach was growling and he wanted to take a mid-day break, but the smoke might no longer betray the real position of the robbers' nest if he waited an hour or two. He decided to split up his troops, sending the lightly dressed auxiliaries on a wider reconnaissance while he and the hoplites continued more or less straight toward the smoke, using the forest for cover as best they could.

The air was heavy with heat, and there seemed to be an inordinate number of insects in this forest. They slogged their way forward, checking at every opportunity for the tell-tale smoke to be sure they were still on course, but it was often lost from view as long as they were in the forest. Roughly two-thirds of the distance to the "fortress," the trees started to thin out. Another hundred yards ahead of them was a barren, open slope littered with loose rocks and patches of low-lying scrub-brush, thorn and thistle.

Agesandros was already calculating he would have to leave the platoon here, watching the approaches to the apparent robbers' nest, when from the left ahead of them the auxiliaries burst into the open. They were evidently making a dash toward the fortress.

Agesandros cursed loudly. He hadn't given orders to attack, just to circle around and investigate the lay of the land.

But already the leading man had fallen with the sickening, abrupt and backward motion of a man hit by a missile of some kind. The next man beside him cried out and bent over, clutching his thigh. The rest of the men crouched down with audible shouts of alarm. Some managed to find cover behind larger boulders, and those nearest the forest edge on the top of the spur of land from the south made a dash for the trees.

Agesandros gave the order for the platoon to form into a narrow phalanx. He pulled his shield off his back and slipped his left arm into the brace fitted on the inside. He pulled his helmet down over his face and drew his sword.

Around him the other members of the platoon were doing the same. In a few seconds they were ready and waiting tensely. Agesandros glanced at his men; only their eyes shifted inside the helmets, which now masked their identity and feelings. He glanced again to the slope ahead of them. The line of rubble and the wafting smoke waited, as silent and apparently dead as before. No cries, shouts or threats were hurled from it. The air was still and oppressively hot.

Agesandros hesitated. They would be attacking uphill and across rugged, uneven ground. They had no archers or javelin throwers to force the defenders to seek cover. They would be exposed to whatever missiles the enemy had from the time they came in range. But they were all in armour, their vital organs protected by leather or bronze, and they had broad shields.

On the slope ahead of them, one of his own auxiliaries twitched in obvious agony. His arms clawed at the earth and his legs flailed as if he wanted to get them back under himself, but couldn't. Agesandros gave the order to move forward, and they advanced as a compact unit out of the cover.

It was hard to keep close formation on the rugged ground. Little gullies and boulders forced the phalanx to part now and again, but they were almost abreast of the wounded auxiliary when the first arrow whistled into the earth just ahead of them. With a shout, Agesandros ordered the phalanx to lift their shields up, and the drill of a lifetime served them well. As if the formation were one man, the shields came up, clacking together. They advanced in the shade of their own shields and the thin rain of arrows clattered harmlessly on the wood.

As they passed the wounded auxiliary still writhing in the dirt to their left, Agesandros cast him a glance. It was Leon. Blood was soaking his chest and an arrow shaft stuck out of his throat.

Agesandros almost faltered, but the discipline of 20 years of drill was overpowering. He kept step with the advancing phalanx, up the slope toward a wall that was manned by maybe a half-dozen archers.

In another 20 minutes it was over. The hoplites advanced, immune to the increasingly frantic defensive efforts. The defenders could not hear how heavily the hoplites were breathing, nor see that they were drenched in their own sweat from the efforts of advancing up the steep slope in unison. All they saw was the implacable, invincible advance of an armoured unit as if it were a single beast. The defenders' nerves gave out before the phalanx even reached the foot of the wall from which they were firing. First one, and then another, and finally all the rest fled. The phalanx mounted the wall in a ragged line, by no means as perfect as it should have been, but the robbers were in flight and did not take advantage of the daylight that briefly appeared between the shields of the attackers.

Once over the wall, the attackers found themselves in a clearing with a pit for a fire over which a pot hung. Some low wooden sheds were constructed off to one side; chickens fluttered about in agitation; a sow with piglets grunted in a muddy pen. The fleeing robbers were scrambling over the opposite wall. Agesandros gave the order to break formation and pursue. About half the men still had the breath and energy to give chase, but a few of the older men stopped where they stood to catch their breath. Agesandros ran forward, but he was not a particularly good sprinter and a handful of men were ahead of him over the opposite wall. By the time he was over it, three of the robbers had been spitted, one was still struggling with a hoplite who seemed determined to take him alive, and two others were half-scrambling, half-rolling their way down the slope, their escape certain.

Satisfied, Agesandros turned and made his way back to Leon. By the time he reached him, several of the auxiliaries were already clustered around. They had laid him out and the arrow was no longer sticking out of his throat, but Agesandros was greeted with the words, "The arrowhead's still inside, sir. The shaft came out headless." The speaker held up the bloody shaft as he spoke, and Agesandros glanced at it with a grimace. Typical cheap arrow; the heads often came off. He went down on one knee beside Leon.

Leon was conscious and he moved his head when he felt Agesandros' shadow fall over him. Blood was streaming over his chest, bright and glistening. His throat worked and the blood flowed faster. "Sir—"

"Don't try to speak," Agesandros ordered. He slipped one hand under Leon's head to hold it up off the rocky ground, and his eyes searched for other wounds. There was only the one, but it was enough.

"Tell—Niobe—"

Agesandros snapped his head to look at Leon. Was that what this was all about? The insubordinate attack, which had cost him two casualties, was nothing but an attempt to win the heart of a stupid slave-girl? Agesandros wanted to take Leon by the shoulders and shake his brain back into place. Just because that worthless, conceited hussy had made Leon feel he was beneath her, Leon had tried to be a hero.

Someone handed Agesandros a cotton cloth, and he put it to the base of Leon's neck. It seemed hopeless. They couldn't possibly staunch the bleeding without cutting off his windpipe or forcing the arrowhead deeper into his throat. Agesandros looked around at the faces crowding in. Not only did the auxiliaries look down at him, but many of the hoplites as well. Leon was well-liked.

"We have to get the arrowhead out," Agesandros announced.

"We better get him back down to the battalion. Maybe Sostratos can help him." Sostratos was the closest thing they had to a surgeon. He was helot barber and medic in one.

Someone brought a blanket from the robbers' fortress and they managed to get Leon laid out on it. Then someone else found a ladder and they converted this into a stretcher. Various men took turns carrying the improvised stretcher and Agesandros walked beside it. Beside him, the experienced veteran who had commanded the auxiliaries tried to explain that the attack wasn't his fault; Leon had insisted. Leon would have attacked alone if they hadn't agreed to support him. From the spur of land on which they approached, they had been able to see right into the little enclosure behind the fortress. They had seen that there were just a handful of men squatting around a cooking fire. Leon had been possessed with the idea of attacking. They couldn't talk him out of it.

Agesandros couldn't stomach any more excuses. "Shut up."

"But, sir," the man whined, "I only wanted to explain—"

"What? That you aren't fit to command even a slave hardly old enough to be an eirene? Get out of my sight before I hit you."

The man seemed to melt away instantly.

Their approach had been noted, and they were met by Klearchos and Ikarios before they actually reached the battalion camp. "What happened?" Klearchos asked, while Ikarios took one look at Leon and went for Sostratos.

"The auxiliaries circled around and saw into the robbers' nest. Only a half-dozen men were squatting around a cooking fire, and they took it into their heads to attack at once."

"Alone? Without orders?"

Agesandros nodded grimly. Leon made a blood-choked, slurping sound. "We can talk later," Agesandros told Klearchos.

Sostratos loomed up on the other side of the stretcher. "Put him down right over there—in the shade," the barber-medic ordered.

"The arrowhead is still inside," Agesandros greeted him. "You have to get it out."

"Let me see," the helot answered, bending over the patient.

Agesandros stood waiting. Around him the crowd changed. The auxiliaries and hoplites who had been on the raid dispersed to drink, eat and tell what had happened. Others came to see how Leon was.

Sostratos probed with fingers, gently turning Leon's head to one side and then the other. He kept shaking his head. Finally he went back on his heels and looked up at Agesandros, shaking his head. "I can't get it out, sir. I don't have the tools or the skill. It's in too deep. If I try with my fat fingers, I'm more likely to shove it deeper—maybe cutting off his wind or his vocal cords. I can't see well enough and I don't know enough to cut him open more without killing him."

Agesandros just stared at the barber. Leon was bleeding to death before his eyes, and there was nothing he could do?

"We could have him back in Sparta by nightfall," Ikarios remarked, nodding toward the main road beside them. "Pharax might be able to save him." Ikarios had been in Agesandros' old platoon and had been with him when Pharax was wounded and lost his leg.

"Can we carry Leon that far?" Agesandros asked.

"Of course we can carry him. The question is whether he'll survive it."

"That's what I meant," Agesandros retorted.

"He's certain to die here."

"I can smear his throat with honey and bind it," Sostratos offered. "That will both disinfect and slow the bleeding somewhat, but you'll need to keep his head raised a little."

Agesandros looked around and sent two of the men standing about to fetch the other company commanders. Ikarios meanwhile was saying, "Send a runner to Pharax. He can wait at Alethea's kleros."

Alethea's kleros was just off this road and a good five miles closer than the city.

Ramphias and Klearchos approached. "I want to send him back to my kleros. Maybe Pharax can save him. And the other wounded man as well. We can send them both back."

The company commanders nodded agreement, but Klearchos added, "Take him back yourself, Agesandros. You'll need to replace him for the rest of this season at least. We can remain here and mop up the rest of the robbers. At least half of them weren't even there. If we're lucky, their comrades won't be able to warn them, and we'll catch them as they come in."

Agesandros looked at Ramphias, who just nodded agreement.

Agesandros did not waste any more time. They were at most 15 miles from his kleros, most of it downhill. If they set off at once they could be there by sunset. He could be back with the battalion by this time tomorrow. Or, given that he had to find a replacement for Leon, it could take another day, but no longer than that. He nodded and ordered Sostratos to bind up Leon as best he could and get him onto a proper stretcher, while he fetched Leon's knapsack in which all their personal things were stuffed. Taking this on his own back and slinging the shield over the knapsack, he set off with a party of eight, four hoplites and their attendants, enough to all take turns bearing the stretchers.

CHAPTER 13

Leon was still alive when they finally reached the turnoff to Alethea's kleros, but he was no longer conscious. Torches burned a welcome at the foot of the drive and flanking the entrance to the gate, indicating that Ikarios' runner had warned Alethea of their impending arrival—and Mika was waiting for them, too. Her white chiton stood out in the darkness of the orchard. She darted out, her face as white as the wool of her chiton. "Master? Is Leon still alive? Will he make it?"

"He's alive. Is Pharax here?"

"Yes, Master. He's been here since dinner."

Agesandros nodded. He was tired as they all were, but this was also home, and it felt good to be here despite the circumstances. After the dust of the road, it was particularly good to smell the moist earth of cultivated orchards. And tonight he would sleep between clean sheets with his soft, sweet-smelling wife in his arms....

Mika was gazing at Leon, and her face was so strained and her eyes so wide with worry that Agesandros laid a hand on her shoulder and offered the only comfort he had. "He's made it this far. If Pharax can get the arrow-head out...."

Mika looked up at him, tears glimmering in her eyes. As always, she was candid to a fault. "But what if he can't? Master, it's so unfair!"

Indeed it was, Agesandros thought bitterly. Leon's only words so far had been for Niobe, and it was Mika waiting here with tears in her eyes.

The helots poured out of the kitchen and a murmur of subdued greetings filled the evening air. Agesandros nodded in acknowledgement, but led the stretcher-bearers up the steps and under the colonnade into the main house. As they moved along the side of the peristyle toward the sickroom, Agesandros heard Sybil call, "They're here!" from the gallery.

In the next instant, Kassia and Pharax and Alethea poured out of the andron, where they had evidently been waiting. Kassia rushed forward to look at Leon, gasping at the sight of him, and looking up with frightened eyes asked, "Is he....?"

Pharax was behind her, and he reached automatically for one of Leon's wrists, feeling for the pulse. But Agesandros was staring at his wife.

Alethea managed a weak smile, but she felt very self-conscious, and Agesandros wasn't making it any easier on her. He was staring at her as if she were a stranger—or deformed into something hideous.

"Why didn't you send word?" Agesandros at last got out, still staring at her as Pharax took over Leon, leading the stretcher-bearers the last few yards to the little sickroom at the back of the peristyle. Alethea shrugged, and Agesandros covered the distance between them. One hand went to her swollen belly, the other to her cheek. She looked strained and exhausted. There were dark circles under her eyes, and the skin around her mouth sagged as he had never seen it before.

"Aren't you pleased?" she asked, her voice tight. She was going to die to give him a son, and he didn't even look happy.

"I don't know. Are you all right?" And with that question everything was all right again. He cared more for her than for a son. Why had she doubted it? If sons had been that important, he would have married a younger woman.

"I'm tired all the time," she admitted, not daring to tell him that it was more her fear of death that wore her out than the weight of the burden in her womb. She added in a soft voice, reaching out a hand to his face, "It's good to see you." The smell and feel of him even calmed her fears a little. His strong, hard hand lay on her growing belly and it seemed to tame the deadly beast inside, turning it back into the innocent child it was. For the first time since she had admitted to herself she was pregnant, Alethea wanted the baby she was carrying. She wanted to give Agesandros a son.

She lifted herself on tiptoe and kissed him on the lips. But then she remembered the reason he was here. She looked toward the sickroom. "How badly is Leon hurt?"

Agesandros still stood with one hand on Alethea's swollen belly and the other resting on her shoulder, but he followed her gaze toward the sickroom. He pulled his lips back in a grimace. "He attacked without orders—all for the sake of that slave-girl Niobe."

"Niobe? She's not worth his little finger," Alethea declared.

"I know," Agesandros sighed. The stretcher-bearers were coming out of the sickroom, and they could hear Kassia promising them dinner and wine. She indicated the andron to them, and announced to Alethea as she swept past that she would go to the kitchen and inform Phoebe of their guests.

Agesandros followed her with his eyes. "What's got into her?"

"Oh, Sybil thinks I can hardly take a step anymore, and Kassia has taken over the household. You must be as tired and hungry as your men," Alethea realized, and she slipped her arm around his waist and guided him into the andron.

Pharax reported that he had extracted the arrowhead, even before the men had finished dinner.

"Will he live?" Agesandros asked, sitting up sharply and daring to hope for the first time.

Pharax, who was still on his feet, scratched at his beard with his left hand and poured wine for himself with his right. "I don't know. I've bound up his neck and the bleeding has almost stopped. That honey may well have saved his life, as it both stopped the bleeding and may have drawn out the worst of the poison already. But he still has lost a great deal of blood, maybe too much. Nor can I be certain the wound won't fester despite the honey; if there was too much filth on that arrowhead, it will infect his neck from the inside. If it swells too much, it will cut off his wind and he'll choke to death. Nor can I be absolutely sure I didn't damage his vocal cords in the process of removing the arrowhead. Last but not least, there's the problem of feeding him. I don't think he should be given solid foods for several days, maybe even a fortnight. He'll have to be kept alive on broth."

"That's not a problem, surely," Agesandros protested. Ever since he had seen Leon with the arrow sticking out of his throat, he had been thinking about him as if his death were inevitable.

"A problem, no, but it will be hard for him to get his strength back. I'd say his chances of recovery are at best 50/50. Much will depend on his own will to live."

Pharax gave Mika very careful instructions on what to do. Mostly she was just to watch Leon, listening to his breathing and taking his pulse regularly. If either changed significantly, she was to ring a little bell he gave her. He would come at once, since a bed had been set up for him in the armoury which lay just beyond the sickroom. If Leon came to himself, Pharax said he would most probably be very thirsty, and Mika was to help him drink. "But only very little and very slowly," Pharax warned, as Mika gazed at him wide-eyed and frightened. "You must hold his head up with your left hand and tip the water into his lips with your right. Are you sure you can manage? I only need to lie down for a few hours. You can wake me anytime."

"I can manage," Mika insisted stubbornly.

Pharax took a deep breath. There really was nothing he could do for either patient at the moment. The man with the leg wound lay snoring on the other bed, contentedly drugged by neat wine. His leg wound had been cleaned and sewn up.

It made most sense for Pharax himself to get some rest in case his skills were needed later for Leon or another patient, but he felt a little guilty leaving Leon entirely in Mika's care. She was very young for one thing, had no training, and she was clearly very attached to Leon. That meant her nerves were strained almost beyond what they could take—but it also meant she would do her utmost.

"If you find yourself falling asleep, just ring the bell and I'll come relieve you," Pharax suggested at last. Mika nodded, but her lips were set as if she would rather die than admit she was too tired to watch over Leon.

Mika was glad when the surgeon finally left her alone with Leon. In her mind, the other man didn't count, since he was sleeping soundly. She waited, sitting on her hands until she heard Pharax close the door of the armory. Then she got up and went to the bedside. They had removed his bloodstained clothes and the bloody sheets from the operation. He lay naked, bedded in fresh white linen, his neck bound in cotton bandages showing only a small patch of blood. Mika reached out and gently touched his arm, but drew back at the feel of it. It was cold and clammy. In terror, she held her breath and forced herself to hold his wrist. She closed her eyes, and then let out her breath with relief. The pulse was there, faint but steady. She put his hand back on his chest and bent to kiss his forehead. "You have to get better, Leon," she whispered. "You have to. I love you, Leon. Do you hear? I love you. And when you're well, you'll see. The warts are going away. The master surgeon has found a cure, and they're much smaller and some are gone away completely. Oh, Leon, don't die! Please don't die!"

After a bit, Mika brought the chair directly beside the bed. Now she could sit and hold his wrist in her hand, feeling his pulse. As long as she could feel that, she told herself, everything was all right. She felt as if her heart kept pace with the faint flutter between her fingers. Then she thought that the pulse felt like the wings of a butterfly. She closed her eyes and pictured a pretty butterfly. She pictured being pretty, if only the warts continued to fade. Of course, with Leon here, she wouldn't want to wear the ugly yellow ointment. But it was working. If she used it just a few more months…. The pulse! She held her breath and felt for it with every nerve of her body. Yes, it was still there. She let out her breath.

From the window opening toward the walled orchard behind the house came the cheeping of the crickets. It was a peaceful sound, and Mika was tired. She stood and started pacing about the room to keep herself awake. Every third round, she stopped to feel Leon's pulse. Each time, she held her breath in terror for a second, and then relaxed. Once she risked running to the bath opposite and splashing her face with cold water to help keep herself awake.

Gradually the window became a rectangle of grey, and from outside came the first trilling of a blackbird. A little breeze came in and lifted the hairs on Leon's forehead, which had at last dried of sweat. He stirred and a low sound came from his throat—half moan, half whisper.

Instantly Mika was beside the bed, wide awake. "Leon? Leon? Do you want something? Are you thirsty? I have water here." Already she was reaching for the shallow kylix, which she could tip on his lips with one hand.

Leon's eyelids fluttered, but then he went still with a deep sigh.

Mika put the kylix back on the table and brushed his hair from his forehead with her hand. Suddenly she was seized with panic that life had left him with that last sigh. "Leon?" She reached for his wrist almost roughly, but the pulse still beat. Maybe even stronger than before.

Mika breathed out again, and she replaced his hand and stroked his forehead. "Leon, I'm right here. I'm watching over you. If you need anything, I'm right here."

His head shifted slightly. His eyelids moved but did not open. His lips parted and he breathed out "… -iobe."

Niobe was sorry to hear Leon had been wounded and sincerely hoped he would recover, but she didn't see that there was anything she could do to help. After all, the surgeon was here, Mika and Sybil were both helping him, and she was left with all the extra work of having Agesandros home with eight of his men and the two patients and the surgeon. All the bloody linens from the two wounded men had to be washed, and of course the latrines were over-used and Kassia chased Niobe out to clean them with malicious eagerness. Niobe knew that Kassia only did it to humiliate her. She could just as easily have sent Glauce or Eunice, but Kassia always insisted that Niobe do this most repulsive of tasks.

She thinks it makes her a queen, Niobe thought hatefully, as she tried to swish out the latrines with water while holding her breath. Niobe hated Kassia more than anyone else in the world. She had stolen Anaxilas from her, and now she did everything in her power to humiliate and demean her. She's jealous of me, Niobe told herself again and again. She must see that if I had my hair and could dress in fine clothes, I'd be prettier than she—not to mention that I know how to please a man as that Amazon never will!

Niobe went to the stream and settled herself on the bank, her feet in the cool water. Then she bent over and plunged her hands in up to her elbows. After a few minutes she felt the rushing water had at last washed the last fumes of the latrines away, and she lay back and closed her eyes to the sun. It was really too warm to lie in the sun—it would burn her skin and make it even darker than it already was—but it was pleasant for the moment with her feet in the cool stream.

It was almost 15 months since she had been captured, she calculated. More than a year of slavery, humiliation and abuse. The tears welled up in her eyes just thinking of it. She was just 17 and unless something happened to rescue her, she would be a slave all the rest of her life. She would be like Sybil—fat, gouty, arthritic and single, living only to serve others. Like Kallisto, said a tiny, faint voice in the back of her head, but she frowned angrily and waved irritably at a fly buzzing about her face. With Kallisto it had been different. Kallisto had loved her like a daughter. Kallisto had wanted to serve her. Kallisto had never looked on it like a burden. And why should she? She had lived in a royal palace, and had often eaten the leftovers from the royal tables. She had had a good bed at the foot of Niobe's own and she had always had good clothes—sometimes even things the concubines and wives no longer wanted. No, Kallisto had had nothing to complain about, since she had had Niobe for a mistress rather than a spoiled teenager like Kassia!

The buzzing fly was irritating her too much and Niobe sat up sharply, waving her arms furiously at the persistent insect. She couldn't even lie down for a few minutes without all of nature conspiring against her!

Angrily, she got to her feet and looked about for some other escape. If she went back to the house, she'd just be given more work to do. But her stomach was growling. It was almost lunchtime. At least all the other men of Agesandros' battalion had dispersed to their own homes this morning. Even the man with the leg wound had limped off on his master's arm to spend the night at their own kleros. Only poor Leon, Pharax and Agesandros were still here. They didn't make that much extra food to prepare. Niobe decided to risk going back to the main house.

She soon regretted it. First Kassia wanted to know what had taken her so long, then Phoebe made her churn butter, then she was sent to help Mika (to *help* her own slave!) with the pressing. Mika hadn't said one civil word to her since their fight the night Chloe had died. Today Mika narrowed her runny, red eyes at her, but didn't even say hello, much less thank you.

It was late afternoon before she was finished with the pressing, and by then Agesandros was back with a strange young man he had engaged to replace Leon for the rest of the campaign season. The newcomer moved warily and kept away unwanted inquiries with a dark, brooding look. He had a square face covered by an unkempt beard and thick lips. He was anything but handsome, and his taciturn nature underscored his unattractiveness.

By dinnertime, Glauce was whispering to Eunice and Mika that Agesandros had picked him up at the jail. "He was sentenced to death for murdering his wife's lover," Glauce whispered excitedly, "but Agesandros said if he proved himself, the sentence would be commuted to slavery."

"He'll just run away at the first opportunity," Eunice countered.

"What opportunity? All the other attendants will be watching him. Besides, he's still in love with his wife and wants to go back to her."

"How do you know all that?" Phoebe demanded with a snort. "You made it up."

"No, I heard the master telling the mistress!"

"What? Eavesdropping when you should have been working? I should have known," Phoebe snorted angrily.

"I wasn't eavesdropping. They were talking normally."

The conversation was cut short by the newcomer's arrival. The helots sat down together for their dinner and with tentative questions attempted to draw the newcomer out, but he just grunted, frowned and then told them bluntly, "Stop interrogating me! You ain't got no right to. It ain't none of your business where I come from. I'll be gone tomorrow."

So they stopped trying to get to know him and withdrew, offended, into their own circle. After dinner, the men settled down around the hearth while the women did the cleaning up. Sybil ordered Mika to bed. "You didn't sleep all last night!" she declared in a scolding tone. "You go up to bed right this minute."

"But Leon—"

"You let someone else look after Leon. He's going to be here for some time to come. Now go on! Do as I say."

"Shall I sit up with Leon?" Glauce offered at once.

"You've got the washing up to do," Phoebe interceded angrily, "and the master will be wanting something when he gets in." Agesandros had taken the hounds and gone hunting with Kassia after he'd brought back his new squire.

"I'll look to Leon myself," Sybil announced, adding vindictively to Niobe, "and *you* could give Glauce and Eunice a hand with the washing up rather than sitting on your hands as usual!"

No sooner was the washing done, however, than Kassia and Agesandros came clattering into the courtyard amidst a pack of panting, happy hounds, carrying a doe. The successful hunters had to be greeted, of course, and everyone poured out into the courtyard with hastily lighted torches to admire their kill. Suddenly, at this advanced hour of the night, there was more work to do. While Orsippos and Hygetos together set about cleaning and gutting the doe before hanging the carcass from a meat-hook, Lampon had to get the dogs fed. Kassia and Agesandros were hungry and thirsty, too, not to mention that they were both bloody from their kill—especially Agesandros, who had carried it home over his shoulders. While Phoebe, Glauce and Eunice fussed with getting a meal ready for the hunters and served wine, Mika helped to clean up Kassia with a sponge and wash her feet and legs in a basin as she excitedly told her mother about what had happened.

Kassia had never looked so much like an Amazon as now, Niobe noted bitterly, wishing again that Anaxilas could see her with blood smeared on her arms and her feet covered in mud and even dung. Her hair was wind-blown and her face flushed from sheer blood-lust, Niobe noted with disgust. And this unnatural, boy-like creature wanted to be a queen? It was so absurd, it would have made her laugh if she hadn't been so tired.

"What are you standing around gawking at?" Phoebe asked irritably. "Give the master a hand in the baths."

Niobe started. Helping a *man* bathe was something she had never done before. Men generally went to the public baths or if they bathed at home, then with the assistance of their wife. But of course, the precious "Lady" Alethea couldn't be expected to do something like that, since she was 6 months pregnant. Niobe thought resentfully of the way she had been made to scrub floors and carry water when she had been in the same way. Resentful still, she followed Agesandros to the baths. His shoulders were soaked with deer blood that was starting to dry and flake from the trickles it had left on his upper arms. He had sweated hard, too, and his feet were no less filthy than Kassia's had been.

With distaste Niobe took the filthy chiton from him as he pulled it off over his head, and with an unconscious grimace she picked up the loincloth he stepped out of. She put both pieces of clothing in the waiting wicker hamper and started mixing the water in the tub, her back to his nakedness. When the tub was filled, she backed away, still not looking at him, and said, "I'll fetch fresh towels and a clean chiton for you."

Agesandros ignored her as he settled into the tub and started splashing the warm water over his shoulders to get the blood off.

Niobe collected the towels from a cupboard in the next room first, and then, taking an oil lamp, went upstairs to the master bedroom to get one of Agesandros' clean chitons. Here all was still and silent, since the rest of the household was still busy with the hunters or their kill. Because she did not serve Alethea regularly, she had to open more than one chest looking for Agesandros' chitons, and she couldn't resist looking at Alethea's peplos and himations while she had the chance. Alethea had some very beautiful things, even if she did not wear them often. But Niobe didn't really have time to try them on as she would have liked. She knew someone would notice she had been gone and start harassing her again. So she took one of Agesandros' chitons and returned to the baths.

It was only as she re-entered the baths and saw Agesandros lying back comfortably, letting the steaming water relax him, that the idea overcame her. Agesandros! How had she failed to notice it before? Agesandros was the most virile man she had ever encountered. A good ten years younger than the ageing, grey-haired Aristomenes and no mere youth like Anaxilas. Agesandros had the scars of manhood and the firm, tanned body of youth, and magnificent golden hair and a thick, curling beard, and—by all the gods—this was the man she *should* have been married to.

Aristomenes had run away *from this man*, abandoning his young and gentle bride to rape and slavery. With sudden vividness she remembered the way Agesandros had looked that night, flanked by Anaxilas and Leon. His simple armour had been humble beside Anaxilas' splendour, and yet he had cast the prince in his shadow. He should have claimed me, Niobe remembered with a cry of inner outrage. It was his right. Remembering how his eyes had scanned the captives and then come back to focus on her, Niobe was certain that he *would* have claimed her—if only Anaxilas hadn't come between them. Anaxilas had said he wanted her and Agesandros had bowed to the wishes of his prince. He had wanted her, she was sure of it. His eyes had looked on her with burning desire. She had been frightened of it—naïve and inexperienced as she was. She had preferred Anaxilas—then. Not anymore.

She set the chiton and towels aside as silently as possible. Agesandros had not heard her enter. He was dozing in the bath, oblivious to the world. She set the lamp down on a shelf and untied her belt. She laid her belt on the shelf beside the lamp and then pulled off her peplos and the chiton underneath. Naked, she advanced toward the bath and stood looking down at him. The water was still and clear. She could see his beautiful body through it, barely distorted by the soft surface undulations of the cooling water. She hesitated only a moment longer, and then she stepped into the bath and sank down on top of him with a sigh.

Agesandros had drifted off to sleep. He woke with a start, disoriented to find himself in a bath at all, much less with a strange woman pressing up against him. It took him several seconds before he even remembered who she was, and then he shoved her aside angrily with a growl and stood straight up, water cascading off his body to splash on her. "What the hell do you think you're doing? You filthy slut!"

Niobe's elbow and hip had been bruised by the violence with which he'd flung her aside, against the tiles of the wall. But it was the rage in his face that frightened her. It was worse than all the brutal lust of Lampis and his sons.

As Agesandros moved from instinctive self-defence to conscious understanding of what had happened, his rage grew. "You worthless tramp! You whore! Leon nearly killed himself to win your respect, and you can't even wait to see if he recovers! I should have you flogged. I should—!" Agesandros couldn't think of any punishment bad enough for what she had done. He could still picture vividly the way Leon had twitched in agony with the arrow sticking out of his throat. He saw him again on the stretcher, drenched in blood and pleading, "Tell Niobe …"

"You filthy, stinking Messenian whore!" Agesandros climbed out of the bath red with rage. With his back to her, he grabbed a towel to rub himself dry.

"You don't understand," Niobe whined from behind him, sobbing audibly. "I was only doing what I was ordered to do. Since the mistress can't service you, she said that—"

Agesandros had her by the throat before she could even finish. "Don't lie to me, whore!" His eyes, green and gold and glinting with fury, were just inches away from hers. "Don't you ever lie to me about my wife or I'll kill you!" For a moment he even considered doing it. Just closing his fingers harder and holding them shut until this worthless, spoiled creature was no more bother to anyone. But he had never killed a woman, not deliberately anyway. He flung her backwards so that she splashed back down into the water, her hands going to her bruised throat, her eyes wide and her face white with speechless terror.

He grabbed up his chiton and pulled it over his half-wet body and buckled his belt around his waist. At the door to the baths he stopped and turned back on her. He could see she was trembling so violently that she shook the water of the bath, creating little waves that caught the dim light of the lamps, making it dance with light. "You call yourself a king's daughter, but you act like a bitch in heat. Worse: you think that men and women consist of nothing more than the parts hung between their thighs. Well, maybe that's all *you* are, but there are others of us with other parts. Get dressed and go back to the helots' hall. I'll decide what to do with you before I leave in the morning."

Agesandros did not tell Alethea about what had happened until they were in bed together. His indignation was undiminished and he kept saying, "Leon did it all for her! He nearly got himself killed and he might yet die! Pharax says he's not out of danger. Think what it will do to his will to live if he finds out!"

"That's why we can't punish her or send her away," Alethea said very softly.

"What? Are you mad? You can't let that slut stay in the household a day longer! She's like a bitch in heat! She's probably been doing it with all the helots—" He broke off; Alethea was shaking her head. He frowned. "Are you so sure?"

"Fairly. She thinks herself too good for helots—or slaves. You—you are an officer, a hero, the man who defeated her husband. She thinks you're good enough for her, but not the others."

Agesandros let out an oath (which Alethea preferred not to understand) and sank back onto the pillows beside her. He stared at the ceiling. "This is the thanks she gives *you* for rescuing her from that horrible helot you told me about—trying to seduce *your* husband. Don't you feel any rage towards her?" Agesandros looked over at his wife in utter bewilderment.

Alethea smiled and stroked his face. Then she kissed him. "Rage? No. I feel—" She paused to analyze her feelings and after thinking about them a moment continued, "I feel very, very lucky to have a husband that could turn down such temptation—with me in this condition."

Agesandros sat bolt upright in outrage. "Temptation? You think I could be tempted by a bitch like that? She's nothing compared to you!"

He lay down again and pulled Alethea into his arms. "Alethea, Alethea, she's so far beneath you. She's—let's not even talk about her. You can't seriously think I might have been tempted?" He sounded genuinely offended.

Alethea twisted around in his arms to give him a reassuring kiss. "Not anymore." They fell silent in each other's arms. Agesandros shifted his hand to Alethea's belly. He hesitated and then asked a little timidly, "Is everything all right? Pharax—"

"What?"

"Pharax said I'd, ah, over-done things."

"What's that supposed to mean?"

"He thinks it's twins."

"What does he know? He's a man."

Agesandros didn't answer.

Alethea held her breath, trying to hold the thoughts back, but she couldn't. The midwife had said the same thing. She didn't have the strength to give birth to even one child. She could never bear two. It was too much. All her fears, suppressed since Agesandros had arrived the day before, were instantly back with her.

Agesandros, sensing her tension, held her tighter and kissed the top of her head. Agesandros knew how much it had hurt her that Eury-anax, her first husband, had not come to her even when Niko was born and she, an inexperienced young bride, thought she was dying. He hastened to reassure her. "It's going to be all right, Alethea. I promise you, I'll be here. I don't care if we're storming Mount Ithome. If you send for me, I'll come at once—even if I have to ride a damned horse to get here in time. I'll be here. I promise."

Alethea nuzzled deeper in his arms, but she didn't dare turn to face him. If she did, he'd see that she was crying. It was simply unbearable to love and be loved so much—and know you are going to die soon.

PART III
A SPARTAN QUEEN

SPARTA, LACEDAEMON

IN THE 2ND YEAR OF THE 30TH OLYMPIAD
THE 8TH YEAR OF THE SECOND MESSENIAN WAR

CHAPTER 14

Only very, very slowly—just as Pharax had predicted—did Leon start to recover, although by no means did he start to regain his strength. On the contrary, he seemed to be fading and shrinking before their eyes, but he was conscious for longer periods of time and his large dark eyes followed whoever was in the room. Mika, Sybil, Glauce and Eunice all took turns taking care of him. Even Phoebe brought him the soups and stews she made extra for him, scolding him into eating more when he tried to turn away or shook his head. "I made this just for you, young man!" she admonished, scowling. "Do you think I have nothing better to do than cook things for you to turn your nose up at? I went to a lot of trouble to make that soup and you are going to eat it all—every last drop!"

Leon didn't have the strength to resist her, so he ate. But despite Phoebe's best efforts he didn't have much appetite. And he said so little that they at first thought he had lost his voice entirely. Finally he started whispering—here a "thank you" to whoever was helping him or a timid request for water. At some point he asked if Agesandros was gone, and he looked shaken when told that Agesandros had been gone for over a week and had a new squire.

Alethea visited him at least twice a day, and it was to her that he made his first real attempt to speak. His voice was scratchy and raw and seemed lower than before. "Mistress," he managed.

Alethea broke into a smile and took his hand, exclaiming happily, "You *can* talk! I will have to tell everyone! Pharax will be so relieved. He was feeling miserable for having done a bad job!"

"Mistress, has something—happened—to Niobe?"

The smile froze on Alethea's face and her thoughts ricocheted about in her head wildly. He had noticed she did not visit him. Would it be better to lie, to pretend she was ill or had been sold? If only she *had* sold the worthless bitch! Then she could pretend she was dead. Or should she tell Leon that she had had some kind of accident and sell her at once? But surely Leon would find out? He would never forgive her for lying or selling Niobe. Alethea was not good at lying. Even now, Leon seemed to read her thoughts, and he turned his head away and closed his eyes.

What excuse could she possibly give? "She—she gets faint at the sight of blood. She was so distressed when they brought you in—"

"Never mind," Leon croaked out in his ruined voice, without opening his eyes.

Alethea stood helplessly looking at him, and couldn't think of a thing to say. She wanted to tell him that Niobe wasn't worth a single thought. That he should forget about her. The other maidens of the household were all better, each in her own way, and if he didn't like them there were scores of others on other kleros to choose from. She wanted to tell him what she thought of Niobe, but she couldn't. It would hurt him too much. So she let it be and tiptoed out of the chamber with a heavy heart.

By evening, his condition had already taken a sharp turn for the worse. Phoebe reported that she couldn't get him to eat no matter how she badgered him, and she wasn't angry when she reported this to Alethea, she was frightened. "He's not just refusing; he doesn't seem *able* to eat. He seemed to want to, but his eyes rolled back in his head and he sank back as if he was too weak."

They sent for Pharax at once, of course, and by the time the surgeon's apprentice arrived, Leon was drifting in and out of consciousness, much as he had at the very beginning. Only now he was weaker from the almost two weeks in bed. With Alethea, Kassia, Mika and Phoebe crowding the little chamber behind him, Pharax took Leon's pulse, checked his eyes and tongue, and probed carefully around the wound. Of course he found nothing.

Alethea went in search of Niobe. When she at last found the slave-girl, she was rubbing oil into her skin as she got ready for bed. The way Niobe tried to hide the oil suggested to Alethea that she had stolen it, but she had no time to deal with that right now. "I want you to come down to the sickroom as once," Alethea ordered in an unusually harsh tone of voice.

"Why? Has something happened?"

"Leon is dying—for love of you, you stupid girl! If you'd show him just a trace of kindness, maybe he would at least *try* to live!"

Niobe started, but then she took the himation she had woven for herself with left-over wool from Alethea and draped it carefully and elegantly as she had been taught in her father's home. Next she paused to brush out her short hair and fix it with a little tortoise-shell comb she had "found" somewhere. At last she followed the impatient Alethea down into the sickroom.

Here the others—even Mika—backed away from the bed to let her approach Leon. Niobe approached at a leisurely pace with a smile playing triumphantly on her lips. At last they had recognized she was something special; at last they looked up to her.

She went to the bed and called softly, "Leon? Leon? It's me, Niobe."

Mika saw the way Niobe's name and voice penetrated to Leon's unconscious, and he stirred at once. His spirit strained back to the living. His head turned toward the sound of her voice. His lips moved, apparently forming her name in hope.

"Leon, do try to get well," Niobe urged in a casual tone of voice, as if speaking to an acquaintance with a head cold. "You're the only one in the whole household who has ever been kind to me," she added with more feeling. "You're the only one in all of Lacedaemon who understands me," she declared most emphatically. Niobe was speaking for the others, not the patient, and she was enjoying it. "I'm sure they'll be much meaner to me if you die and there is no one to defend me."

Leon stirred again; his eyes fluttered open but couldn't seem to focus. He was looking for Niobe, but she didn't lean nearer to make it easier for him; that would have spoiled the regal pose she had struck, with her head high and her himation so carefully arranged.

Leon was fighting for consciousness and almost made it. Certainly he managed to whisper "… iobe," but then his eyes rolled back and he went still again, as if he'd sunk back into unconsciousness.

Niobe smiled triumphantly. "See?" she asked the others as she turned to face them. No one dared challenge her. At the door she paused to cast Mika a little, sneering smile, and couldn't resist remarking, "Did you think he would recover for the sake of a toad like you? You've probably only made him sicker, hanging your ugly face over his bed day and night."

Mika was too hurt to defend herself. She cried out in pain as if she had been struck physically, and it was Kassia who slapped Niobe across her face with all the fury Mika should have felt. Alethea, shocked by her daughter's reaction as much as Niobe's remark, hissed, "That's enough!"

Kassia turned on her mother in outraged protest, "Mom! You heard what she said—"

"Shhhhh!" It came sharply and simultaneously from both Pharax and Alethea, while Phoebe took Niobe roughly by the wrist and dragged her out into the peristyle. They could hear Phoebe berating her and Niobe whining in protest as Phoebe drove her back to the helot's quarters.

"Mom—" Kassia started again.

"Shhhh!" Alethea answered, "see to Mika."

Kassia wanted to protest—but the sight of Mika, who had crumpled up onto the floor, her face in her hands, was too much for her. She went down on her knees beside the slave-girl and threw her arms around her. "Don't cry, Mika. It's not true. You know it's not true! If anyone has kept Leon alive, it's been you—every bit as much as Pharax. No one has cared for him more or better than you!"

Mika sobbed harder, managing between gasps to say what they all knew. "But—he—doesn't—want—me! He wants—her! Just b—because she's—p-pretty."

"Kassia, take Mika outside and fetch her wine," Alethea directed softly but firmly.

Kassia understood and nodded. She got back to her feet and then bent and pulled Mika up. Mika was too shattered to resist. She let her mistress lead her out of the chamber and into the walled orchard behind the house.

Alone at last with Pharax and the patient, Alethea cast the surgeon's apprentice a glance. He was holding Leon's wrist and watching him closely. Alethea approached the bed. "Is there nothing we can do?" she asked.

Pharax shook his head and sighed. "You did the best you could. It was a good thought. Niobe *did* help him at first—if only...." Pharax sighed. Leon had at some level of consciousness heard the entire ugly little scene. Pharax had seen him flinch when Kassia slapped Niobe, and then he had rolled his head back and forth and groaned as if in pain.

Alethea leaned over Leon and put her hand on his forehead. "Leon? Can you hear me? Listen! I'm going to set you free." The thought had only just come to her. It was all she had left to offer. If he were no longer a slave, maybe Niobe would not look down on him so much. And maybe the thought of freedom would give him something live for. "Did you hear me? I'm going to free you."

"Mistress?" His eyes opened wide and he focused on her with complete clarity. She was leaning directly over him, making it easier for him.

She was so relieved to meet his lucid eyes that she broke into a wide smile and took both his hands in hers. "Do you understand, Leon?

From today forward you're a free man." She was utterly unprepared for Leon's response.

"Don't throw me out!" he croaked out, and his eyes were full of terror rather than gratitude. "Please! I have nowhere to go! I have nothing! What will become of me!?" His voice scraped and scratched, and his hands clutched at hers so hard he was hurting her.

"You'll be free, Leon," she tried to reassure him. Somehow he had misunderstood her. "You'll be free and can buy Niobe—"

"Please, Mistress, please!" His face crumpled up and he started crying like a child. "Please don't send me away. Please don't throw me out. Please, please, let me stay. I'll do whatever you want. Just don't throw me away."

Alethea abruptly saw the six-year-old clinging to his mother as *she* sold him into slavery. She knelt on the floor beside the bed and despite her swelling belly, she managed to pull Leon into her arms. She guided his head to her breast and held him to her, letting his tears soak her bodice as she rocked back and forth as best she could. "How could you think I'm throwing you away, Leon? I'm not sending you away! I would never do that. This is your home. No one is ever going to make you leave. Oh, Leon!" She looked over his head buried in her breast as he sobbed and clung to her and gazed helplessly at Pharax. Somehow everything she did went completely wrong.

The small of her back was aching and the circulation to her feet was being cut off; so when the worst of Leon's crying was past, Alethea managed to drag herself off the floor, turn herself around and sit on the bed all without letting go of Leon. She took Leon's head onto her shortened lap and laid one arm across his chest, and with the other hand she wiped away the tears still trickling from the corners of his closed eyes. He was clearly trying to get control of himself. He held his breath to stop from sobbing, and then gasped for it all the more desperately when he could hold his breath no longer. In between, his body shuddered, almost as if from a chill. She was losing him. Alethea held him closer and stroked his face as the tears started to spill out of her own eyes. She started talking softly.

"Do you remember? The first year you were here? Trying to mow the hay? We had lost all our livestock in the raid, but I was obsessed with getting the hay harvest in—and no one had the courage to tell me I was mad. You'd never used a scythe before and got horrible blisters on your hands. But you were ashamed to show me. Niko had to tell me about them. Why was that, Leon? Why are you afraid of me? Nobody else is—certainly not Phoebe and Niobe. Mika was at first. When she tried to burn the warts off her hand, she was afraid to show me the damage she had done to herself. Sybil had to come to me. But she's learned to trust me, I think....

"She's a good girl, Leon; I'm so glad you sent her to me. It's a comfort to think she'll be here when the baby—or babies—come. I can picture her playing with them and kissing away their cuts and bruises. It's a comfort to think she'll be here to help. Phoebe's not the kind, you know, and Sybil is too old now to keep track of small children. Kassia will be gone by the time they're born, and Eunice is being courted by a young man. Did you know? He's an apprentice to the blacksmith. He'll be able to support her. So soon I'll have to replace her, too.

"And the last thing I need is another captive like Niobe. She just can't accept that she's a slave now and has to do her share of the work. She tries to make poor Mika do her work, ordering her about as if Mika were still beneath her, and Mika already does more than her share.

"Mika's a willing worker and she's bright, too. People don't notice that at first, but when you think she didn't speak a word of Greek three years ago, you have to admire how quickly she has mastered it. And not just that, but she's learned to do a hundred different tasks she never did in her wild homeland. Most of all, she's curious. She asks questions about everything—now that she knows she'll get an answer rather than a blow to her ear, as other masters gave her.

"She was sold by her own uncles. Did you know that? And then sold again and again by impatient masters and mistresses who never gave her a chance—just because she was ugly and often didn't understand what they wanted of her.

"Agesandros is having trouble with his new squire. He sent word the other day...."

Pharax slipped out of the sickroom and limped out toward the walled orchard. It was dark now, and the crickets were cheeping and screeching in an insistent chorus. On the steps down into the orchard Pharax paused, taking in with admiring eyes the sight of the orchard bathed in moonlight. He spotted the two maidens sitting side by side on a marble bench. As he passed the little house altar, he could smell and see a puddle of wine in the shallow bowl and guessed that Kassia and Mika had made an offering for Leon's life. As he approached, they both looked up at him wide-eyed.

Mika's face was still swollen and streaked red from crying, but she was composed. Kassia had never looked more beautiful. She'd pulled her hair out of its bonds and combed it with her fingers out of her face, so it fell freely about her shoulders catching the moonlight. As always, her beauty intimidated Pharax, and he faltered.

"Is he going to make it?" Kassia asked, bridging the gap created by his own diffidence.

"I—don't—know. But if anyone can save him, then it is your mother." Pharax shook his head in wonder. "The skill of the greatest surgeon on earth is nothing compared to the healing she does for the soul."

"It was *her* stupid idea to bring Niobe down—" Kassia protested, but Pharax raised his hand to silence her.

"It wasn't a stupid idea at all—it worked. At least initially. It was the sound of Niobe's voice and her presence which brought him back from the very edge. That Niobe is so unworthy of him is not your mother's fault—"

"But she knows Niobe is a selfish bitch—"

"Yes, but your mother couldn't know that Niobe'd be so stupid and vindictive as well. Kassia—" Pharax was standing before her and trying not to notice that his heart was beating faster and his hands sweating just from being near to her in the dark—"Your mother is such a kind, caring woman that she isn't *capable* of anticipating something as heartless as what Niobe did tonight. It just didn't occur to her that someone could say something that cruel—much less in a sickroom with a young man fighting for his life."

"So why did she get mad at *me*? I only gave Niobe what she deserved."

"Niobe deserves to be branded in the middle of her forehead—something to teach her that beauty isn't everything! But that's not the point. Your mother rightly feared that the scene would have a negative impact on Leon. He'd only barely started wanting to live, and then you attacked the girl he loves—"

"I only did it because of—"

Pharax held up both hands. "I know." He turned to look at Mika. "Are you all right, Mika? Your face is much better. You know that, don't you? The ointment *is* working this time. If you keep using it another month or two, I'm sure all the warts will be gone."

"Thank you, Master Surgeon," Mika replied, her eyes swimming in tears, "but it doesn't matter any more. Leon doesn't care if I have 100 warts or none at all. He only cares about Niobe."

"I don't think that's true, Mika," Pharax declared solemnly. "It may be true that he has fallen in love with Niobe—undeserving as she is. But he cares what happens to you, too. He came and thanked me for helping you, you know. He said to me it was so unfair the way people made fun of you for something that wasn't your fault." Pharax risked a glance at Kassia. "When he thanked me for helping you, Mika, I finally understood why Kassia once said Leon and I were similar. At the time, I admit, I was a bit offended—being compared to a slave and a runaway at that. I've learned, meanwhile, that it was a compliment."

Kassia looked down at her hands, embarrassed. Maybe it had been a compliment once, but in the meantime *she* had come to value the surgeon's apprentice more and more.

Pharax directed his attention to Mika again. "Leon does care about you, Mika, and I know he was very happy to have you looking after him. I think, in fact, that you should help the Lady Alethea now. She shouldn't stay up all night, not in her condition, but she won't leave Leon unless you're there to take her place and watch over him. Will you do that? Even knowing that Leon loves Niobe and would rather it was her watching over him?"

The tears spilled out of her eyes, but Mika held her head up and wiped them away angrily as she stood. "Of course I will. I'd do anything to help him or the Lady Alethea." She started back toward the house, but halfway there she paused and turned back on the Kassia and Pharax to add defiantly, "But don't expect me to be nice to Niobe!"

Usually Agesandros brought his battalion back to winter quarters only after the rest of the army was home, so no one was really expecting him yet. The first snows had dusted the peaks of the Taygetos and then faded again in the heat of the day. Thunderstorms swept down the Eurotas valley day after day, tearing the leaves from the trees and leaving huge puddles on the roads and in the orchards. The streams were suddenly alive again after all but disappearing in the summer drought. Now the snow on the tips of the Taygetos grew and stayed, then slowly spread downwards into the forests. Throughout the city people started to prepare for the return of the army, but the advance guard had not yet wound its way through the narrow passes and started down into Lacedaemon when the sight of a chariot smashing through the puddles of the driveway and lumbering up in front of Alethea's kleros took the household completely by surprise.

The massive chariot—with elaborately carved wagon, bright painted wheels and four high-strung horses—creaked to a halt and then rolled backwards as the horses fussed and flung their heads about, almost rearing. It was Agesandros' cursing at the driver that gave him away. After staring with an open mouth for a moment in disbelief, Glauce rushed into the courtyard shouting, "The master! The master is home! In a chariot!"

The other helots poured out of their workplaces—Mika and Sybil from the washhouse, Eunice and Phoebe from the kitchen, and Hygetos from the workshop. Lampon and Orsippos were in town at the market and Leon was out tending the livestock, but the household helots stared in confusion while Glauce continued into the main house, still shouting her message.

Niobe was listlessly sweeping the walkway of the peristyle and looked up with a start. Agesandros was the last person on earth she wanted to see. She hated him even more than Kassia, and at once she put the broom aside and looked for a place to hide. Kassia leaned over the railing of the gallery and called down to Glauce, "Are you sure?"

"Of course I'm sure! He's out front in a huge, four-horse chariot."

"No, I'm not. I'm right here," Agesandros announced from the peristyle. He turned his helmeted head up to Kassia. "Where's your mother?"

Alethea was already coming out of the women's hall. She could not run to him, only waddle awkwardly. She was so big with child that she was certain now that it was twins, just as Pharax had said months ago. Agesandros' eyes, too, went first to the prominent belly, but then he settled on her face and took it in his hands to kiss her before pulling back and saying loudly with a glance up to Kassia, "Come see what I've brought you! Come!"

He was like a little boy in his eagerness, and with his arm around Alethea's waist to help propel her forward, he rushed her back out through the courtyard to the waiting chariot. The rest of the household already stood about staring in wonder at the chariot and the four fretting and sweating horses—from a respectful distance. On her mother's heels, Kassia let out a little gasp and exclaimed in wonder, "They're beautiful! They must be racehorses!" She started forward toward the horses, but the driver shouted in alarm, "Stand back! They kick. Stand back!"

Indeed, the nearest of the four had flattened his ears and turned his head toward her maliciously. Kassia hesitated, but Agesandros was declaring proudly, "I took it off an Elisean ambassador!"

"Oh, Agesandros! You didn't!" Alethea was horrified. Violation of the immunity of ambassadors was a sacrilege. It would bring terrible punishment from the gods. Her hand went instinctively to her unborn children.

"What?" He looked at her innocently.

"Violate the immunity of an ambassador. Please—"

"Of course not. The ambassador is fine—except for having sore feet from walking home, perhaps. I only took his chariot. I knew how much you've missed having one since the raid. And I thought this would suit you." Agesandros was so proud of himself and his prize that Alethea didn't have the heart to tell him the truth: this heavy, over-sized, gaudy chariot was useless to her. It would get mired in the least amount of mud, was too wide for the narrow back alleys of the city, would be unmanageable in tight corners, and was utterly useless for driving across fields as she had done with the light, hardy vehicle her father had given her. Worst of all, it needed four horses, and all four of the magnificent beasts fretting at the reins were clearly high-strung stallions. The kind of horses, as Kassia had quickly recognised, that one kept for racing. They would eat huge amounts of oats and hay, require constant care and exercise and were apparently dangerous as well. Alethea had never driven more than a two-horse chariot and none of the others had done even that.

She lifted her face to give and Agesandros the kiss he expected and happily returned, and then she walked carefully around the chariot. As she appeared to look with admiration at the details, Alethea tried to think of some way of breaking the news to her husband gently. The only practical thing to do with this representative state chariot was to give it to one of the two kings in exchange for a practical vehicle and two sensible, manageable horses, preferably geldings.

At this point Leon emerged from the yard behind the kleros and stood at the fringe of the crowd, evidently uncertain of the reception he was going to get from Agesandros. He was well enough now, but had not yet recovered his full strength. Nor had he consciously spoken to Agesandros since he had flagrantly disobeyed orders, led an ill-conceived rush at the robbers' nest and nearly got himself and the others killed. He was very nervous about how Agesandros would treat him now. Moreover, not having met the man Agesandros had taken in his stead, he also looked nervously at the driver of the chariot, thinking that this was the man who had replaced him. The man was too evidently competent for Leon's comfort. He waited, mentally discarding one greeting after another, and almost hoped that Agesandros wouldn't notice him.

Agesandros did. He at once took in that Leon was on his feet, but looked weak and pale. Worse, however, he looked uncertain of himself and sober. Agesandros liked him better when he was smiling and at ease.

"So there's the insubordinate, lovesick youth who abandoned me to the miserable ministrations of a sullen, untrained criminal," he greeted Leon, scowling.

Alethea caught her breath and looked over in alarm, as protective of Leon as she would have been of one of her sons. But Leon smiled at Agesandros in relief. If Agesandros complained about his successor, he had a chance of being restored to his old position. He quickly replaced the first smile of relief with a solemn expression, and advanced to face his punishment. "I'm sorry, sir. It won't happen again."

"What? The insubordination or the being lovesick part?"

"The insubordination, sir."

"Pity. That's the part I can deal with better."

Alethea finished her "inspection" of the chariot and slipped her hand into Agesandros' elbow to draw his attention away from Leon and the unspoken, unpleasant topic of Niobe. "It's really very impressive, Agesandros. I don't think even our kings have something as fancy as this. In fact, it's so—well—ostentatious—that I'm not sure if it would be appropriate for me to drive about in it. People might think I'm being arrogant. You know how sensitive people are. Displays of wealth are scorned nowadays, and to drive about in a chariot finer than either of the kings—"

"It's a prize of war. I took it in Sparta's service. Besides, Kassia is going to be our queen." He cast his stepdaughter a glance that seemed to contain grudging acceptance of her decision.

"That's not the point. It could make people jealous, and that's dangerous." Alethea leaned her head on his naked shoulder and remarked, "There are times when the pretence of humility can reap more than an insistence on one's rights. If I were to *give* this chariot to my uncle, for example, I'm sure he'd be delighted to have something better than the Agiads."

"But you've been complaining about not having a chariot for as long as I've known you," Agesandros protested, disappointed that his gift had not been as well received as he had expected.

"Indeed; but I can't drive a four-horse, and nor can Kassia."

"That's why I kept the driver, too," Agesandros announced smugly, indicating the man still holding the reins.

Alethea spared the man a glance. He was no longer a youth and he had a scar on the side of his face and along his right arm, probably from an accident. But he met her gaze with almost a sneer, and he was very well dressed with long hair. She didn't like the arrogant way he looked back at her. Another slave like Niobe, she thought with an inner groan, one who evidently thought himself better than his masters. "That was very considerate of you, but—can he do anything besides drive? There are so many repairs that are needed, I was hoping we could afford a slave with building skills—"

"Better," Agesandros announced, laying his arm across her shoulders again and pulling her to him. He could see she was worried, and he was so pleased to be able to reassure her. "We took over over 100 slaves, and the other two men who were my portion—big, strong Ethiopi-ans—I plan to give to Leoprepas in exchange for him building a proper house on my kleros. But we can have any repairs you need to have done here taken care of first." Leoprepas was a perioikoi who made his living from construction.

"That is an even better gift than the chariot, Agesandros," Alethea declared seriously. "With children on the way, it's not right to plan to stay here forever." What she meant, but couldn't say, was that Agesandros could not stay on Niko's kleros after she was dead. He would have to raise his children on his own kleros. Alethea pretended her concerns were more frivolous, adding, "It will be wonderful to build our own house the way we want it."

Anaxilas was only two days behind Agesandros, and Anaxilas wasted little time after his return before calling on his intended bride. He too rode up in a fine, if less extravagant, chariot, and he had gone to much trouble with his appearance as well. He had spent the morning at the baths getting cleaned, oiled, shaved, and having his finger- and toe-nails filed and his hair trimmed. He was darkly tanned from the sum-mer campaigning, and the polished bronze of his breastplate and greaves contrasted brilliantly with his dark skin. His muscles bulged on his arms and thighs, and at the sight of him stepping off the chariot

Niobe felt her pulse quicken. But he did not see her in the shadow of the colonnade; his eyes were focused like a famished man's on Kassia.

Kassia had been warned. Anaxilas had had the courtesy to send a slave with word that he would be calling in the afternoon. She had—unbidden—bathed and changed into one of her prettiest peplos. She even accepted the necklace and bracelet her mother offered her. Mika had been called to help her put up her hair. By the time Anaxilas arrived, she looked much as she had on the day he had noticed her on the stage. Ten months had done little to her face, but there was an indefinably greater maturity to her stance and greater dignity to her movements as she came forward to welcome him.

Kassia had a kylix of wine to welcome her bridegroom, but Anaxilas tossed it aside impatiently, remarking, "You're all the wine I need." And in the next second he had pulled her to him and covered her mouth with his hot, ardent kiss. Kassia wasn't prepared for that. She had dressed and prepared herself to greet a prince, not a lover. His grip was tight and hard and frightening. No one had ever held her like this before. No one had ever kissed her like this before. This had nothing to do with the tentative, shy, tender kisses she had exchanged with her cousin on the steps of the mill.

She resisted instinctively, and just as instinctively Anaxilas held her tighter. Niobe, watching from the shadows of the colonnade, smiled with satisfaction. She had known it. Kassia would never please Anaxilas, but he would tame her before he discarded her and looked for his pleasure elsewhere. He was too proud not to break her first.

At last Anaxilas had had enough, and he drew back with an expression that seemed to waver between annoyance and pleasure. "I would have expected more enthusiasm after such a long time," he told his bride disapprovingly.

"We hardly know each other!" Kassia answered indignantly, still trying to catch her breath and not only pulling back but wiping his kiss off her lips.

"That's what I'm here for," Anaxilas answered with a grin, "to get to know you."

"By smothering me so I can't even get a word out?" Kassia countered sarcastically.

"But I love every word—no matter how silly—that comes out of that sweet, moist mouth." Anaxilas was focusing on her moist, pink lips and meant exactly what he said. "Better still, I love the lips when no sound comes out of them at all."

Kassia frowned. She hated nothing more than having her person ignored in fascination with her body. She turned her head aside so he couldn't stare at her lips. She looked toward the house, hoping for rescue from her mother or Agesandros, but Alethea had not left her loom when the word came of Anaxilas' arrival and had furthermore forbidden Agesandros from leaving her side. "The two young people have to get to know one another," she had declared firmly. "They can't do that with you and me following them about. Nor is your scowling at Anaxilas going to do anything but make him resent you more. We will stay right here," she said, returning her attention to the loom.

"What are you looking for?" Anaxilas asked, following her gaze and frowning. If Agesandros came out now and tried to interfere, he'd kill the man, he thought to himself.

"Nothing. Let's go somewhere and *talk*," Kassia suggested, trying to regain her composure. This was the man she was going to marry very soon. She *had* to like him. "Tell me about the campaign. Where were you? Did you have many battles?" Kassia was leading him out of the courtyard, back down the drive into the orchard.

Anaxilas was delighted. He decided that her resistance had been caused by *fear* that Agesandros or her mother or the slaves might be watching her. Clever girl! She wanted to get him into the orchard where no one would see them. So he smiled broadly and fell in beside her while answering her questions readily.

As he spoke of where he had been and what the vanguard had done, Kassia started to relax a little. She had been unnerved by his kiss, but she told herself she should have been flattered. She tried to concentrate on what he was saying and ask questions that would help her to know him better. She paid little attention to where he was gently guiding them, until he stopped and announced, "This is a good place."

"What for?" she asked innocently, looking about. They were in the middle of the orchard. The ground was littered with the yellowed leaves of the near-naked mirabelle trees. As far as she could see, there was nothing special about this place.

Anaxilas smiled and said, "To do what we came here for."

"Talk?" she asked, cocking her head.

"You are enchanting!" Anaxilas cried out, and was about to enfold her in his arms again and kiss her when he had a better idea. "Wait!" He pulled his scarlet himation off his shoulders and spread it onto the ground. "Come, let's lie down."

The word "lie" set off alarm signals to Kassia. Why should they lie down to talk? "Why?"

Anaxilas couldn't be bothered arguing with her any longer; he was too hot. So he wrapped his arms around her and pressed his kiss on her lips until her neck creaked. She struggled more violently than before, and Anaxilas—annoyed by so much coquetry—used an old soldier's trick. He abruptly let go of her, and while she still gasped for breath and tried to step back, he bent and sliced at her knees from behind. She fell with a painful thud on to her buttocks, and Anaxilas grinned down at her.

Kassia looked up at him, flushed with fury. "How dare you?!" she spit out furiously, already struggling to get back onto her feet.

Anaxilas was quicker. He knelt astride her and pinned her to the ground, holding her shoulders down with his hands. "You are irresistible when you're angry, do you know that?" He kissed her again, using the weight of his chest to hold her in place so he could pull up her skirts with his hands.

Kassia had gone to the Spartan agoge as a girl, and she had an elder brother. She brought her knee up hard and fast, and while Anaxilas doubled up in pain and grasped his outraged genitals, Kassia sprang to her feet. By the time he could sway to his knees, still half blinded by tears of pain, she was halfway to the house, her skirts held so high he could see her naked calves as she ran.

Anaxilas let out a string of curses, but to chase after her was unthinkable. He'd make himself a laughing stock for slaves! The bitch! The misleading little bitch! He knew virgins could be fickle and coquettish, but this was going too far. She might have done him real harm! The little bitch! Now, no doubt, she'd go running to Agesandros and would make up stories about him. What did he care what Agesandros thought? Agesandros didn't control her. And she certainly wouldn't be able to play these tricks on him in his own home! Cursing, he gathered up his himation and was preparing to go and collect his chariot when he caught a glimpse of something moving at the corner of his eye. His first thought was that Kassia had come back—still playing coquette. But the next instant he realized that the woman coming toward him was too tall and full-figured for Kassia. She was vaguely familiar, but a slave with short hair, and then it came to him—Aristomenes' concubine, the one he'd sent home last summer and enjoyed last winter. What was her name?

"Kassia is an untamed Amazon," Niobe declared languidly as she stepped nearer.

"Ah—ah—" he searched for the name, and then dismissed it as unimportant—"where did you come from? I mean, what are you doing here?"

"Your grandmother sold me. She thought you were becoming too fond of me."

Anaxilas frowned darkly. He hated being treated like a little boy. It was none of his grandmother's business who he slept with. Why shouldn't he sleep with a slave he'd captured? Suddenly he remembered, too, that it was his grandmother who had pointed Kassia out to him. His grandmother had been trying to manipulate him all along. She *wanted* him to marry Kassia. Some dynastic game she was playing, no doubt. He was supposed to sleep with an untamed, spoiled wildcat just to please his grandmother? Well, he *would* do that, but there was no reason why he shouldn't have this woman, too! It was perfectly normal for princes in other cities to have concubines. Why not in Sparta, too?

Anaxilas surrendered to Niobe utterly—thinking that he was again subjugating a slave. Believing he was proving his virility and mastery, he in fact let Niobe make love to him any way *she* liked. While telling himself that he was insulting Kassia by taking her slave in the very place and time he had planned to make her his, he was wax in Niobe's expert hands. And while Anaxilas bucked and groaned in a frenzy of lust beneath her, Niobe gazed with a satisfied smile at his fragile, pale-haired bride trembling with indignation and shock in the shadow of a tree.

CHAPTER 15

Kassia did not know who to turn to. She couldn't go to Agesandros and admit that he was right. How could she ask for his help when she had so rudely told him her marriage was not his business at all? She cringed at the memory. She had been so arrogant, reminding him that she was the daughter of the noble, heroic Euryanax. She had all but called him an upstart whose marriage to her mother was only tolerated, not really accepted. No, she couldn't turn to Agesandros *now*. Besides, nothing had changed. Agesandros had nothing to say about her marriage. He was not technically her relative. He could not help her, even if he wanted to.

Uncle Leobotas was the only one who could speak for her, and the thought of going to him was more terrifying still. She was certain he would have no understanding for her feelings. She wasn't rightly sure she *understood* her feelings herself. Was she angry with Anaxilas because he had tried to force himself on her, or because he had taken her slave instead? How could she be angry about both?

One way or another, Kassia was sure Leobotas would raise his eyebrows and inquire just what she expected of her bridegroom. Why shouldn't he take her slave if she rejected him? And why indeed had she rejected her bridegroom? Surely she knew what marriage entailed? Surely she knew that Anaxilas had asked no more of her than he, as her husband, had a right to ask? What game did she think she was playing?

She could already hear the head master's cool, patient and yet admonishing voice saying, "You are not a child anymore, Kassia. You consented freely to this marriage." Indeed she had. That meant she had *consented* to being deflowered by Anaxilas. What right did she have to deny him? None. And Leobotas would tell her so.

And since she'd had no right to deny Anaxilas, she had no right to complain about what he'd done with Niobe. Niobe was just a slave. What he'd done with her was not even adultery. It wasn't worth mentioning—Leobotas would tell her that. He hadn't done it under her roof, and if it had been under her nose, that was her own fault for going back.

Why had she gone back? Had she intended to apologize or at least explain herself, or had she only wanted to express her outrage verbally? Kassia, trembling, knew it had been the latter.

She had run almost to the house and then, ashamed to face everyone, she'd stopped. As she stood indecisively at the edge of the orchard, she had decided that running away made her a coward. She wasn't afraid, she told herself—she was furious. She'd turned on her heel and marched back into the orchard in a rage. She had been determined to make Anaxilas *listen* to her. But she never got a word out. Anaxilas had silenced her yet again.

Now she wandered about between the stream and the mill, confused and trembling and shivering, and it was getting dark already. Soon she would have to go in and face everyone, and they would all look at her and ask why her best peplos was torn and dirty. Or worse, they *wouldn't* ask her. They would just smirk and exchange winks and nod, thinking she had done what Anaxilas had expected her to do. What everyone apparently expected a bride to do.

Why was she the only bride in the world who didn't want to do it? Chloe had wanted nothing more from Niko, and apparently Niobe was just as eager. Even Alethea herself was more than happy to take Agesandros to her bed, or she wouldn't be in the condition she was in now.

If only she weren't! Kassia would have gone to her mother, if only her mother hadn't been so weak and frightened of what lay ahead. But how could she possibly go to her mother now, when she was so exhausted and worn down with worry and so terrified of death? Kassia couldn't bring herself to burden her mother with any more problems, much less one of her own making. She knew her mother would take her side, but what could she do? Kassia had consented. Leobotas had signed the papers—with the king. Kassia was as good as married already. Her mother couldn't change that. Her mother could only sympathize, and that would weary her more, and then she wouldn't have the strength when her time came....

Kassia dragged her fingers roughly through her hair and stared at the house crouching at the foot of the snow-tipped mountains. She had to go in soon. The smoke blowing gently away from the kitchen was laden with the smell of roast pork. If she didn't go in soon, someone would come looking for her. What was she going to say when everyone stared at her and asked about the afternoon? Wouldn't they notice she wasn't flushed with happiness? But if they did, her mother would start to worry. She mustn't find out, Kassia told herself, combing her hair with her fingers with a different determination, and tying it at the back of her head. She had to pretend everything was all right.

As expected, they all stared at her as she joined them for dinner, but she tossed her head and pretended she didn't notice. She asked about the meal; she talked in a rush about the weather and the horses and the hounds; anything but Anaxilas. And although her mother looked at her very strangely and reached for her hand, asking, "Are you all right, Kassia?" Kassia insisted that everything was "fine." She jumped up after dinner and fled to her chamber to "write," giving no one a chance to interrogate her further. She took refuge in her own chamber and bolted the door.

She sat on the floor with her back to the door and held her knees in her arms. What was she going to do? What could she do? She was promised to Anaxilas. She would have to marry him, and he would do to her what he had wanted to do today. He would do it. Why was she so afraid of it? Other women enjoyed it. Had she been afraid of Damonon doing it to her? No, but then she hadn't really thought about it. They had kissed and she had felt like a woman for the first time, and he had been warm and strong and comforting. That was all. At least all that she could remember….

Now when she closed her eyes, she saw Anaxilas doing it to Niobe. It turned her stomach. Why? She had seen Niko and Chloe in much the same spot and pose once. It had embarrassed her and she had hastened away. Yet the image had haunted her for months afterwards—and not with revulsion. Rather she had been fascinated—and ashamed of her fascination. Niko and Chloe had seemed transported to another world as they lay together, but Anaxilas and Niobe reminded her only of the livestock. She shuddered.

He hadn't listened to a word she'd said! He hadn't once asked her about her summer. He hadn't even asked if she was well or asked after her mother, much less asked about her poetry. He hadn't taken the slightest interest in anything about her at all! The rage was coming back, bubbling up to overpower her shame and fear. He didn't know a thing about her and he didn't *want* to know her. So why did he want to marry her?

It could only be for her so-called "beauty".

Kassia hated her beauty with abrupt violence. She took her nails and dragged them down her face like claws. Maybe if she destroyed her face—if she took a hot iron to her cheek like Mika had once done to her hand—maybe if she had an ugly scar marring her forehead or her nose—he wouldn't want her anymore. Anaxilas could call off the wedding, just as Leobotas could. It was only Kassia and her mother and Agesandros who were helpless. Kassia wanted to scream, but at that moment she heard voices in the gallery.

She held her breath. It was her mother's voice, concerned and pained. "What do you think he did to her?"

"That bastard—" Agesandros cut himself off, sighed, and then found words to calm his wife. "He didn't have to *do* anything. Kassia probably just discovered what an unmitigated ass he is and is more than distressed at the thought of being married to him. She's not stupid, after all."

"No," Alethea agreed, and Kassia sat tensely, holding her breath and trying not to move even an eyelid. She could feel her mother looking at the door. She felt as if her mother's eyes could see through the wood. Her mother's sympathy made her want to cry, but how could she take advantage of her like that? She bit on her lip.

"There's nothing we can do," Agesandros told Alethea gently. "Come to bed."

Kassia could hear the gallery groaning and creaking under her mother's heavy footsteps. Tears of self-pity slithered out from under her eyelids and down her cheeks. It was so unfair! She was going to be taken from these people who truly loved her and given to a beast who coveted only her outer shell.

If only she were as ugly as Mika, this wouldn't be happening to her, she thought, resting her head on her knees and giving into her tears at last.

Before Anaxilas had time to call again, Kassia sent Mika into the city with a message for Queen Eupolia. Kassia wrote to her great-aunt candidly that her mother was ill and frightened of this unexpected pregnancy so late in life. Kassia begged to be allowed to stay with her mother until the birth was over.

Queen Eupolia nodded with approval. "An excellent young lady," she said to herself as much as to Mika, who stood waiting for a reply. Then turning to the slave directly, she ordered, "You may tell your mistress that I approve of her devotion to her mother and cherish her all the more for it. It demonstrates that she understands the meaning of duty. We can only assume she will be as good a queen and wife as she is a daughter. Of course she should stay with her mother until this difficult pregnancy is over—one way or another."

In Sparta, winter was when roofs were repaired, fences and walls mended, irrigation ditches and fountains dug, rooms and terraces and floors added to houses, and barns or sheds built. For the more complicated and skilled tasks, perioikoi workers were hired. Simpler tasks were done by the master and his helots. And even when professionals were brought in, the owner usually lent a hand to be sure things got done right and before the campaign season started.

There was, therefore, nothing odd about Agesandros working in an old, threadbare chiton with a spade in his hand, but the sight of a hoplite in bronze and crested helmet starting up the drive to Alethea's house made Agesandros scowl in displeasure nevertheless. He wasn't expecting visitors and he wanted to be left in peace. He had work to do here and he did not want to have to go into the city for any reason. Alethea was too close to her time. Sybil said the labour could start any day now. He tossed his spade aside, wiped sweat out of his face with the back of his arm, and then strode out to intercept the hoplite. "Are you looking for me?" he called out.

The hoplite was a young man, just a year out of the agoge, by the name of Talthybius. Agesandros knew him only fleetingly. He was the younger brother of a man Agesandros had served with half a decade earlier. Talthybius looked surprised as Agesandros emerged out of the trees to stand in front of him. That annoyed Agesandros. Did the young man think he had no right to be at his wife's kleros?

In fact, Talthybius was simply intimidated. Agesandros was a good ten years his senior. He was an officer, while Talthybius was just an ordinary hoplite. When Talthybius had been only an eirene, Agesandros had already become a legend by destroying Aristomenes' secret camp in the Taygetos. Agesandros was also a good head taller than he was. Talthybius was confused to find him blocking the way—even if at the moment he was dressed and smelled like a helot. "I—ah—wanted to speak to the Lady Alethea," he explained himself with obvious embarrassment.

It was the wrong thing to say. Agesandros frowned more darkly. "What business do you have with my wife? She's not well. Anything you came to say to her, you can say to me."

Talthybius wasn't sure about that, but he didn't know how to talk his way around this peremptory officer who blocked his way. So he admitted, "I came about a slave. One of your wife's slaves. I want to buy a certain Niobe."

"Niobe? How do you know about Niobe?"

"Ah—Anaxilas has told me about her. He said she was—ah—good. But he's going to marry soon and so he can't keep her for himself. I thought I could—ah—well—you don't want her for yourself, do you?"

Agesandros' first instinct was to knock the grin off Talthybius' acne-studded face for insulting him—not to mention Alethea—by such an insinuation, but fortunately he had long since learned not to follow his first impulse. The fact was, Niobe was more than worthless to Alethea, and he was delighted at the prospect of getting rid of her. He had wanted to get rid of her ever since she'd made that disgusting attempt to seduce him. But Alethea had only bought her for Leon, and what would he do if they sold her?

"Come inside and let's talk about this." Agesandros indicated the house at the end of the drive. He led the way back, taking Talthybius right to the andron, and after ordering wine and fruit to be brought to the guest, he went to wash up and change into a clean chiton. Then he returned to the andron and settled himself on the couch opposite

Talthybius. "So you want to buy Niobe. What are you prepared to offer?"

Talthybius cleared his throat awkwardly. He had come prepared to negotiate with Niobe's owner, Alethea. He had brought things he thought a woman would want—notably jewellery and a mirror. Somehow he didn't think these things would interest Agesandros. "Well, ah, well—I have—well, what do you want for her?"

"I need a slave-woman who is milking. My wife will be brought to childbed soon and I've been told she will have twins. I don't want her to have to nurse entirely on her own."

Talthybius' eyes widened and he stammered, "Where am I supposed to come up with that? I wouldn't even know where to look."

"The slave markets in Tegea or Gytheon would be good places to start," Agesandros snapped back, with obvious annoyance at so much lack of imagination. "If you can't manage that, then I would expect another able-bodied young slave who can replace Niobe in all her duties."

"All of them?" Talthybius asked with a little smirk.

"Fucking isn't one of her duties, if that's what you mean; it's an extra-curricular activity which she engages in with too much enthusiasm. Do you have a slave woman who can work hard in the household?"

"I—I can find one, sir." (The "sir" slipped out automatically if inappropriately under the circumstances.)

"Good. Then as soon as you've delivered her and I've agreed she's suitable, you can take Niobe."

"Thank you, sir." Talthybius sounded genuinely relieved.

Just three days later Talthybius was back with a black woman of indefinable age, but nursing a baby. Proudly he pointed out she was "wet" and so exactly what Agesandros had ordered. Agesandros had told Alethea about the deal by now, and she came down to interview the prospective replacement. The fact that she was indeed nursing, however, made the decision easy. Alethea, certain that she would not be alive to nurse her own babies, was desperate to provide for them. They agreed to the trade, and Niobe (who had not been warned) was turned over to Talthybius immediately.

Alethea was both surprised and even a little offended that Niobe made no protest at all against the transfer. She shrugged, packed her belongings into a little sack, and then walked out behind Talthybius without a backward glance or a good-bye to anyone. "You'd think we'd mistreated her," Alethea remarked, baffled by her behaviour, but Agesandros insisted, "Good riddance!"

Then Agesandros went in search of Leon, who was helping Orsippos to clean the leaves and other rubbish out of the drainage pipes from the fountain. Leon, as always, was working with a will, although this was dirty, wet work and unpleasantly cold at this time of year. When Agesandros called to him, he washed his hands clean in the splashing water and wiped them dry on his chiton as he came to face Agesandros. "Sir?"

"I have some bad news for you."

Leon waited, tense but unmoving.

"I just sold Niobe. She wasn't pulling her weight, and we traded her for a woman who is nursing. You know Alethea is expecting twins. I wanted her to have a wet nurse. I'm sorry things worked out like this. We did what we could for her, but she just couldn't accept her new status."

"Yes, sir," Leon managed very softly. What could he say? He had seen with his own eyes that it was true, and Agesandros and Alethea had the right to do whatever they wanted with their property. What they had done for him was more than most slaves would dream of asking. Yet the thought that Niobe was gone, sent away where he could never see her again, still shook him. It meant he would never have the chance to show her what he was worth. He felt as if he had just been kicked in the gut. "May I ask where she was sold, sir?"

"I sold her to Talthybius."

"Who's that, sir?" Leon ventured, still numbed by what had happened.

"He's a peer—not a helot or even perioikoi. There's no reason to think he will abuse her."

"No, sir," Leon agreed, defeated. "Is that all, sir?"

"For the moment." Agesandros didn't like the way Leon was taking this. He looked as if he'd been beaten. Leon returned to his task and Agesandros sighed and returned to his own.

Niobe was not afraid of the future. She was certain that if Alethea or Agesandros had wanted to send her somewhere horrible, they would have done that long ago. She had spent a few sleepless nights worrying about what Agesandros was going to do to her after that disastrous night when he had rejected her love. When nothing happened, however, she realised that Agesandros was all bark and no bite. He was completely under the thumb of his ageing, ineffective wife. Niobe felt only contempt for Alethea. Sometimes she even pitied her. She was obviously older than her husband and couldn't hope to keep his affections forever. She let her children, particularly that brat Kassia, walk all over her, and it was Phoebe more than Alethea who ran the kleros.

Niobe had learned that she had nothing to fear from Alethea, unlike Queen Eupolia, and as a result she respected her less.

As she walked beside Talthybius, she eyed him sidelong. He was slight of build and looked somewhat weak for a hoplite. She wondered that he had survived the infamous Spartan agoge—but probably it wasn't anywhere near as hard as they pretended it was. Talthybius was still suffering from juvenile acne and it made his face quite unattractive. Niobe rather hoped he wouldn't expect her to kiss him all too much.

They reached the outskirts of the city and Talthybius led her down a street away from the acropolis. They passed a large gymnasium and palestra, where young men and youths poured in and out and the sound of shouts and cheers spilled down the steps. They passed behind a stadium and then turned into a side street. Abruptly they stopped before a small shop selling tin trinkets—the kind used by the poor as offerings to the gods or given to small children to play with.

Talthybius nodded to the perioikoi sitting on a high stool behind the counter, and the man jumped up and came around to let them in the door to the house itself. He grinned at Niobe. "We got everything fixed up for you," he winked; "my wife will wait on you." He pushed open the door and shouted a name into the corridor.

The interior was unexceptional: a narrow corridor led to a cramped, cobbled courtyard onto which a half-dozen rooms opened. "It was the best we could find in so little time," Talthybius explained with an apologetic shrug. "But it's ideally located. Anaxilas can visit you when he comes to the stadium to train his team."

"Anaxilas?"

"Of course. Didn't you know? I'm only his agent—so Alethea wouldn't know who had really bought you."

Niobe felt her heart start to soar. She had won! She had truly won! Anaxilas had bought her and set her up in her own house. True, this was hardly a palace, and there was much work to be done to make it suitable. But there would be time for that later. The important point was that she was clearly here to be his concubine, not an ordinary slave. To Talthybius she turned her head regally and announced, "I suspected, but I wasn't absolutely sure."

The shopkeeper's wife emerged, drying her hands on her apron, from a wooden door that seemed to give access to the courtyard of the house next door. "Are you the prince's woman? Welcome, welcome. My husband and I live just next door. I'm to cook and clean for you. We've fixed up the bedroom. Where are your things?"

Niobe turned to Talthybius, "Didn't Anaxilas send clothes and things so I could outfit myself properly?"

"Ah—no—did he say he would? Oh, well, ah—here." Her manner was so imperial that Talthybius feared he might have forgotten something. He didn't want to displease Anaxilas. He wanted the prince to look on him as a loyal, trustworthy friend. He wanted the prince to remember, long after he had become king, how he had helped him on this delicate mission. So Talthybius removed the buckle from his own belt and handed it to Niobe. It was a knot of Herakles in solid silver. "Buy what you need with that."

Niobe looked at the buckle somewhat sceptically, but it was clear that the poor Talthybius didn't have anything else of value on him except his sword. She would have to make do with the buckle.

By the time Anaxilas arrived, Niobe had made the most of what she had. The perfume was the cheapest of rose oils and she hadn't been able to find henna at all, but she was bathed and oiled and scented and dressed at last in a gown that flattered her. She had decided on her strategy as well. At the sight of Anaxilas she ran to him, threw her arms around him, and stretched up to kiss him, babbling the whole time, "Thank you, thank you! I can never thank you enough for rescuing me! I promise, you'll never regret this! I'll always make you happy. You'll never, never regret rescuing me!"

Anaxilas was flattered. He had never been a hero before. No woman had ever been grateful to him like this before. Grateful, aroused, and seductive all at once.

Later, when he collected himself and his things to leave, Niobe was far too clever to beg him to stay. She was not really sorry to see him go, but she said wistfully, "If only I had something pretty to wear on my neck and wrists, I'm sure I'd please you better."

Anaxilas laughed and smacked her buttocks teasingly. "Not very subtle, but I take the hint. A bangle or two, some earrings, a necklace—all the things you were used to as Aristomenes' concubine—that's what you want, isn't it?"

"Oh, no! Only you!" Niobe hastened to assure him, throwing her arms around him and kissing him hotly.

He laughed and was gone, but he brought her a bead necklace the next day. And every day thereafter he added a little something to her growing collection. It became a little game. He would say, "Nothing today—unless...." And he would think of something he wanted her to do to or for him. Or, as she grew more self-confident, she would turn the game on its head and tease him at the most critical moments, "What will you give me, if....".

Then one day Anaxilas announced, "I'll be getting married soon. My mother-in-law went into labour today, and as soon as it's over Kassia won't have an excuse to put our marriage off any longer."

"If her mother dies, she'll be in mourning. You can't marry during mourning, can you?"

Anaxilas shrugged and bent to pick up his clothes. "That means that at the latest, I'll be married in 12 days. And if the old bag doesn't die, it could be as early as the day after tomorrow. I've been made to wait long enough. I will take my bride from her mother's house at the first possible moment."

Niobe didn't know what to say, so she wisely held her tongue. Anaxilas twisted around to look at her. "You aren't jealous, are you? You've got no right to be, you know. I have to get heirs on someone like her. It has nothing to do with us."

Niobe nodded and told herself that Kassia would never please him. Never. After he had tasted Kassia's frigid embrace, he would crave his sweet Arcadian mistress more than ever. But it was hard not to be a little nervous, remembering what had happened the first time Kassia had entered his life....

CHAPTER 16

Alethea's labour began mid-morning. She felt the first sharp contraction and broke out into a sweat of terror at once. It was starting. Or rather, it was over. This was the beginning of the end.

Her heart cried out in protest: it couldn't be. Not yet! She had so much she still wanted to do and see. So much to tell her children. And Agesandros. It was too soon. She wasn't ready.

Yet she had known it was coming. Known that it couldn't be much longer. She had known, and still she wasn't ready.

Is anyone ever ready to die? Her father, longing for his cave in the months after her mother's death, perhaps…. But inwardly she screamed back at the gods: That was different! My love, my Agesandros, is still alive.

He was so very much alive. She could hear him even now as she grasped the column supporting the roof of the peristyle. He was talking to Lampon in the armoury, getting things sorted out so they could do some repairs to the outer wall, which had developed cracks. Agesandros had enough energy for a whole battalion, Alethea thought with a smile, and then the next contraction hit her.

She grabbed the column more tightly, clinging to it for life itself, and stared at her garden. It was not at its best. The roses were all tipped with brown from the nightly frost and only the autumn snowdrops were blooming freshly. Why couldn't she have been granted another spring? But then she would have wanted another summer, and then the fall when Agesandros came home.…

Sybil was beside her. "Has it started?"

"Yes." That was all. She couldn't manage any more.

Sybil's arms seemed surprisingly strong, and her slow steps were no longer too slow for Alethea. Together they waddled carefully around the peristyle and Alethea gave it one last, longing look before she entered the "sickroom"—the room in which Chloe had died. The last room she would see in life.

Sybil got her to the waiting bed. It was made up with fresh, clean sheets, waiting for this moment for weeks now. Sybil helped her out of her peplos, helped her to lie down, propped up the pillows and covered her with the sheet. "Now you just relax," Sybil cooed, "and I'll take care of everything else."

Suddenly Kassia was beside her, looking frightened. "Mom? Has it started? Are you in labour?"

"I think so, maybe not—" but the contractions came again, and she could only gasp and grab the edge of the bed.

Kassia looked pale as a ghost, and Alethea tried to smile for her. "It's nothing to worry about. All women go through it. I gave birth to you and your brothers. There's nothing to worry about. Fetch the midwife for me—you can take the chariot and team. Get some practice." Her uncle had, as expected, sent her a practical two-horse chariot and no less than two teams of sensible horses in exchange for the ostentatious chariot and race horses Agesandros had captured. Kassia had only just started learning how to drive, but that didn't matter. Alethea wanted her out of the way right now. It was hard enough on the girl that she would soon lose her mother. She didn't need to see how painful it was.

Kassia was gone, but abruptly Agesandros was there. He looked angry, but Alethea knew him well enough to know it was only worry covered over with a scowl. She managed a smile for him, too, and reached out to touch his face. She wanted to remember his face in all eternity. In the dark gloom of the underworld, she wanted to be able to close her eyes and see his face.

"Is there anything I can do?" he asked, and the words were a stab to her heart because they were so typical of him. From the start, he never showered her with empty words of love. He had always given consistent concrete help instead. Her father had raised her to judge a man by his actions, not his words, and Agesandros had never failed her—but there was nothing he *could* do to help her now.

She grabbed his hand and tried not to let the self-pity overwhelm her. This was no time to weep. Not yet. "Knowing you're here is everything. Just stay near enough to—to come to me if I call for you. Will you do that?"

"I'll wait just outside—in the walled orchard.." The walled orchard was on the far side of the sickroom—away from the busy peristyle. "If you want me, just call my name.… Are you sure there's nothing else I can do?"

"Niko and Sandy. I'd like to—" She cut herself off. She wanted to see them before she died, but only when it was certain that she was dying would they be let out of the agoge. She mustn't admit yet that she was dying. "Let them know it's started."

Agesandros nodded, holding her hand firmly.

"But keep Kassia busy," Alethea instructed. "There's no need for her to see this too intimately."

Agesandros nodded again.

The new African slave slipped silently into the room. She had said hardly a word since she had joined the household almost ten days ago. Now, too, she came wordlessly, with a bowl of warm water and fresh towels. There was something both efficient and calming about the way she settled down to attend her new mistress, but she gave Agesandros unambiguous glances of disapproval. This was no place for a man, her looks said sternly.

Alethea squeezed Agesandros' hand. "Give me a kiss," she begged.

He bent and kissed her on the lips, then the forehead, and then he drew back only a little and stroked her cheek with the back of his hand. "I know this is going to be hard on you. It must be like facing a flogging. You know it's going to hurt like hell and there's no way out of it. The sooner it's over, the better. And this way you get everything over with at once. Two children are enough. We won't have any more. Pharax says there are ways—"

Alethea nodded and kissed the hand she was clinging to. "You should start thinking of names for them. I think they're both boys."

"But I wanted one of each—"

She clutched at his hand in pain this time, and Agesandros waited until the spasm was past. Then he bent and kissed her again. "I'll be waiting just outside."

Kassia dutifully brought the midwife and then she went for Pharax. Her mother hadn't sent for him, but she had promised long ago that she would fetch him. Unable to stand in a chariot, he followed her in his own cart. It was mid-afternoon when he arrived. Alethea had been in a labour only about 6 hours. Everything was going fine, according to Sybil, who stood in the doorway and did not want to let him in. Agesandros came in from the orchard and demanded, "Do you think you can help?"

"If everything's fine, no. If something goes wrong, yes." He met Agesandros' eyes.

"All right. Sybil, get out of the way."

The African exclaimed in obvious horror at the sight of a man—not even the husband—entering the birth-chamber, but Alethea whispered, "It's all right. He's a surgeon."

Agesandros went back into the orchard and leaned against the wall of the house. From the window above his head came the murmur of voices and then, at all too frequent intervals, the sharp screams and gasps of his wife in agony. He didn't move, but his fists balled until they ached. He'd release them and they would ball again on their own.

Kassia joined him. She sat on the bench nearby and held her hands in her lap.

"How long does this go on?" Agesandros asked his stepdaughter abruptly.

"It varies from birth to birth. Chloe died after 36 hours—"

"I don't want to hear about it! Don't you remember your brother's birth?"

"Remember, no, but I was told it took more than a day with Niko and only a few hours with Sandy. But then with Sandy Mom was in shock. They'd just brought her my father's corpse—"

"I know. I heard about it. The head on top of a heap of other parts.... You didn't see it, did you?"

"No, Orsippos kept Niko and me away until my grandfather had put the pieces back together and made it look like a decent corpse, wrapped in a red himation."

"Do you think if I rushed in and gave your mother another shock, it would speed things up?" Agesandros asked half in jest and half seriously. "I could put on full panoply and charge in beating a spear on my hoplon. If you think it would help, I could shout that the Messenians are attacking."

Kassia smiled weakly. At least he *wanted* to help. Her father had kept as far away as possible. And Anaxilas? He had let Niobe miscarry his baby without lifting a hand to help or showing any remorse. Kassia shuddered and looked up at the sky over the orchard. It was luminous with dusk.

Mika slipped into the garden carrying a tray. "Unoma is much more help than Niobe was," she praised the new slave. "She's done all the running back and forth with water and linens. I thought you might need something to keep your strength and spirits up." She held out the tray. It was laden with bread, cheese, wine, pomegranates, dried apricots and fresh figs.

Kassia thanked her and then asked her to fetch a warmer himation. Clutching the wool about her shoulders, she sat with Agesandros and they both picked at the food listlessly. Waiting.

As the night darkened, the midwife started to get nervous. She glanced resentfully at Pharax, but she didn't know what to do. Alethea had dilated properly and the head of the first baby was properly positioned, but it was as if, she whispered in an agitated voice, it was being held back by its twin. The African woman had started to chant incantations, apparently to her own gods. Phoebe and Sybil took turns wiping the sweat from Alethea's face and murmuring encouragement to her.

Alethea heard the midwife and Pharax whispering in the corner. She reached out her hand. "Pharax?"

He rushed over to her. "What can I do?"

"Nothing. I knew this would happen. I'm too old. I'm too weak. Please. Send for my sons. I want to see them once more."

Pharax's eyes widened with each word. Nothing was more fatal than surrender itself. He had watched Chloe die, fighting to the very last for her life and that of her baby—but if Alethea gave up, it was hopeless.

"You mustn't say that!" he protested, seconded loudly by Sybil and the midwife. "You mustn't think that! Come, the baby is positioned correctly. It's ready to come."

Alethea shook her head and closed her eyes. Tears glistened on her eyelids. "I know. But I don't have the strength to push anymore."

A spasm of pain swept over her, shaking her out of her surrender for a second, tearing a scream out of her, and making her clutch at whatever she could grasp—the side of the bed on one side, Phoebe's hand on the other. Pharax looked around at the faces of the women in terror. They were resigned. No, worse: they were in mourning already.

Abruptly it was clear to him. They, too, had expected this. They had never really believed it would go any other way.

The spasm was past, but Alethea's face was still twisted with pain. She didn't even bother to open her eyes. "Please, Pharax. Please let me see my sons again. I'll hold out that long. But send for them. Have Kassia drive—" The scream was torn out of her again as if by surprise, and it ended in a whimper that was as much emotional as physical pain.

Sybil was hushing Alethea like a child and wiping her with a damp cloth, but Phoebe looked at him accusingly. "Won't you do what she asks?" she demanded reproachfully. "Is that too much to ask? Send for her sons. Who knows how much longer she can last?"

Pharax staggered out of the sickroom on his crutch. "Agesandros!" He shouted. "Agesandros!" He lurched his way forward, the closest thing to a run that his one leg allowed him. Before he'd reached the steps down into the orchard, his ex-commander loomed up before him in the dark. "Agesandros," Pharax gasped from the exertion. They stared at one another. "She's asking for her sons."

It was Kassia who screamed "Noooooo!" and pushed past them both to burst in on her mother.

"I thought you said you could help!" Agesandros flung at the surgeon's apprentice like an accusation. "You said if things went wrong—"

"I can! At least, I *think* I can, but I've never done it before. Agesandros—" He cut himself off, afraid of what he was going to ask. "Agesandros, give me permission to cut the babies out of her."

"What do you mean!? Butcher my wife—"

"Not butcher! Save her! Let me remove the babies as I would a sick appendix or an arrowhead! You've seen me do it. You know I can. I can cut open her womb without destroying any vital organs. I don't promise you the children, but I can save Alethea—I think. Let me *try*."

Agesandros did not take long to consider. He was used to making battlefield decisions. He knew how easily they could go wrong, but also that thinking too long only made the chances of success slighter. "Do it."

"You have to back me," Pharax warned, knowing the women would throw him out if he tried to do this operation without Agesandros' authority. Agesandros nodded.

Pharax turned about and clumped back into the chamber with Agesandros at his back. The African woman raised her voice in a howl of protest and the midwife too shouted, "Go away! Go away! This is no place for you! There's nothing you can do."

Agesandros waved the women aside irritably. He went down on his heels beside Alethea, who was clinging to Kassia's hand. Kassia looked over at him, her face streaming tears. "Alethea, listen to me."

She shifted her eyes from Kassia to Agesandros and her face crumpled up. "I'm sorry, Agesandros. I hoped I'd manage to give you at least—"

The next contraction wracked her and she half-sat up, her teeth clamped, and her hands clutching so hard that Kassia gasped in pain.

Agesandros jumped to his feet in alarm and looked about at the way the women calmly went about their various tasks. The midwife checked on the progress and shook her head. Sybil wiped Alethea's face and the African woman brought her a fresh cloth. The contraction was over and Alethea fell back onto the soaked pillow. Phoebe signalled to the African woman to replace it, while Alethea rolled her head back and forth and then took a deep breath and focused on Agesandros again. "I'm sorry. I'm so sorry, Ag—I—I thought—I wanted—to give you at least one of—"

"Listen to me!" Agesandros leaned over the bed and grabbed her by the shoulders. "Listen to me! I'm not going to let you die. Do you understand? I'm not going to just stand here and watch you die! I've told Pharax he can operate. Do you understand?"

Alethea looked at him through a daze, but Kassia understood. "Can you do it?" Her question was directed at Pharax and there was so much hope in her voice, that both Agesandros' and Pharax' courage was strengthened. Kassia clearly believed he could do it, and that made Pharax not only determined to try, but almost confident of success.

"You want to cut the babies out?" Alethea asked in a weak voice.

"Yes, we want to cut the babies out."

Alethea closed her eyes and nodded. She understood. If she were going to die anyway, they might as well save the babies. It was good so.

But not yet. She opened her eyes and grabbed Agesandros' hand fiercely. "But my sons. You'll let me see them first?"

Agesandros glanced over his head at Pharax. He made a helpless gesture. He didn't dare wait, but he knew, too, that thinking her sons were coming would give Alethea something to stay alive for, help her not to surrender. Pharax mouthed inaudibly, "Tell her yes," and Agesandros assured his wife, "Yes. You'll see your sons."

Reassured and relieved, Alethea turned her attention to her daughter. "Kassia, there's so much I wanted—" The next contraction came, and Kassia and Agesandros waited tensely on either side of her until it was over. Sybil wiped her face, and then Alethea focused again on Kassia. "If Anaxilas—disappoints you—in any way. Don't—stay with him. You can always come home." Alethea's parents had promised her this when she married Euryanax against their better judgement. She wanted Kassia to have the same security. But Kassia would be an orphan, while she had had both her parents. She turned again to her husband with new urgency, almost desperation. "Agesandros, promise me—promise that—that you'll take Kassia back if she wants to leave Anaxilas."

"Mom! Don't even think about that now—" Kassia protested, while Agesandros assured her in a firm, decisive voice, "Of course. Kassia will have a home with us as long as she lives."

"But if I'm not there—"

"Stop it, Mom! You're going to be there! Didn't you hear what Pharax said? He's going to cut the babies out—"

Alethea wasn't paying any attention. She had focused all her concentration on Agesandros. "And Leon. Leon, too. I promised him we wouldn't ever throw him out. No matter what mistakes he makes, you must forgive him—for my sake, Agesandros."

"Leon is closer to me than a brother, Alethea. Surely you know that?"

"And Niko, don't forget to—"

The next spasm of pain overwhelmed her, and Agesandros looked impatiently over his shoulder for Pharax. But the surgeon was nowhere to be seen, and so he turned to stare at the midwife, who was squatting at the end of the bed and peering professionally at her patient. She shook her head again. "It's being held back by the other baby."

"Sandy, too," Alethea gasped out, demanding Agesandros' attention again. She didn't have the strength for complete sentences. She had to hope that Agesandros understood what she meant. He should look after her orphaned sons. They would need a father more than ever when she was gone.

From the doorway, Pharax was gesturing to Kassia. Agesandros jerked his head to Kassia for her to go to the surgeon. She bent and kissed her mother's forehead and excused herself. "I'm going to go for Niko and Sandy now, Mom. We'll be back as soon as we can."

Alethea squeezed her hand, said "thank you," and then let her go. But when Kassia had taken only a few steps, Alethea called after her, "Drive carefully! Don't let the horses get away from you."

"I can manage them, Mom," Kassia assured her, backing toward the door. There she stopped and looked up expectantly at Pharax.

"I need help," he admitted candidly. "We need to give your mother a sleeping drug. I'm sure you have the ingredients here, but I don't know where to find them. If I tell you what to do, can you manage—?"

"I can do that," Mika announced from the hallway, and in surprise they turned to look at her. "Let Kassia go for the young masters. She's the only one who can drive. But Leon and I can help you, Master Surgeon."

With relief, Pharax saw that Leon was standing behind her. The latter nodded solemnly, adding, "Just tell us what to do, sir."

Pharax took a deep breath. Although the night was cool, he was sweating profusely. Never had an operation been so important to him.

He always wanted to save lives. Each patient was important. But Alethea was much more than that. He didn't think he could live with himself if something went wrong and he had to live with the knowledge that he had failed her. Not to mention that he'd never be able to face Agesandros again. He gave rapid, clear instructions to Mika to make up a drink that would put Alethea to sleep quickly, and then turned to Leon.

"I need much more light. I need a table for my instruments and a deep bowl of water in which to wash my hands and instruments during surgery. I—" he hesitated but then decided to risk it, "need some one to hold and pass me my instruments as I work. Dexippos can do that, but sometimes I need someone to hold things steady as I work—in the wound, I mean. Dexippos can't manage that, and I hate to ask Agesandros.…"

"I can do it," Leon assured him seriously. "The Lady Alethea saved my life *twice*. If there's anything I can do to help, I will."

"Good man." Pharax clapped him on the shoulder once. "Start by finding a suitable table, and as many lamps and lanterns as we can put on the shelves or can hang over the bed."

Leon set off at once.

When Mika returned, Pharax took the deep kothon, filled to the brim with the sour-smelling mixture, into the sickroom. At the sight of him carrying the drink, a murmur of protest went up from the women. Phoebe shook her head and said in a low, bitter voice to Agesandros, "After all she's done for you! I can't believe you're going to do this! Aren't you even going to let her say goodbye to her sons?"

"Get out!" Agesandros ordered, his nerves shattered.

Phoebe left with dignity, her face rigid with hatred. As she passed the new African slave, this woman too got to her feet. For a moment she hesitated, her glances shifting rapidly from her owners to Phoebe. Then she shook her head and started chanting to her herself as she hastened to follow Phoebe out into the peristyle. She seemed not to entirely understand what was going on, but she did not like men in a birth-chamber, and she recognised Phoebe's authority in the house-hold. If the men were taking over and Phoebe was leaving, so was she.

Next the midwife announced with an undertone of alarm, "I won't be party to this! I came here to deliver a baby, not commit murder! No one can say I sanctioned this. You're my witness, Phoebe," she called after the woman who had already left. "Phoebe!? You'll bear witness for me, won't you? I didn't ask for this!" She grabbed up her things and fled.

It was Sybil who made the most fuss. She still stood at Alethea's head, wiping her face with a damp cloth, and her gaze shifted from Agesandros to Pharax. "You can't do this! You've got no right! She loved you more than anything in the world. You can't just carve her up like she was dead already! You can't cut her up like a carcass! Agesan-dros! If you let that man take a knife to Alethea, I will curse you! I will call the furies down upon you, so that you cannot rest one minute from this day forward!" Sybil was working herself up more and more with each phrase. Her face was flushed with emotion and her voice was already tight and shrill. "I will call the curses of—"

"Sybil, stop making such a fuss." It was the young but firm voice of Mika, coming into the chamber with a hydria of steaming water in one hand and one of cold water in the other. She clunked them down on the floor, and stood to comb loose strands of hair out of her face with her hand.

Sybil stared at her in sheer astonishment before setting off in a new tirade. "You impudent girl! Who do you think you are? Don't you know what is going on? Don't you understand—"

"The Master Surgeon is going to save the mistress, not kill her, Sybil," Mika declared with absolute faith. "He'll save her just as he cured me."

"You stupid girl!" Sybil wailed through her tears. "This isn't about a few warts! Don't you see? All they care about is the babies. They only want to save the babies. They're going to cut the babies out and leave our poor, dear Alethea to die!" Sybil's resistance had collapsed into sheer despair. She was sobbing hopelessly, and Mika left the water standing on the floor to go and throw her arms around Sybil. "They're going to kill her," Sybil sobbed between gasps for air, as Mika—small and frail as she was—deftly steered the fat old woman away from the bed. As she passed Pharax, Mika nodded to him and mouthed, "I'll be right back." Then she took Sybil's arm over her shoulders so she could better support her, and led her out of the chamber.

Pharax and Agesandros were alone with Alethea. The latter was clinging to Agesandros' hand and staring up at him with an expression somewhere between terror and adoration. "Don't be angry with her, Agesandros—"

For a moment, Agesandros' fury was so overpowering that he actually started, his hand jerked, and he caught his breath. He wanted to shout at Alethea that he had every right to be angry. He was trying to *save* her life, and he was insulted that they all assumed the opposite. But in that moment her face contorted with agony and she lifted her head from the pillow. The cords of her neck stood out sharply as she pressed with all her failing strength against the children still in her distended womb. All the anger was instantly gone, and Agesandros felt only fear and confusion.

Suddenly he missed Sybil and the African woman with their cooing and soothing words. Beads of sweat had formed on Alethea's forehead and glistened on her neck, but there was no one to wipe them away with a clean, cool cloth. Agesandros' hand was cramping in Alethea's grip, and still she writhed and let out short, gasping moans. Even as she eased back onto the pillow, her face was twisted and tears mingled with the sweat. "It's all right," she whispered. "I can't take it any longer. It's all right. Tell them I love them. I won't stop loving them even when I'm dead—"

"Damn it, Pharax, do something!"

Pharax was already there. He pressed the kothon to Alethea's lips with his right hand and helped lift her head with the left. Alethea didn't resist. Her desire for an end to the pain was momentarily greater than her need to see her sons. Did she really want *them* to see *her* like this? What could she possibly say to them that they didn't already know? But then the thought occurred to her that they might blame Agesandros for her death. With the kothon half empty, she hesitated. She wanted all her loved ones to stay together, comfort one another, and support one another when she was gone. Maybe if it were her dying wish that her sons not reject Agesandros.... But she had already sipped too much of the drink, and her eyes rolled back in her head. Pharax had to shake her awake to make her drink the rest. He did not want her coming to prematurely. Alethea drank because he poured the liquid down her throat and she would have choked on it otherwise. She drank without really knowing what she was doing. She failed to swallow the last mouthful; it spilled from the side of her mouth when Pharax set her head down.

Agesandros was staring at him, but Pharax had driven all doubts from his consciousness. He was seized with a fever of determination. He looked about sharply. He needed light and to get set up—and Leon was there, hovering in the doorway, apparently awaiting only a signal. Dexippos was with him. Together they carried in a table, and then while Dexippos unloaded his master's pouch and set things up as he knew his master wanted them, Leon started carrying in and lighting all the lamps he had collected. Mika, too, was back now. She brought the water to the head of the bed, then rapidly collected all the soiled linens lying about where Sybil and Phoebe and Unoma had left them. She removed them from the room while Leon brought a big bronze basin for the surgeon to wash his hands in. He mixed water from the pitchers Mika had brought. Mika returned with a stack of fresh napkins and took up Sybil's station as if she had done this dozens of times.

Pharax glanced at her. She was so patently determined to help that it was not his right to question her. "Mika, I may need you to wipe away the blood as I work. Can you do that?"

"Of course. I'm not afraid of blood."

"Good girl. Then come stand beside me."

Pharax glanced up at Agesandros. He was rigid and pale, but he was evidently also determined to stay right here. That irritated Pharax for a moment. It was not going to help him to have Agesandros' hawk-like eyes watching his every motion. But he forced himself to forget his own vanity and concentrate on the task alone. He closed his eyes and conjured up the image of Chloe's corpse. He held his breath, remembering each detail as vividly as he could. Then he asked Dexippos for the scalpel.

Kassia went to Niko's barracks first. As eirene, he commanded a class of 10-year-olds and no one had to give him permission to leave his post—he simply risked disgrace if his charges took advantage of the situation and attracted the attention of the authorities with some prank that was too cheeky or got themselves in real danger. Fortunately, they were all sleeping soundly when Kassia arrived. Niko did not ask any questions. When he registered that his sister had woken him, he slid off his bed, grabbed his clothes and left the barracks. Only after they were out in the street, as he pulled on his clothes, did he ask what this was about.

"Mom's in labour and Pharax is going to try to cut the babies out of her."

"Why?"

"Because she'll die otherwise, just like Chloe did!" Kassia hissed, outraged at her brother's stupidity.

"But why? She didn't have any trouble with us—"

"How do you know?! Besides, it's twins and she's over 40. Surely you knew how dangerous it was? *She's* been terrified of it ever since she found out! Surely you noticed?!"

Niko only looked perplexed and guilty. His sister shamed him as he registered he had been much too concerned with proving himself in this critical last year before citizenship. He had been home to visit even less often than usual—particularly after Chloe died. He'd been too ashamed to look Phoebe and Orsippos in the eye. No, he hadn't noticed his mother was terrified. She'd seemed so calm and comforting, just like always.

"You are a bonehead sometimes!" Kassia told him definitively, and Niko couldn't even defend himself. "Mom thinks she's dying and has sent for you and Sandy."

"What can we do?"

"Have you lost half your brains playing ball or what? To say goodbye, of course."

"But I thought you said Pharax—"

"He's going to *try*! But he's never done it before. Maybe he won't do it right. And if he can't save her, no one can. Will you hurry! We have to get Sandy."

Niko had not realised his mother was in danger, and so the shock went deep. He started to follow Kassia to the waiting chariot, then realized that he might not be back before dawn. His sense of duty made him stop and turn back. "I've got to ask Thersander to look after my class." Before Kassia could stop him, he slipped back into the barracks. It didn't take long for him to get another eirene to agree to fill in for him, however, and then he was back. They drove together to Sandy's barracks.

Here Niko did the negotiating with Sandy's eirene, and soon Sandy appeared, yawning and bewildered. "What's happening?" he asked his elder brother, scratching himself sleepily.

"We're going home."

"Why?"

"Because Mom sent for us," Niko told him simply.

"She's having the babies," Kassia added.

Sandy looked over at her wide-eyed. "So what's that got to do with us? Isn't Agesandros there?"

"Agesandros is there, but Mom wants to see us," Niko told his younger brother, adding in a voice now used to commanding younger boys, "and that's enough reason for you. Stop being impertinent!"

Although it was now the darkest hour of the night, the entire kleros was still wide awake. Sleepy and a little grumpy, Lampon came out to the stables when they drove into the yard. "You go on in," he told the three young masters. "I'll see to the horses."

In the courtyard, light spilled from the open kitchen door, where the entire household was collected around the hearth. The men looked as if they had come from their beds, the women as if they had not seen them yet that night. Wine was on the table as were the remnants of a meal, half-eaten. Kassia noticed that the midwife was with the household.

At the sight of the children in the doorway, Phoebe straightened. "Well, thank Hermes for that! Go quick. She's not dead yet!"

Niko broke away from his siblings, sprinting into the house toward the sickroom, without a thought for anyone but himself. How could he have failed to notice what his mother was going through? Why hadn't he come home more often? Why hadn't he come last time she asked? Suddenly he remembered how often she had asked him if he couldn't "find time" to visit. He had had too many excuses. He had been too self-important, and she had always accepted. But now—only now—he saw how sad her smile had been when she accepted his decision. How could he have been so blind? So selfish?

"Mom!"

"Not now! Get back out there!"

"You've got no right—"

"I'll teach you to obey a peer, eirene! Get out!"

"Your mother's not conscious, Niko. Wait outside." Pharax spoke without stopping what he was doing, and Niko couldn't see his mother because Pharax and Dexippos and Mika were blocking his view.

Kassia came up behind him and pulled him away. "We have to wait out here." They sat down in a row on the marble bench outside the sickroom, facing their mother's precious garden.

Abruptly the frail wail of a baby burst out of the window over their heads. Niko was on his feet first, and then the other two; but before they could move, Mika rushed out to them shouting, "Help! Get Unoma! Fetch Unoma and Phoebe! Help!"

Niko sprang away with Sandy on his heels, while Kassia turned on Mika. "What is it? What's happening?"

"The babies! The umbilical cord of one was wrapped around the throat of the other. One's alive, but the other has been choked by his brother. Maybe Unoma—"

"What about Mom?!" Kassia shook Mika furiously. "What about my mother!"

"I don't know!" Mika wailed, the strain finally getting to her, too. "I don't know!"

Unoma and Phoebe, trailed by Glauce and Orsippos—and probably everyone else as well—were running up the side of the peristyle. Mika pulled herself together and took the older women back into the chamber. Kassia stood in the doorway, her brothers behind her. In the light of the lamps it was hard to see. Two small, slimy, and bloody things were passed to the serving women. One was screaming to make your hair stand on end and struggling so hard that Phoebe could hardly hold onto it, slippery as it was. The other, the limp one, was grabbed by its feet by the African woman. She held it head down and smacked its tiny bottom and just when Kassia was about to protest, a wail went up from it.

Before she had time to rejoice, Pharax was shouting over his shoulder, "Get them out of here. I need light and air and quiet!"

Kassia backed quickly out of the way, as Phoebe and Unoma took the little infants straight to the baths and set about cleaning them up. Sandy was beside her asking, "What are they? Boys or girls?"

"What difference does that make?" Kassia asked irritably, her ear cocked to the other room, where Pharax was giving urgent-sounding orders to Dexippos, Leon and Mika.

"Boys," Phoebe answered Sandy's question. "You have two little brothers."

"More brothers! Just what I needed," Kassia declared as if disappointed, but her attention was riveted on the room behind her.

"Squeeze, Mika! Harder! Agesandros!"

"Where?"

"There. More light! Mika! Dexippos!"

"Here."

Kassia could tell by the urgency of Pharax's tone that something was wrong. And all she could do was stand there listening. Or could she? With abrupt resolve, she turned and walked into the sick chamber. The stench was what struck her first, and then the blood apparently everywhere, and then the faces—pale, skeletal and frightened—hovering around the bed. Her mother's face was peaceful and waxy, as if she were already dead, but Kassia could see for herself that her blood was pulsing. Agesandros, his hands drenched in blood, was trying to hold an artery closed, while Pharax worked to replace everything and Dexippos prepared needle and thread. Mika was working without instructions to wipe the blood away from where Pharax was working, and Leon was holding a lamp directly over the bed to give as much light as possible. Kassia didn't see what she could do—except give Mika a clean cloth.

She lost all sense of time. She did not know how many cloths she passed to Mika, although the basket for the dirty napkins was overflowing, when she heard Pharax say, "Agesandros, you can let go now."

Agesandros grunted and seemed to have difficulty letting go. His fingers were stiff from holding the artery. He pulled his hand back slowly, staring. But the blood no longer spurted. His eyes went to Pharax, but the surgeon had no time for him. He wasn't finished yet. Agesandros slowly straightened and his eyes came to rest on Kassia. Only now he he register that she was there. He nodded to her, a little nod of respect, and then his eyes went back to the operation.

Mika backed away from the table. After a moment, as if dazed, she bent and collected the cloths that had fallen on the floor. She put them into the basket. "Are there any clean linens left in the whole house?" she asked Kassia in a whisper.

"I don't know." Kassia was still staring. Pharax was closing the wound now. Surely he wouldn't do that if Alethea were dead. But she could see no pulse, no breath, nothing.

Mika left with the dirty linens, but Kassia stood staring like Agesandros and Leon. And then Pharax stepped back, and his peg leg slipped on all the blood and fluid on the floor, and he crashed down onto his back with a cry of surprise. Kassia was the first to reach him. "Are you all right? Did you hurt yourself? Pharax?"

Pharax gazed at her in wonder. "What are you doing here?"

"She's been here for the last hour—ever since the babies were cut out."

"Pharax?"

He was struggling to get back on his feet, but he was trembling too violently, and he fell back down.

Leon set aside his lamp and went down on his other side. Supporting him and yet holding him still, he urged, "Just relax, sir. Catch your breath. You've been on your feet for at least three hours straight."

"Don't just stand there gawking! Get wine, water and something to eat for the surgeon!" Agesandros ordered his stepsons, both of whom stood gaping in the doorway.

"Pharax?" Kassia still held his shaking arm. "Is she going to make it? Is my mother going to live?"

Pharax shook his head. "I don't know." He dropped his head on his arms and whispered again, "I don't know."

CHAPTER 17

The images and voices were confused. Darkness and pain alternated with an almost blinding light. The light was attractive. It offered peace and harmony of excruciating intensity. Oblivion. In the darkness with the pain, however, were the familiar, loving voices of Kassia and Agesandros, Niko and Sandy, and Leon and Mika and Sybil and others. How can anyone want pain? But it was proof of being alive, wasn't it? The spirits and shades, the immortals, felt no pain. And it wasn't all pain and darkness. The stroke of gentle fingers, the touch of lips to lips, the scent of rosemary....

Alethea smiled before she opened her eyes. She felt sun on her face and someone tucking warm wool around her arms. She was being jostled, too, that's why the pain had shaken her awake, but it was worth it for the sun and the scent of rosemary. They were carrying her into her garden. She heard Agesandros' irritable voice. "Set her down near the roses. If she comes to, I want her to see them first."

The jostling stopped and still she kept her eyes closed, enjoying the feel of the sun on her face and listening to the voices around her. "You should get some rest, Father. Sandy and I can sit with her." She smiled to hear Niko call Agesandros "father."

Agesandros didn't answer. Nor did he move. She could feel him looming over her, casting a shadow on her chest. Kassia was singing in her sweet, high voice, very softly. She was singing an ancient lullaby, something Alethea had once sung to her rather than one of the songs she'd written herself or one of the rousing marches the Supreme Polemarch had written recently. Sandy told Kassia to "shut up," but Agesandros countered him. "Let her sing. Her mother loved to hear her sing."

Kassia's voice was lulling Alethea back to sleep. She was exhausted, and it was enough just to know she was alive after all. If she died now, she died not in agony but in peace, with her loved ones around her. But why should she die now? There was so much she had to live for. She wanted to be there for Kassia, if her marriage proved as bad as she expected. And she wanted to see Niko get his cloak and shield. And Sandy still needed her, even if he were the only one among them that didn't admit it. She wanted to grow old with Agesandros....

"Your sons, master." It was Phoebe's voice. "Don't you want to see your sons? You have to send word to the Council of Elders that you have sons."

That did it. Alethea's eyes snapped open. "Sons? Two of them? Are they alive?"

The commotion was almost too much. Suddenly they were all crowding around, hanging over her, blocking out the sun and the roses. Niko and Sandy were disclaiming their love loudly, Kassia burst into tears, Sybil started crying praises and thanks to the gods, and from behind them came the wailing of newborn infants. Alethea focused on Agesandros. He had caught up her hand and held it, his eyes brimming with unshed tears, and she smiled at him, until Unoma jostled her way through the others to show her the two little red bundles—one bald-looking and one black-haired.

Alethea reached out to them in wonder. She had not once dreamed that she might live to see them. She took one in each arm and looked from one to the other and then up at Agesandros with so much pride and joy that she looked almost young. Tears were trickling down his face, but he still couldn't bring out a sound.

Everyone—except Agesandros—was talking at once. Niko was apologizing for not visiting more often. Sandy wanted to know what she was going to call his brothers. Sybil was explaining that the dark-haired baby's umbilical cord had been wound around the fair-haired baby's neck. This was what had prevented the birth. Phoebe announced that Unoma had saved the fair-haired baby's life. Alethea smiled up at the African woman and then handed the babies back to her. "Thank you." To the others, she admitted somewhat ashamedly, "I'm still so tired."

The black woman took the babies without comment, while the others hastened to assure her she had every right to be tired. They started urging her to get some rest. Now that it was clear she would live, Niko and Sandy had to return to the agoge. The household, once they'd seen for themselves that she was back among them, had to feed the livestock and get on with their other tasks or get some sleep. Leon and Mika and Sybil were all but sleeping on their feet, and while Sybil bathed Alethea in tears of relief, Mika and Leon only timidly wished Alethea well before slipping away to their own beds. Finally there were only Kassia and Agesandros left. Alethea smiled and reached out a hand to each of them. "Thank you," she said ambivalently, and then closed her eyes with a contented sigh and went back to sleep. Only now did Kassia have time to remember her impending wedding.

At Agesandros' bidding, Niko took word of the birth of his half-brothers to the Spartan Council, and it was just after noon that a delegation of elders, three men including Leobotas, arrived to inspect the infants. The function of the delegation was to certify and record the birth of children eligible for the agoge and citizenship. The delegation also had the unpleasant duty of ordering the exposure of children with any kind of defect that would prevent them from becoming productive citizens. According to Spartan law and tradition, a deformed or sickly infant, that would not be able to endure the agoge or serve in the army, could not be allowed to live at all.

Agesandros was sound asleep when the delegation arrived, and he had to be woken. Still somewhat groggy with sleep, he came into the armoury where—for some reason—Phoebe and Unoma had brought the infants for inspection. On the damaged wall, all the weapons had been taken down and stacked in the far corner. On the other walls, the shields, spears, swords and bows of Nikolaidas' ancestors hung—most notably the panoply of his father.

The first thing one of the councilmen said was: "This is highly unusual, Agesandros, son of Medon—to register your sons' birth on another man's kleros. Your sons should have been born on your own kleros—"

"You obviously haven't seen it. You wouldn't let your wife give birth in a barn either!"

"Agesandros!" Leobotas reproved him sharply.

Agesandros just moved forward to stand beside the three elders. Phoebe held the dark-haired baby out first, and the blankets were opened to expose the squirming infant. The three men inspected him clinically but with approval. He was well formed and the volume of his cries gave evidence of his robust and healthy lungs and heart. Satisfied, they nodded and asked Agesandros his name. Agesandros hadn't thought about it. He hadn't had time. He certainly wasn't going to name the boy after his own drunken father and at that moment, he couldn't even remember Alethea's father's name. He had never known her father. Her brother had done his best to prevent the marriage. For a moment he considered honouring Leobotas himself, but then he wondered if he should honour the surgeon who had saved both the infants and Alethea.

"Do you expect us to wait here all day?"

"Areas," Agesandros decided spontaneously, remembering a poem that Tyrtaios had written about twins. Tyrtaios, the Supreme Polemarch, more than anyone, he decided, had made this day possible; he had saved Agesandros from disgrace and turned him into a hero that even Alethea's brother could no longer scorn. And he had written a poem about twins, one dark and one fair, like Castor and Polydeukes.

The elders understood his reasoning. They nodded approval, and the name was recorded on the wax tablet they had brought with them. Then Unoma held out the second infant for inspection. This baby was not only fair, he was notably smaller than his brother, and his neck still seemed far too small for his head. He whimpered and whined, rather than bawling out his indignation, at the cold, probing fingers of the old men. The old men frowned, and for a heartbeat Agesandros thought they might reject this infant as too weak.

"My wife nearly died to give him birth. If Pharax hadn't managed to cut them out of her, she *would* have died. I'm not going to go in and tell her that after all she's gone through, you've decided to kill one of them."

The three men gazed at him with expressions varying from astonishment to disapproval. Leobotas looked annoyed, but answered with a glance to the others, "You won't have to. Is this the wet-nurse?" He indicated Unoma.

Agesandros nodded, and the elders signaled approval before handing the baby back. "What name?"

"Apollonides," Agesandros replied as expected.

The women were sent out with the babies, and Agesandros led the elders to the andron for wine and a snack. As they walked along the peristyle from the armoury, Leobotas caught Agesandros' arm. "Where is Kassia? I have a message for her. Her bridegroom has sent word that he will come for her tonight."

"Tonight? But Kassia is exhausted. She was up all night helping her mother—she helped during surgery itself!" Agesandros stressed, full of pride and admiration for his stepdaughter.

"Steady," Leobotas warned, with a significant glance at his fellow councilmen. "We know your opinion of Anaxilas. Don't let it blind you. Kassia has been promised to him, and he seems to feel he has been kept waiting long enough already. He wanted to marry her last spring, remember, and had fully expected to carry her home shortly after his return with the army. He is in no mood for even another day's delay. He *will* come for her tonight. The best you can do is make sure that Kassia is ready for him."

Kassia took the news calmly. She was sitting on her bed, her hair a mess, when Agesandros broke the news to her. She had dark circles under her eyes from the sleepless night, but she nodded and said, "I expected as much."

Agesandros' head was full of comments—all of them insulting—about Kassia's bridegroom, but he kept them to himself. It would hardly help Kassia now to hear what he thought of her husband. Besides, she already knew. Instead he started, "Your mother—"

"In Persephone's name, don't breathe a word to Mom! She'll only worry about me. Don't mention a thing to her! It will be soon enough for her to find out when it's over!"

All Agesandros had wanted to say was that her mother wasn't up to preparing her, but clearly she already knew that. Again Agesandros had the feeling he had underestimated his stepdaughter. She was far ahead of him.

"Should I send Sybil and Mika to you?"

"No, not yet. Let them sleep. They did more than me."

"It wasn't their mother," Agesandros reminded her. "You were the most courageous of all of us. I know we've had our differences, Kassia, and you—rightly—resented the way I tried to interfere with your marriage, but I want you to know that I—I—admire you. I think—"

"Agesandros!" She leapt up and flung her arms around him with the impetuousness of youth, completely taking her stepfather by surprise. She gave him a quick kiss on the cheek, but then drew back. "Thank you. Thank you for *everything!*" She seemed to want to endow the word with a wealth of meaning that she could not articulate, and Agesandros could not grasp it all. He sensed only her intensity and sincerity. He started to open his mouth, but she cut him off. "Please. Not now, and don't take this wrong, but I want to be alone for a bit—before it all starts."

"Of course." He went to the door of her chamber, but then stopped to look back. Kassia sat on the edge of her bed, her hair in disarray and her shoulders sagging, as she stared at her hands in her lap. "Kassia, are you sure there's nothing I can do?"

She looked up with a start, as if she had already forgotten him. She gazed at him and bit on her lower lip as if she were considering asking something of him, but then she shook her head decisively. "No. No, there is no way you can help. But thank you for asking."

This time she watched him leave and listened to his footsteps retreating along the gallery. Only when she heard him start down the stairs did she return to her thoughts. Only one thing was absolutely certain in her mind: she was *not* going to marry Anaxilas. She would kill herself first. She would not let him plant his seed in her, so she could writhe in agony as her mother and Chloe had. Chloe and her mother had loved the fathers of their children. But for her it would be completely different. She would hate the planting as much as the harvest. She couldn't bear the thought of Anaxilas touching her—anywhere. She couldn't bear the thought of him kissing her again. She shuddered physically with revulsion. She hated Anaxilas.

When she had agreed to the marriage, she had never met him. She had not known about hate. She had had no reason to fear. And she had not been in love with someone else. She had not believed she *could* love again. But now her teenage love for her cousin seemed only a childish fantasy, whereas her love for Pharax was overwhelming.

When had it started? It seemed as if it had always been there—from that first meeting at the olive harvest, when he had shown so much interest in Mika. But not until last night, when she saw him all but collapse after saving her mother from certain death, had she admitted it to herself. When Pharax fell over onto the floor after the operation, Kassia had felt her heart in her throat. She had suddenly known that she loved him—funny red beard, flabby arms, paunch and all. She would not be afraid if *he* were claiming her tonight. She would not even be apprehensive. She wished it were Pharax who was coming for her tonight.

Kassia was on her feet, pacing about her chamber like a caged wildcat. Why shouldn't it be Pharax? Why shouldn't he claim her tonight—before Anaxilas got here? If she were already gone when Anaxilas came, he couldn't claim her. If she were to wake up tomorrow in Pharax's house, in Pharax's bed, it would cause a brief scandal. It would humiliate Anaxilas—but he deserved it. And she would be safe. Anaxilas would never stoop so low as to beg her return after she was "besmirched" by someone else.

Pharax! Pharax! Pharax! He was her salvation. All she had to do was tell him what was facing her. Surely if he knew that she hated Anaxilas and was afraid of him, he would offer to rescue her? Of course he would—just as Agesandros had asked if there was anything he could do.

Invigorated with hope, Kassia took a comb to her hair, changed into a fresh peplos, and then ran barefoot down to the guest room where they had put Pharax to bed after the operation.

She knocked on the door loudly, "Pharax? Pharax? It's me, Kassia. I have to talk to you."

"What?" He sounded drugged and sleepy still. "Wait. Stop. Just a minute." She could hear him whispering to Dexippos, and then after a moment, the slave opened the door. Pharax had apparently hastily pulled a chiton over his head, but he was still barefoot and his hair was standing on end. His face was puffy from sleep, and he yawned even as she entered.

The sight of Kassia, with her freshly brushed hair cascading over her shoulders, made him struggle to his feet. "Kassia, I—I—"

"I need to talk to you. It's urgent."

"Is your mother—"

"Mom's fine. She woke up briefly and now she's sleeping soundly. She even held her new sons, and you would have thought she wasn't a day over 20. And the Council has accepted both of them, even the one that nearly got choked to death in the womb. So you see, you did it. You really *did* save all three of them."

Pharax's expression was so amazed that Kassia wanted to kiss him. "I couldn't have done it without your help," he stammered out, remembering how he had almost lost Alethea after the babies were removed.

"The others did more," Kassia admitted modestly.

Pharax had been thinking of the others. He had not noticed Kassia until it was over. But what did it matter? She had certainly been there, and in some way she must have helped the others. He nodded and smiled at her. "I know, but I couldn't have done it without all of you—Leon holding the light hour after hour and Mika, never fainting or turning away, never slow or clumsy. She, as much as I, saved your mother's life." He took a deep breath. "I wasn't sure. I wasn't sure...."

"Pharax, I've come to you about something else. Don't think I'm callous, but they just sent me word that Anaxilas will come for me tonight."

She saw him start and catch his breath. He looked away and licked his lips. He couldn't seem to find anything to say. Kassia had seen enough. He was distressed by the news just as she had expected him to be.

"Pharax, I don't want to marry him."

Pharax's head snapped back. "What?"

"I hate him. I haven't told anyone about this—not even Mom or Agesandros—but when he came back from Messenia, the very first time he called on me, he—he tried to force himself on me." She gazed at Pharax as she spoke, watching for the slightest change in expression.

Pharax stiffened, but he said nothing. He seemed to be holding his breath.

"It's not just that, Pharax. That wouldn't have been so bad, if only he had *talked* to me first. But he didn't want to talk to me. He didn't even ask how I was or how Mom was or what I'd done all summer! He didn't ask if I'd written anything—much less ask to see it, though I had everything ready for him!" As she spoke, her indignation returned. She spoke in a breathy flood of outrage, and Pharax stood holding his breath and wishing with all his heart he wasn't a flabby, one-legged surgeon but the fleet, strong hoplite that he had once been.

"Anaxilas doesn't care about *me* at all!" Kassia concluded. "He doesn't even see me as a *person*! All he sees is my *outside*." She uttered the last word as if it were something filthy and repulsive.

"I'm so sorry," Pharax whispered. Why couldn't he have been wrong about Anaxilas?

Kassia was frustrated and growing desperate. She had told him how horrible Anaxilas was. She had told him she hated him. She had told him she didn't want to marry him. She could see that Pharax was distressed by what she had told him. Why didn't he offer to help her?

"Pharax, I *can't* marry him. I just can't."

"Have you told Agesandros that?"

"No, of course not. He's not my guardian. He can't stop the marriage. Leobotas is my guardian, and Leobotas would never understand. You must see that? Besides, there isn't time to go to him. Anaxilas will be here tonight! I have to run away, Pharax." Surely that was explicit enough, she thought hopefully, gazing at Pharax with anticipation. She held her breath as she waited for him to say the words that would save her.

Instead Pharax retorted in open alarm, "But where would you go? Would your uncle take you in? I can't picture Charillos—"

"Uncle Charillos is the last person who would help me. No, I can't turn to my family." Why was he being so dense?

"But who else can you turn to? You can't just run away. The mountains are filled with outlaws and runaways and rebels. Kassia, you're just a maiden—"

"I know! That's why I need your help!" She was near to tears of frustration because he still hadn't caught on. It humiliated her to have to *ask* for his help.

"My help? But how can I help?"

Why didn't he see? Why didn't he understand? In desperation, she had to sink even lower. "Take me away with you before Anaxilas comes! Marry me!" As she spoke, she moved closer to him. She looked up at him with desperate, hopeful eyes, and her lips were moist from wetting them in her agitation.

Pharax drew back in horror. She was so beautiful! He couldn't think of touching her. He was too unworthy. He had a peg leg and a paunch. The very though of her seeing him naked shamed him. No, he couldn't take something as perfect as this. He had no right to.

"What is it?" Kassia asked, mortified. He had drawn away from her. He had rejected her. She didn't understand. "Don't you want me?" she asked, bewildered. All her life she had been told she was beautiful and desirable. And suddenly, at the most critical moment of her life, the only man she wanted didn't want her.

"Kassia! How can you ask something like that?! You are another man's wife. You will be my queen. I—I can't just run away with you!"

"Why not? I don't want to be another man's wife. I don't want to be Sparta's queen. Pharax, please!" She forgot the humiliation of begging. She was only aware of her desperation. This was her last chance, her last hope, Pharax had to agree to marry her. "Please marry me, Pharax, please!"

Pharax was more horrified than ever. She was starting to cry. She was still so young, so fragile and delicate. Her beauty had never been more touching. Every instinct of his body screamed for him to take her in his arms, to kiss away her tears, and promise her that everything would be all right. But his mind warned him that it would be madness. His courage failed him. "I—I—can't," he stammered out helplessly. "I—I—" Whatever he had intended to say, he didn't get it out.

Kassia turned and fled. She ran blindly at first. Away from the scene of her humiliation, away from the first man who had ever rejected her, away from her shattered hopes. She got out of the house by the walled orchard, and ran barefoot past the barns and stables and down to the river. She stared at the rushing water, splashing bitterly cold, and she paused. Her feet were cold already, and her teeth started to chatter. She glanced up at the leaden sky hanging low over the Taygetos, obscuring the snowy peaks. The sun that had shone this morning on her mother in the garden was obscured again. Winter had closed in once more. The day was short and already drawing to a dreary end. And with the darkness would come Anaxilas. He would take her aboard his chariot and rape her somewhere between here and the city. She was sure of it. He would not even wait to get her home to a soft bed. He would rape her as he had all the women he'd captured or purchased.

And Pharax didn't care. The tears streamed down her face. That was the worst of it. Pharax didn't care. She didn't mean anything to him. Not any more than Mika or her mother. He didn't want her for his bride.

The gurgling of the river penetrated to her consciousness like the voices of the dead trying to communicate. Damonon! She had promised herself to him. She had promised to come to him. And she had failed him. But he had not failed her. He had come for her, for he had a better claim than Anaxilas. He would take her for his bride and save her as Pharax had refused to do. She let out a sigh of relief as she understood at last how she would escape Anaxilas. She considered the stream. But it seemed too uncertain to her. The cold would make her struggle. She wouldn't be able to keep still under water. No, she couldn't imagine drowning herself. She turned and walked back to the house, back in through the door of the walled orchard that she had left open. She paused by the house altar. She removed the bracelet she was wearing and placed it on the altar. "Please help Mom to understand," she whispered. Then she hurried.

The dusk was closing in fast. Everyone would be gathering for dinner. Sybil and Mika would be awake. Agesandros would tell them that Anaxilas was coming and they would come looking for her. She had to act fast. She slipped into the house, hesitating in the corridor before risking a dash along the side of the peristyle to the armoury.

The room was poorly lit by only a single window and the door. The window faced the orchard and was shaded by trees. The light from the peristyle was nearly as poor. It took a moment for her eyes to adjust, but then they scanned the room and found what she was looking for. Her father's arms.

She went and carefully pulled the sword from its sheath. The sound of the iron sword rasping in the scabbard seemed so loud that she jumped and looked hastily about herself to be sure no one else had heard. But she was alone. She tested the blade. Out of respect to her father and so that it would be ready in an emergency, it had been sharpened before it was hung up. No one had used it since. It was as sharp as a weapon could be.

It was also cold in her hand. The blade was cold. It made her shiver. She stared at it with a strange feeling in her stomach. The urge to urinate was undeniable. She licked her lips.

From the peristyle Sybil was calling for her. "Kassia? Kassia? Come get something to eat, child. You'll need your strength tonight."

No. She wouldn't. She took the handle in both hands and pointed the tip of the blade at the bottom of her rib cage. Long ago, during the Messenian raid, her mother had taught her about killing herself. Don't risk a stomach wound, she'd warned; go for your heart. She was glad the Spartans used short swords. A longer one would have been hard to hold. She yanked her arms forward.

They gave her a state funeral, as if she had been a queen. The entire city turned out, remembering the sweet voice of the soloist and the fragile beauty of the child-poet who had made them all weep with her ode to the dead in this Second Messenian War. They came in black and they ordered their helots to wear mourning as well—although the laws required that only for the kings. They spoke about her with awe, remembering that she had flung herself hysterically upon the corpse of her cousin when he had been killed in the raid on the agoge. And they whispered how she had tried to take her life then, too.

The Supreme Polemarch honoured her with an ode set to music that was unique because of the absence of a soprano solo—because it marked the death of his soloist. Sung entirely in alto and in a minor key, the melody haunted everyone who heard it.

King Anaxanidras spoke of her as his "child" and his son and heir, her would be father-in-law, Archidamos, of his "daughter." Queen Eupolia said Sparta had a lost a "great queen" and treated her grandson as if he did not exist. It was unfair.

Anaxilas' grief was boundless. She had killed herself rather than marry him. Everyone knew it. They whispered that she had learned about Niobe, that she had been unwilling to play "second" to a concubine, to a slave. Anaxilas knew better. He knew that she had rejected him not because of Niobe, but for himself. And that hurt him more than anything. Niobe could be discarded --indeed, he had already sold her to an Egyptian slave trader. But how could he change what he was? The answer was surprisingly clear: he had to stop being everything that he had been before. He had to start his life over again....

Only Pharax knew that Anaxilas had not killed her, he had. If only he had had the courage to do as she had asked of him that fateful night, she would not only be alive, but his wife. Pharax knew the price of his cowardice. He would live alone the rest of his life. He would never take a wife. He would not sire children. He would live only for his medicine, remembering always what he might have had....

When the incense and the choruses and the official mourners were gone; when Niko and Agesandros together had lovingly put Alethea back to bed; when all that was left was a fresh mound of earth under a tamarask tree by the mill; Mika went down to cry alone.

With all the kings and princes, queens and priests and polemarchs paying their respects, she had not been given a chance. Mika sat down on the steps where Kassia had once exchanged innocent kisses with her cousin, on the steps where they had waited together for Pharax to dig up Chloe's corpse. Mika sat clutching her knees to her chest, her chin on her knees, and she remembered Kassia. She remembered her saying she hated being beautiful, and rejecting make-up and elaborate hairstyles. She remembered that Kassia, more than anyone else in the household, had made sure she smeared the ugly yellow ointment on her face.

Mika felt her face. Beneath the tears her skin was almost smooth. Not beautifully smooth like Kassia's unblemished skin, but the warts were gone. All that was left were some dimples and low bumps. She wasn't beautiful—not like Kassia or Niobe—but she wasn't ugly anymore, either. And it was because of Kassia.

Kassia had treated her like a friend, she remembered. Kassia had taken her side when Niobe ordered her about or insulted her. Kassia had slapped Niobe for her. And Kassia had let her help in the surgery, not shoving her aside, but serving her.

Mika was crying so hard, she didn't notice at once that someone had come to sit beside her—not until Leon put his arm around her shoulders and pulled her to him. He held her tight and let her cry onto his chest for a long time, and then he said, "The most beautiful thing about her was that she taught me to love you, Mika."

HISTORICAL NOTES

I. ON THIS NOVEL

All the characters in this novel are fictional and so are the events described. They are the products of research about the period, and the events are, based on that research, plausible. For example, we know that on the one hand the Greeks were capable of highly delicate operations such as cataract removals, but on the other hand, most Greek doctors knew so little about gynaecology that they believed the womb wandered about the inside of a woman's body causing other organs to malfunction. It was widely assumed that a woman's fertility was greater during menstruation, and that intercourse was the best cure for all forms of female illness from hysteria to asthma. Sparta, however, was the one city in ancient Greece where women's bodies were not mysterious and hidden. Because Spartan girls were fed like their brothers, required to exercise and did so in the nude, I think it is fair to hypothesize that Sparta was likely to be the first city in Greece where more sensible gynaecology was practiced. We know for a fact that caesearians were being performed by the age of Julius Caesar.

The fact that captives became slaves is one of the more distasteful aspects of ancient Greece. It is only a matter of using one's imagination and the power of empathy to understand what an enormous trauma this must have been—particularly for sheltered young girls such as Niobe. On the other hand, the nature of people—as ancient sources repeatedly make vivid—has not changed very much in 3000 years. Niobe, Mika, Alethea and Kassia are people I have known—only the costumes and manners and circumstances have changed, not their fundamental character.

II. ON SPARTAN WOMEN

The high status, education, and economic power of women in Sparta shocked and horrified men throughout the rest of the ancient world. Aristotle speculated that the entire decline of Sparta in the later half of the 5th century BC was attributable to the license of Sparta's women.

Spartan girls enjoyed the same food as their brothers and were required to engage in sports while receiving public education. Girls in other Greek cities were more likely to be killed at birth, were then fed less and less healthy food than their brothers, and were confined to a few dingy, smoke-filled rooms for their entire lives—rarely getting fresh air or sunshine much less exercise of any kind. While most Greek women were illiterate, Spartan women were possibly more literate than their men. There are recorded cases of Spartan women being the students of the philosophers, and there are many references to their written messages to their sons. Archeological evidence supports a comparatively widespread degree of literacy.

Spartan laws prohibited the marriage of girls before they were at an age to "enjoy sex" and Spartan girls generally married in their late teens or early twenties, whereas in the rest of Greece fathers were urged to marry off their daughters as soon as they started menstruating—as early as 12 or 13. In Athens women could neither inherit nor control property, but in Sparta they ran the family estates thereby controlling to a large extent their husband's and son's status. Economic power has always bestowed status.

Please visit my website: **www.elysiumgates.com/~helena** for more information about Spartan women and some suggested reading.

III. ON SPARTAN SEXUALITY

The archeological evidence for Sparta suggests so far that, just as ancient commentators described, there were no brothels within the city of Sparta itself. Spartan men interested in purchasing sex had to travel to one of the outlying perioikoi communities. Even more telling is the almost complete absence of pornographic depictions on artifacts, such as are abundant in both Athens and Corinth. On the other hand, some of the most important and lovely pieces of Spartan sculpture depict couples sitting side-by-side. Regardless of who the figures were intended to depict (Helen and Menelaus, Chilon and his wife, a Spartan king and his queen), what is significant is the greater importance given to depictions of a man and wife side-by-side, i.e. in partnership, compared to depictions of sexual intercourse. This is particularly notable when one considers that female nude figurines appear in Sparta in the Archaic period, whereas it was not until the Hellenistic period that the female body was shown nude in other parts of Greece. The naked Spartan figurines reflect the fact that Spartan girls and women exercised in the nude, and so the female body was familiar and not an overtly erotic image.

Contemporary literary sources from Sparta itself are almost non-existent, but the poems of Alkman, written in the second half of the 7th century BC, are an important exception. Among other works are the lyrics of songs written to be performed in public at festivals by girls' choruses. Alkman also wrote poetry expressing his own adoration of the Spartan girls he worked with. He was considered by ancient scholars the first "love poet"—a notable distinction for the poet whom the ancients also viewed as "the most Spartan"! None of Alkman's texts can be classed as pornographic, but many modern commentators assert that because the texts of the lyrics, designed to be sung by girls' choruses, praise the girls' beauty, that the songs were lesbian in nature. This is nonsense. Boys' and men's choruses sang about bravery and girls about beauty—because those were the virtues that each group, respectively, was expected to strive for and which their elders wanted praised at public festivals. What the texts—and the fact that Alkman was so revered in Sparta—do tell us is that the Spartans enjoyed light-hearted music and tributes to female beauty in a public context—not merely in the back alleys of the red-light district.

In contrast to these sparse, native records, ancient observers of Sparta in the Archaic and Classical periods generally have a great deal to say about Spartan sexual relations. Herodotus, for example, is always happy to provide some juicy little story about a man who covets a close friend's wife, or who steals a rival's bride just before the wedding, or the king who loved his barren wife so much that he refused to set her aside even for the sake securing the succession to his throne. Notably absent in all these tales is a single mention of a Spartan with a male lover.

Xenophon, an Athenian who served with the Spartan army and sent his sons to the Spartan agoge, describes at length three aspects of Spartan sexuality in the Classical period. First, he explains that Spartan laws required men and women to marry in their physical prime and not when too young (for girls) or too old (for men) and that they should be initially restricted in their sexual contact so as to not to become "satiated" but rather *to enjoy* sex together. Note that there is explicit emphasis on the desirability of the *female* partner enjoying sex as much as the male. Second, Xenophon explains that Sparta's laws allowed a wife of good repute to have a sexual relationship with another Spartiate of good character. Although Xenophon stresses that this is to take place with the husband's consent, it is obvious that this was not always the case. And third, he describes at great length the practice of youths still in school having an elder mentor to guide and advise them, but he stresses emphatically that this relationship was not as "elsewhere in Greece." On the contrary, according to Xenophon, Sparta's laws made it just as disgraceful for an older man to molest a boy as for parents to have sexual intercourse with their children or brothers with their sisters.

Aristotle, writing later still, has even more to say about the greed and avarice of Spartan women. Indeed he goes so far as to attribute Sparta's decline to the power and wealth of her women—stating that undisciplined females are always the result in warlike societies which do *not* esteem homosexuality.

In conclusion, contemporary sources suggest that Sparta was not a particularly homo-erotic society and certainly there was no institutionalized homosexual behaviour upto the mid-5th century BC. On the contrary, in Sparta women's sexuality was not only recognized but respected and to a degree encouraged. Rather than being something frightful and dangerous, which male relatives needed to vigilantly guard (as in the rest of Greece), female sexuality was a positive factor which contributed to healthy children and so to the well-being of the state.

IV. ON SPARTAN MARRIAGE

To appreciate the unique aspects of Spartan marriage it is helpful to remember what marriage was like for elites in other ancient Greek cities. The comparison is with Athens, because we have the most reliable information about Athens, and the focus is on the aristocratic elite because only they were not craftsmen or labourers, had the luxury of household slaves and so are comparable in terms of social position and life-style to the Spartiates.

Athenian men generally did not marry until their early thirties, but it would have been a rare Athenian man who went to his marriage bed without extensive sexual experience. For a start, it was common for boys to be the objects of the homosexual attentions of men a few years older. These relationships were considered "honourable liaisons" and could have pedagogical benefits when older lovers took an interest in their protégé's education. It is interesting to note, however, that in the many erotic depictions on Athenian pottery the boys are not portrayed enjoying the experience, but rather stoically enduring it.

Once an Athenian male reached maturity and citizenship status, he ceased to be the object of sexual desire and became a predator. He might select a boy or youth of his own class, reversing the roles of a few years earlier, or he might take advantage of the vast array of sexual wares offered for sale in one of the liveliest trading centres of the ancient world. (There is considerable evidence that one of the principal wares that brought Athens her wealth was slaves.) These included prostitutes of both sexes ranging from the cheap varieties offered in streetside stalls to outrageously expensive courtesans, who limited and selected their clientele. In between were all the various kinds of male and female "entertainers" who performed at the symposia that young men of wealth attended on a more or less regular basis.

Eventually, the need for an heir would induce a man, by many accounts reluctantly, to marry. In order to do so, an Athenian would look about for a man or family who was politically useful to him or who could be counted on to pay a good dowry, and inquire about possible brides. It is highly improbable that a prospective bridegroom would have glimpsed any of the bride-candidates, because these (as we shall see below) were kept carefully guarded inside their homes and only seen in public on rare occasions, when they were carefully segregated from all strange males. The marriage negotiations would have been conducted with the prospective bride's male guardian. After the dowry was paid to the groom, the bride would have been collected and removed to the groom's house in a joyful ceremony accompanied by singing, music, dancing and feasting.

From the groom's point of view, except for the presence of a wife in his household, very little else changed. Nothing stood in the way of his continued attendance at symposia or his patronage of brothels. In fact, a man was perfectly in his rights to also contract with a poor man for his daughter to come into the household as a concubine—and of course, an Athenian man was within his rights to sleep with any of his slave girls. The contract of marriage was significant only because only sons by the legally registered wife could be enrolled as citizens of Athens.

Athenian girls were married as soon as they started to menstruate. This meant that most brides were roughly half the age of their husbands. Athenian girls were reared in their houses on a diet smaller and less nutritious than that of their brothers, lacking meat, fish, spices and wine. They were kept indoors, without exposure to direct sunlight or physical exercise, received no formal education and were usually illiterate. They were taught that women should speak as little as possible, and certainly not in the presence of men.

Once an Athenian maiden reached sexual maturity, she knew that her male guardian would marry her off, but she had no say in the matter. Normally girls were married to a complete stranger—a man they did not see until the day he came and took her away from her home, family and everything she had known until then. She was removed to a strange house, sometimes far away from her parental home, and surrounded by strangers. She might share the household with her husband's mother, sisters, and even his concubine(s).

Here she was still not allowed control of money worth more than a bushel of grain, and it was considered a disgrace for her to be seen standing in the doorway of her house, much less in the market or elsewhere. Talking to a strange man was cause for scandal—until she was old enough to be a grandmother. She might leave the house only to go to the childbed of a neighbour, to attend a wedding or funeral, or to take part in religious festivals.

It is estimated that on average women in Athens were brought to childbed six times in their lives, and that infant mortality ran between 20 and 40%. Even more devastating are frequent references to exposing children. A father could decided to kill any child that seemed an unnecessary financial burden. Because of the need to provide a dowery for daughters, and given the low value placed on women generally, it is fair to assume that—as in other cultures from China to Afghanistan today—girls were far more likely to be left to die than boys.

Last but not least, if a woman was raped or seduced, her husband was required by law to divorce her. Even if a husband was understanding or devoted, Athenian law mandated divorce or the man lost his own citizenship.

Turning at last to Sparta, the picture is dramatically different. Spartan boys left their parental homes at the age of seven to start their public education in the agoge. At age 21 they changed the barracks of the agoge for the barracks of the army, so it was not until age 31 that they could at last move into their own home or kleros and live with their own families. This fact has led many modern scholars to impute widespread homosexuality to Spartan men, but it ignores entirely the reality surrounding those barracks.

First, even as small boys, Spartan males spent much of their time out of doors playing, hunting, riding, and swimming. And everywhere the boys went they encountered the female children of their class because, unlike Athenian girls, Spartan girls were required by law to go to public school just like their brothers. The girls, too, were required to go to the public playing fields, race-courses, and gymnasiums in order to learn to run, wrestle, throw the discuss and javelin. The girls, like their brothers, swam in the Eurotas to cool off. And the girls exercised and swam in the nude just like their brothers.

In addition to sport, Sparta was notoriously "devout"—which meant, among other things, that Sparta honoured the various gods at a series of festivals throughout the year, some of which lasted days. These festivals included processions, athletic contests and horse and chariot racing—all for *both* sexes. A chariot race for women is specifically mentioned at the three-day Hyacinthia, for example. There were also dancing and singing competitions. Again, the girls were expected to perform just as the boys were. Again they sometimes did so in costumes that were (from the perspective of foreigners) "scanty," and sometimes they danced nude.

Because Sparta was a small society (at the peak of its power, under Leonidas I, there were just 8,000 male citizens of all ages), by the time youths reached adolescence they had seen all their prospective marriage partners engaged in a variety of activities and dressed in everything

from what passed for formal dress in Sparta to nakedness. It is important to stress that they hadn't just seen them. No Spartan law or custom suggested that women should be silent, while many foreign
accounts decried Spartan women's outspokenness. Boys and youths of
the agoge were expected to be still and respectful in the presence of
their elders, and girls were too—but not with each other! No one who
has raised or worked with teenagers can truly believe that Spartan
youths and maidens played, hunted, swam, rode, sang and danced
side-by-side from age seven onwards without talking to—and flirting
with!—one another. The bigger question is rather how the Spartan
school authorities and parents kept the entire system from getting out
of control.

One answer may well be that they didn't. Since Spartan marriage customs (from the early Archaic and into the mid-Classical period) for-
bade dowries and there was no religious component to the marriage
ceremony, the Spartan marriage practice may have in fact amounted to
elopement. According to contemporary sources, the Spartan marriage
ceremony was as follows: the bride shaved her hair like a boy (of the
agoge), donned men's clothing (presumably the chiton of the agoge)
and waited alone in the dark. The bridegroom came alone and surrep-
titiously after curfew, "took her" (but not necessarily home!) and then
stole back to barracks. That sounds suspiciously like two young lovers
trying not to be caught by the officers of the law patrolling the city
streets, because they were up to "something" of which the authorities
did not approve! No complicated and mysterious "cross-dressing" ritu-
als are required to explain the custom if it is looked at in this light.

Plutarch claimed—and has been quoted by historians ever since,
apparently without anyone pausing to reflect—that as a result of this
surreptitious marriage custom, men "might even have children before
they saw their own wives in the day." Nonsense! As I have pointed out
above, Spartan bridegrooms would have seen their future wives by day
almost daily from the time the girls were seven. Furthermore, they

would have seen their *brides* as often as they liked by day afterwards too! Young matrons were just as free to engage in sports, riding and driving or to go to market or hang about the temples as their younger sisters—especially if they were not yet in charge of a kleros! It may be true that young Spartan couples did not risk making love in broad daylight, but given human nature, I sincerely doubt it.

Alternatively, of course, Spartan law and authorities really were stronger than the forces of human nature, and Spartan youths and maidens dutifully did what the law required of them. This required that a youth still in his prime (still on active service, aged between 21 and 30) select a suitable girl of good character "old enough enjoy sex" (interpreted as 18 onwards), that he first got her father's permission and that he then took her alone in the dark of night before returning to barracks. Not so difficult to live with even for ardent lovers....

Under the circumstances, it is safe to say that the necessity of seeking sex outside of one's class and age-group was considerably reduced in Sparta. Since the city policy prohibited brothels inside the city but the youths and boys had to sleep in barracks located inside the city, their opportunities to visit such establishments were far more restricted than in other cities. As to women of a lower class, these consisted of perioikoi and helots. It appears that the perioikoi, like other Greeks, kept their women locked inside their houses in their own communities and gave the Spartiates little opportunity to seduce them. Because perioikoi were free, any use of force against them would have brought the Spartiate severe punishment. It probably didn't happen often. As for the helots, even these were far less accessible to Spartiate men than chattel slaves were to other Greeks. First, they lived in the countryside, often far from the city, and second, they were not private but state property. Because they were not chattel slaves and could marry and have children of their own, they lived in their own houses surrounded by their own families, including fathers and brothers. This made them far less vulnerable than female chattel slaves. Obviously, Spartiates could easily use force against these male protectors as well as the girls themselves, but in doing so a Spartiate would have been damaging *state* property and would have been liable for punishment—if it were without good cause. Whether Spartan magistrates would consider a youth's passion for a helot girl sufficient justification for damaging valuable workers is, in my opinion, dubious. Despite the tales of "hunting helots," the fact is that these incidents are only recorded from the late 5th century onwards as the situation in Sparta deteriorated rapidly. At all times, the Spartan economy depended on helots so heavily that it is inconceivable that there were widespread slaughters—except in very unusual circumstances. Furthermore, the Laconian, as opposed to the Messenian, helots were largely loyal. They would not have been so, if there were widespread rape and violence against them.

From the woman's perspective no less than from the youth's, marriage in Sparta was never to a stranger. Spartan girls had watched, cheered, jeered and flirted with the bachelors of the city from girlhood onward. They knew them all by name, patronymic and reputation. If a girl's father came home and announced he had a suit for her hand from one or another young man, she would have an opinion. Nothing in Spartan law or custom prevented her from voicing it. Whether her father listened to her was another matter, but it is not likely that a Spartan man would force a husband on a daughter over his *wife's* opposition—and she, no less than her daughter, would know all about the eligible bachelors from watching them on the playing fields and dance floors. In short, Spartan girls might not have chosen their husbands, but they had a good chance of vetoing a truly distasteful candidate.

As a wife, at least after her husband retired from active service and went to live on his kleros, a Spartiate woman took over control of an estate, household, and the family finances. She also had control of her children until they reached the age of seven and her daughters again from puberty to marriage (as it is widely presumed that they no longer lived in the agoge during this stage). Because she had helots, no Spartiate wife was required to do any menial tasks, and if she managed a prosperous estate she had the money and time for personal pleasures such as horse- or dog-breeding and hunting. She continued to go into the city not just for festivals but to go to the market or fairs and to exercise, since women were encouraged to remain fit into old age just as Spartiate men were. If her estate was a significant distance from the city, she drove a cart or chariot to get there, and once in the city she met with friends and family and spoke to whomever she pleased without discredit.

There is no reason to think that Spartan women, on average, had more or fewer pregnancies than other Greek women. They probably had more live births and lower infant mortality because they were older and healthier when they conceived, ate better during pregnancy and fed their infants better afterwards. A Spartan mother's sons did, of course, have to pass the inspection of the elders. If a male-child had some deficiency that made it doubtful whether he would be able to develop into a young man capable of taking his place in the line of battle, the elders could order it exposed. But a mother had the assurance that this would only be done because of a physical fault, not on the whim of the father. Furthermore, there is no evidence that girls were subjected to the same test.

While it is impossible to generalize about what a Spartan—any more than an Athenian, or American—marriage was like, several features are clear. The partners were more equal in age and education than their counterparts in other parts of Greece. They were not strangers when they came into the marriage, and in the majority of cases they would have *both* consented in some way. They would have had a longer or shorter period of quasi-marriage, when they were not living in the same household and the wife was not yet in control of the estate, but within a few years, they would set up house together. Henceforth, a man and his sons' citizen status depended upon his wife's good management of the family estate since a failure by the kleros to pay mess or agoge fees would have resulted in the loss of citizenship for father or son respectively. It is therefore not surprising that in this household, the wife ruled supreme and alone. It is inconceivable that a concubine was allowed to live in it, or that "flute girls" came to entertain the husband and his friends. Altogether, this was a good formula for a marriage based on mutual respect and partnership.

One last point. It is widely assumed that "because the men were away so much of the time" Spartan women basically lived in a world of their own and related mostly to other women. The alleged "frequent absence of Spartan husbands" is cited as an explanation for lesbianism and adultery. This is astonishing when one considers that even men on active duty did not drill all day—probably not more than a few hours—and that dinner at the messes did not last as long as the symposia of other Greek cities. On a normal day, it is probable that Spartan husbands were away from home less than the average working man today, who leaves home at 7 or 8 am and returns only after a commute and an 8 hour workday some 10 hours or more later. The evidence suggests, furthermore, that during the frequent festivals, men and possibly even the boys were with their families—all day. How much of their free time—and Spartan men, far more than the tradesmen and craftsmen of other cities, had plenty of it—was spent with their wives depended on the relationship itself, just as it does today. As for Sparta's frequent wars, until the Peloponnesian war these were purely seasonal and the campaign "season" was short—two to three months at the most. Again, in modern times many men travel on business, reserve duty, or to pursue their own hobbies for that many months out of every year. Few Spartan women saw so little of their husbands as the wives of men on duty in Iraq, Afghanistan or serving with the navy today.

None of which means there were no unhappy marriages or no opportunities for women to become interested in other men. What is noteworthy is that in Sparta there were no official sanctions against adultery. Helen, the most famous of all Spartan women, ran away from her husband and lived with a younger man for ten years causing a war with immense loss of life—and then returned to Sparta, resumed her duties as queen and "lived happily ever after." She was honoured in Sparta with monuments, temples and festivals—despite her adultery. Other real Spartan women, including queens, got away with adultery with impunity as well.

It is hardly any wonder, then, that the rest of the ancient world viewed Spartan women as licentious and detestable. But then again, as Leonidas' wife Gorgo tried to explain in her much-quoted quip: Spartan women were who they were because Spartan men were strong enough and self-confident enough to appreciate them.

GLOSSARY OF GREEK TERMS

Agoge

The Spartan public school, attended by all boys from the ages of 7 through 20 and by girls for a shorter period—probably from 7 until they had their first period. The agoge was infamous throughout Greece for its harshness, discipline and austerity, however not—as many modern historians would have us think—to the exclusion of the arts or intellectual training. On the contrary, ancient commentators claimed that "devotion to the intellect is more characteristic of Sparta than love of physical exercise." Furthermore, although the children lived in barracks, they were also introduced to democracy early by being organized into "herds" or "packs" which then elected their leaders. Their instructors were the 20-year-old youths on the brink of citizenship, the eirenes.

Andron

The chamber in a private house where symposia were held. It was often provided with permanent benches or shelves built against the walls for the guests to recline upon.

Chiton	The basic under-garment worn by both men and women. It could be long or short, belted or unbelted, bound at one or both shoulders. Slaves seem more likely to have worn it clasped only on one shoulder, and "short" chitons for mature men were also associated with "unfree" status.
Cythera	An ancient stringed instrument
Eirene	A Spartan youth, aged 20, on the brink of citizenship and serving as an instructor in the agoge.
Ephors	Executives of the Spartan government elected from among the citizen body for one year. Any citizen could be elected ephor, but no citizen could serve in this capacity for longer than one term. The ephors at this time were still viewed more as civil servants or administrators. Later, after Chilon's reforms, they became much more powerful.
Gerousia	The Council of Elders in Sparta. This body consisted of 28 elected members and the two kings. The elected members had to have attained the age of 60 and were then elected for life. Although this institution was highly praised by commentators from other parts of Greece, who saw in the Council of Elders a check upon the fickleness of the Assembly, the senility of some Council members and the "notorious" timidity of the Council were often a source of frustration among younger Spartans.

Helots	The rural population of Lacedaemon, descended from the original settlers of the area. Helots were not slaves. They could not be bought and sold. They were, however, similar to serfs in medieval Europe, as they were not free to leave Lacedaemon. Furthermore, they were required to give 50% of what they produced to the Spartiate estate-owners. While this requirement may seem harsh, it is important to remember that it was far less than what the rural labourers in other Greek city-states paid; since the latter were slaves, they gave up 100% of all the fruits of their labour. Much has been made of the fact that the Spartans in at least one recorded incident—but by no means "regularly," as some commentators assume—rounded up and killed the "best" helots. The recorded incident dates to a much later period, one in which increasing unrest among the population made rebellion a real threat.
Himation	The long, rectangular wrap used by both men and women as an outer garment.
Hoplite	A Greek heavy infantryman.
Hoplon	The round shield carried by a Greek heavy infantryman.
Hydria	A pitcher for water.
Kleros	The land allotment granted each Spartan citizen on maturity as a result of the Lycurgan Reforms. These were allegedly large enough to provide for a man and his immediate family, and according to tradition there were 6,000 of

these allotments, providing a citizen body of equal size at the time of the Reforms. Another 3,000 were added in the next century.

Kothon

A drinking vessel similar to a modern mug, distinctive to Sparta. In most of Greece, drinking cups had two handles; in Sparta, just one.

Krater

Large jars of pottery or bronze for mixing water and wine to the desired level of alcoholic content.

Kryptea

The Spartan "secret police," made up of young citizens who were tasked with keeping rebellious helots under control. In later centuries this was the body which "murdered" helots without warning in the dark, but the roots of the organization date back to unrecorded history, and my hypothesis is that it dates from the Second Messenian War and was then more comparable to a modern Special Forces unit.

Kylix

A drinking vessel with a low, shallow bowl on a short stem. These could be quite large, requiring two hands to hold, and were often passed around at a symposium.

Lacedaemon

The correct designation of the ancient Greek city-state of which Sparta was the capital. Lacedaemon consisted originally of only the Eurotas valley in the Peloponnese, know as Laconia. In the late 8th century BC, the valley to the west, Messenia, was captured and remained part of Lacedaemon until the 4th century BC. There were a number of other cities and towns in Lacedaemon, but the bulk of

	these were inhabited by perioikoi rather than Spartiates. The Spartiates were concentrated in Sparta, because of the requirement of attending the messes on a nightly basis.
Lochos	The main subdivision of the Spartan army, variously compared to a regiment or a division.
Lochogos/Lochagoi	The commander of a Lochos; Lochagoi is the plural form.
Mastigophoroi	The assistants to the headmaster of the Spartan agoge, responsible for maintaining discipline among the boys attending the agoge.
Melleirene	A Spartan youth, aged 19, about to become an eirene, or two years from citizenship.
Paidonomos	The headmaster of the Spartan agoge.
Palestra	A public place for exercise, particularly wrestling
Pentekonter	A two-decked, fifty-oared Greek warship, predecessor of the trireme.
Peplos	The most common indoor garment worn by women in Greece at this period. It was basically a single rectangular cloth, folded vertically in half and sewn up the open side. It was held on by clasps over one shoulder or—if a hole for the second arm was made in the folded side—by clasps at each shoulder. Spartan women continued to wear this garment after it was out of fashion elsewhere, and the fact that they let it slip up to the thigh for greater ease of motion earned them the (derogatory) epithet of "thigh throwers."

Peristyle	A courtyard surrounded on all sides by a colon-naded walkway.
Perioikoi	Non-citizen residents of Lacedaemon. Like the helots, the perioikoi were descendants of the non-Greek native population of the area prior to the Dorian invasion of the Peloponnese in roughly 900 BC. The perioikoi enjoyed free status and ran their own affairs in their own towns and cities, but had no independent state, military or foreign policy. The perioikoi—like the metics in other Greek cities—were required to pay taxes to the Lacedaemonian authorities. They also provided auxiliary troops to the Spartan army. Since Spartiates were prohibited from pursuing any profession or trade other than arms, the perioikoi had a (very lucrative) monopoly on all trade and manufacturing in Lacedaemon.
Pilos	A felt cap worn under the Greek battle helmet, or as a head covering against the cold; also worn by helot attendants without helmets.
Polemarch	A military commander.
Spartiate	Full Spartan citizen; that is, the legitimate son of a Spartan citizen who has successfully completed the agoge, served as an eirene, and been admitted to the citizen body at the age of 21.
Stoa	An open, roofed area supported by columns. In its simplest form, it is little more than a portico built against a building. More elaborate buildings, such as Pausanias describes in his travel guide to Greece, might have several rows of pil-

lars. They could be round or rectangular in shape, and Pausanias reports on several of these structures in Sparta, most built at a later date than described in this novel.

Syssitia — Spartan "messes" or "dining clubs." Adult Spartiates were all required to join one of the many existing syssitia when they attained citizenship at age 21. Thereafter, they were required to dine at these messes nightly unless on military duty or hunting. The existing members of each syssitia had to vote unanimously to admit an applicant. Recent research suggests that membership in the various syssitia may have been based on family ties or clan relationships, but this is not certain. They were not, however, merely military messes based on military units, and they were explicitly designed to encourage men of different age-cohorts to interact. Each member was required to make set contributions in kind (grain, wine, oil, and so on) and was expected to make other gifts, particularly game, in accordance with their means. Failure to pay the fees was grounds for loss of citizenship, and failure to attend the meals without a "valid" excuse (such as being out hunting) could result in fines or other sanctions.

ABOUT THE AUTHOR

Helena Schrader earned a PhD in History with a biography of the German Resistance leader who initiated the plot against Hitler on July 20, 1944. Her study of women pilots in WWII, *Sisters in Arms*, was released in 2006. She has published two novels set in WWII and to previous novels on Ancient Sparta. (See: www.helena-schrader.com) She is an active Foreign Service Officer.

978-0-595-47067-
0-595-47067-X

74794642R00195

Made in the USA
San Bernardino, CA
20 April 2018